Gestation

Unborn Hostage

Richard Henegan

iUniverse, Inc.
New York Bloomington

Gestation
Unborn Hostage

Copyright © 2009 Richard Henegan

All rights reserved. No part of this book may be used or reproduced by any means, graphic, electronic, or mechanical, including photocopying, recording, taping or by any information storage retrieval system without the written permission of the publisher except in the case of brief quotations embodied in critical articles and reviews.

This is a work of fiction. All of the characters, names, incidents, organizations, and dialogue in this novel are either the products of the author's imagination or are used fictitiously.

iUniverse books may be ordered through booksellers or by contacting:

iUniverse
1663 Liberty Drive
Bloomington, IN 47403
www.iuniverse.com
1-800-Authors (1-800-288-4677)

Because of the dynamic nature of the Internet, any Web addresses or links contained in this book may have changed since publication and may no longer be valid. The views expressed in this work are solely those of the author and do not necessarily reflect the views of the publisher, and the publisher hereby disclaims any responsibility for them.

ISBN: 978-1-4401-6603-7 (pbk)
ISBN: 978-1-4401-6601-3 (cloth)
ISBN: 978-1-4401-6602-0 (ebook)

Library of Congress Control Number: 2009935865

Printed in the United States of America

iUniverse rev. date: 10/2/2009

Introduction

Gestational age is a very important piece of data in every pregnancy, but its origin is often misunderstood. Most people assume it is the baby's age when in fact it is two weeks plus the fetal age. This is because the length of a pregnancy is calculated from the last normal menstrual period, which occurs about two weeks before conception in most cycles.

The common description used by medical personnel who deal with pregnancy is given in menstrual weeks and days. For instance, a pregnancy that is fourteen weeks and two days is written as 14W2D. This is actually two weeks more than the fetal age but since the last menstrual period is known in most cases, this is the reference point used, since the date of conception is not as reliable.

CHAPTER ONE

Four Weeks, One Day (4W1D)

Annatha lay sprawled out limply on the hard tile floor in the bathroom, her face pressed against the cool ceramic side of the toilet bowl. Surprisingly, it felt good against her sweaty brow. She felt flaccid, like the Raggedy Ann doll she played with as a child. Her stomach heaved involuntarily again, and she fought the nasty-tasting acid reflux surging towards her throat. It appeared her digestive system was merely a trampoline now that kept bouncing everything she swallowed back up, climbing higher and higher until it reached her mouth. She gagged on nothing in particular and a shudder wracked her body. *What the hell*, she wondered aloud, *is going on?* Disgusted, she stared at her sweaty palms and wiped them on her light green velour pants.

Three days ago when this illness began, she thought it was a stomach virus and stayed home in bed. It was a reasonable assumption: she felt bone tired, chilled, and her mouth erupted like a stuttering volcano almost all day long. The persistence of the same symptoms for more than two days now was unusual, as the stomach flu had never lasted over a day before. The drained, ragdoll feeling was probably from the constant puking, but she was tired of being bedridden. It was like Superman getting a

1

continuous intravenous kryptonite solution, without the cool outfit. All in all, she was sick and tired of being sick and tired.

Before heading for the gut dump, the name she had given her toilet the past two days, she had been scouring the Internet for medical help. On WebMD she had typed in her symptoms and one of the top hits had been pregnancy. To say this had caused a sinking feeling in her gut didn't come close to describing her reaction. *Sixteen and pregnant?* In her mind, that wouldn't simply be a disaster; it would more than likely be a teenage Armageddon. Sure, there was always abortion to make such a predicament disappear, although she had never thought of it in terms of herself, only as agreeing in principle with a woman's right to choose. The other alternatives of adoption or keeping it if she were pregnant weren't even on the table, but an abortion didn't miracle itself into one's life. There was the telling of the parents, getting the money and then having the procedure. The last item on the list seemed like a cake walk compared to the first two. Her real father had died last year and his replacement, born of her mother's desire for material comforts, was a monster. Brandon, her stepdad since she turned twelve, was a Microsoft software engineer and part-time animal killer.

She wanted to blame his dastardly deed of putting her cats to sleep two weeks ago for this possible misfortune, if indeed she was pregnant. However, her dad's words always haunted her when she tried to skirt responsibility. After a round of finger-pointing when she got into trouble, she would reluctantly remember him admonishing her to take one hundred percent of the responsibility for her actions in any situation, even if she was only partly to blame. He begged her not to follow in his footsteps and to learn this lesson sooner rather than later to avoid years of self-pity. It was a lesson he had passed on from Alcoholics Anonymous, where he sobered up during the last year of his life. Ironically, the day after receiving his sixty-day chip, he was diagnosed with cirrhosis of the liver, a fatal consequence alcoholism had seen fit to bestow upon him. Of course, the topic that prompted his advice on responsibility in the first place had been Brandon. It was always Brandon, but her dad had a way of helping her through these times.

She felt a rising tide of liquid in her throat and quickly placed her head over the side of the smooth bowl to spit a wad of slimy green fluid into the toilet. Maybe she was being possessed, she thought in a half-hearted attempt at humor to lighten an otherwise miserable situation. That last offering looked a lot like the vomit spewing out of Regan's mouth in *The Exorcist*. Her dad had taken her to see it at the drive-in, a ritual repeated often as they both enjoyed horror films. The night she saw *The Exorcist* for the first time, a heavy rain pounded on the car roof and fogged the windows. Her dad had to keep the windshield wipers on so they could see. He didn't seem to mind and told her it added to the creepiness. The memory stirred her senses, and she could almost smell the familiar aroma of her dad's cigar-drenched upholstery mixed with his leathery aftershave. Oddly enough, it had always been a comforting scent and she longed to inhale it again. God, she missed him.

Back to the real world, Annatha asserted and slumped against the toilet. If she was pregnant, she had no real friends at school to confide in. Her classmates were all too busy trying to look like the skinny MTV mannequins that danced on the music videos. She didn't see herself as uncool--far from it--but she didn't go for redefining herself to match the mindless media babes that other girls in her class used as role models. Unfortunately, that made her a kind of nerdy freak in their eyes, but so be it. She fed her soul by painting and loving her cats, and Brandon had taken half of that from her.

She teared up again as she thought of Buster and Spanky being dropped off at the pound and going to their deaths like defenseless Jews at the Nazi death camps. Without her knowledge, Brandon whisked them away after Annatha left for school and didn't tell her what had happened until it was too late. They were already gone. All because he didn't like the fact her picture on her MySpace profile showed cleavage. She enjoyed wearing cute clothes, and cute clothes for a sixteen year old showed cleavage and some skin between the shirt and jeans. His reaction struck her as over the top, since she didn't mimic the street whore look other girls her age on MySpace seemed to go for.

Annatha heaved a large sigh and grabbed the side of the toilet. She struggled to raise herself up and turned on the cold water tap at her sink. Resting one hand on the countertop, she brushed her long auburn hair out of her eyes. *Jesus,* she thought, *I look like a raccoon.* The mascara she put on so carefully this morning had been no match for the salty tears that smeared her makeup each time a wave of nausea hit her. She washed her face with soap and water and scrubbed around her eyes until the skin was red. Looking in the mirror after she dried off, it was hard to decide which look was worse; the raccoon or the zombie, night–of-the-living-dead creature that stared back at her now.

The tank top she was wearing was drenched with sweat, and she shook it to air out her sticky skin. Then she pulled it tightly against her chest and examined her breast size. She winced, as they were tender when she applied pressure. *That's new,* she thought, *and wasn't it on the list of pregnancy symptoms from the WebMD site?* Her breasts were a B cup and with her small frame, she was a size 32B. The new bras were good at pushing them together so she could sport a cleavage. It wasn't so much to attract men as it was that she enjoyed showing them off since they had taken their sweet time, finally appearing when she turned fourteen. Her dad had not approved of the revealing attire either, but he didn't kill her cats. He had explained that she was advertising an attitude, and that attitude said "I'm easy." She had disagreed vehemently, but in the end, his disapproving look had spoken more words than anything he could have said aloud. After his death, Annatha had briefly regretted her juvenile defiance, but she couldn't take it back and her dad always told her guilt was a destructive emotion, so she had decided to let it go.

If he was still alive she could go to him with her dilemma, but given her current situation, she would have to handle this alone. First things first, she reminded herself while she measured a strip of toothpaste on the brush and began cleaning the foul taste from her mouth. Tomorrow, after the vomiting gave her a reprieve, she would go by the drugstore and get a urine pregnancy test. Then she would know once and for all if she was pregnant or simply dying of a terminal disease.

Shedding her tank top, Annatha slipped into a night shirt, climbed into her bed and snuggled cold feet under the pink and green floral quilt. Thankfully, she had this room that served as a refuge from her family. No one bothered her here, so this is where she spent most of her time. There was no family time, watching movies with popcorn and Milk Duds; the only thing they did together was eat. She had learned to scarf her food down quickly to avoid any more contact with Brandon than was absolutely necessary. Her mother pretty much left her alone, as she was too busy with her social events. The resentment Annatha carried against her was that she never took up for her only daughter, no matter how cruelly Brandon spoke to her or how unreasonable his punishments were. When he finally told Annatha about the fate of her cats, her mom had sat silently, sipping on her nightly martini. It was a familiar escape she had indulged in every night for some time now. Funny how she had left her dad because of his alcoholism and Annatha believed she was headed for the same fate. She'd probably drink, too, if she was married to that ogre, she reflected as she opened her Dell notebook and waited for the browser to open.

Annatha entered Yahoo messenger, logged in as *sassybrat18* and chose a Washington State chat room. She was curious to see if *legaltenderguy* was on tonight. She had not seen him since the night she met him online two weeks ago. Putting her head in her hands, she rode a wave of nausea that had jumped out of nowhere. She cursed softly, as she didn't want to be forced out of bed again after getting cozy under her blankets.

Damn, girl, what were you thinking? Annatha scolded herself as the chat room screen reminded her of the ill-fated night that was the cause of her suspected predicament. Full of anger after the news about her cats, she had gone online two weeks ago on a Saturday night when her mom and Brandon were on vacation in Belize. She had vowed to get revenge against her stepdad by sleeping with someone she met online and springing the news on him the next time they fought. This brilliant plan was, of course, hatched after she had downed two shots of tequila from the downstairs bar.

Navigating to another chat room, she began searching the ID column on the right. She remembered how the smooth-talking *legaltenderguy* had swept her off her feet that night with his charm and empathy for her loss. He told her he had cats and couldn't imagine how he would feel if someone had them put to sleep. In her inebriated state, she had been drawn to him like a tractor beam and agreed to let him send a cab to take her to his hotel near SeaTac airport. Fortunately, her stepsister Dee had gone to a party with her friends that night. Brandon had coaxed her into watching Annatha while they were gone. Dee was a brilliant 4.0 student and soccer star. She attended Pacific Lutheran University in Tacoma and was the apple of Brandon's eye. As far as he was concerned, she could do no wrong, and he constantly threw her accomplishments up to Annatha as a role model for her to emulate. It could have made her hate Dee, but Annatha actually liked her. She was fun, smart and treated her well. But Brandon's favoritism made it almost impossible to feel close to her. She suspected her stepsister might break a confidence she divulged in order to curry favor with her dad.

The cursor stopped over an ID name *legaltenderstud* and Annatha felt a knot in her stomach. *Was this the same guy?* She watched the chat room dialogue and quickly came to the conclusion it wasn't. This pig was asking all the females in the room to show him their boobs on cam. *Legaltenderguy* had been courteous and respectful, which was why she had decided to IM him and set herself on course for their rendezvous.

The thirty minute cab ride from her home on Mercer Island to the airport was not enough time for her to sober up and back out. Besides, she didn't have enough cash to pay the driver and couldn't use her credit card, as Brandon had forbid her to do so unless she was buying gas. He gave her a printout every month of her purchases with the ones he questioned highlighted in yellow. She sarcastically referred to it as his CIA intelligence report, as it was calculated on an Excel spreadsheet.

Annatha continued her chat room search. So far there was no sign of her one-night stand. It wasn't something she was proud of, but there was no taking it back now. She recalled after she arrived at the hotel, *legaltenderguy* paid the taxi driver and escorted her to the hotel bar. He was what she would call "hot" for his age. About thirty-something, tall, well-proportioned with short, thick brown hair, he was very charming and polished. He was dressed well in a pair of tight jeans and an Eddie Bauer pullover shirt. She found herself staring at his deep blue eyes through the alcoholic stupor and was surprised how attracted she was to him despite their age difference. Most likely, the tequila had something to do with her perception. The waitress wouldn't serve her drinks because of her age, but Thomas-his real name, she learned after introductions--ordered doubles and shared with her. After a few potent servings, he had her well-lubricated for a trip to his hotel room.

Annatha also recalled she was a little too drunk to remember much, but his experience was obvious compared to the few episodes of sex she had with a high school senior six months before. Thomas had taken the precaution of asking her how old she was and she lied that she was eighteen. She also lied about being on birth control. Her father had taken her to Planned Parenthood so she could get on a birth control pill, but for reasons she couldn't recall at the moment, she stopped taking them after his death. The following morning she had awakened alone in the hotel room and Thomas was gone. A sweet note and cash for cab fare were next to her neatly folded clothes on the dresser. In the light of sobriety and a God-awful hangover, it had only made her feel cheap.

The chat rooms were busy as usual, but *legaltenderguy* was nowhere to be found. Annatha closed her laptop and fell back on her pillow, staring at the drab, textured ceiling above her. *Tomorrow is "P" day,* she thought. If she was pregnant, there was only one thing to do: Contact Thomas and let him know of her condition, then see if she could guilt him into paying for an abortion. That way the problem would be taken care of and no one would be the wiser. Her plan to tell Brandon about the liaison with a stranger seemed almost suicidal now that she wasn't high on alcohol. The only thing she would accomplish would be to stir up a hornet's nest, and she wasn't willing to face his wrath in her current state. No telling what he would do, maybe even kill the neighbor's dog. She frowned. Truthfully, he would probably take away her car, and she definitely didn't want that. It represented some degree of freedom to her, and shocking him with news of a sexcapade while he was on vacation wasn't worth the consequences.

Despite her desire to think through her options if she couldn't find Thomas or if he refused to help, fatigue overwhelmed her and she fell fast asleep.

Chapter Two

Four weeks, Two days (4W2D)

Wendy Malloy absently studied the heavens from her clinic office as she waited for her last patient of the day. Gloomy clouds scurried across the sky, dumping showers in fits as they nervously moved west. The frequent breaks in the cumulus parade allowed brilliant sunshine to bathe the earth, steaming the heated grass. She squinted against the bright light and quickly closed the blinds.

Her previous patient had DNKA'd (Did Not Keep Appointment) and she had a few minutes alone. With the extra time, Wendy decided it was time once again to take stock of her life. Taking stock was one of her best character traits, she felt, as it always focused her perspective on what was happening and where she was going. The last time she summoned this exercise was when she decided to take the job at this clinic. It seemed like a good option, counseling patients about abortion, hoping one would decide to adopt their unborn child and she would be in the perfect position to offer herself as an adoptive parent. Things weren't working out that way after two months, frustrating her plan, which was why she needed to rethink the whole process.

Wendy's stock-taking had been born of necessity when she

underwent surgery for infertility and was told afterwards her pelvis looked like a Hershey's chocolate factory. *Nice description by the doctor,* she recalled. The large chocolate cysts on her ovaries were due to endometriosis and were the death knell of any hopes she had of conceiving a child the old-fashioned way. Seth, her husband of ten years and an orthopedic surgeon in Seattle, had refused to proceed any further with assisted reproduction, namely in vitro fertilization. His declaration that "no child of his would be conceived in a Petri dish" had pretty much squashed any further hopes she had of conceiving at all. To add insult to injury, Seth already had a bun in the oven with an operating room nurse who was ten years younger than Wendy and apparently very fertile.

Of course the inevitable heartache, divorce and grasping onto anything to hold herself together followed. She began to spiral downward, unable to accept Seth's infidelity and rejection, not to mention her barren pelvis. Her behavior became unsettling to her coworkers in the Labor & Delivery ward where she worked. She would find excuses to take babies from their mothers and sit rocking them in the nursery. The feel of a tiny newborn against her body seemed to soothe her broken heart and lift her shattered spirit. After a particularly humiliating session with her nurse manager about the numerous complaints from mothers about their babies disappearing with a nurse they characterized as kind of weird, she had retreated to the sparsely furnished apartment where she had moved after the separation and cried out for help to the God of her childhood.

There, alone in the darkness, sobbing on the floor, she had felt a kind of strong breeze blow against her hair. It was if she was on a mountain top and the howling wind picked up her broken heart and carried it away from its emotional desolation. Next, a sudden peace had engulfed her and she felt at that moment everything would be all right. Despite abandoning Him for many years, her Lord and Savior, Jesus Christ, had taken her in His arms and rescued her weary soul.

At that moment, her stock-taking was born. She had been

given clarity of mind just by turning her will and life over to God. The gift would not be forgotten or wasted. Immediately, she had begun the task of reviewing her situation and realized being around newborn babies was stoking the flames of her depression. Taking the money from her divorce settlement, she had bought a three acre farm just outside of Olympia and moved away from the devastation she had suffered in Seattle.

Immersed in farm life, she spent her time gardening and caring for the animals she kept buying. Her favorite time with them was when they were small. Nursing small chicks, kittens and puppies was absolutely therapeutic for her and quenched her thirst for a baby of her own. Fulfilling this need was good and bad: good because it was spiritual food; bad because she was collecting quite the small animal zoo and it required a good deal of her time. They weren't her only pastime, either. She had planted a vegetable garden. Digging in dirt, the warm sun on her back, she loved to drink in the aroma of the rich soil and fertilizer. Wendy relished the experience of eating vegetables she had grown herself. It was quite a feeling of accomplishment.

Despite these diversions, she often had to stop her mind from racing over scenarios where she could get her own child somehow. This was most difficult at night, when she was all alone in the house. She prayed often to have the thoughts removed, but she decided after months of trying that God must have a plan for her to get a baby or He would have rewarded her pleas to remove this obsession.

Thus, another stock-taking had been born. After a year's hiatus without a job, she had decided to go back to work. Following the application process for her current position, she firmly believed God had led her to this clinic. The physician was looking for an RN to counsel patients who came in seeking a pregnancy termination. Wendy abhorred abortion and felt it was an abomination; however, she realized after leaving the job interview that one of the options discussed during a pregnancy counseling session was adoption. Surely one of the patients would see this as the preferred way to go and Wendy would be there to offer herself as an adoption candidate. It wasn't exactly ethical, but that didn't seem to matter to her. She would simply resign if called on it. There were plenty of RN jobs to be found. With this new resolve, she had called the doctor and accepted the position.

Now, two months later, she had begun to doubt this was God's will. If it was, He was surely testing her. Time after time, the unwilling mothers had rejected her adoption speech and chosen to terminate their pregnancies. It infuriated Wendy but she had managed to hide her feelings thus far. Many times she had gone home and furiously weeded her garden to vent her anger at the wanton killing of babies she witnessed day after day. She wasn't directly involved in the abortions, but it still left a bad taste in her mouth, not to mention the fact these women had become pregnant accidentally, something she had failed to do on purpose.

Wendy felt her blood begin to boil at this last train of thought and she quickly mumbled a prayer to stave it off. The intercom sounded and startled her from her reverie. Her last patient had arrived.

****

Annatha threw her purse on the bed and carried the Walgreen's bag into the bathroom. She had purchased a pregnancy test, after choking down breakfast for her Mom's benefit, to find out once and for all if she was pregnant. Prying open the box, she removed the kit and set it on the counter. She looked around and spotted a green cup with a yellow daisy floral pattern her mother had purchased at Bed, Bath and Beyond. Annatha managed a wry smile. *This must come under the Beyond category,* she mused. Little did her mother know what it would be used for in the future.

Despite the fact instructions on the box directed the user to pee on the test strip, Annatha was not having any of it. She would pee in the cup--much easier to hit--and then dip the strip into her urine. The toilet was cool against her skin, so she ran some water to facilitate the process. First she voided a little to see where the stream would be, then positioned the cup underneath and proceeded to fill it up halfway. Even using her method, Annatha felt some urine splatter on her hand and her face scrunched up.

"Gross," she muttered in disgust.

Not able to finish the process without washing her hands, she quickly stood up and ran water over her fingers. Drying them off thoroughly, Annatha retrieved the test strip and carefully dipped it into the urine. When she withdrew the strip, it immediately morphed into a deep blue plus sign.

Annatha closed the toilet seat and plopped down hard. *It was final now, she was definitely pregnant.* She stared at the test strip in her hand for several minutes, thinking of the effect this would have on her life. Unable to fight the tears that were welling up involuntarily, she blinked hard and tried to think again of her options.

Options, she thought ruefully, *what fucking options?* This pregnancy had to be stopped quickly and without involving anyone she knew. The money her father left her was in a trust until she reached eighteen, so she had no financial means to do this herself. The only hope she had was getting Thomas to agree to pay for it. She knew next to nothing about him; he could be married for Christsakes. There was no other choice but to follow this plan and if he said no, well, she thought, she'd jump off that bridge when she came to it, as her dad used to say.

Mentally exhausted from the stress of anticipating this moment, she exited the bathroom and fell into bed. Tonight, she'd look for Thomas on the internet and try and set up another meeting with him. She couldn't tell him why, so she'd have to pretend she wanted to have sex again. Her thoughts raced as fatigue grabbed her and shoved her into a deep sleep.

****

Wendy steered her Volvo into the long driveway leading to her home. Tall evergreens lined the way and hid the house until the gravel drive ended in a large circle. Her home was a ranch style two bedroom. The cedar siding was capped off with a forest green metal roof. A porch swing was to the left of the door on her covered porch, and baskets of brightly colored flowers were hanging all along the eaves.

On her way home, Wendy had fought the exasperation created by her last patient. She was only fifteen and covered with tattoos and piercings. Completely oblivious to the gravity of her situation, she had chewed gum and texted on her cell phone during the interview. When Wendy brought up the alternative of giving her baby up for adoption, there was no sign of acknowledgement in her vacant stare. Pressing her further, Wendy had even asked her to put her cell phone down and patiently repeated the adoption speech. The young girl had finally shown some emotion and demanded she stop talking about adoption. She had lectured Wendy that she came to have an abortion and resented her bringing up anything that would make her feel guilty about it. It was all she could do to keep from slapping the girl across the face to knock some sense into her. Surprised at the thought of striking a patient, Wendy knew she needed to rethink what she was doing and vowed to do so after dinner, with a glass of wine.

Bart, her golden retriever, came out from under the porch to greet her. Wendy stopped and petted him, stroking his head firmly with her fingers. He loved when she did that. Bart followed her into the house and took his usual position in front of the TV, where Wendy had a large pillow for him to lie on. The cats emerged from the hallway that led to two bedrooms and a basement, strolled over nonchalantly and began rubbing against her leg, purring their welcome as she began to prepare dinner.

The microwave whirred into action and Wendy decided that she would have a glass of wine with dinner. She walked down the hallway and opened the basement door. The previous owner had put a deadbolt on it and it could only be opened with a key from the hallway entrance. Wendy never locked it; all she kept in the basement was her wine stock. The cool basement air greeted her as she reached up and pulled the string for the overhead light. She could navigate down the wooden stairs without injuring herself now.

Next, she flipped on a wall switch at the base of the stairway that controlled the main light and stopped dead in her tracks. The wine rack was in its usual place about halfway down the finished wall on the right, but she saw the rest of the room in a completely different way this time. There were no windows. It had a small furnace that could heat the room and two electrical outlets if needed. It was plenty big enough for a bed, a television and some kind of recliner chair. Even better, it had a small bathroom with a shower and toilet for some reason known only to the previous owner. Not quite able to comprehend why her mind was going in the direction it was, Wendy continued to study the layout, and an unexpected plan began to formulate in her brain. This was divine inspiration, she realized, and grabbed a bottle of wine. She couldn't wait to get through with dinner and sit down at her computer with a glass of chardonnay to flesh out the details. A prayer of thanks tumbled from her lips as she climbed the stairs again.

****

Annatha was finally back in her room. She had suffered the sarcastic comments of her mother and Brandon at the dinner table about how pale she looked. It was tempting to shock them by saying how she always thought pregnant women had a special glow about them. Not so tempting she would dream of saying such a thing; nevertheless, it was a nice private fantasy.

She slipped into a night shirt for comfort and jumped onto her bed, sitting cross legged in front of her laptop. She rubbed the touch pad, the login screen appeared and she entered her Windows password. Yahoo messenger was already on her desktop and she signed in. Her stomach gurgled and she looked down at it.

"Not now," she commanded, "I have work to do."

Browsing the usual chat rooms, Annatha searched for *legaltenderguy* in the ID column on the right. It was Friday night and many of the chat rooms were full. This made it difficult but not impossible. Unfortunately, she had not added Thomas to her friends list so she couldn't tell if he was online. She checked the dropdown menu that allowed a search for a specific chat ID, and typed in *legaltenderguy*. The screen changed to Washington chat room five, and miraculously she was able to enter the crowded room. She decided to wait for a few minutes to see if Thomas recognized her *sassybrat18* ID. Watching the dialogue scroll on the left, she saw Thomas was flirting with a female chatter. *Another victim*, she mused. He seemed really nice when she met him, but it could have been the booze. Most likely he was a player. For her plan to work, he had to be a player with something to lose, she thought.

Annatha realized there was no way he was going to notice her, if he even remembered her, while he was engrossed with his current prey. She double clicked his ID and an IM window opened. Not wanting to seem too eager, she typed "How's it going, Thomas?" Using his name would let him know she was someone who knew him. Annatha had already looked at his Yahoo 360 and all of the information was likely fictitious, as his name in the profile was Justice Served. So the only way she would know his real name would be that they had met. It wasn't long before he replied.

"Hey girl!"

He doesn't remember my name, she realized. This might be harder than she thought.

"You don't remember me, do you?" she responded.

"You obviously remember me. Where did we meet?"

She considered her reply. *Might as well let it all hang out*, she thought.

"At the Doubletree by SeaTac a couple of weeks ago."

There was a pause. *Jesus, does he screw that many women?* She saw at the bottom of the IM window that he was finally typing.

"Okay, sorry, I remember you now. It's been a long day."

Not the kind of greeting she was hoping for, Annatha thought as she rolled her eyes, *but it was a start.* Boldness was the key, so she persisted.

"I was hoping we could meet again."

This time the reply came quickly. "That sounds great, sweetie, but I'm leaving in the morning and won't be back until Monday."

Sweetie? Annatha cringed. She hated being referred to as sweetie; especially since Brandon often used it with Dee, his daughter. Shaking her head, she realized Thomas's excuse was a definite wrench in her plans. More disturbing was the prospect it might just be a subtle way of blowing her off indefinitely. *Was this the bridge she should jump off?* Her heart sank momentarily before she remembered the whole reply. He told her he was coming back Monday, which left the door open. Oh well, she was hoping to resolve things this weekend but that was not to be. *Don't give up,* she encouraged herself. A few more days only meant she had to be more patient. She began typing her reply.

"Monday would work for me, too. I had a really good time and just thought we should hook up again, but if you can't, no sweat." *There, not too eager but a definite opening.*

"Sounds great, I had a good time, too. How do you want to work this?"

Annatha exhaled. She hadn't realized she was holding her breath. *Phase one complete,* she thought. After she gave Thomas her cell phone number, they agreed to meet at the Denny's by SeaTac around noon on Monday. Thomas was busy in the morning with a deposition but had the afternoon free. The location was Annatha's idea, as she wanted a public place to break the news to Thomas. If she went to his hotel room he would want to have sex right away and she was not in the mood. Fortunately, he didn't question her choice of meeting at a restaurant.

She had to suffer through another half hour of idle chat with Thomas, but it was well worth it. From time to time, he tried to steer her towards turning on her cam and having cyber sex, but she politely declined with the excuse that she looked gross. *What a dirty old man,* she mentally gagged after saying goodbye. No matter, he used her and now she was using him. Monday, she would pitch her need for financial help to have an abortion and pray that he bought it. She logged out of chat and closed the laptop. *You're in a fine mess,* she scolded herself, then headed into the bathroom and buried the pregnancy test evidence under some tissue in her trashcan. The maids would never check the bottom of her bathroom trash liner. She washed out the floral ceramic cup with soap but knew she would never be able to drink out of it again. Her dad always said that urine was sterile when he told her she could pee in the river while he was fishing. Somehow, this information didn't make it any less gross.

After she tidied up in the bathroom, she brushed her teeth and gagged at the taste of her toothpaste. Everything made her gag, it seemed. Swallowing against the nausea, she returned to her room and opened a window. The crisp night air felt good against her face and thankfully diminished the wave of sickness that dwelled in her stomach. Something else was living there too, she suddenly realized. Shaking off this unpleasant revelation, she turned off the light and returned to her bedroom. She burrowed under the covers and positioned her face to feel the breeze coming from the open window, hoping the brisk night air continued to counter her nausea. Her mind was racing as she schemed about how best to approach Thomas on Monday. It was another hour before she finally fell asleep.

****

Thomas glanced over his shoulder at the naked young woman lying face down in his hotel bed. *She'll probably be there until morning,* he frowned. *Can't be helped, son,* he reminded himself, *when you pour alcohol down them to loosen them up, they have to sleep it off.* He admired the contour of her shapely ass for a moment before returning to his laptop. Taking a draw from his cigar, he exhaled slowly and watched the thick smoke linger in the still room air for a moment before wending its way towards the open window. It was a no smoking room but he didn't care. They allowed adultery, why not smoking?

He closed the IM box from *sassybrat18* and puffed slowly while considering the transaction he had just completed. One of his rules in this game was never to capture the same prey twice. It was simple. Strike quickly and only once: the chances of injury were less. And this was a game to him. The chat rooms were his Serengeti plains and quarry was plentiful. He stalked the rooms, looking for weaknesses that would allow him an advantage. Not just anyone would do, either. First, he checked their profile and then, before launching his final attack, he asked for a cam viewing to confirm their pic wasn't somebody else. Younger women, legal age of course, but under twenty-one were his primary targets-- the more attractive, the better.

Now his rule was being bent for a particularly cute young thing he recalled from a few weeks before. She wasn't sexually outstanding, but then she had been pretty soused, he recalled. Thomas stood up, walked over to the open window and stuck his head out. Bathing in the balmy night air, he stared absently for a few minutes at the procession of flashing lights from rows of aircraft dutifully lined up for their landing approach at SeaTac. It felt good and he needed to clear his head while this thought process continued. A flattering thought crossed his mind that she was choosing to see him again, and he was fifteen years older than her! *You've still got it, Tommy!* He puffed out his chest to the noisy street in front of the hotel. Vanity was a powerful drug and it was clouding his judgment, but the other aspect was also exciting. She would be sober this time and much more responsive. Adjusting his boxers to free a growing erection, Thomas briefly wondered how Laurel would be affected if she found out. Thus far, his wife had been clueless, but he had been flawless in his ability to conceal his activities away from home.

His recent promotion to medical malpractice had afforded Thomas the ability to travel often for depositions. He shuttled between home in Denver, Salt Lake City and Seattle for expert testimony to use against the defendant hospitals, physicians, or whoever he named in the lawsuit. At first, he had focused solely on the case, working at night on deposition questions and organizing testimony. However, this still left hours where he had nothing to do but watch television, and trolling local bars was not his thing.

Thomas retraced his steps and plopped back down in the desk chair, then positioned his feet on the edge of the bed. The young lady didn't even stir. His laptop displayed the same chat room he had been in when Annatha IM'd him. This was where all of his adventures had begun. Fooling around on the Internet, looking for ways to pass the lonely nights away from home, he had stumbled upon Yahoo Messenger and the world opened up. There were thousands of people online, talking about anything and everything. Flirting, stripping, masturbating and cybersex were commonplace. At first he was overwhelmed. Bit by bit he found his way into more savory rooms, although his initial foray was in the role playing rooms. It was interesting and seemed harmless, but the typed dialogue, though stimulating enough to help him masturbate, didn't satisfy his need for more intimate contact. Plus the fantasy requests from some of the participants were getting too bizarre even for him.

Enter local chat rooms. These were online bars where males and females vied for each other's attention. Everyone was either drunk or stoned or worse. The lame come-ons by the classless boys were embarrassing to him as a man, and he quickly realized his chat entries impressed the girls in the cheap seats. They would IM him and ask where he was and if he was married, followed soon by "why don't we meet sometime?" His marital status didn't seem too important to most, but he kept that a secret, as he did most everything else. He would admit to being an attorney, not a far stretch from his chat ID, but anything else was either a lie or omitted.

Strangely enough, the more he did it, the more he wanted to do it again. It was definitely a contest, as he soon realized the easy ones were just that--easy. He was after more interesting game, and applying his charm and skills resulted in double the satisfaction if he bagged a more elusive prey. It was odd, he reflected as he watched his latest victim's shapely back heave slowly up and down as she slept, it never occurred to him when he married that he would be involved in something like this. Seven years with Laurel, most of them good, didn't seem to enter his mind when he left Denver. The smell of the hunt was powerful and seductive. He couldn't resist.

All of this was a risk because the firm wouldn't approve of his extracurricular activities on the road, not to mention the devastating effect it would have on his marriage. Laurel would certainly divorce him and take his three year old son Nicholas with her. The years of slogging through college and law school, enduring his first job at the firm in family law and all the sleaze that entailed; now rising junior partner with a four thousand square foot home in an upscale Denver neighborhood, usher at his church, devoted father and son-in-law--all would be sacrificed due to his hunger for out-of-town sex. Despite this self-knowledge and insight into his behavior, Thomas felt like he wasn't hurting anyone that didn't find out. And he would see to it they didn't.

The only computer he ever used for his clandestine activities was his business laptop, and it stayed at work except when he took it with him out of town. Laurel would never have access to it. He scanned it every day for key loggers and other spyware, dutifully deleted his Internet files, and his cell phone bills came to the office. It was a foolproof plan.

Thomas moved to the edge of the bed, sat next to the young woman's sleeping body and stroked her soft, youthful skin. *This was why he did it,* he thought, *it afforded him a trip back to his own youth when the girls had flat abdomens, perky breasts and velvet skin.* Laurel was no slouch. After her pregnancy, she had worked hard to get back in shape, but when nursing was over, her breasts had headed south and the stretch marks on her loose abdominal skin from Nicholas marked her as sexually second-hand in his mind. He knew it was a shitty secret about himself, one he wasn't proud of. That didn't make it go away. It did not result in his seeking an affair at first, but it definitely decreased his carnal desire for his wife. For two and a half years after Nicholas was born, he had dutifully stayed faithful to Laurel, even though there were opportunities with clients when he handled divorce cases.

Six months ago all of that changed. One of his family law clients arrived for her appointment with a two year old son who had cerebral palsy. Thomas found out that she had never looked into any negligence on the part of her obstetrician that would have resulted in her son's brain damage. After the divorce was final, he had approached the managing partner about letting him handle the medical malpractice case for this client as she trusted him, etc. The partner agreed and Thomas found an expert to interpret the fetal heart rate tracing as abnormal enough to suggest oxygen deprivation for a prolonged time. All he had to do was produce the child in a wheelchair with his affliction speaking loudly to the jury. The doctor's insurance company had deep pockets and that was all it took for the jury to award his client a multi-million dollar judgment. This success catapulted Thomas into his new position and that's when the travelling started. Laurel wasn't happy about it at first, but she had her hands full raising Nicholas as a stay-at-home mom after quitting her job as a CPA. She was very independent before Nicholas, but after her source of income disappeared when she resigned from her position, a certain amount of dependency and clinginess began. The trips away from home were therapeutic at first for Thomas, as he had time to himself. But it had evolved into his current activity and he was able to compartmentalize this part of his life with expert rationalization. It was a skill a lawyer had to possess to survive in the business he or she was in; Thomas had just translated the same savvy to his personal life in order to avoid guilt.

The motionless body of tonight's conquest never reacted to his hands on her skin, so Thomas finally gave up. The sex was over for tonight. The stirring he felt in his crotch would have to wait until Monday to be satisfied. He took the last few puffs from the cigar and held it under the tap, listening to the sizzle as the cool water contacted the hot, glowing tip. Moving back to the desk, he began to compose a note on the hotel stationary that he would leave her for when she awoke in the morning. He counted out five ten dollar bills and placed the note and the money in an envelope. Then he folded her clothes neatly and placed them on the desk. He had to think for a minute what her name was and then wrote "Jackie" on the outside of the envelope and tossed it on her pile of clothes. *She was definitely a hotty,* he smiled, *well worth the effort.* Shedding his boxers, he slid under the covers and switched off the bedside lamp. *All in all, a good trip,* he thought drowsily as sleep overtook him.

CHAPTER THREE

Four Weeks, Four Days (4W4D)

It was forecast to be a hot, dry July day in Olympia. Wendy shed her church clothes as soon as she arrived home and dressed in her gardening attire. The light, airy cotton pants felt good after wearing constrictive hose all morning. A loose fitting blouse and wide-brimmed straw hat finished out her grubby clothes ensemble. She glanced in the mirror to adjust the hat and her gaze lingered on her reflection. Measuring five foot eight and a trim one hundred thirty pounds, she was still in good shape for her late thirties. There were a few pesky wrinkles radiating from the corners of her dark brown eyes that etched deeper when she managed a smile with her shapely, thin lips. Prominent cheekbones were the one feature she inherited from her dad and gave her face a rather statuesque quality.

  Wendy knew with flattering clothes she would appeal more to members of the opposite sex and attract the interest of a prospective mate, but that had been the furthest thing from her mind since the devastating divorce from Seth. Leaning forward, she frowned and pulled a gray hair spiraling out from under the straw hat. Even though she avoided dressing for potential dates, her desire for a youthful yet dignified appearance wasn't going to allow the aging strands to dwell in her light brown hair. Otherwise, she would wind up looking like one of those granola eating, tree hugging, hairy armpit Evergreen College faculty female professors with their natural look and that just wasn't her style. *Enough silliness,* she chided her reflection and strode down the hall and out the front door.

The house was still cool from the night before, and the warm wave of air that washed over her when she stepped outside felt soothing. It was the initial phase of her weekend summer ritual and elicited a Pavlovian-like response that allowed a calmness to settle in. The elevated garden she had worked so hard to build last year was situated between the house and a pole barn, also trimmed with cedar siding. Tall fir trees surrounded the house and kept the sun's glare from her eyes for the moment, but as she walked toward her destination, the arboreal cedar curtain melted in front of her, giving way to bright sunlight that temporarily blinded her so she stopped, waited a moment for her eyes to adjust and continued.

Before she reached the tool shed behind the house, Wendy stopped by the chicken coop and opened the door. The first one out was her Rhode Island Red, followed shortly by the two Andalusians. Their feet started scratching immediately, looking for worms and other insects, clucking in low tones as if they were gossiping among themselves. Next she opened the door to the shed and gathered the tools she would use, along with a foam knee pad. She left the door open to air it out, as noxious fumes from the bags of fertilizer were intense in the closed-off space.

When she reached the elevated garden, she stopped to admire her handiwork. The precise geometric arrangement had the appearance of rows of houses in a sprawling suburb, and the packets stapled to a small stake at the head of each row heralded like tiny billboards the particular vegetable poking up through the sod. Repeating furrows between the plants were like hometown streets where children might play.

She noted with pride the leafy radish blooms signified they

were ready to harvest, as did the cucumbers. The chives in her herb section were coming along nicely, too. The scent of rich soil filled her nostrils and she drank it in. In her mind, this was like soaking in a hot bath with scented candles lining a tub filled with bubbles. The soothing affect was the same.

Wendy sighed as the image evaporated and she prepared for the not so soothing task of tackling the pesky weeds. She placed the cushy knee pad at the beginning of a row, maneuvered it with the toe end of her garden clog, and dropped down in position. As she began working her trowel in the rich soil, her mind wandered to stock-taking again. This was one of her favorite places to indulge in this vital exercise. While mindlessly performing the dull chore, her conscious brain became an open receptacle, approaching a meditation-like state with passive feelings. This process was effective because it prohibited her from judging any thoughts or ideas that surfaced, which protected her from being swept into the emotional chaos expectations always produced.

The first subject that surfaced had to do with basement upgrades she had accomplished yesterday, since it was the most recent event in her life. In response to what she believed to be divine inspiration, Wendy had transformed the downstairs room into a self-sufficient studio apartment. Bedroom furniture was acquired at a yard sale, along with a mattress and box spring. There was already an outlet for satellite reception, so she had moved her bedroom TV and satellite receiver downstairs. They worked perfectly. Next was a trip to Wal-Mart, where toiletries, towels, wash rags, soap and shampoo were all purchased and put away in the basement bathroom. It had a toilet, sink and shower: everything needed by a long term occupant. A locksmith had installed one deadbolt with a keyless entry on the basement side. She wanted two but his bid was too much to drill into the steel door a second time for that.

The only difficult item was the refrigerator. It was only the size of a mini-bar in a hotel room, but it was bulky and required some engineering expertise on her part. She strapped it on two pieces of plywood with duct tape, and used them like a sled to lower the refrigerator down the wooden stairs. Walking it back and forth across the floor, she managed to place it where she wanted. *If you can't fix it, duct it,* she smiled.

Wendy decided to remove her blouse. She still had a sports bra underneath and privacy was not a problem this far from the road, with nothing but thick fir trees guarding the front line of her property. The sweat on her shoulders and back grabbed at the material and made it difficult to negotiate over sticky skin. Exasperated, she inverted it and threw it on the grass behind her. She relished the psychological therapy weeding the rows in her garden afforded her, especially today, but she couldn't feel peaceful with sweat trickling down her torso like creepy, crawling insects. Retrieving her shirt, she used it as a towel and wiped away the unwelcome distraction, then continued her mental inventory.

The crux of a plan that had been divinely revealed to her Friday night required that Wendy resort to more direct tactics if she was to ever going to have a child of her own. Exactly what those tactics would be still eluded her, but she felt the clinic was at the core of an answer that waited to reveal itself in the not-too-distant future. She didn't feel like she could see the future; it was more that she could sense it.

The endless parade of godless pregnant girls that filed in and out of her office was getting to her. None of them wanted to be pregnant, or stay pregnant, for that matter. Their solution was to rip the living organism inside of them out as easily as Wendy uprooted the unwanted weeds from her garden. No more, she thought as she pulled out the final clover patch in the second row and placed it in a bucket; her patience had worn thin. Drastic measures would be necessary and indeed, she believed with every ounce of her being that God would send her a messenger very soon to help fulfill His plan, and it was up to her to recognize this divine emissary.

A whispered prayer for help and guidance escaped her lips as she felt the overwhelming odds against what she was trying to accomplish. The acquisition of a child of her own had been an unreachable goal for so long, she dared not get her hopes up too high. After her surgery, when the infertility specialist had relayed the bad news, Wendy felt so utterly helpless. And the added insult to injury of her husband fathering another child behind her back had been like a shot through the heart. There was still a festering wound there. Moving away, quitting her job and focusing on her small farm had only provided a small Band-Aid. The only thing that could fill it again and make her feel like a whole woman was to cradle her very own child in her arms and quench her maternal thirst once and for all. Whether it was related by blood meant little to her at this point, as the child would know only her as its mother. That would more than suffice to stave off the unending emotional pain she dealt with every single day.

A faint clucking behind her caused Wendy to turn around. The chickens had found their way to the rich dirt in her garden. She took a short break to watch them work. They would scratch the soil busily, first one clawed, dinosaur-like foot and then the other, until a juicy worm was exposed. In the blink of an eye, a head would dart down and hungrily grab the hapless creature with its beak and swallow in a single motion. If they weren't fast enough after capturing the worm to swallow it, another chicken would zero in and the struggle would end with each getting a partial meal. As she watched them, a metaphor occurred to her regarding her current situation. She too would have to pounce quickly and without hesitation when the situation she was waiting for presented itself. No one else could see what she had captured or she would lose her prize. Half measures just wouldn't do if she hoped to succeed.

The wheels came off her serene reverie at that point and tears of hope and pain welled up and her vision blurred. She wiped her eyes with the front of her sports bra and decided to momentarily abandon her tedious chore. Scooting forward off the knee pad, she moved it onto the rye grass next to the garden, then laid back and rested her head on the foam cushion. Sprawled out on the cool lawn, she shaded her eyes from a blazing sun. The tears continued unabated and moved like a new river over dry land, finding the path of least resistance on her dirt-stained skin. She felt the cold, wet intrusion of a single drop that found its way into her right ear. Her arms felt heavy, as did her heart, so she ignored the unpleasant sensation. It was nothing compared to the suffering she had endured from a childless life.

Years of raised hopes dashed, resurrected, only to be dashed again haunted her. At long last, a sliver of hope pierced the dismal abyss she had wallowed in for so long. It had been born of her unexpected inspiration two nights ago. God had revealed a way she could save a life and heal her own heart as well. When, not if, the opportunity presented itself depended solely on His grace. She had faith in that. Slipping her feet out of the garden clogs, she burrowed her heels into the refreshing grass and felt an inner strength taking hold. *Buck up*, she scolded herself. This was very likely going to demand unwavering belief in her Maker, as well as determination and courage to pull off. Lying there in self-pity wasn't going to accomplish anything. A resolute determination replaced her mournful expression and she hoisted herself up. Brushing the dirt off of her pants, she spied the chickens by their coop.

"Here chick," she clucked her tongue, "Mom's got some treats for you." They turned their heads and formed a little train behind her as she headed for the garden shed to retrieve their feed.

****

Annatha turned down the gravel driveway leading to her grandmother's house just outside of Monroe, Washington. The rocks peppered the undercarriage of her Honda Civic like popcorn off a skillet. She had not called ahead, so she wasn't sure if Nana was home, but she decided that morning she needed a break to do something besides vomit and sleep all day. Not having a definite plan, she just knew a few hours with her horse would rescue her from the troubled whirlpool she was thrashing about in. Since her father had died the preceding November, she had not had the heart to visit or ride at his mother's mini-ranch in the Snohomish valley, but a change of scenery was called for and this was the first place she thought of. The entrance was lined with tall firs and a white rail fence that guided her to the circular drive in front of the rambler with sunflower yellow siding where Nana lived alone. The car came to a stop and she waited as the dust cloud that followed her swept over the car and dissipated slowly in the still summer air.

When she stepped out of the car, the familiar smells welcomed her and she stood for a moment, waiting for her stomach to react. Fortunately, it didn't seem to mind and even welcomed the scent of a freshly mown field of orchard grass. She headed for the front door and rang the pewter bell that was fastened to the side of the door frame. It was never clear to her why Nana didn't own a doorbell. The loud tones echoed around the covered porch but quickly fell silent, and only a slight breeze stirred the wind chimes hanging above a cedar swing. *Probably still with her church folks,* Annatha decided and headed for the barn.

Before reaching her destination, curiosity got the best of her and she detoured around the side of the metal structure to check on her dad's '68 Mustang parked along the side under an eave. Nana kept it protected from the elements with a large gray tarp. She lifted the front cover and admired the chrome grill and metallic blue paint job on the hood. Her dad had spent countless hours working on the car and always referred to it with pride as "cherry," bestowing upon it the name of Cherry Blue. It was sleek and sporty, and the midnight blue paint sparkled in the sunlight almost as brightly as her dad's eyes when he was behind the wheel. The rebuilt engine screamed around sharp curves and frightened her at first, but after getting used to it, she relished the excitement. They had taken Cherry Blue on scores of day trips with the top down and the wind in their faces along winding roads that looked like fur lined corridors in Mount Baker National Forest. Before he lapsed into an irreversible coma, her dad ordered his mother to give it to Annatha when she felt the time was right. Last month Nana promised her she could have it for Christmas this year if her driving record was perfect. The thought of possessing a car that Brandon couldn't take away from her was intoxicating, not to mention she would have something her dad poured his heart and soul into. She would take such good care of Cherry Blue. Several long months would need to pass before her dream came true; she sighed and replaced the cover before resuming her original course to the barn.

Once inside, the familiar blend of horse manure, grain and hay opened the door to Annatha's memories of her dad. The nostalgia was double-edged. It brought almost overwhelming sadness that he was gone forever, and with him, their time together. On the other hand, the happy memories softened ever so slightly the harsh reality of her loss. After he sobered up a year before his untimely death, they had spent many weekends helping Nana around the small ranch and riding on the hundreds of acres of Weyerhauser logging roads adjacent to the property. Despite the fact the heavy scent of horse manure should be unpleasant, Annatha didn't mind it. Now, cow pies or dog and cat shit were a different story altogether.

The large door allowed in some light, but the sun was on the other side of the barn, so she waited for her eyes to become accustomed to the dimly lit interior. She listened quietly for any sound coming from one of the six stalls that lined the cement walkway. After a few moments, she knew the horses were all in the pasture because they couldn't help pacing around when someone entered their territory, waiting to see if it was a predator or friend. Striding purposefully, she emerged from the rear of the barn into the fenced pasture where three horses were grazing. Immediately, their heads shot up and studied the intruder who had just invaded their domain.

The closest one was Annatha's quarter horse, Magic. The great thing about owning a horse was it didn't matter what their name was before you acquired them, you could call them anything you wanted and over time, they would respond to it. When her father brought her to Nana's on her fourteenth birthday and opened the stall to reveal her gift, Annatha had felt like her dad had pulled a rabbit out of a hat, thus the name Magic. He was a ten year old bay gelding with three white socks and stood an even fifteen hands, just the right size for her. His large brown eyes that studied her now had melted her heart the first time she laid eyes on him.

The other two were also geldings, but her dad's was almost eighteen years old. He was a dark brown, sixteen-hand quarter horse with a black mane and a white blaze between his eyes. You couldn't find a more gentle horse. Her dad had called him a nag breed gelding and said that nags were the most underrated breed in the world. They never did anything to hurt you and even though they might not be the fastest horse on four legs, they got you where you wanted to go safely. Nana's brown and white paint almost shrugged when he saw her and went back to grazing.

Magic slowly walked a few yards towards Annatha and then stopped, waiting for her to make a move. Her dad's horse, Sam, didn't hesitate; he plodded over slowly and stood in front of her, shaking his head up and down once as if to say hello. It was then that she decided Sam needed some company and slipped the halter she had grabbed in the barn over his head and took the lead rope in her right hand. "Sorry, Magic," she apologized to her horse, who seemed dumbfounded she wasn't taking him. Then she turned and walked into the barn, Sam plodding alongside her. Once inside, she cross tied him in the grooming stall.

Brushing Sam was easier than she thought it would be. Obviously, Nana had been grooming him regularly. While she pounded the dust out of a saddle pad, Annatha wondered what feelings her grandmother had when handling her deceased son's horse. Satisfied it was free of any small stones that would rub a sore on Sam's back; she hoisted the pad with some difficulty over the oversized gelding. The leathery saddle's smell filled her nostrils as she grabbed the horn in one hand and the cantle with the other and hauled it over the massive back, carefully positioning the front skirt over his withers. She cinched the saddle tightly and secured the flank belt, then slid the snaffle bit easily into his mouth and lifted the bridle over the ears. One sign of a horse with good ground manners was how much one could mess with their ears, and Annatha felt like she could yank on them with a pair of pliers and Sam wouldn't protest. Gathering the reins, she exited the barn with Sam in tow and stopped short as she noticed Nana's green Ford pickup pulling up behind the Civic.

When she emerged from the truck, there was a wide grin on her hard face. Nana's appearance was typical of a woman who had worked outside most of her life. Of medium height, her wiry figure was deceiving in a T-shirt and Wrangler jeans. She could haul a bale of hay onto a truck bed as easy as the teenage boys who were hired to help "hay" the field every summer. A John Deere hat hid the shock of white hair underneath. She kept it short because it was easy to wash and dry every morning before doing her chores.

"Hi Nana," Annatha greeted her cheerfully.

Gathering her granddaughter in her arms, Rose Wolcott squeezed hard and said, "It's about time you came to see me, Annatha Bannanatha."

Annatha both hated and loved the fact that Nana called her such a cheesy name. It made her feel like a little girl every time, when she was trying so hard to be seen as a young woman. But in fact, she didn't really mind; it was familiar and comforting at the same time.

"I thought I'd ride some today," she said weakly through the strong grasp around her chest.

Rose pulled away and studied her. "So, you didn't come to see me after all," she winked. She reached out and stroked Sam's nose. "I'm sure he'd appreciate some attention after all this time."

Annatha immediately recognized the blank stare on her Nana's sun baked face. She was looking a million miles away. "Why don't you come with me?" she asked.

"I'd like to," Rose replied as her gaze snapped back to the present, "but my right knee is locking up on me and sitting in a saddle is almost unbearable. That damn doctor always has the same remedy for my ailments. If it hurts to go like that, Rose," she feigned a deep male voice and moved her leg up and down, "don't go like that." Annatha laughed.

"You and Sam go have a good time," she motioned with her head. "I need to unload the grain I just bought for the boys. Come on in when you get back and we'll have cold lemonade and some juicy chick chat."

"Deal, Nana," Annatha smiled and turned to cinch up Sam one more time before climbing into the saddle.

"Make him work, girl," Rose called after her as she headed down the drive towards the road. Annatha waved without turning around and kicked Sam gently to pick up the pace.

A half a mile or so later they were far enough down the trail that she couldn't see any signs of civilization. The foxgloves were blooming in an array of colors that lined the logging road. Annatha's favorites were the white ones with a dollop of pink in the middle. Sam would make a half-hearted attempt to grab some long grass on the side of the road from time to time, but Annatha just jerked the reins and said no. After the umpteenth time, she turned his head and walked him in a tight circle for a few minutes. This was a maneuver horses hated and worked very well when disciplining them. Her dad had taught it to her. After the brief lesson, Sam never tried to eat on the run again. Annatha felt sorry for him: it was like leading a hungry person through a buffet without letting them eat, but it wasn't good to let a horse get distracted so it was necessary.

Sam knew the way as well as Annatha did and after an hour they reached the top of a vista. The trees had been logged, so the view was spectacular. She could see Mount Rainier to the south and Mount Baker to the north. Despite the fact it was July, there was still plenty of snow on them and their beauty always left her in awe. She climbed down to stretch her legs, threw the reins over

Sam's neck and let him graze on the lush grass. Annatha climbed onto a large boulder to view the Cascade Range more clearly. She inhaled a deep breath of the warm summer air and drank in the scenery. This was exactly what she needed. Despite the dark cloud over her the past few days, the bright sunlit peaks of the jagged volcanic mountains soothed her soul as always. The only sad part was her dad wasn't there to share it with her as he had so often in the past. She never quite grasped what he meant when he told her that this was his spiritual church. He often spoke of the spirituality he had found working the steps of AA, but it was like listening to a foreign language to her. It had given him peace and the strength to not drink again, and that was all that mattered.

Annatha admired the majesty of the mountains that carved the horizon, and a determination grew inside not to pile one tragedy on another by becoming a single, teenage, poverty-stricken mother. She never prayed, but she felt close to her dad in this place and silently asked him to help her have the strength to see this through. A whole life lay ahead of her, but it would be forever changed if she was burdened with raising a child before she finished her education. Despite the fact she was planning to terminate the existence of the life she bore inside her, Annatha had never been more certain she was making the right decision. She had nothing to offer this baby, and would most certainly be kicked out on the street only to bounce from one bad situation to another. That was no way to raise a child. No, she would get beyond this, and move forward without looking back. One day she would be ready for a baby. This was not that day.

A feeling of peace settled in and she walked back over to Sam and hoisted herself back into the saddle. She laid the reins across his right neck and the horse turned left and headed back down the trail the same way they had come. Annatha realized she was thirsty and couldn't wait to taste some of Nana's cold lemonade. She kicked Sam more forcefully, and he broke into an easy lope. Annatha fell into the rhythm of Sam's body as he moved down the trail. Warm air fluttered through her hair and she drank in the breathtaking moment atop the powerful gelding her dad once rode. *Nag breed,* she smiled. *This guy was no nag.*

Chapter Four

Four Weeks, Five Days (4W5D)

Meredith glanced up from her card hand when she heard Annatha clear her throat at the entrance to the entertainment room. She had a few friends over and was playing bridge after feeding them a light lunch with martinis for dessert.

"Yes?" she asked cheerily.

Annatha rolled her eyes. Her mother made her sick the way she acted in front of her socialite friends. "I'm going to the movies and won't be back until late," she said.

"Get something to eat while you're at it," her mother frowned. "You look like an x-ray."

"Thanks, Mom," she replied icily. "Love you, too."

Meredith turned to her company and shook her head. "Raising teenagers is like trying to nail jello to a tree." Polite laughter erupted and they resumed their game.

Annatha was already heading for the front door and wondered if her mother's last remark was going to make her any more nauseous than she already felt. Making a critical comment about her weight in front of people who didn't even know her was so rude; she had almost bit her tongue in half to keep from firing back a nasty retort. Too bad she didn't get off her dead ass and offer her some of the food she had prepared for the people who were most important to her: rich housewives. She closed the door and decided it was best to ignore the underlying anger at her mother's offensive behavior; she had more important issues to deal with today. The long-anticipated Monday rendezvous was upon her.

Negotiating heavy traffic on the floating bridge over the calm, deep blue expanse of Lake Washington, Annatha wondered how her meeting would go with Thomas. Her life would never be the same if she couldn't get rid of this pregnancy without her family finding out. Even though she was loved by Nana, she would definitely not want to be burdened by Annatha moving in after being thrown out by her stepdad. There were many times she would call her grandmother after her mom first married Brandon, crying and begging to let her come live on the ranch. Nana had listened patiently every time, then firmly explained to her that life was hard, and what we are and what we are to become depended on how we dealt with adversity. Annatha had definitely not wanted to hear that. She wanted to be comforted and invited with open arms to move in with Nana. There was one time she always regretted when she got so mad at being told once more to basically buck up, she yelled, "No wonder Dad drank so much" and slammed the phone down. It was some time before Nana spoke to her again.

Her thoughts wandered to the impending rendezvous with Thomas. *Would he be understanding?* He seemed so kind and compassionate when she unloaded her troubles that night in chat. Most likely it was bait to get her into the sack, but she had to believe he wasn't all bad. How would she tell him? "I'm pregnant and it's yours" seemed the most direct way. Would he believe her? Glancing in the mirror, she hoped the makeup hid her pale features. *Morning sickness? Hell,* she thought, *the all-day sickness has taken a toll on my features.* She stared at her colorless skin that mimicked the appearance of Morticia from *The Addams Family* sitcom without her beautiful, dark eyes. *God,* she moaned, *I look like I just got released from a Nazi death camp.* She decided to heap on some more foundation to give her face some semblance of color and hide the dark circles under her eyes. Thomas just had to help her. She sighed in desperation as she juggled her attention between the makeover and negotiating I90 traffic. She hoped he didn't go all gallant on her and want to get married. "He's probably married, dumbass," she said out loud.

The really weird thing in this mosh pit of trouble she was being tossed about in was the fact that she was really pregnant. Annatha still had trouble getting her mind around this reality. There was a living organism inside of her and she desperately wanted to get it out of her body. She had nothing against motherhood, just not at her age or circumstances. Abortion had never been a topic she had given much thought. There was always the women's rights issue embraced by her schoolmates whenever the discussion came up, but more importantly, the moral aspect of terminating a pregnancy had never suffered a debate in her mind. She cracked the window and breathed in fresh air, hoping it would quell the queasy feeling in her gut. It wasn't clear if the pregnancy or the looming showdown with Thomas was making her nauseous right now, but her stomach was doing a weird dance and she wanted it to stop.

The exit to SeaTac airport loomed ahead and she turned on the blinker before exiting the interstate. *It's almost show time, girl,* she whispered under her breath. Then out of nowhere, a weird thought that this would make a good reality TV show suddenly popped into her head as she slowed down for a red light. *You're an idiot,* she scolded herself in the mirror.

****

Thomas Loftin was browsing in the lingerie section of Victoria's Secret at South Center Mall near SeaTac airport. The morning had gone well for him. He had been brilliant at the deposition. So brilliant, in fact, he had gotten carried away and it lasted longer than planned. He was running late but he wanted to get something sexy for Annatha to wear. It wasn't easy trying to pick out the correct size. He recalled her breasts weren't particularly large, but she had a nice trim figure and would look killer in something sheer and tight. He decided dressing naughty for him was the least she could do since he had agreed to meet her a second time, something he had never done before. The sales girl had good taste but she was making it difficult for him with so many choices. To make matters worse, she insisted he touch every item she selected. They were all so silky smooth and his tactile preference was not the issue. A sexy color and revealing style were the choices he focused on.

Finally, he made a decision and quickly paid for it with cash. No sense in risking a credit card bill being discovered by Laurel, even though she had not paid attention to their finances since their son was born, despite the fact she was a CPA and numbers were her life. Glancing at his watch as he hurried through the mall, he discovered he was running behind about fifteen minutes. After looking forward to this meeting all week, he wasn't going to let it slip away, so he pulled out his iPhone and scrolled down to SeaTac, the ID name he had entered for Annatha's cell phone number. He pressed enter and waited.

The cell phone ring tone sounded and startled Annatha. She had just taken a booth at Denny's after waiting a few minutes. Thomas was not there yet and she was just beginning to wonder if he was going to show. Glancing at the number on the display, she didn't recognize it; the area code was 303. Suddenly a feeling of dread washed over her. *He's going to cancel. God, what am I going to do now?* she groaned and pressed the answer key. She placed the phone against her ear and tried to squelch her growing dread.

"Hello?" she tried to sound normal.
"Annatha, it's Thomas, how are you?" he sounded upbeat.
"I'm fine," she replied. "Where are you?"
"Only a few minutes away, babe; sorry I'm running behind."
She hoped Thomas didn't hear the air that just rushed out of

her lungs in relief. "No worries," she managed meekly, "I have a booth so I'll see you when you get here."

"See you in a few, I …," his voice was cut off suddenly and the line went dead.

Annatha glanced down at her cell phone and realized the battery was dead. *Goddamit,* she swore, swept up her purse and headed for the door.

"I'll be right back," she informed the waitress, who had a puzzled expression. "I need something from my car."

"Okay, hon," the waitress smiled.

Plugging in her cell phone to the car charger, Annatha dialed the last call on her phone.

"It's Annatha, Thomas," she said quickly when he answered. "Sorry, my phone went dead. I had to go out to my car and plug it into the charger."

"I thought you changed your mind," he teased her. "Just leave it in the charger; I'm almost there. You're not going to need it for a few hours."

Annatha rolled her eyes at the last remark he made, then checked briefly to be sure the battery was charging before returning to her booth. The strong smells of coffee and food cooking filled her nostrils again and her gut began protesting loudly. She jumped up and headed for the bathroom. Fortunately, it was a false alarm, as she only dry-heaved a few times. Stopping in front of the mirror on her way out, she primped one last time before returning to the booth.

Thomas strode through the door just as she slid into the vinyl covered bench. He was scanning the other side of the Denny's. Annatha's first thought was he looked pretty hot for his age, what she called a "Crombie Mod Bod" after the well known clothier Abercrombie and Fitch's modelesque male bodies. He was wearing a forest green, long sleeved crew neck shirt with a white T-shirt underneath and neatly pressed jeans that hugged his athletic legs. She raised her arm slightly so when he turned her way he spotted her at once. A big smile dressed his face and he swaggered over to where she was sitting. He leaned over and planted a kiss on her cheek, then sat down on the other side of the table.

A river of fear moved rapidly into Annatha's brain; it was a loud, rushing sound and quickly overwhelmed her senses. Unable to stave off the torrent of anxiety that had suddenly swept over her, she struggled to clear her head and comprehend what Thomas was going on about. But the driving sound crescendoed in her ears at the same time her view of Thomas's face narrowed and she could only make out his lips moving, as if she was watching a movie screen through a cardboard toilet paper roll. It was useless, she realized as she struggled again to shake loose the panic seizing her brain. She knew she would be incapable of making small talk before she dropped the bomb; if she didn't let it out now, she felt her head was going to explode from the churning apprehension she was helplessly fighting against.

Through the din, she heard her name being repeated and struggled to focus. With a great deal of effort, she finally understood he was calling her name over and over.

"Annatha," he repeated firmly this time.

She blushed and the intense racket in her head ceased immediately, as if he had grabbed an arm and pulled her to the bank, saving her from being swept away.

"Are you okay?" Thomas questioned her softly, looking around the booths to see if anyone had heard him raise his voice as he called her name repeatedly. *What the fuck is with this kid?* he thought. She looked pale, thin and very distracted. Jesus, she was the one who called him so what gives? Even though he had been looking forward to an afternoon tryst with this cute, petite, auburn-haired chick, he was tempted to get up and run out of the restaurant, then drive away quickly and not look back. His butt had just lifted slightly from the cushioned vinyl bench to begin his exit when she finally spoke.

"Thomas," she blurted out, her eyes welling with tears, "I'm pregnant and it's yours."

Stopping his planned retreat from the restaurant, Thomas

suddenly felt as if an opposing attorney had just presented evidence that blew his case out of the water. His mind was racing now, wondering how he had let himself be drawn into seeing a woman for the second time, a rule he had made early on. *It's water under the bridge now*, he scolded himself. *This shit will need to be dealt with if it's true, and dealt with quickly and quietly.* He studied her face. Tears had made their way down her cheeks and rested against her upper lip on one side.

"I thought," he croaked, cleared his throat and started again. "I thought you were using birth control."

Annatha felt a giant weight was lifted after announcing her news. She felt a little calmer now, especially since Thomas didn't immediately question her about his paternity in the matter. A salty taste in her mouth made her realize she was crying, so she grabbed a napkin and wiped her face.

"I was," she lied and squeezed the napkin in her fist. "I'm so sorry this happened."

"And you're sure it's mine?" he blurted out the inevitable question.

There it was, but to his credit, it wasn't his first response, she thought.

"Yes, I'm sure," her voice was more measured now, resolved. "I haven't been with anyone else in six months."

Thomas hesitated. There was much he wanted to say but he had to tread carefully now; this young woman had the power to cause him a good deal of trouble if he made her angry.

"Okay, Annatha," he said in a softer voice. "I'm not blaming you; accidents happen." Before he could continue, the waitress appeared at their booth, smiling broadly.

"What can I get you two?" she beamed.

Thomas looked at Annatha. She had grabbed a menu and glanced at it briefly.

"Coke," she said and closed the menu. The waitress turned to Thomas.

"Ice tea for me," he replied.

The waitress gathered their menus and disappeared, the smile gone after taking their puny order.

"So you have lured me here, so to speak," Thomas continued carefully, "which means you must want something from me."

Annatha shrugged but didn't deny his accusation. She gathered herself for the pitch she had gone over in her mind a hundred times in the past few days.

"First of all," she began, "I'm not going to have the baby." The relief in Thomas' face was obvious after her opening sentence. Good, she thought, just what she had hoped for. "I wouldn't have even called you if I could have an abortion without my stepdad finding out," Annatha admitted. "I don't have any money for an abortion, which is the only reason I even wanted you to know. I hoped you would help me get this thing done and over with as quickly as possible."

This is a best case scenario, Thomas rejoiced silently. She wasn't asking for anything more than his help terminating the pregnancy. Suddenly, the thought crossed his mind she might not be pregnant and just wanted to milk some money out of him for a Wii. *Jesus Christ you idiot,* he chided himself for having such suspicions*, most people aren't as devious and manipulating as you are.* She seemed sincere and he just needed to suck it up and do the right thing.

"Just in case you're wondering if I'm a greedy kid trying to shake you down," she seemed to read his mind and reached in her purse. She retrieved something and sat it on the table in front of him. It was her pregnancy test strip. "Since you're a lawyer," she continued, "here is exhibit A."

The corner of his mouth rose slightly with her last remark. This kid had a sense of humor despite her crappy situation, he mused as a grim smile forced itself onto his face. He weighed his options silently as always, never wanting to feel he was painted into a corner by anyone. There was always the scenario where he just got up and walked out of Denny's and drove away, leaving this unfortunate girl behind with her problem. The hole in this option was that she had his cell phone number from his earlier call, although he could ditch it and get a new number. However, there was the possibility she could have it traced by a professional. Giving her the cash would mean there would be no physical trace that they ever met. The downside to this was she could change her mind and cause God knows what kind of trouble for him. If he interjected himself into the process and made certain she had the abortion, all would be erased and his life would be back on track. Not to mention, the unfortunate girl's life would also be back on track. After all, he did share some responsibility for her predicament. However, going with the option that gave the opposition their first choice had never been his style.

"What if I walk out and tell you this is your problem, since I was told you were using birth control?" he asked coldly.

Annatha felt her throat go suddenly dry, as if she had just swallowed a bucket of sand. Despite the fact she had rehearsed this scenario in her mind countless times the past few days, she had hoped it wouldn't come to this. However, alone with her thoughts last night, her practical side had reminded her she had to be ready to play hardball if needed. She deliberately reached into her purse and retrieved her driver's license. Placing it flat, she slowly pushed it across the table top until it rested directly in front of Thomas.

"I didn't lie about birth control," she studied his face as she measured her words, "but I lied about my age. I'm not eighteen Thomas, I'm only sixteen."

If her display had affected him she couldn't tell. *Damn, he's got a good poker face,* she marveled but continued to press. "Which means that if I go to the police there is a pretty good chance I could have you tracked down through the hotel records," her voice cracked slightly, unaccustomed to threatening anyone but her parents.

Despite the direct threat, Thomas admired her spunk. The evidence to back her statement was right in front of him and he could see she was not bull-shitting him in the least. *Tough broad, he thought.* She had an ace in the hole after all. He wasn't surprised at the false age she gave him that night; fighting it in court wouldn't be too difficult, but the effect on his life would be devastating, which left him with only one choice if he wanted to avoid messy.

"Point taken," he surrendered and pushed the license back to Annatha, "although I wasn't serious about leaving you all alone with this. I was mostly thinking aloud."

That's a load of crap, Annatha thought, but she felt a growing confidence that her daring ploy had worked and he was going to help her.

"So what way would you feel most comfortable with giving me the money?" she asked.

Thomas reached in his back pocket and produced an iPhone. He held up one hand, gesturing for her to wait for his plan to reveal itself. He Googled pregnancy in Washington and selected the choice for problem pregnancies. There was a link to abortion clinics. He didn't want to take the remote chance they would walk into a clinic where a gynecologist he had sued or deposed was working, so he scrolled down to the ones listed in the Tacoma area. He couldn't recall filing a claim or deposing any doctors from that city. After several calls, he wasn't having any luck getting Annatha an appointment that day, and he was due to fly back to Denver that evening.

Annatha listened as Thomas tried in vain to make her an appointment for that afternoon. The fact he was taking care of this so quickly was heartening. She felt it would be too good to be true to have this over with today.

When his last call failed, Thomas swore under his breath and placed the iPhone in front of him. Maybe a Seattle clinic would be best, despite his reservations.

"No luck?" Annatha asked.

"I tried Tacoma to keep this thing private for you," Thomas rubbed his eyes thoughtfully. "No one has an opening today."

She had not considered location before now, but far away

sounded better than closer. Never knew who you might run into.

"Try Olympia," she suggested, "that's only an hour away."

Retrieving his phone, Thomas searched in Olympia and only found two clinics that advertised doing terminations. He was fast losing hope this could be resolved today, but he dialed the first number anyway. To his surprise and relief, the receptionist reported a cancellation had just been made and if they could be there within the hour they could have it. Thomas agreed and inquired about any fees for the process. She provided the information and he hung up.

"Okay," Thomas announced as he replaced the iPhone in his pocket, "here's the plan. I'll follow you to the nearest airport park and ride. We'll leave your car there and I'll drive you to the clinic and bring you back before I have to catch my plane this evening. You might get a sedative or something and you shouldn't drive yourself." He didn't know if this was true or not, but it afforded him the opportunity to make certain she went through with it.

"Thank you," she said gratefully, "you're doing the right thing." With that she got up, leaned over and kissed Thomas on the cheek.

Lord, he thought, *I'm being congratulated on my moral character by a teenager.* He just nodded weakly and walked after her to his car.

"Why can't we leave my car here?" Annatha squinted against the bright sunny day.

"It might get towed."

They drove to the nearest park and ride. Thomas paid the attendant in advance and then stopped at the first ATM he saw after leaving the lot. He withdrew five hundred dollars and when he returned to the rent car, he entered the clinic address in the navigator menu and the computer guided them to their destination in a flat, monotone voice. The trip was quiet, as neither had much to say that had not already been said. They were both on a mission and their focus was consumed with it.

Fortunately, the traffic was light and they made the trip in under an hour.

Thomas pulled into the professional building parking lot off Lilly Road on the east side of Olympia. Despite his announced plan, he had no intention of hanging around while Annatha went through an abortion. His task was done. He would give her money for the procedure and transportation back to the park and ride. Annatha had convinced him she would go through with it by driving with him with no other way back.

"Annatha," Thomas called to her and she turned around. He was standing by the side of the car, his door still open. "Please come here."

She walked back to where he stood and could tell the plans had changed by the look on his face.

"I can't do this with you," he apologized. "I have a flight to catch. Here is enough cash for the abortion and if you call the airport shuttle when you're done, they can drive you back to the Park and Fly. There's enough money here for that, too."

"You've done enough," she reassured him, despite the fact even a stranger for company with what she was about to go through would have been comforting. She took the cash, turned and headed for the entrance to the clinic.

Thomas watched her go through the front door. *It's over,* he breathed a sigh of relief. Now he had a plane to catch. All he could think about as he pulled back onto the main road in front of the office building was that his "no repeat encounters" rule would never be broken again. If he had steadfastly followed this simple canon, his life would never have suffered the upheaval it had today.

****

Wendy was gazing out the window that overlooked the parking lot. She spotted a small foreign car and observed the two people who were talking on the side of it. *The man seems a bit older than the girl; could be her dad,* she decided. She certainly hoped it wasn't the baby's father. It could be her work-in this afternoon. When the scheduled patient had cancelled, Wendy planned on leaving early to take a walk in Tumwater Falls Park. She could feel desperation creeping in, despite her hopeful affirmations the day before. A connection with nature and God would have done her good, but shortly after the cancellation, the receptionist informed her she had worked in a patient who seemed desperate to be seen that day. Sunset was after 9 pm, so she would go after work.

The thought of facilitating another fetal death was pushed far down for now and Wendy prepared the pamphlets and materials she would need to counsel her patient.

****

Annatha entered the building with mixed emotions. Thomas had come through with the money and even arranged to pay for the shuttle ride back to her car, but it would have been more chivalrous of him if he had stayed and helped her through the process. Alone and nervous, Annatha keenly felt the loss of her father. He would not have approved of what she had done, but he would have been there to walk her through each step. She checked the note Thomas gave her with the doctor's name on it and opened the glass door where it was stenciled in gold letters.

The cool air conditioning inside the office raised goose bumps on her bare arms, or maybe it was fear of the unknown that caused them. She wasn't sure but shrugged into her sweatshirt hoody to keep warm. The receptionist who greeted her when she approached the front desk looked younger than her and had eyebrow and nose piercings. Her white face was framed by jet black hair and Annatha surmised she was Goth. *Appropriate choice for her line of work,* she thought.

Her dry mouth opened to return the receptionist's less than enthusiastic welcome but nothing came out. Clearing her throat, she tried again. "My name is Annatha Wolcott and I just called to schedule this appointment."

Immediately, a clipboard was thrust in front of her and the

receptionist instructed her to fill out the forms, and then asked for her driver's license.

Annatha took the clipboard and looked up at the last request. "Why do you need my driver's license?" she asked.

"To confirm ID, Miss, its office protocol," she said drily.

Retrieving the license, Annatha handed it over and took a seat. She glanced around but no one else was in the waiting room. The walls were decorated with scenic photos of natural wonders displayed against burgundy wallpaper. Not knowing what she expected, the beautiful pictures looked out of place to her in an office where people came to end a pregnancy. *Well, what did you think.* she asked herself, *there would be pictures of wailing women and dead babies?*

Shaking off this image, she filled out the form, returned it to the receptionist, and retraced her steps to the bench and sat down. There were magazines on the table in front of her, but reading at this point would have been an exercise in futility. Her stomach churned angrily from the anxiety she felt and she noticed her hands trembled slightly when writing down the information on the form. There were two things she managed to be thankful for despite her fears: privacy laws and no parental consent was needed for her to have an abortion.

After a brief wait, the door next to the reception desk opened and a tall, attractive woman with medium-length light brown hair wearing blue scrubs stepped out. Annatha felt the woman's steady gaze sizing her up for a moment before she spoke.

"Annatha?" she asked, despite the fact there was no one else in the waiting room. "I'm Wendy," she continued, "please follow me."

Annatha stood and dutifully followed the nurse into the hallway. They dispensed of the usual intake routine, recording weight and blood pressure results.

"My office is across the hall," the nurse pointed at the doorway. "Please go in and have a seat; I'll be right with you."

Wendy watched the young girl as she followed her directions.

She wondered silently where the man was she saw her with in the parking lot. He wasn't in the waiting room and when she went in an exam room that had a window overlooking the parking lot, she saw the car was gone. *My mistake,* she admitted, *he wasn't the girl's dad, most likely he was the FOB* (Father of the Baby). Wendy shook her head in disgust and then studied the billing form. There was no listing for an emergency contact. *That's odd,* she thought. It indicated to her the girl didn't want her family to know what was going on, which made perfect sense given the age difference she witnessed in the parking lot.

Wendy felt light-headed, so she leaned against the wall next to the window. She noticed she was breathing more rapidly than normal and her heart was pounding. Deliberately, she closed her eyes and willed the unwelcome anxiety to dissipate. She had to think this through carefully. The girl was all alone, with no support person, and her family had no idea where she was. It was a perfect setup. All she had to do was gain the girl's confidence by coming to her emotional rescue.

She opened her eyes and stared at the brilliant blue sky, believing in her soul such a beautiful day had to be an omen. *This might be the opportunity foretold over the weekend,* she considered. Sure it was only a rudimentary plan that had no meat, but preparations in the basement had been completed as an act of faith. Could God have placed the opportunity in front of her so soon to fulfill His will? First, Wendy told herself, she had to convince this girl she only had her best interest at heart. After all, wasn't it in the girl's best interest to save her from going through with the horrible deed she was planning? *That's your take on it,* she reminded herself. *The girl might not see it that way just yet.* She knew without a doubt the girl's unborn child's best interest would be served by saving its life, but if she presented this fact without laying a proper foundation, the whole thing could blow up in her face. Gathering herself together for what could be a pivotal moment in her life, Wendy strode out of the exam room and entered her office with a motherly smile on her face.

"Okay, young lady," she began, "what can I do for you today?" Wendy studied the girl's face closely. She was very pretty, with deep green eyes accented by thick, auburn hair that fell halfway down her back. Her figure was wafer thin and despite the beauty of her emerald eyes, they looked troubled..

"I want to have an abortion," Annatha said the words out loud for the first time.

Wendy didn't flinch at the response. She began by asking when her last menstrual period was, if she had a positive pregnancy test, and other medical history questions. She noted the girl answered each query directly but with no extra information. Wendy knew she was very nervous and that could work to her advantage.

"Have you considered other options?" she looked directly into Annatha's eyes with this question.

"At sixteen?" Annatha's voice suddenly filled with emotion. "I have no options."

Wendy paused for a moment, allowing the girl to regroup. *So you're crying because you have no options,* she thought sarcastically. *Who cries for your baby?* Reminding herself that such recriminations were not helpful at this point, Wendy assumed a nurturing tone when she spoke.

"Does the father know about your decision?" she asked.

Annatha wiped her eyes and replied. "Yes, he's paying for this but he was just a one-night stand and doesn't even live in this state."

"I see." Wendy observed with a gaze that held no sign of judgment. Her personal reactions must be hidden during the interview if she hoped to win the girl over. Besides, the next line of questioning would be crucial.

"What about your parents," Wendy said softly, "do they know you're pregnant?"

A cloud descended over Annatha's face and her brow furrowed. "They don't know and they wouldn't give a shit anyway," she replied sternly. "Sorry about the language."

"No problem, go on," Wendy waved off her apology.

"I hate my stepdad. My mom doesn't care what I do as long as I stay out of her way, and my real dad died six months ago." Annatha paused, surprised she was revealing so much information, but the nurse had kind eyes and seemed concerned. "If I told them," she continued, "my stepdad would put me on a bus to Alaska with a one-way ticket."

"That's sad," Wendy said sympathetically and reached over and patted her trembling hand. "I'll help you through this, Annatha, that's what I'm here for."

The kind gesture surprised Annatha. It was motherly and caring, but in addition, completely unexpected from a total stranger. She looked into the nurse's eyes and was amazed to see they were brimming with tears. Annatha felt her despair melting in the compassionate gaze that was fixed on her now. She reflexively turned a palm over and squeezed the nurse's comforting hand.

After a few moments, when Wendy felt the bonding was proceeding as planned, she released her grip and straightened up in the chair. She feigned composing herself while studying the copy of Annatha's driver's license displayed on her LCD screen. The address was a Mercer Island residence. *Rich folks,* she thought.

"You live on Mercer Island?" she asked, daubing her eyes with a tissue. "Sorry," she apologized quickly, "I don't usually do this."

"Yes, we do," Annatha replied. She was caught off guard by the nurse's emotional reaction.

A plan had been forming in Wendy's mind during the interview, and she felt it was divine in origin. It wasn't the first time inspiration had been given to her by God. She realized the next few minutes would determine whether or not she could convince this girl to come home with her. Her approach had to be a mixture of vulnerability and savior. It would take some finesse.

"I know you're anxious to get this over with, hon," she began in her most empathetic voice, "but we can't do it today. There's lab work and an ultrasound that need to be done and there is no one here to do them now. Also, you have to be fasting after midnight before the procedure." She purposely avoided offering help at this point to see if the girl would approach her to come up with a solution. "We can't do the medical abortion because you don't want to have a problem after you get home and risk your parents finding out what you've done."

Annatha's head fell and she stared at the floor. She had been so relieved Thomas agreed to help her when that hurdle was crossed. Then a stroke of luck at getting an appointment today lifted her hopes that it would all be over with soon. Now she was being informed she couldn't have an abortion today. What the hell was she going to do now? She felt abandoned and alone, despite the nurse's emotional support. Her mind whirled like a cyclone, searching for options that didn't include her family. She supposed she could take the shuttle back to her car, return home and then come back tomorrow, but she might not be able to drive after the procedure.

"Will I need a driver after the abortion?" she asked.

Wendy didn't think the girl had a ride since the man she spotted her with in the parking lot had left. *How was she planning to get home*? It wouldn't be prudent to admit she was spying on Annatha in the parking lot, though.

"Did you drive yourself here?" she asked with a faked, clueless expression.

"No, the baby's father did but he had a plane to catch. He gave me money to take a shuttle back to SeaTac airport, where I left my car."

"Well, you can't drive yourself home tomorrow after the procedure, since we give you sedation that lasts hours," Wendy replied. She guessed the girl was trying to figure out a way to get back to the clinic without anyone finding out. If she decided on that plan, any chance she had of convincing her to come to her house today would vanish. She had to act quickly.

"Can I make a suggestion?" she said softly and leaned forward.

Annatha nodded weakly, without looking up. She was running out of options.

"I don't normally get involved with patients," Wendy continued in a low tone, "but I can help you out if you let me."

Her head rose with this last offer as Annatha wondered what the nurse had in mind.

"I live alone and have an extra bed at my place. You're welcome to stay there overnight." Wendy paused to see if there was an immediate rejection through body language from the girl. Seeing none, she continued. "I'll drive you here tomorrow, you can have the abortion and then I'll take you back to your car when the drugs have worn off, or you can call the airport shuttle as originally planned. The choice is yours." Her intent was to coax the girl in one direction and simultaneously allow her the option of how to get back to her car. Adolescents responded better if they didn't feel cornered.

Annatha was stunned at first. This was totally unexpected. The nurse seemed genuinely concerned about her situation, but this was going above and beyond. Besides, she knew nothing about her.

"Why would you do that?" she asked curiously.

"I went through something similar at your age," Wendy lied, "and it would have made all the difference if someone had supported me." The "I've been where you are" card was a good one, she knew, and it was time to play it.

"Really?" Annatha replied with a puzzled look. "You got pregnant when you were sixteen?"

"Fifteen," Wendy lied again and touched Annatha's arm. "I know how you feel," she stroked her skin gently, "and I would be grateful if you allowed me to help you through this."

It was certainly an extraordinary offer, Annatha thought as she mulled it over. Even though the gesture was touching, she felt awkward about spending the night with a total stranger. However, it would solve her seemingly hopeless dilemma about how to have the abortion tomorrow without involving anyone else. For some reason, this nurse seemed truly interested in helping her, so she finally made the decision to let her and deal with being uncomfortable for one night. Maybe this was what her dad used to call grace. He defined it as an event that arrived from nowhere at just the right moment to save you from something bad.

Annatha quickly formulated a plan in her head about how she could spend the night away from home without arousing suspicion. She decided to call her Mom and tell her she was spending the night with Nana. This could work, she thought, and felt a rising hope that the nightmarish ordeal would be over with soon after all.

"You don't really know me," Annatha met Wendy's gaze. "Are you sure you want to do this?"

"Don't give it another thought," Wendy smiled broadly. "I'll get the medication we use to help dilate your cervix overnight and we can leave now." She knew the sooner she got Annatha in her car, the less time she would have to change her mind. "You can wait for me at my car in the parking lot; it's the navy blue Acura at the end of the row adjacent to the street." Wendy didn't want the Elvira look-alike receptionist to see them leave together in case anyone traced Annatha to the clinic. The girl would go out the front door, and she would leave through the back entrance. "Here are the keys; you can let yourself in."

"Okay," Annatha agreed, took the keys and headed for the parking lot.

Wendy didn't take long to reach the car and climbed into the driver's seat. She was overjoyed Annatha was there. Trying not to sound paranoid, she grabbed the seatbelt strap and casually asked, "Can you duck down? I don't want my doctor to see me taking a patient with me. He'd ask too many questions and I could get in trouble."

Annatha complied and rested her head between her knees. The inside of the car felt like an oven and the leather seats were as hot as a frying pan. She could feel beads of sweat forming where her thick hair blanketed the skin on her neck, but Wendy turned on the air conditioning and soon she could feel the cool air blowing on her. Annatha flipped her head sideways to expose the sweaty skin on her neck and an icy sensation replaced the uncomfortable heat.

After a block or so, Wendy let the girl know she could sit up. They drove in silence for a while, each deep in their own thoughts. God had finally granted her fervent wish and Wendy allowed the ecstasy to wash over her like a pristine waterfall in a tropical jungle. The stage was set at home. Everything was in place. She couldn't make any mistakes now. The baby's life depended on it. *My baby,* Wendy corrected herself. Finally, after all the years of suffering, she would have a baby, even though it was not born of her womb. It would be the product of her heart and her faith in God. Nothing else mattered. The implications of this last thought fed her euphoria and she struggled to keep it to herself.

"If you want to listen to music," she willed herself into the present and turned to Annatha, "you can pick whatever station you want." She hated teen music. In fact, she hesitated to even call it music, but she would endure this sacrifice to appease her baby's vessel. To her surprise, Annatha chose a station that played blues. An appropriate genre for her passenger's current state of mind, Wendy mused, and not a bad choice either. She liked blues, too.

Annatha leaned back and listened to the soulful sounds of the radio station she chose. She felt odd driving home with a woman she had just met today, but she didn't have much of a choice. Despite the unfamiliarity she was experiencing, she felt they had bonded somewhat, especially since the nurse had been through a similar episode in her life.

Shit, she suddenly remembered, she didn't have her cell phone and needed to call her mom at some point in the evening so Brandon wouldn't go postal on her for not asking permission.

Even though she had failed to come home in the past without calling when she was angry with Brandon, she had paid dearly for her defiance. She certainly didn't want to suffer through a harsh grilling from her stepdad when she showed up tomorrow.

"Can I call my Mom when we get to your house?" Annatha asked as she turned down the volume. "I don't want her calling the FBI."

"Certainly," Wendy replied cheerfully, "I have a land line you can use. My cell phone doesn't get reception there."

"Where do you live?"

"On a few acres near Capital Forest."

"My Nana has a small ranch near Snohomish. It's so peaceful there. I'm telling my Mom that's where I'm staying tonight."

Wendy nodded. "Is Nana is your dad's mom?"

"Yep."

"That's nice." Wendy glanced at the girl. She seemed comfortable enough. It would make everything easier if she remained in that frame of mind. "Are you hungry?"

"My stomach hasn't been hungry for over a week," she said, "and today hasn't helped any."

"Well," Wendy slowed to a stop, "I'll pick some fresh vegetables and we'll make a big salad and feed you a scrumptious meal before you have to be NPO."

"NPO?"

"That's the term we use for fasting before a procedure," Wendy answered. "It's a Latin phrase, *nil per orem,* that means nothing by mouth."

"Oh," Annatha said absently and returned the volume to normal. The kindness of this nurse was sweet and weird at the same time. She was like a younger crazy aunt. Even gave her the option of listening to her own music, something that never happened before, including with her dad when he was alive.

****

Thomas squirmed in his vinyl seat at gate A5 in the American

Airlines terminal at SeaTac. Usually, he was busy at his laptop, making last-minute notes from his deposition. His mood was not light this particular evening. The day had been anything but predictable. He wasn't used to being played by a teenager. Annatha had set him up nicely and came well prepared to get what she wanted. He could tell she was nervous but it hadn't stopped her from laying all her cards on the table. It wasn't exactly extortion but certainly felt like it. On the other hand, he was lucky she had been so adamant about getting an abortion. If she had taken a different tack ... he shuddered unconsciously at the thought. Laurel would certainly have left him, faced with such a debacle, and he would have been disgraced at the firm. No more out of town trips, if they kept him on at all.

There was no thought given to putting a stop to his philandering on these trips. Life was too dull without the challenge of luring a young woman into his bed. The opportunity to do so only came around a couple of times a month, and he slogged through his droll life as a well-respected attorney, father and husband by playing this game. It was somewhat foolish of him not to wear protection, but he hated the way a condom felt. A second child was in the planning stages since Nicholas had just turned three. Maybe he should convince Laurel to go ahead with it now so he could get a vasectomy and avoid another unpleasant scene such as he had today, he resolved.

The announcement to begin boarding interrupted his thoughts and brought him back to the present. He still had not decided what to do about his cell phone. Annatha had his number and even though he was almost certain she had gone through with the abortion, he couldn't take a chance she might contact him in the future. She still had no idea what his full name was or where he was from. Getting rid of the cell phone would ensure his anonymity prevailed.

When the gate agent asked for first class passengers to board, Thomas made a beeline to the restroom across the walkway. He found a large trash can in the corner and looked around. Only one person was in a stall, and no one could see him. *Damn*, he swore, *that guy's taking a crap. How can anyone crap in an airport bathroom*? He resorted to mouth breathing only to avoid inhaling the foul stench through his nose, and pushed open the top of the receptacle. Holding the iPhone with his shirt sleeve so his bare hand was protected, he buried it underneath the mass of paper towels. After depositing the phone, he washed his hands thoroughly and wiped off the sleeve where it touched the trash. Returning to the gate, he greeted the agent with a thin smile while she scanned his boarding pass.

"Welcome aboard, Mr. Loftin."

He grunted and walked briskly down the jet way where the strong smell of aircraft fuel greeted him. *Shit*, he muttered, *that's better than the stink I just encountered in the restroom*. Satisfied he had erased any chance of appearing on Montel for a paternity test by ditching the iPhone, he settled into his first class seat and ordered a scotch.

****

Wendy drove down a two lane road surrounded by tall fir trees. Wild foxgloves were in bloom here also, and Annatha fondly recalled her ride on Sam the previous day. They looked like ornaments with tiny bells hanging daintily from the branches. The car slowed and she heard the faint chime of the blinker. They turned down a gravel driveway, also bordered with fir trees. It was at least a block from the main road, and the house didn't appear until they reached the circular driveway, similar to the one Nana had. It was a one story cedar surrounded by neatly manicured flower beds. The rhododendrons were reluctantly shedding their soft pink blooms but two azalea bushes were still adorned in brilliant red. There were flower boxes sitting on the porch rail with brightly colored gardenias and spilled-over, reaching trails of tiny blue buds. It appeared the nurse had quite the green thumb, she thought. For reasons unknown to Annatha, the small, quaint little house painted by foliage reminded her of the story of Hansel and Gretel without the candy. *You're weird*, she thought, *what the hell was that about?*

"Here we are," Wendy announced as she unlocked the doors.

Annatha smiled thinly and exited the car. A gravel walk way led to the porch stairs and she followed Wendy to the front door. Wendy unlocked the door and opened it, stepped aside and motioned for Annatha to go in.

The front room was large with a comfy-looking couch, recliner, coffee table and small TV at the far end. A farm-style table with six chairs filled an alcove next to the entrance. Looking right, Annatha could see an open doorway that led into a kitchen decorated with all the fashionable country home accessories. The appliances were stainless steel and the countertop looked like cement. Ahead was a short hallway that had three doors on the left and one on the right. Annatha heard Wendy's keys clatter against the wood tabletop and turned around to tell her host how comfortable the house felt.

"Make yourself at home," Wendy said politely before Annatha could relay her compliment. "I'll get dinner started."

She noticed Wendy seemed a little formal, not as friendly or nurturing as she had been earlier. *Maybe she's not used to company,* she guessed. The nausea had improved today after the meeting with Thomas, and she felt like she could use something to eat for the first time that day.

"Thanks," she nodded and decided to skip the compliment for now.

"Have a seat on the couch; the remote is on the table if you want to watch some TV. I have satellite reception so watch what you want." She waited until Annatha had settled in and made sure she was able to work the remote, then turned and disappeared through the front door and headed for the garden.

Annatha nestled into the soft cushions. She suddenly felt very tired. The anticipation of and finally meeting with Thomas had taken its toll on her, not to mention the emotional rollercoaster she had been subjected to after securing the clinic appointment only to find out the abortion could not be done today. Her dad used to call it bone-weary to describe how he felt from his cirrhosis and Annatha could relate to that saying now.

The quaint decorations and soft earth tones of the room were very soothing, and her eyelids felt heavy. The coziness of her surroundings was a sharp contrast to the contemporary coldness of her mother's decorations at their mansion on Mercer Island. She blinked rapidly, fighting the urge to drift off to sleep.

Absently channel surfing, Annatha stopped when she landed on the Science network. There was a special about the Universe and her geek side was attracted to anything that had to do with astronomy. Despite her desire to watch the program, she must have dozed off, because she was awakened by a pleasant aroma. The nurse must have returned while she slept and started dinner. She heard her stomach gurgle with hunger pangs from the culinary scent. *Damn, girl,* she almost laughed, *she can probably hear it in the kitchen.* Fully awake now, she remembered the phone call to her mom.

"I don't mean to interrupt, Wendy," she called from the couch, "but can I call my mom while you're cooking?"

Wendy appeared in the doorway. "I just checked the phone and for some reason my service is screwed up right now. But don't worry, this happens all the time and it should be working again soon."

Why would she check the phone before I even asked? Annatha wondered. She shrugged off the unease this caused, sure she was just being paranoid. Wendy seemed like a very organized person and most likely was just trying to be helpful by reminding her to call her mom until she checked the phone and realized it wasn't working. She would just call later, she shrugged, after they finished eating. Besides, even if she didn't call her mom, she'd probably surmise she had gone to Nana's anyway, but it would be nice not to face Brandon's wrath after having an abortion. *It was doubtful she would check on her by calling Nana, but if she did and it made her worry, tough shit.*

Her eyes focused again on the TV to forget about calling her mom. The earth was being struck by a large celestial body that would result in the creation of our Moon. Annatha felt a hand on her shoulder and she realized she had dozed off again.

"It's time to eat," Wendy said softly, "the second door on your left down the hallway is a bathroom if you want to wash up."

Walking down the narrow hallway, Annatha glanced to her left through an open door that led to a bedroom. The bed was neatly made, with a pastel green quilt dotted by red and pink roses. A small computer desk was in the corner. Everything was country décor and very tidy.

Closing the bathroom door, Annatha shed her jeans and sat on the toilet. It seemed like gallons of pee came out and she wondered how she had gone so long without relieving herself. Up until today, she had been peeing every hour on the hour. It must have been the constant tension that blocked the urge, she decided. She finished and stood in front of the sink, wondering if the eyes staring back at her from the mirror would ever again look rested. Splashing cold water on her face after washing her hands, Annatha struggled to wake up from her brief nap. She noticed a spark of alertness while the icy well water dripped into the sink. Satisfied this was all she could do for now, she dried her face and hands, then returned to the kitchen alcove and stood behind a chair. The table was already set. A glass of wine was in front of one plate and a glass of milk in front of the other. *Obviously mine,* she thought. Wendy must have done it while she was sleeping.

Wendy entered the room with two steaming bowls of pasta and red sauce. She returned to the kitchen and reappeared with a large salad bowl and homemade dressing.

"Have a seat, hon," she motioned. "I picked the vegetables from my garden," she declared proudly and winked. "The spaghetti sauce is my secret, so don't ask for the recipe."

Annatha devoured her food while Wendy mostly picked at hers, talking idly about her cats, the chickens and how difficult it had been to keep rabbits out of her garden. She nodded politely during the conversation but said nothing.

Despite her constant chatter, Wendy was studying the girl carefully while she ate. *She's obviously famished,* she noted, *because she finished every last morsel.* The fact the girl had a ravenous appetite was a relief; it meant she was comfortable which definitely worked to her advantage.

"Finish your milk," Wendy smiled.

Annatha grinned shyly. "Okay, Mom," she kidded and gulped down the rest.

The plan was going so well thus far, Wendy marveled. It had to be the will of God that brought this troubled child to her. Still, there was a loose end she wanted to explore before putting her plan into motion because once she had stepped over the line, there would be no going back. *Your demeanor has to be matter of fact, Wendy,* she reminded herself. If the girl suspected she was prying too much, there could be an unwelcome confrontation. She pushed her chair back, stood up and began clearing the table.

"I've been thinking about what you said about your home situation at the clinic," she began nonchalantly, while gathering the dishes. "So your mom remarried after your dad died?"

"Nah," Annatha replied, "my mom left my dad a few years before he died. He was an alcoholic and she finally gave up on him and filed for divorce. She got remarried about six months later to my stepmonster."

"It must have been hard on you to have an alcoholic father and watch your parents split up like that," Wendy said sympathetically.

"Not as hard as living with Brandon the terrible," she frowned. "Besides, my dad got sober about a year before he died of cirrhosis, so we had a good relationship that last year."

One more piece of information should suffice, Wendy

plotted. "So I'm surprised you're not closer to your Mom after all you've been through."

Annatha had wondered the exact same thing; if it weren't for Brandon that might be true. Her mother was a different person after she left Annatha's dad. The two of them had started to bond in their common struggle to make ends meet on their own, but her mom caved and began looking for a man to support them. She couldn't take the lower middle class existence as a result of being a single mom. Brandon had represented wealth and comfort, apparently something her mom could not do without.

"One would think so," she agreed bitterly, "but I'm obviously not important enough to her or she would have chosen a better husband over a rich husband." She paused then said as an afterthought, "Or no husband at all."

Estranged from her mother, Wendy surmised from the last remark, just what she wanted to hear. "Well I can certainly understand why you don't want your parents to know," she began her observation that would cement the girl's trust. "Your mother would likely not support any decision you made to show her allegiance to Brandon."

She gets it, Annatha realized, *smart lady*. "You're a lifesaver, Wendy," she said gratefully. "It was very kind of you to help me out like this."

Wendy shrugged. "I wish someone had helped me when I went through my abortion," she repeated the untruth. "My parents were awful and said some nasty things I never forgave them for." Convinced she had hooked the catch best suited to her plan, she resumed clearing the dishes and announced, "That's enough depressing conversation for one night." Annatha began to help but she waved her off.

"You're a guest, hon," she smiled. "I've got this. You go rest; you're obviously very tired."

Returning to the spacious couch, Annatha turned on the TV again while Wendy worked in the kitchen. When she was finished, the nurse settled into the recliner with another glass of wine.

"Mind if I watch CNN?" she asked.

"God no," Annatha replied. "It's totally okay."

Wendy cringed slightly. She hated the word totally. Question to clinic patient … *so you're sure you want an abortion over adoption?* Answer … *totally.* It rolled off their tongues so casually, yet it contained a brutal permanence that most likely escaped their frivolous minds. She shrugged off the brief flash of irritation and instead returned Annatha's response with a thin smile.

She opened the satellite on-screen guide, scrolled down to CNN and selected it on the remote. Another wildfire was raging in Southern California, fueled by the Santa Anna winds.

Sleep was caressing Annatha's eyes during the news, and she fought to stay awake, since it would be rude of her to fall asleep.

Wendy watched her peripherally and knew she needed to go to bed soon. She looked exhausted. She reflected how all the pieces of the puzzle were now in place. Divine providence had interceded and delivered a baby inside of this girl who planned to take its life. It was only fitting that she would be the one to save it.

She sipped her wine and considered how she would approach Annatha in the morning when she told her she couldn't leave. The wine was soothing her nerves, which allowed her to think more clearly. It would not be a pleasant scene, she knew for certain, but she had to overwhelm Annatha by demonstrating how futile resistance would be. She knew most of it would be played out spontaneously and no amount of rehearsing could prepare her for the intensity of the girl's response, but certain facts must be communicated forcefully and ruthlessly to drive home the hopelessness of her situation. Once the dust had settled, Wendy would try and establish a different kind of relationship and try to forge an alliance between them to work together for the sake of the baby. Despite this fervent hope, she knew none of it was going to be easy.

"I'm going to change," Wendy announced after the weather report. "I'll be back in a jiffy and we'll get you off to bed."

She soon returned wearing a pair of yellow cotton pajamas and a nightshirt folded across her arm. "Something for you," she gestured to Annatha with the nightshirt. "Follow me."

Annatha stood behind her as she produced a key and unlocked two dead bolts in a solid metal door. Wendy suspected the girl might ask why she was putting her in a room secured by a steel door with two sets of deadbolts but had prepared for this.

"The couple who owned the house before me had a very expensive wine collection in the basement," she said without turning around. Shoving the door open, she reached inside and pulled the string to turn the light on over the stairs. "Watch your step," she warned and started down.

Taking the steps carefully, Annatha couldn't see the room well until Wendy disappeared briefly and flipped on a second light. With slightly more illumination, she could make out the walls were a bright yellow and against the right side, a twin bed with a yellow floral quilt was positioned half way down with a flannel blanket neatly folded at the foot. The bed had one nightstand with a smaller antique lamp that Wendy switched on and then turned to face Annatha.

"This is my guest room," she gestured with both arms. "Make yourself at home. There's a fridge in the corner over there, but it only has water in it. You can't drink anything after midnight though, remember?"

Annatha nodded, still scoping out the basement. In the middle of the room, there was a recliner, and a small TV was positioned to view from the chair. It appeared to have a satellite receiver similar to the one upstairs perched on top. Next to the recliner was a rather high tech looking floor lamp made of metal with a rectangular housing. A portable tray was wedged between the floor lamp and the recliner. It had a functional look but did not exude the homey feeling she experienced upstairs. The wall décor definitely wasn't consistent with the rest of the house. There were framed photographs of various Washington landmarks; Mount Rainier, the eruption of Mount St. Helens, and a river scene with dense foliage surrounding a small waterfall. The air was cold and dank and she shivered involuntarily. *Oh well, it's only for one night,* she reminded herself wearily.

"Here's the bathroom," Wendy called to her from the doorway.

Walking over, she looked inside and saw it was a three quarter bath with a shower, but no tub. There were hand towels neatly displayed that matched the quilt on the bed, and various toiletries, even a toothbrush, on the sink counter. Annatha's brow furrowed slightly. It was as if Wendy was expecting someone.

"I know," Wendy noticed the forehead crease on the girl, "it looks like I was expecting someone, but my sister and her kids come to visit often and they sleep down here. I have an air bed for the boys. I don't blow it up until they're here," she winked. The lies just kept on rolling out of her mouth, she cringed. The Lord would forgive her, though.

Annatha breathed a little easier. It seemed a little creepy at first, but again, her host had a simple explanation that put her at ease.

"You have nephews, then."

"Yes," Wendy replied as she exited the bathroom, "and they're a handful." She pointed to a small white desk to the left of the bathroom door that was partially hidden in a dark shadow cast by the staircase. "In case you want to read before sleeping, I have some magazines on the desk."

Annatha nodded numbly and plopped down on the bed. "I doubt I could read more than three words," she sighed. "I'm beat."

Good, Wendy rejoiced silently, just what she wanted to hear. Returning to the bed, Wendy motioned for the girl to move, then pulled back the quilt and fluffed the pillows. She reached in her shirt pocket and pulled out a small baggie. "This is ginger root," she held up the small herb, "it's good for pregnancy nausea. You just chew it. It might come in handy in the morning."

Wendy placed the herbal remedy on the nightstand and started to leave. She stopped just before she reached the first step and turned. "I'll be upstairs if you need anything. I don't close the door to my bedroom. Just please knock so you don't scare me half to death."

"Okay," she replied sleepily and began to remove her top. "Thanks again, Wendy; see you in the morning."

"Goodnight Annatha," Wendy said in her most endearing voice. "I'll wake you up when it's time."

She climbed the stairs and left the basement door open. Then she walked into her bedroom, removed her slippers, switched off the bedside lamp and waited in the dark. A half an hour later, she crept softly to the basement door in her bare feet and started down the wooden stairs. Despite her best efforts they creaked, no matter how gingerly she pressed her feet against them. The sound echoed loudly in the basement and she paused to listen after each step. Halfway down she could finally make out the girl's deep breathing. She was fast asleep. Now all she had to do was get out of there without waking her up. Carefully negotiating the stairs on her way back up, she had no luck avoiding the squeaky groans each time her weight tested a step. With only a few left to scale, Wendy grabbed the railing for support, then stretched out her right leg and hoisted herself up on the top step, skipping the ones in between to avoid a repeat of her noisy entrance. Once back outside in the hallway, she eased the steel door shut and quietly locked the keyed and coded deadbolts. Pressing her ear against the door, she didn't hear the girl stirring and exhaled a deep sigh of relief. *It's done.*

Wendy felt giddy. She had waited so long for this day and now God had provided her with the opportunity to have her very own child. It was only months before it would be born, and now it was safely locked in her basement. Annatha seemed like a sweet, well-mannered girl and she had suffered some tragedies in her life. However, she was planning to take her baby's life, and Wendy couldn't let that happen when she wanted a child of her own so badly. She believed in her soul God had chosen her to rescue this unborn human being from a horrible death and at the same time save the girl from making a decision that would haunt her and damn her immortal soul. However, there was still the morning to deal with and she knelt by the side of her bed to pray for strength.

****

Meredith finished her gin martini and left the empty glass on the bathroom counter. When she came out of the bathroom, Brandon was propped up on his side of the bed, feverishly pecking at his laptop, oblivious to his surroundings. His overweight six foot five frame devoured most of their bed. A half-finished can of Red Bull was perched precariously on his nightstand, most likely because he wasn't paying attention to where he placed if after slogging down a huge gulp of the highly caffeinated beverage. *Must have a software problem,* she surmised. His salted blonde hair was rumpled and looked like an unkempt hedge was planted around his balding crown. His reading glasses were perched on the edge of his considerable nose and his green eyes glared menacingly at the screen, as if daring it to display anything but what he willed. Sliding carefully under the covers, she waited patiently until the pecking stopped.

"Annatha's not home yet," she interjected before he started up again.

Brandon glanced at her wordlessly and resumed typing.

"She went to the movies with her friends around noon," she continued, ignoring his body language, her words slurred from the alcohol. "I haven't heard from her since."

Brandon took his glasses off, annoyed at her persistence, not to mention he could tell from her speech she was inebriated. "She's probably whoring around and taking drugs," he replied angrily. "She has no respect for herself or anyone else, and I'm going to ground her smart ass when she gets home. She'll see who really owns that car of hers." Replacing his glasses, he returned to his laptop, signaling the conversation was over.

Despite her gin fog, Meredith was a little concerned. When Annatha didn't come home after one of her rebellious confrontations with Brandon, she was usually at her Nana's, but she had just phoned Rose, who denied her granddaughter was there. Meredith didn't suspect her of lying because she had never refused to disclose the information before. Expecting Brandon to get up and do something was out of the question and she was in no condition to look for her, either.

Underneath the concern she felt was simmering anger that her daughter was acting out again. Her rebelliousness had strained her relationship with Brandon so many times she had lost count. Tomorrow would be another knockdown, drag-out fight between Annatha and Brandon when she got home. It was a scene that had become all too familiar. However, she preferred her daughter arrive safely, even with the inevitable fireworks, than not arrive safely at all. She tried to reassure herself Annatha was fine, but her maternal worry meter was rising.

Chapter Five

Four Weeks, Six Days (4W6D)

Annatha opened her eyes to a cold, almost pitch-black room. It took her a minute to get her mind around where she was. She finally remembered the nurse's invitation to stay over and glanced around at the unfamiliar surroundings. The only illumination was from a small nightlight plugged into an outlet next to the bathroom door. *Thank God for that*, she thought. Her stomach was signaling an imminent eruption so she threw back the quilt and flannel blanket, swung her feet over the side of the bed and eased onto the thin carpet. She padded quickly across the room and made it to the toilet just in time. After emptying her gut of a disgusting yellow slime, she rinsed out her mouth with water. There was a faint but distinct bloody taste to the water that caused another round of retching. She realized it was probably iron from the well water after examining her mouth for blood in the mirror. Checking her watch, she saw it was five after seven. Might as well shower, she decided.

Returning to the bed, she looked around for her clothes. It was hard to remember where she put them last night, and then she spotted them draped over the back of the recliner. She grabbed the baggie from the nightstand, stuffed a healthy morsel in her mouth and went back to the bathroom. The ginger root tasted awful but she chewed it slowly while the shower water warmed up. By the time she stripped and got in the shower, her stomach felt a little less queasy. It surprised her that something could actually help her feel better. No matter, after today the symptoms would disappear and she could have her life back. After her shower, she wrapped her body with one towel and fashioned a turban around her wet hair with another. When she opened the bathroom door, Wendy was busy making the bed. She was wearing a terrycloth navy blue robe that covered everything down to her ankles. Thick socks ducked into deerskin slippers that were open heel.

"Good morning." She turned when Annatha came out of the shower and pressed the heavy robe down with both hands.

"Good morning," Annatha replied. Her clothes weren't on the back of the recliner anymore. When she reached the chair, she noticed they were neatly folded on the seat. The portable table wedged between the lamp and chair last night was in fact a TV tray, and was propped open in front of the recliner with a bowl of fruit and a full glass of milk on its surface. *That's odd.* She was confused as to why Wendy brought her food when she wasn't supposed to eat after midnight. Opening her mouth to ask what the deal was, she realized the nurse had turned back around to finish the bed. Tucking in the quilt, her host methodically folded the flannel blanket.

Shyly, Annatha shed her body towel and began dressing. The nurse she hardly knew was still preoccupied, but there was something weird going on. She had been so adamant about the eating thing yesterday. Pulling the zipper up on her jeans, Annatha sat down in the recliner to put on her socks and noticed out of the corner of her eye that Wendy must have completed her task because she was perched on the corner of the bed with her legs crossed.

"We need to talk," she announced when she saw the girl staring at her curiously.

Annatha noticed a flat tone in Wendy's voice that had not

been there before and she felt gooseflesh on her arms. She couldn't decipher if it was a chill in the room since she just finished showering and her hair was still wet, or the change in demeanor the nurse displayed now. "Okay," she replied. Not meeting her gaze on purpose, she wriggled a foot into one of her shoes.

"I haven't been completely honest with you," Wendy began. "I have never been pregnant. I've always wanted a family with a loving husband and children, but God saw fit that I would never have those things."

It sounded like a rehearsed speech to Annatha but she decided not to interrupt with questions just yet.

"I tried for years to become pregnant," she continued, "but I was diagnosed with severe endometriosis, a condition that destroys your reproductive organs and prevents you from getting pregnant. Mine was also causing so much pain I had to have a hysterectomy."

Annatha forced herself to look at Wendy's face now. She didn't know where this was going but her gut told her it couldn't be good. Her eyes softened and when she spoke this time, there was despair and heartache dripping from her words.

"My ex-husband left me because I couldn't have children, and ran off with a younger woman he got pregnant while we were still married." Wendy was looking past Annatha during this part of her speech, but turned to face her before she continued.

"So you can imagine how upsetting it has been for me to watch all the women and girls who came to the clinic get pregnant so easily and then decide to have an abortion."

An internal red flag began to wave and a gnawing sensation gripped her stomach. Annatha still didn't understand what the point of all this was, but the deceit about being a pregnant teen and now this confession were making her very uneasy and she squirmed in the recliner. The stairs leading to the basement door were behind her and she briefly considered making a run for it. However, the nurse was obviously distraught and she decided to give her a few more minutes to make sense.

Wendy continued, but this time her voice trembled. "Time after time, I've watched unborn babies killed by mothers who didn't care one whit about the fact they had conceived a precious life, knowing all the while I was incapable of doing so."

"I can imagine it's been hard for you," Annatha interjected, still unsure why she was being burdened with the nurse's life story and at the same time, feeling a growing knot in her gut, "but what does this have to do with me?"

Wendy's gaze met Annatha's confused stare. She allowed this last question to dangle for a minute before stating the most ominous line Annatha had ever heard.

"I believe God has sent you to me," she finally declared. Her face had assumed a more pious demeanor now.

Annatha felt herself on the verge of freaking out. *What the fuck did she mean God sent me to her? Sent me to her for what?* She didn't even need to know the reason why; it was time to get the hell out of there.

"I want you to drive me to the clinic now," she managed in her bravest voice. Annatha shed the towel, shook out her wet hair and jumped up to retrieve her purse. She accidentally knocked the tray table over and the contents spilled onto the carpet.

"I can't do that, Annatha," Wendy replied coldly, ignoring the mess on the floor. "God has sent you to me and I can't let you go through with the abortion."

That was it. She had heard enough to know the kind nurse she met yesterday wasn't playing with a full deck. Annatha grabbed her purse and started for the stairs. Fuck her, she swore, she'd walk to the goddamn clinic if she had to. At the top, she paused in front of the closed steel door and discovered a keypad she hadn't noticed last night, along with a second keyhole. She grabbed the knob and turned it with her hand, but when she pulled the door didn't budge. *The bitch has locked me in,* she realized. Annatha struggled a few more times with the knob and finally hit the door with her fist in frustration. She dropped down exhausted, breathing heavily as she sat on the top step. A sense of crushing desperation over her predicament gripped her. Trying to gather her thoughts, her mind raced wildly in a vain attempt to figure out what this crazy woman had in mind. After a few minutes she resolved this was not happening, and stormed back down the stairs ready to do battle. Wendy was methodically picking up the fruit. Annatha watched in amazement as the nurse wordlessly went into the bathroom, washed the food and returned with the used hand towel. She casually dropped to her knees and began mopping up the milk. Still stunned by the sudden turn of events, Annatha stared blankly at the woman on the floor who was performing a menial task after informing her guest she was being kidnapped. She must be seriously deranged.

"Why is the door locked, Wendy?" she demanded, her voice trembling with angry fear.

The nurse paused from her chore, and in a matter-of-fact tone, replied evenly, without looking up. "It's simple, Annatha, I can't let you leave. You're carrying my baby."

Annatha staggered back against the steps. She couldn't believe what she was hearing. At first she was speechless. Desperately racking her brain for some way out of this, she found herself unable to quickly process a rational response due to the nurse's shocking pronouncement, uttered with no more feeling than if she was reading a recipe.

She did realize any kind of decorum with her host was now gone. The gloves were off. "It's not your baby, you fucking psycho!" she screamed. "It's mine."

Wendy stood and faced Annatha after placing the towel over the spilled milk. "You were going to kill your baby, remember?" Her eyes flashed angrily.

This last remark released some primal defense mechanism inside of Annatha and she crouched slightly as a predator would before an attack. After sizing up her adversary's physical attributes, she instinctively knew she was outmatched in a toe-to-toe fight. Her eyes darted around the room, taking inventory of the contents and any weapon that might be available to her. It was her only chance to overpower her captor.

Watching Annatha closely, Wendy slipped her right hand into her robe pocket and guided it through the wrist strap attached to her mace, gripping the can tightly once the strap was secure. It seemed clear the girl was plotting some way to subdue her and make her escape. As if on cue, Annatha made a sudden break past Wendy and grabbed the bedside lamp. She wheeled around and in the same motion, brandished it above her head with both arms; her eyes were dark and glared menacingly at their target.

Unsure of how effective the object above her head would be in disabling Wendy, Annatha started to launch the heavy lamp towards her enemy but stopped momentarily when she saw her right hand emerge swiftly from the robe pocket and almost simultaneously became aware of a hissing sound. Her face exploded with burning pain and her throat felt like an airbag had deployed in it. A lava flow of tears, snot and saliva poured out of her face as she staggered back. She dropped the lamp to free both hands in a reflexive defensive maneuver to protect her eyes. The attempt was in vain, as the noxious spray had already done its job. She fell to the floor groping for the bedside table but her arms were useless as uncontrollable muscle spasms from the pain frustrated her efforts. She wanted to scream but her throat was too swollen to make a sound. Without warning, she felt strong hands pulling her up and then steering her towards the bathroom. The shower was turned on and Wendy bullied her inside.

"This will help," she grunted and released her grip. She took a step back and watched while the girl poured water into her eyes and mouth, gargling and spitting furiously. A lack of sympathy for the suffering she had caused Annatha was easy as she focused on what her baby would have endured with an abortion. In fact, truth be told, she was enjoying this a little too much. She noticed for the first time since discharging the mace that she had a slight burning in her eyes and skin. It occurred to her she might have released it too close to her target. Wendy turned on the sink faucet and splashed cold water on her face.

Annatha felt the burning start to ease as she soaked her face with the frigid shower water. Her whole body was drenched, along with the clothes and shoes that covered it. She didn't give a shit. That was brutal. After about five minutes, the nurse turned off the water and handed her a towel.

"Get the fuck away from me," she cried angrily.

After drying herself as much as possible, she returned to the room and sat on the side of the bed, then placed the wet towel over her face. It was painfully clear the option of escaping by means of physical force was out of the question for now. She was a prisoner of this insane nurse unless she could figure some other way out. Muttering every four letter word she could think of into the thick cloth towel her face was buried in, she cursed herself for being lured into this situation in the first place.

To say the last week had been a living hell for her was the understatement of her life. Puking and worrying, baiting Thomas and finally getting the money, then trusting Wendy to help her terminate the pregnancy so she could resume her life--and now she had this shit to deal with? The wheels of her young life had come off their tracks and she was clueless how to proceed. Was it possible to reason with this woman? As frantic as her situation was, she didn't want the nurse to know the terror she felt at that moment. Covering only her eyes with the damp towel, afraid the burning would return, she struggled to speak in a calm, reasoned tone.

"Look, Wendy," she managed thickly, "you don't have the right to keep me here, even if I was planning to have an abortion. Remember Roe vs. Wade?" She was surprised at her voice: it sounded like she had swallowed a frog.

Wendy had resumed soaking up the milk from the carpet. Finished, she righted the tray table as she stood up and replaced the washed fruit. "That was a godless decision, child, made by godless lawyers. Since that decision," her eyes flashed again and her voice climbed an octave, "there has been wholesale slaughter of unborn babies in this country. The Jewish holocaust pales in comparison to this massacre." She composed herself and cinched the robe sash tighter, then continued evenly. "I answer to a higher power and He has ordained me to save one of his precious souls."

Holy shit, this woman wasn't playing with a full deck. Annatha groaned in despair. There was no way she could dissuade someone with such fundamentalist fervor from their deranged beliefs. Recognizing any attempts to pursue a legal argument would only fall on deaf ears, she decided to try a different tack. She removed the towel and tried to focus on the nurse's face. When her vision cleared a little, she took a deep breath.

"Look," she spoke firmly this time her voice sounding more normal, "I would be willing to carry this baby and let you adopt it, but I don't want to be trapped in this basement for eight months. My mom will be sick with worry."

"Really," Wendy replied sarcastically, "your mother sick with worry? That's not the woman you described to me last night. Besides," she continued, "you'd change your mind and I can't take that chance. Abortions are performed into the third trimester in some states and I would have no guarantee you wouldn't go behind my back and terminate the pregnancy."

Annatha plopped back onto the mattress and slammed both fists into it, unable to control her frustration. She rued the fact that her single act of rebellion had led to a set of circumstances she could never have imagined. How she wished she had just told Brandon and her mom she was pregnant and weathered the storm. It would have been like enduring a heavy rain fall instead of a tornado. Instead, due to her reluctance to disclose the pregnancy for fear of reprisal by her stepdad, she was imprisoned in a crazy woman's basement with a pregnancy to deal with now. In retrospect, it was a bad choice to say the least.

The girl's mini-tantrum, followed by silence, signaled the discussion was over for now and Wendy breathed a sigh of relief.

"Try to eat the fruit. I cleaned it for you and put more milk in the refrigerator. If you spill it again, you can clean it up or smell sour milk for eight months," she added drily. "Also, there are some pot pies in the freezer for lunch. You can heat them in the microwave on top of the fridge."

Annatha was lying motionless on the bed, her eyes closed. Wendy touched her leg and said firmly, "Look at me, Annatha."

Annatha squeezed them tighter, which only caused them to burn again. To avoid inflicting more pain on herself, she opened them reluctantly and glared at her with an irate look that communicated a mixture of defiance and hopelessness.

Wendy could see the girl's rebellious eyes were still swollen and bloodshot. She brought the mace out of her robe pocket and held it up for the girl to see.

"There's no point trying to escape. Every time I come down here this will be around my wrist, ready to use." Wendy inserted her right hand through the opening in the strap to demonstrate. "The keypad on the door has a six digit code and will disable itself to further attempts after three tries until I reprogram it. There simply is no way out for you. When this is all over, you will be free to go when I say so. I'll fill in the details when your due date is much closer."

Walking towards the stairs, milk-stained towel in hand, Wendy turned in front of the first step and glanced back at Annatha, sprawled limply on the bed. "Look at it this way, child," she said piously, "if you think about it, you might find redemption over the next few months."

All Annatha could manage to reply was a weak, "Fuck you." She watched the nurse through painful tears as she climbed the stairs. The metal door slammed behind her, the sound echoing in the small basement, and Annatha started involuntarily. Next she heard the deadbolt locks as they clicked into place. Disbelief at what had just transpired permeated every cell in her body. She turned over, buried her face in the brightly colored quilt and sobbed uncontrollably.

****

Wendy glanced in her rearview mirror as the house disappeared from view. Phase one was completed, she thought with growing satisfaction. The girl was safely locked down. She wasn't going anywhere without her permission. The mace had been an unexpected bonus because it drove home the point that the girl was no match for her. Now her challenge would be to work on the girl psychologically so that she wouldn't be too stressed during the pregnancy. After her initial reaction of shock and horror, Annatha would be groomed to rely on Wendy for sustenance and companionship. This would afford her the opportunity to gradually convince the girl that bucking her situation constantly was not in her or the baby's best interest.

The next phase would be to convince her coworkers she was pregnant. She checked her purse to make sure she had brought the Ipecac along so she could feign morning sickness at the clinic. It was disguised in a Benadryl bottle so no one would be suspicious if her purse accidentally spilled its contents.

Everything was going according to plan thus far. For the first time in years, Wendy felt in control of her destiny. Acquiring a baby like this was far from the normal process nature employed, but God had chosen her to save this unborn fetus and His generous reward was allowing her to keep it as her own. A dream once dreamed that had turned into a nightmare, now was within her grasp. Her Lord and Savior would make certain nothing got in her way and she would obediently do His footwork.

****

Annatha lay in a heap on the floor next to the bed, too exhausted to cry anymore. Her body still shuddered with leftover spasms that she couldn't control, just like the dilemma she found herself in. The slamming steel door had cemented the helpless nature of her plight. Regret over meeting Thomas in a fit of rebellion was unrelenting and again she cursed herself for the immaturity that led her to this place. Her course of action after discovering the pregnancy was reasonable and deliberate, and there was no way she could have foreseen the kindly, helpful nurse she met at the clinic would be off her rocker. But when all was said and done, she had no one to blame but herself. She certainly wanted to point an accusing finger at several people in her life as responsible for driving her into this hellish position, but as her dad always said, you also have four fingers pointing back at you.

In an attempt to uncover some minute detail that would keep her from being stuck in this basement for eight months, Annatha mentally retraced her steps from the previous day. There had to be something she left behind that would help find her once her mom notified the police she was missing. It didn't look good. Her car was at SeaTac airport and would eventually be discovered, but there wasn't any evidence there she could think of that would lead an investigation to Wendy's clinic. Thomas had covered his tracks nicely by not going inside, and she had not told anyone about their rendezvous. *What about her laptop? Would a CSI team be able to locate Thomas by scanning her hard drive? Would they think of that?* She had read some about computer forensics online as a hobby, but the wily attorney probably knew all of that, too, and very likely was an expert at dragging a digital bush behind him to cover his tracks. That avenue of potential discovery was most likely a dead end.

She realized reluctantly that if there was any way out of this, it would be up to her to find it. Wendy was a little scary physically because she was so tall, not to mention her mental instability and that horrid can of mace. Annatha knew she would first have to overcome any intimidation she now felt around the nurse following the sudden and effective attack she launched earlier. There might be a way to outwit her, she hoped, or if the right circumstance presented itself, perhaps she could catch her off guard and overpower her. This wasn't a *Die Hard* movie Annatha reminded herself; she had no formal training in how to plan such a surprise attack. It was a reality that the much-stronger nurse with an effective weapon would be almost impossible to take out unless she found something to counter this advantage. For now, it looked like she would have plenty of time to devise a plan for that scenario.

Next, there was the vexing problem of all those deadbolts, but at first glance that seemed to be a no-brainer. There was no way she could get that door open unless she had the code and a key. She tried to convince herself that nothing was impossible and evaluated her chances of incapacitating Wendy somehow and procuring a key. *Dumbass,* she scowled. Even with a key there was still the keypad code, and a comatose person would not be able to reveal it. *Clever woman, despite her craziness,* she admitted grudgingly.

Don't give up, Annatha, she chided herself. She'd been a fighter all her life and this was no time to give up. Wendy's psychological instability just might be an opening she could take advantage of at some point. If she was mentally ill, a chink in her armor might become apparent at some point, or maybe she would crack up at the clinic. That would be a disaster, though, because no one else knew she was down here.

At any rate, she knew she would have to stay on her toes in case an opportunity presented itself for her to outsmart the nurse or find a means of escape at a moment's notice. If only she had been able to call her mom, the number could have been traced. Now the phony dead phone story made sense. Wendy knew this, too, and would not have allowed her to call anyone for fear of being traced.

Wait a minute, she remembered suddenly, Thomas called her cell phone and they could trace him from that once they located her car. He would know the last place he left her when the authorities found him. It might take a while, but she felt some relief that there was a very real possibility she could still be found.

God, Thomas will be furious, she frowned. Too bad, he bore some responsibility for the predicament she was in. After all, he just dumped her off at the clinic even though he promised to see her through the process. He deserved any scrutiny that came his way.

Gathering herself up from the hard rug floor she trudged, crestfallen, over to the recliner and sat down wearily. Wendy had replaced the cup of milk and added a bottled water. Maybe putting something in her stomach would mute the utter despair she felt. She chewed the cantaloupe slowly to see how her stomach would react. As usual, it rebelled and a wave of nausea hit her hard. She quickly made her way over to the nightstand and grabbed another ginger root. The effect was almost immediate this time. She noticed a sample bottle of prenatal vitamins was on the nightstand, too. Wendy must have put it there before she left. Annatha picked up the bottle and threw it across the room. *No fucking way was she going to do anything healthy for her or the baby.* She didn't want it yesterday and certainly didn't want it now.

Annatha returned to the chair after the brief outburst and tried to quell the rising tide of rage she was experiencing. The admonishments from the loony nurse about her killing the baby were way out of line. Who was she to pass judgment? Abortion was legal; kidnapping wasn't. Besides, she knew without a shadow of a doubt she wasn't ready to be a parent. Her own experience with adult parents had been less than perfect.

Taking a sip of water, her thoughts drifted to her dad. How different things would be right now if he was still alive. This horrific affair would have only existed in a nightmare to be thankfully vanished when she awakened. But it wasn't a ghastly dream and she longed for the comforting father whose sober wisdom spawned a rebirth in their relationship the final year of his tragic life.

She recalled how before he started attending AA, things had gone from bad to worse. From the time she was eight up until she was fourteen, her father had been a raging alcoholic. Every night until their divorce her parents played out the same sick game. Her dad would start a fight when he arrived home from work, and her mom was all too willing to wallow in it with him. After the yelling went on for a while, her dad would tell her mom to fuck off and leave the house, which is what he wanted to do in the first place. It was a classic manipulation so he could go to a bar and drink without having to listen to her rag on him. He used the fights as an excuse to leave, but the simple fact was he couldn't make it through one day without getting shit-faced. After he left, Annatha would retreat to her room, because all her mom did the rest of the night was sit in front of the television and whimper like a lost puppy. Initially, she had tried to comfort her mom but soon realized she was assuming the role of a parent. This revelation caused her to launch an odyssey into solitude that continued to the present time. She would go to her room when her dad got home and get lost in her music and books, headphones firmly inserted with the volume up to block out the noise. One night after watching a movie about the creation of the atomic bomb, she began to refer to her room as the bunker. Looking around, she almost managed a wry smile. She was certainly in a bunker now.

Not everything was bad during her dad's drinking days. She resumed her train of thought. When he got home from the bar, no matter how drunk he was or how late it was, he would always come to her room and give her a kiss on the forehead. The smell of stale alcohol was thick when he leaned over, but oddly enough, whenever she smelled the odor now, it seemed somewhat soothing because of this nightly ritual. She knew he went and slept on the couch afterward. The next day when he arrived home from work, the sick jousting would resume and always culminated with the same result.

Her mom played the victim until she temped for Microsoft to make some extra money when her dad was let go from the accounting firm due to his drinking. There she met Brandon and had an affair with him, using it as a vehicle to leave her marriage. This triggered a rapid downhill slide for her dad, until he ended up homeless, panhandling on street corners. After a year of this hell, he found AA and everything changed for him. All was going well during his first year of sobriety, until he was diagnosed with terminal cirrhosis and died shortly after her fifteenth birthday.

During the brief period Annatha got to know her dad without alcohol in his life, he became her confidant. He had an easy, live-and-let-live attitude that always made her comfortable about spilling her venomous thoughts towards Brandon and her mom. Never once did he criticize them in front of her; instead, he would constantly prod Annatha to think of ways she could deal with the situation by changing her attitude. His talk of acceptance, tolerance and detachment sounded good, but in the trenches with Brandon, she found herself helpless to resist the temptation to lash out and rebel. Still, she had placed a good deal of stock in what he had to say. On occasion, advice was given when she asked for it, but mostly he would just share his life experience with a story that would help her understand the futility of her way of thinking. It was maddening and helpful at the same time.

Just the opposite interactions took place with Brandon and her mom. They would viciously criticize her dad even after he got sober. Brandon never missed an opportunity to refer to him as "that lush." This only made her hate him more and lose respect for her mom because she never once stood up for her ex-husband.

The past wreckage repaired, Annatha and her dad had forged a pretty good relationship before he died. Despite the unfairness of having a terminal disease diagnosed just when his life had turned around, he had remained brave and avoided any displays of bitterness, something she admired him for to this day. She wondered how he would have reacted to her news that she was pregnant. *Not to be*, she reminded herself as she slowly plucked the juicy grapes and ate them. They felt cool in her mouth but the mace had fried her taste buds and the aftermath was akin to scorched earth, which made it impossible to detect any flavor. No use fantasizing about how her dad would have greeted her behavior, she thought as she idly clucked her tongue on the roof of her mouth, hoping to awaken some nerves. He was gone and she was stuck with the reality that Brandon and her mom were the two persons responsible for finding and saving her. Not a promising prospect at all.

****

Meredith was pacing fitfully around Annatha's room, looking for any clues as to where she might be. Awakened at 3am by the neighbor's dog, she had tossed and turned for an hour or so, then gave up and made some coffee before climbing the stairs to her daughter's room. If her worry meter had been rising last night, it was pegged this morning. Annatha's room wasn't clean but it approached the definition of tidy. Nothing seemed unusual or out of place to Meredith. She raised her cell phone up to eye level to see the display and redialed her daughter's cell phone. Once again after five rings she got her voice mail greeting. Annatha was a plain vanilla kid, she reflected as she replaced the cell phone in her robe pocket: no frills, not even a unique ring tone or clever greeting. Except for her drama with Brandon, Annatha was mature for her age, which was why she felt so unnerved at 6am as she parted the curtains and gazed down at the large composite redwood deck sprawled across half of the back yard. A gazebo in one corner of the deck sheltered a hot tub. The sun was up and the wild birds that lived on the island were attacking the feeders she stocked weekly; they fussed at each other and postured for a dominant position. A rising sun sifted rays through the tall firs and highlighted their instinctive rituals. It looked to be another beautiful summer day on Mercer Island. *Goddamit, Annatha,* she swore softly to herself, *where are you?*

It had not escaped her thoughts, sitting alone on Annatha's bed earlier, how Brandon would react to her child missing. He did not like disruption in his life, especially if the source of the upheaval was her daughter. Each day he entered coded programs and they reacted predictably if he inputted the correct language, and unfortunately, that was his expectation for life. When something went awry, it wasn't as easy as debugging a program or adjusting a line of code. It was messy and unpredictable and the result was a barrage of accusations and finger-pointing at everyone around him--everyone except Dee, his only daughter.

Since awakening, whenever she had the urge to dial 911 and report Annatha missing, Meredith had balked. Was she willing to open a Pandora's Box and unleash the wrath of Brandon? Yet there was the possibility her daughter was in trouble, and despite the almost constant antagonism between them, Meredith just wanted her home. Her one hope was that Annatha had rebelled and stayed at a friend's house, hoping to worry her mother as payback for her perceived "conversion to the dark side," as her daughter liked to describe her marriage to Brandon. The rub was, she honestly didn't know if Annatha had any friends. If she did, they never came over. Whenever she went out, Meredith never asked her where she was going or with whom. It was so damn peaceful when she and Brandon weren't at home at the same time, it had never mattered to her before.

Another possibility was that she spent the night with her Nana although it was a long shot. Rose Wolcott, her ex-mother-in-law, never let her granddaughter get away with worrying her mom. Rose would always phone to let Meredith know her daughter was spending the night. There was usually a tone of disapproval in her voice, likely the result of Annatha railing about Brandon, but she never butted in. They weren't on the best of terms, but Rose had told her she was right to leave her son; she just disapproved of the way she did it. Brandon had insisted she not go to her ex-husband's funeral and she had complied to avoid dealing with another prolonged spell of his silent treatment. Her failure to support her daughter during that time was a sore point with Rose, too.

Removing the cell phone from her pocket again, Meredith had to step away from the window, as the glare from the sun made it impossible to see the screen. In the shadows, she scrolled down to Rose's number and hesitated. If Annatha wasn't there,

Rose would be upset and insist she call the police. She closed the phone again and jammed it in the robe pocket, frustrated at her indecision. *Maybe more caffeine would help,* she decided, and went downstairs to pour another cup of coffee.

Sitting in the brightly lit breakfast nook, she sipped on the hot beverage slowly and tried to think of other options. The morning sun toasted her back and the coffee warmed her insides to the point she had to slip out of the thick robe. Her pajamas were light cotton and when she removed the robe, she felt a tiny trickle of sweat on her back.

"That smells good."

Meredith startled and looked up to see her stepdaughter Dee standing at the coffee pot. Delilah was her first name, but Brandon had always called her Dee. She was beautiful like her mom. Tall, with a trim, athletic body and thick blond hair that highlighted her large baby blue eyes, she was everything one could want in a daughter. A consistent straight-A student and soccer star, she had won a scholarship to Pacific Lutheran. She had an apartment on campus but was staying with them for a few weeks during summer break.

"Help yourself," she replied and waited for her heart to slow down after the unexpected appearance of her stepdaughter.

Dee poured herself a cup of coffee and walked toward the front door. "I'm going to get the paper," she called over her shoulder.

Meredith watched her leave and wondered if she knew where Annatha was. It was doubtful, since she and Annatha weren't close. Dee never expressed any animosity but always had an exasperated look on her face when Brandon and Annatha went after each other. The favoritism Brandon showed for his daughter angered Annatha, but Dee didn't seem to hold it against her. She saw the treatment her dad meted out and probably understood her stepsister's reaction on some level. However, her attitude was not so tolerant with respect to Meredith. She would always be the "other woman" to Dee since her dad had divorced her mom over their affair. The vicious attacks in court during the divorce by Dee's mom resulted in Brandon hating her with every fiber of his being, though to his credit, he never let Dee see this. *Hell hath no fury like a woman scorned,* she thought wryly as she finished the cup of coffee and got up to get another.

Dee's footsteps on the stairs let Meredith know she had gone back up to her room. They usually avoided being alone together, even though Brandon would be up soon. However, this morning, she felt compelled to go talk to her stepdaughter. She had to speak with someone who knew how Brandon would react if the police were called. Dee was only twenty, but she had a good head on her shoulders and knew her dad well. The burden she felt was weighing heavy on her and Meredith needed to share her fears with someone; Dee seemed to be the logical choice.

Pouring herself a third cup, Meredith climbed the stairs again and hesitated at Dee's bedroom door. She knocked softly.

"Come in."

She opened the door, stepped inside and closed it behind her. Dee was sitting cross-legged on her canopy bed, propped up with pillows, reading the paper. Her walls were painted soft lavender and the quilt was a pale yellow with tiny flowers that mirrored the walls.

"What's up?" she asked. "You look tired."

"Annatha didn't come home last night and I don't know where she is," Meredith blurted out. There, she had finally said it aloud to another human being.

"Did she say where she was going?" Dee asked. Her stepmother's voice sounded frantic and unfamiliar.

"She said she was going to the movies around noon, and I haven't seen or heard from her since," Meredith continued. "I've called her cell phone several times but all I get is her voice mail."

Dee sighed. Her stepsister was up to her old tricks again. Disrupt the family and cause trouble for her dad. A flash of anger shot through her as she could see how worried Meredith was.

Despite the fact this woman had stolen her dad away from her mom, she felt a little sorry for her.

"Let me see what I can find out," she offered and opened her laptop. Typing in some commands, she motioned for Meredith to come over. "Have a seat."

Sitting next to Dee, Meredith watched as she opened her MySpace page and clicked on Annatha's picture from her friends list. Annatha's MySpace page appeared quickly and Dee studied it quietly. Meredith had never seen it before, even when Brandon had made such a big deal about the lewdness of her profile picture. There were only three people on her friends list and Dee was one of them. Odd, she thought, she'd never even considered the two of them as friends. The other two were a boy who was kind of a geeky-looking guy with long hair and glasses, and her ex-husband Bill.

"Who's that?" she asked and pointed at the boy's picture.

"That's Michael," Dee answered. "He's a friend of mine who is a computer nerd. I cyber-hooked the two of them up since Annatha and he have a similar interest in programming."

"Annatha likes to program?" Meredith was incredulous.

Dee smiled. "I know. She'd never let Dad know, but she has written some programs for hacking Windows, most likely out of revenge."

"And you never told him?" Meredith was stunned Dee and Annatha had interacted at this level.

Dee shrugged. "I would never purposely cause a fight between those two, Meredith," she declared flatly.

"Sorry," she apologized. "I shouldn't have asked that question."

"You're stressed," Dee allowed. "Let's see if she has any messages to meet up with someone."

Dee peered at the screen and scrolled down, but the only messages were from Michael and some unknown guys hitting on her by telling her how pretty she was. His messages were brief and contained computer jargon even she wasn't familiar with.

"I don't see anything helpful," she admitted and started to close the laptop.

"Wait," Meredith reached out and stopped her. "Why is Bill's picture on there as a friend if he's dead?" Seeing her deceased ex-husband's picture was creepy but she wanted to know why it was there.

Dee looked at Meredith. "Annatha created a MySpace for him when he was alive so they could communicate online. She must still be maintaining it."

"Can you go to his MySpace page for me?" Meredith asked.

"Sure." Dee clicked his picture and Bill's profile opened.

The page was like a memorial to her ex-husband. The picture Annatha chose was the one taken with him holding her in the delivery room. He looked so young and handsome, Meredith thought sadly. There were several AA slogans and a eulogy written by Annatha. They both read it quietly.

Meredith was struck by the emotion in her daughter's words. For the first time she could feel how devastating Bill's death had been for her daughter, and she wasn't prepared for the lump in her throat it produced. Most likely the fatigue from being up half the night contributed to this unwelcome response, she realized. She quickly brushed off the emotions Annatha's tribute to her dad awakened, like wiping off a mistake on a painted canvas.

Dee remained quiet for a few minutes after reading the eulogy. It was heartbreaking. She couldn't imagine losing her father at such a young age. No wonder her stepsister was so rebellious towards her dad. When she glanced at Meredith to see her reaction, Dee could see the worry and pain that creased her face and for the first time, she felt a knot in her stomach. Maybe something was wrong.

"Have you looked in her room?" she asked.

"Yes," Meredith replied softly.

"Mind if I look?"

Meredith nodded gratefully and got up to go back to Annatha's room. Dee followed. The difference between the two rooms was striking. The walls were chocolate brown and adorned with nature photos taken by Annatha. A pink quilt was rumpled and the bed was unmade. It was the one she had before moving to Brandon's and the wood frame was faded, in sharp contrast to the richly stained canopy bed in Dee's room. Showing her disapproval early on after her mother remarried, Annatha had refused to let her stepdad buy a new bed. He was insulted at first, but soon rationalized it would be one less expense for an ungrateful stepdaughter.

Meredith absently searched through her daughter's dresser drawers again. Dee went in the bathroom and turned on the light. A towel was crammed in the corner next to the sink, and an unplugged curling iron was on the counter. Makeup cases were opened and the mirror was splattered with mouthwash and resembled a Jackson Pollack painting. *Kind of a slob there, Annatha,* Dee thought. She stepped around the toilet and saw the trash can had a box stuffed under some tissue paper. Reluctantly, she dug underneath the tissue paper and turned the box around to read the front. She let out a short gasp. It was a pregnancy test kit. Without hesitation, she emptied the trash can to see if there was a test strip hidden there but was unable to find it. Turning slightly to confirm Meredith was still out of sight, she flattened the box and stuffed it in her jeans pocket. Things were beginning to make sense now, she realized.

At least this meant nothing sinister had happened to her stepsister. However, since she had disappeared it probably meant she was pregnant. When she finally showed up again, the pregnancy would be taken care of or she would bring the father and announce they were getting married and having a baby. She hoped it was the former. Still, if she showed the pregnancy test to Meredith, there would be an element of reassurance, but there would be consequences, too. If revealed, a world of grief would fall down on Annatha because her dad would go berserk. Even if she was planning to have an abortion, he would likely kick her out and her stepmom would be helpless to stop him. Annatha knew this as well as she did. That's why she had chosen to deal with this herself. Dee felt empathy for her stepsister, all alone, trying to handle what must be a difficult situation.

"Anything in here?" Meredith appeared at the door to the bathroom.

Dee jumped at the sudden interruption, but quickly regrouped. She nervously started closing the makeup cases and putting them in drawers.

"Sorry," she said without looking at Meredith, "nothing helpful." Her initial reaction was to keep the information to herself for now. She hoped it was the right one.

Visibly shaken, Meredith helped her tidy the bathroom. They worked silently. After they finished, Dee took her hand.

"I know you're worried," she reassured her, "but I have a hunch we'll hear from her today. If we don't, I think you should call the police."

Touched by her concern, Meredith squeezed her stepdaughter's soft hand. "Thanks for your help, Dee."

****

Wendy put the Acura in park and turned off the ignition key. The house looked the same but would never seem the same. It would forever be the place her baby was born and raised. This thought caused a swell of joy inside her and she smiled. A faint meow came from the front seat and demanded her attention. The kitten she had purchased for Annatha was clawing at the leather seat in a vain attempt to scale it. His tiny paws were flailing against the smooth material, and it looked like he was trying to climb an ice cliff. Wendy laughed and scooped up the determined kitten, cuddling him until he calmed down. She grabbed the animal carrier from the back seat and deposited the small creature inside. Securing her purse over her right shoulder, she needed to use both hands to hold the heavy carrier as she walked from the car to her front porch. The rest of the items would require a few more trips.

Privy to the story of Annatha's stepdad and her cats, she decided at work it might help the girl see her differently if she provided a companion, especially a kitten. There would be many days alone in the basement until Wendy took off work the last month of her pregnancy and a playful friend would help pass the time. She lifted the carrier and placed it on the kitchen table, then went back to the car and retrieved the litter and litter box, food and a few toys she had purchased at the pet store after she picked up the kitten at the pound.

She opened a window in the kitchen to let in some fresh air and the fragrant aroma of wisteria wafted in with the first breeze. Pork chops she had marinating in the refrigerator from the night before were placed on a shallow cooking pan and she popped them in the oven. The home-grown salad vegetables were sliced and tossed expertly as the pleasant odor of heavily seasoned meat filled the kitchen. Wendy didn't detect any sounds coming from the basement while she worked.

After basting the pork chops with the marinating sauce, Wendy emptied the bag of litter into the litter box, then placed the toys and kitten food in a large bucket so she could carry it all down together after dinner. The local news was on and she listened more than watched while arranging the supplies, to see if there was a story about a missing girl from Mercer Island. Thankfully, there wasn't. She placed a few treats in the carrier for the kitten to keep him quiet when she opened the basement door to bring dinner down. The surprise would be ruined if Annatha heard it.

When the meat was done, Wendy arranged a generous piece of the sizzling pork with a bowl of dressed salad on the food tray. She retrieved the mace container from her purse and dropped it in her scrub top pocket then carried the meal to the basement door. A small peephole allowed her to see down the stairs before she opened the door. It was a precaution she had paid to have inserted the weekend before. As she placed her eye against the glass, the steel door was cool against her cheek. She squinted but couldn't see the stairs. All of the lights were off in the basement. Frustrated, she sat the tray on the floor and considered her next move. Annatha could be hiding in the dark on the top step, ready to push her down the stairs, and she would be helpless to defend herself with her hands full. She hadn't taken into consideration there was no switch she could turn on the staircase light with from this side and allow a necessary reconnaissance before she opened the door. Tonight, before going to bed, she'd remove the string that hung down from the fixture. That way it would always be on and illuminate the stairs to avoid any sneak attacks. Annatha would have to break the light bulb to turn it off. If she did, there would be consequences and that would stop. However, the problem of how to scout the basement before opening the door presented an immediate challenge and she needed to find a solution before proceeding.

After a few minutes of planning, Wendy was ready to open the door. Placing the food tray on the floor next to it, she quietly unlocked the two deadbolts while she gripped the knob tightly with her free hand. This maneuver would prevent the girl from turning it once she sensed the deadbolts were disabled and fighting to push the door open. Satisfied the knob was secure, she pressed an ear against the metallic surface, listening for any sound that might reveal Annatha was lying in wait on the other side. A few moments passed, and all she heard was silence. The mace was plucked out of her pocket and readied in her right hand. With her left hand, she shoved the door firmly and swung it all the way open, but met no resistance. At the same time she stepped onto the step and groped for the light string in the dark. Her fingers brushed against the cord and she squeezed it quickly, pulling it at once to activate the light.

Able to see now, she examined the stairs briefly but couldn't see the girl. The door was opened all the way, which made it virtually impossible for the girl to be hiding behind it. With one eye on the stairs, she picked up the tray and bullied the door closed with her shoulder. When she reached the bottom, she could just make out the shadowy features of the basement furnishings, but still couldn't see Annatha. The nearest light she would be able to flip on was in the bathroom to her left. She set the tray down on the final step with one hand while she held the mace tightly in the other. The girl could still be concealing herself so she could launch a surprise attack. Holding the mace in front of her, she moved quickly to the bathroom and switched on the light. Her eyes darted rapidly around the room and it was then she noticed that Annatha was sleeping in the bed. Early pregnancy fatigue was working in her favor, she thought as she breathed a sigh of relief.

Replacing the mace in her pocket, Wendy picked up the dinner she had prepared for Annatha and took it to the table tray in front of the recliner. She noticed the fruit from this morning was only half eaten. *That's not good,* she frowned. Wendy glanced over at the bed, but the girl still hadn't moved. She removed the fruit plate and set the dinner down; still no reaction from the motionless form, only a barely perceptible breathing pattern that moved the comforter slowly up and down. Wendy turned on the bedside lamp, reached over and shook Annatha gently by the shoulder a few times. The girl startled awake somewhat violently. Her eyes blinked sleepily, then widened when she saw Wendy standing over her.

Annatha glared silently at the face of her captor looming above her. Her eyes were clear, but her mind felt thick from sleep. It was like the heavy fog she often witnessed early in the morning over Nana's pond that gradually dissipated as the sun climbed the heavens and warmed the earth. The comforter was launched off of her body with a single kick of both feet. She was definitely awake enough to know she was hot. *How long had she been sleeping?*

You bitch, she swore silently at Wendy, who stood next to the bed, dressed in pink scrubs. *You fucking bitch.* She was fully alert now and a seething rage began to brew again. During her long day of solitude, she had decided it was futile to plead for her release. The nurse was mentally unstable and no amount of reasoning could change that. Hopefully, a plan would emerge or an opportunity would arise that she could use to escape. Until then, she would try to control her temper. It didn't mean she was going to be pleasant, just civil.

"I brought you some dinner," she said cheerily.

"Whatever," Annatha mumbled and sat up in bed.

Her stomach gurgled loudly, protesting the long hours of starvation. She had been unable to finish her breakfast, and the thought of eating one of the pot pies left in the fridge only precipitated a wave of nausea. Not to mention her current situation had squelched any hunger pangs. Forcing herself out of bed, she sat in the recliner and ate quietly. The pork chops were moist and seasoned with something she had never tasted before. They were delicious, she admitted grudgingly.

Wendy watched as the girl attacked her food and felt her body start to relax. *Good,* she thought, *the baby needs nourishment.* The tense muscles in her neck eased slowly and her hunched shoulders stood down from their state of alertness, ready to thwart any attempt by the girl to overpower her. She noticed Annatha was still wearing the night shirt she had provided last night. It swallowed her small frame and she was huddled inside it except for her arms from the elbows down.

"I'll buy you some clothes tomorrow," she promised. "You can't wear that for nine months."

Annatha didn't look up. *It would be a miracle if church lady bought anything remotely stylish.*

"Also," her voice sounded mischievous now, "I have a surprise for you later when I come get your dishes."

"And that will make things all better?" Annatha shot back.

"You'll see," she replied, unmoved by the sarcastic response.

Wendy turned and left the basement. After securing the door she went into the kitchen to fix herself a plate. She carried her dinner into the bedroom and sat it on the desk next to her computer. After a few bites of salad, she wiped her palms on the scrub bottoms she was wearing and cradled the mouse in her right hand. Navigating to the bookmarked website for a midwifery supply company, she selected a birthing cushion. The cushion would be used to help position Annatha comfortably for the birth process. Next she added a supply kit to her cart that contained everything needed for a home birth and filled out the billing information required to order them. The confirmation page appeared and she saved it to her desktop. Next, she typed *empathy belt* in a search engine and found an online website that sold them. They were supposed to let the father experience what pregnancy felt like to the mother. Wendy chewed on a bite of the pork slowly as she read the description. "Now Dad will be able to know firsthand how your center of gravity changes," it read, "as well as the discomfort caused by excess weight on your hips, knees and feet." *What a cheesy idea,* she frowned. *They should have the father pass a watermelon out his rectum if they really want him to experience what the mother does.* Despite her disdain for the product, she knew it would suit her plans. Her hand searched carefully for the stem of her wine glass sitting on the desk while she worked the mouse to order the belt. It only had two sizes so she would have to make some adjustments so that she looked like a pregnant woman whose belly was growing at a normal rate. She wouldn't need to wear anything until about twenty weeks, anyway. Most women didn't show until then with their first pregnancy, which was why so many abortions were done after twenty weeks. A pregnant teen could hide the fact she was pregnant until then but had to come clean once her abdomen began to protrude. The order completed, she saved the page to her desktop and took a drink.

The window in front of her desk faced west. A blaze of pink painted the western sky as the sun retired for the day. *Humans killing their unwanted babies,* she sighed, taking in the beautiful sunset as she sipped the wine. Finally she was saving one and would be able to raise it herself, not some deadbeat single teen that had no business being a mother. She downed the last of her salad and opened Microsoft Outlook. After finishing up her few emails, she glanced at the clock on her computer desktop and noticed two hours had gone by. She gathered her dishes and went to the kitchen to clean up. When the dishwasher was loaded, Wendy gently removed the kitten from his carrier and hoisted the litter box under her free arm. There was no sense of the trepidation she had experienced when opening the door earlier. The stairs were well-lit and empty. She unlocked the deadbolts and gingerly walked down the stairs after pushing the door closed behind her. It would be a disaster if she tripped and knocked herself out. The girl would surely search her pockets for the mace, and that would be an unpleasant scene.

Annatha was watching MTV but didn't turn around. Wendy cringed. *Godless cable channel,* she thought. She set the litter box down and cradled the kitten in her arms. The girl still didn't acknowledge she was there, so Wendy walked over to the recliner and stood behind it for a moment to see if she would become curious enough to turn around. It was like watching a statue. Wendy sighed.

"Can you turn that down for a minute?" She finally broke the impasse. "I have the surprise I told you about."

What does she want now? Annatha wondered. She craned her neck slightly, ready to complain about the request to turn down the volume, but stopped when she saw something furry in the nurse's arms. It was a kitten, she quickly realized, a small, light tan, furry kitten with a smooshed chocolate face, socks on all four legs that matched the color of its face, and large blue eyes.

Wendy stepped forward. The look on the girl's face confirmed this was a good decision. "He's yours," she smiled and handed the kitten to Annatha.

The tiny, soft creature nestled in her arms and Annatha's heart melted. The anger she had felt since last night thawed in an instant. For a minute, she was speechless.

"You are so cute," she finally managed, then cooed and snuggled her nose into the furry head, kissing him repeatedly.

The hole in her soul after losing her precious cats was healed in one fell swoop. The cutest kitten she had ever seen was purring in her arms. She held him to one side in one hand and held out her other hand in front of the kitten's face. To Annatha's surprise, he reached out his paw and placed it in the palm of her hand, just like Buster used to do. It was difficult to keep from tearing up, and Annatha mentally willed herself to retreat from the euphoria she felt. The nurse was definitely playing mind games with her. She knew the story about her stepdad killing her cats and could be trying to get on her good side. She looked at Wendy warily.

"He's really mine?"

"Yes, he's really yours," she smiled broadly, "but you have to train him to use the litter box and feed him." Her voice assumed a stern tone. "You can never change the litter box because you could get a disease called Toxoplasmosis that can cause mental retardation in a fetus." She continued, "And you must wash your hands after you handle him for the same reason. I'll clean the litter box."

I'll bathe in the litter if it causes this baby to be mentally retarded, Annatha thought defiantly. *That'll teach you to kidnap pregnant teens, you bitch.* She shrugged instead of voicing her angry reaction and agreed. "Okay, okay."

Wendy was pleased with her decision to get the kitten. She had never owned animals before moving to the country, but they had been her refuge during many lonely, desperate days. Her cats lived outside mostly and she didn't mind. It kept the mice population under control. A chicken was occasionally taken by the coyotes, but they were cheap and she could replace them easily enough. The power of animals to soothe broken hearts was well-documented so she reasoned it should work in this situation. Annatha needed to maintain a healthy emotional state during the pregnancy for the baby's sake.

"I'll bring you some frozen food you can eat for lunch when I bring breakfast tomorrow," she said while she gathered the dinner tray, this time noting with satisfaction the plate was empty.

Annatha didn't reply; she was on the bed waving a feather Wendy had bought in front of the kitten. He would crouch, then pounce fiercely like an African lion. *That's one happy kid,* she thought and decided not to wait for a thank you. It was a bit much to hope for that. She made a mental note to add a Toxoplasmosis titer to the blood tests she had ordered for Annatha yesterday at the clinic as she silently exited the basement. Since she had owned cats before, she could be immune. If she was, that would relieve Wendy from litter duty.

After adding the girl's dishes to the load, Wendy set the dishwasher and put on a nightshirt. Sitting up in bed, she could feel a cool breeze from the window beside her. She opened the night stand drawer and took out *What to Expect When You're Expecting*, every pregnant woman's bible. Even though she was a labor and delivery nurse for ten years and knew all of the clinical aspects of the birth process, she had never been through a pregnancy before and wanted to know everything she could about the physical and emotional changes Annatha would experience. Also, the knowledge would come in handy when she presented herself as pregnant at work. The first few chapters were read in short order and she set it aside.

Taking a deep breath, a feeling of peace and contentment washed over her. The Lord's plan had gone so smoothly thus far, it had to be divine guidance. In her basement was a fetus gestating inside another woman, a godless heathen to be sure, but an adequate physical vessel to carry and deliver her child. "My child," she spoke the words with awe and reverence. Once it was free of the person who had plotted its demise, she would become the mother who held it, nursed it and ultimately raised it to adulthood. Most importantly, she would provide love and receive the same. It was a dream she had despaired would never come to fruition, although she never totally gave up pursuing it.

She downed the last of her wine and swished it in her mouth to kill the acid taste that still lingered from this morning. Today at the clinic, she had taken Ipecac twice before lunchtime so she could vomit and didn't take any precautions to hide the fact. And despite the fact she hated to vomit, she understood it had to be done if she was going to convince the clinic staff she was truly pregnant. A coworker, Mandy, who worked in billing, was in the break room and heard her getting sick. She had politely asked if she was all right when she emerged from the bathroom. Wendy lied that she had eaten some bad food. Later she would apologize and inform Mandy she didn't want to tell anyone she was pregnant until she was out of the first trimester.

Vomiting was a necessary evil, she knew, and the only thing that got her through was the reason for it. She had never understood bulimics and how they could willingly force themselves to retch just to control their weight. Nothing tasted as bad as stomach contents, and there always seemed to be something in the fetid mix she didn't recognize.

Wendy derailed this train of thought due to its general ickiness and continued to map out her plan in the dimly-lit bedroom. She would tell her doctor and coworkers she was going to a high risk specialist in Tacoma. This would ring true because of her age and the fact she would tell them the pregnancy was conceived by artificial insemination with donor sperm. If a local obstetrician was identified as the doctor who would manage her pregnancy, one of the employees at that clinic might disclose she wasn't a patient if they ran into a coworker from her clinic and was asked how she was doing. Despite privacy regulations, she knew some health care workers weren't above revealing a patient's medical record, especially if that patient was a mutual acquaintance.

Still, it was tempting to tell someone she was pregnant now. Waiting until the second trimester was prudent since she had not even confirmed the girl's pregnancy with an ultrasound exam, but her excitement was hard to contain. It had taken every ounce of discipline she possessed and many small prayers throughout the day to keep it a secret. She would have to continue to do so for the time being.

Her thoughts drifted to the years she spent working in L&D

(Labor & Delivery) at the University of Washington. She recalled the jealousy she felt while watching happy couples have their babies. Even though she knew the emotion was selfish, it wasn't easy to control, and it required a great deal of effort to pretend she shared their joy. At other times, her job was downright frustrating. About half of the moms had not even planned their pregnancies, and some didn't seem to even want their babies. Others were on drugs and child protective services had taken their babies away shortly after they were born. She also observed this same tragedy repeated multiple times with the same hapless mother who couldn't manage to stop using no matter how many times she conceived. It was an abomination as far as she was concerned.

More recently at the clinic, she had witnessed a constant procession of women who made the decision to terminate the lives of their unborn children, unwilling to even consider adoption. They made Wendy sick, and she felt she had every right to judge them for their sins. To defy one of the basic laws Moses brought down from Mount Sinai was unforgiveable. If they truly believed in God, how could they destroy one of His creations? They would face a reckoning with their Maker some day, and He would cast them into the depths of hell.

All of these negative emotions and harsh judgments melted under the glow of her unbridled ecstasy. Things were different now. No more jealousy and frustration to battle. God had seen to that by placing Annatha in her path. She was in charge of her destiny as well as the baby's, and that made her feel powerful, almost omnipotent. But, she quickly reminded herself, all power came from the Savior, and breathed a prayer of thanks.

She hoisted herself out of bed but felt a little wobbly, like she just stepped off a Tilt-a-Whirl ride at the fair so she decided to remain motionless until the rest of the world followed suit. How many glasses of wine did she have? Two was her usual allotment to unwind without unhinging her brain. Maybe that was her third on the desk top; after all, it had been a rather eventful day.

She shrugged. More important tasks had preoccupied her during the evening than how much alcohol she consumed.

The room was stable at last, so she headed into the bathroom, brushed her teeth and gargled several times with mouthwash. It wasn't easy removing the foul taste from the Ipecac's effects, but the wine and mouthwash had formed a synergistic partnership and banished it at last. Examining her face in the mirror, she was curious to find out if the internal joy she felt would surface and alter her external features, bestowing a transcendent glow of pregnancy upon her. Maybe it was wishful thinking or the wine, but she believed it had.

The air felt chilled when she returned to bed, so she lowered the window and buried herself under the covers to warm up. It was time to go to sleep, so she downed an Ambien with her last sip of wine. She decided to read a little further before the sleeping pill kicked in. Opening the book, she breezed through the pages until she found the symptoms most women experienced in the first trimester. It was quite a list. There was fatigue, nausea, sore breasts, frequent urination, mild cramping, mood swings and picas. *We women have to suffer a lot,* she thought sleepily as her eyelids grew heavy and she dozed off with the book on her chest.

****

Dee unlocked the front door quietly and entered the dark house. It was after midnight and the downstairs was pitch black. She groped for the light switch and flipped it on, illuminating the expansive foyer at her dad's home. Making her way to the bottom of the stairs, she turned on the light and returned to the front door and switched off the one in the entryway. She retraced her steps to the ornate stairway but stopped when she heard a faint voice calling her name. Peeking into the kitchen where she guessed the sound originated, she could barely make out a silhouette sitting at the table in the dark. It was Meredith.

"No word from Annatha?" she asked.

"None," a weak reply echoed from the darkened room.

"Have you told Dad?" Her pupils had adjusted to the darkness and she could see Meredith's eyelids were swollen from crying.

"No, not yet."

If Dee had not seen the pregnancy test in Annatha's bathroom that morning, she would be insisting her stepmom 'fess up to her dad. However, the information had relieved any fears that something sinister had befallen her stepsister. She struggled with the dilemma of revealing what she knew to Meredith, since it would alleviate the same fear in her. The lines on her stepmother's face were carved by the pain she felt inside, and it seemed only fair that Dee should share the information with her. Yet it wasn't entirely obvious to her if telling Meredith about Annatha's pregnancy now, which would have an immediate effect on the alarm she was feeling, was preferable to withholding the information a bit longer in the hopes she would know nothing at all about it. On the way home, she had formulated a plan to try and determine what Annatha was up to and find her before she made a bad decision. Meredith would never be the wiser if it succeeded, so she decided to wait until tomorrow. If her scheme didn't pan out, she would come clean. Dee was glad the room was dark so Meredith couldn't see her eyes. She was lousy at keeping secrets and felt certain her face would give away the fact she was hiding something.

"Well," she managed, "I'm sure she'll turn up soon. I'll try Michael to see if he knows where she is."

"Michael?" Meredith was puzzled.

"The guy on her MySpace," Dee replied.

"Oh yeah, goodnight then," her voice trailed off into the hell she was drowning with gin.

"Goodnight."

Dee shut the door after reaching her room and plopped down on the comforter with her legs crossed. She opened her laptop and navigated to MySpace. She found Michael was online. Fortunately he was still on her friends list and she quickly typed an IM and pressed send. He had done her a favor during their senior year in high school when she suspected her boyfriend Josh was cheating on her. Playing her "popular girl approaches geek guy" role perfectly, she had persuaded him to help her spy on Josh's computer. Michael had been all too willing to help out, as he was amazed a girl of her stature was even speaking to him. His only reward would be that she might befriend him or just acknowledge his existence at school. Dee had provided him with her boyfriend's email address and Michael promptly loaded a Trojan on Josh's computer when he opened a fake email sent about a free porn site. The ploy worked handily, as Dee received reports from Michael that unveiled Josh's internet activities, confirming her suspicions that he was seeing someone else and chatting with her almost every night. She had reams of paper documentation that busted the lying bastard when she confronted him. When she got through with him, he had crawled away like a wounded animal.

Michael never asked for anything, so she thanked him and they went their separate ways in the timeless clique system that defined each high school student's status. It was cold, and she regretted it, but this time she would offer to pay him back somehow. There were limits, of course, but they could work something out.

While she waited for his reply, Dee went to his MySpace page by clicking on his image in her friends list and saw that he was working for The Geek Squad. He didn't mention going to school, which puzzled her because he was such a braniac. An IM box suddenly flashed on the screen with his reply.

"Well hello, stranger. You must need a favor."

That's harsh, she winced, although she deserved it. Typing rapidly she told Michael Annatha had disappeared and they had no idea where she was. She wanted to know if he could look at the chat history on her laptop and see if it contained any clues.

"Have you called the FBI?"

Dee paused, one would expect that. How could she explain why they had not?

"I can't tell you why we haven't or Annatha would kill me. I don't think she's been abducted or anything like that, but I can't reveal how I know that."

"Ah, a mystery."

Good, she breathed a sigh of relief, *that means he's interested.* She sent another IM.

"Can you help?"

"I'll need her email addy and you'll have to open an email I send her that will contain a Trojan so I can scan her hard drive."

"Thank you so much," she replied. "Hang on a sec while I get it." She activated Microsoft Outlook and found Annatha's email address. She typed it in the IM box, sent it to Michael, and then quietly headed for her stepsister's room.

She remembered where the laptop was from searching the room with Meredith. It was a good thing, because she couldn't turn on a light. Her stepmom might come upstairs, see her daughter's bedroom light on and think she was home. That would be cruel, not to mention Dee didn't want to try and explain what she was up to sitting alone in the dark with Annatha's computer. She groped blindly and when her hands located the hard shell of the laptop, she picked it up and went into the bathroom, shutting the door behind her so she wouldn't be discovered. Closing the toilet lid, she sat down and opened the laptop, which cast an eerie glow in the dark room. *This feels kind of creepy,* she thought. Shrugging it off, she double clicked the IE (Internet Explorer) icon. She studied the Favorites window on the left side of the program screen, and saw Annatha's Hotmail account was listed. When the email service's website page appeared, the login name and password automatically populated. *That's a stroke of luck*, she exhaled. The inbox contained three messages: two appeared to be spam, but one was from Michael. She selected it and a file secretly downloaded onto the hard drive with a Trojan attached. The laptop would need to stay connected to the Internet for

Michael to do his thing, so Dee replaced it on the bed, plugged in the adaptor so it had power, and set the screensaver to a black page. She stopped at the entrance to the room to check if any light was bleeding under the bedroom door. Satisfied it was safe, she tiptoed back to her room.

She raised her laptop cover; it was still on her MySpace page and there was a new message from Michael.

"Trojan on board," it said, "but the information I find will be withheld unless you go to a Geek Squad picnic with me this coming Saturday."

Wow, Dee smiled, *the boy's grown some balls since high school.* Her smile quickly vanished when she realized her payment was to accompany Michael to a geekapalooza.

"Reluctantly she said yes," was her reply. She owed him that much.

"Good, call you Friday night, but I will need your cell."

Dee typed in the number, wishing she could have him destroy it after the picnic. *You're such a bitch sometimes,* she scolded herself. Well, it was for a good cause if he could help her locate Annatha. Her hope was that she could talk to her stepsister before she made an irreversible mistake like running off with the father of the baby. Abortion was the only good option Annatha had, and even though they weren't close, Dee felt pretty sure Annatha would much rather discuss any options with her stepsister than her mom or Brandon.

****

Thomas carefully closed *Green Eggs and Ham,* as his son was fast asleep after only a few pages. Nicholas looked so peaceful with his eyes closed, almost angelic. Once those eyes opened, though, he more closely resembled the Tasmanian Devil from a Warner Brothers' cartoon. He eased off the bed so as not to disturb his sleeping son and padded softly across the carpet in his bare feet.

Loftin headed directly to the master bath, brushed his teeth, and then removed all of his clothes inside the closet except for his boxers, so as not disturb Laurel. She might be asleep already; she seemed really tired since his return from Seattle. Sliding under the covers in the cool air conditioned room, he turned to face his wife and found her staring at him coyly.

"What?" he demanded. He hoped she didn't want sex tonight. The previous day's news from Annatha was still fresh in his mind and he didn't feel much like going through the motions.

"I'm pregnant, Tommy," she said, her eyes welling with tears. She was only one of a very select few people who still called him that.

Thomas reached out and gathered his wife in his arms. "That's great news, honey," he beamed. While they embraced, he couldn't help thinking of the irony that he had been informed twice in the past two days he impregnated someone, and how different the circumstances were. Life was always playing jokes, he mused. Feeling very macho, he wanted to stand up on the bed and beat his chest like Tarzan, he felt so virile. His sperm were quite amazing little critters, he gloated silently and squeezed Laurel harder.

Chapter Six

Eight Weeks, Six Days (8W6D)

Wendy typed in Annatha's last menstrual period (LMP) from memory and pressed enter. The website she was on calculated the gestational age from the LMP or backwards from the estimated date of delivery (EDD). A slight breeze rustled the sheer curtain on the window next to her desk and she felt it brush against the wet hair on her neck, evoking an immediate rush of goose bumps all over her body. She had just finished taking a shower after arriving home from work and always let her hair "air dry" when she didn't have to be anywhere in public. An involuntary shiver followed and she huddled deeper in the thick robe she was wearing and waited for the website's gestational calculator to return the result. A few moments later the page displayed eight weeks and six days as the girl's current gestational age by her LMP.

Wow, Annatha had been there four weeks already, she marveled while lowering the window almost all the way. The sun was almost completely hidden behind the tall fir trees that surrounded her house, and she knew from experience a brisk wind would soon follow. She hated to close the window because she would not be able to hear the sound made by gusts of wind as they darted through

111

beds of needled foliage that blanketed the majestic branches. It was like listening to a symphony of ocean waves as they crashed repeatedly on a beach. However, her damp hair wouldn't let her enjoy it anyway, so she reluctantly shut it completely.

She decided to file her nails since they really needed a manicure and she had been too preoccupied to notice. It was taking a great deal of patience and effort to deal with the moody teenager in her basement. Even though she was always pleasant and hoped she had scored some points by getting the girl a kitten, she was still the cruel captor and Annatha's demeanor had remained sullen and distant. All she did was eat, sleep, watch TV, and play with the kitten, who was growing along with the fetus inside her. The silence was somewhat disturbing to Wendy, although she had to admit it was not unexpected, given the circumstances. The goal would never be to befriend her, as it could possibly cloud her judgment, given that she would ultimately be forced to deal with getting rid of her after the baby was born. What she wished for eventually was a sort of utilitarian partnership, both working together to have a healthy child.

Tomorrow would be the first test of how cooperative the girl would be. She planned to ultrasound Annatha using the portable unit from the clinic. It would have to be a weekend since she couldn't just walk out the door with it on a work day. If the girl resisted the sonogram, Wendy had some Hydroxyzine, a mild tranquilizer used frequently before the valium revolution, and it wouldn't hurt the baby; she would put in her drink to sedate her long enough to perform a quick exam. It had to be done.

The prospect of finding an abnormal pregnancy had weighed heavily on Wendy since the day she brought Annatha home. One out of five pregnancies ended in miscarriage and if the ultrasound showed an empty uterus, blighted ovum (empty amniotic sac) or even a fetus without a heartbeat, Wendy's dream was over. The thought caused her to shudder slightly. Not only was her dream over but she would have committed a felony kidnapping for nothing. Thus far she had avoided thinking about what action she would take if the pregnancy was abnormal. Instead, she chose to have faith that God would not have created the circumstances for her to save a baby and reward her with the child, then destroy her happiness with a cruel twist of fate.

Wendy shed the towel wrapped around her head and dropped it on the floor along with the negative thoughts she was having. She slipped out of the robe and into her night shirt. Standing in front of the window, she gazed dreamily as rays of light from a setting sun pierced the row of cedars directly in front of her. A multitude of bright, jagged beams danced along with the windblown branches and provided quite a show. They were just like God's grace, she thought, awed by the display of nature's beauty. Like the dogged shards of sunlight, it could penetrate any obstacle and caress you with His love when you least expected it.

In a single moment, the magnificent display of God's creation swept away any doubts she harbored. The baby would be alive and well, she breathed deeply and repeated the affirmation. Her thoughts returned to the following day, when she would finally see her child for the first time. The idea of witnessing this tiny human being she would mother and love forever was intoxicating to her. She took another sip of wine, and drank in the awe-inspiring view to calm her rising anticipation.

****

Carlos shifted uncomfortably in the golf cart as he started his rounds through the parking lot. It was his first day back after four weeks of convalescence from back surgery. He always worked the evening shift as a second job. During the day he worked for a landscaping company where he herniated a disc in his lumbar spine while lifting a rather large boulder. This was an easy job, watching the Park and Fly from 7pm to midnight. Most of the time he gave out tickets and accepted payments from the booth, but he didn't think he could stand all night, so he traded with a coworker who usually drove around and checked the cars on the lot. His foot jumped off the accelerator when he saw a blue Honda Civic parked between a Jeep and a SAAB. Could that be the same one that checked in the day before his surgery? He remembered the car because the girl driving it seemed very distracted. Even more peculiar, she walked over to a mid-size silver-colored foreign vehicle after parking the Civic and drove away with a guy who looked a good bit older than her. At the time, he thought maybe they were having an affair and she needed some place to stash her car out of sight. Whatever her reasons, it seemed peculiar and stuck in his memory for some unknown reason.

Carlos exited the cart and walked over to the driver's side window, cupped his hands to shield his eyes, and pressed his face against the window. The seats were empty but there was a cell phone sitting in a cup holder up front with the charger plugged in. *That's odd,* he winced as he straightened up slowly. His back was protesting the flexion required of it to bend over and peer in. *Something's weird,* he thought and returned to the cart. He drove back to the small hut where the keys were kept.

"Hand me the keys to D24 Jorge," he called out to the attendant. "And the log from July twenty-first, the day before my surgery."

The crew-cut, dark haired retired Marine rifled through the file cabinet and retrieved the log. He handed it over with the keys and asked. "What's up, Carlos?"

"Just take care of that customer," he grunted as a Ford truck pulled up to the booth. "I'll let you know when I know something."

He returned to the car, opened the doors and scoured the interior for anything that might contain the owner's information. Sometimes the insurance verification and or registration were kept in the glove compartment, but not this time. *Dammit,* he swore under his breath, *what the hell have these guys been doing while I was gone?* The log had a notation that the girl would be returning later that day or the next day. Somebody should have noticed this discrepancy weeks ago. He unzipped the pocket in his jacket and fished out his cell phone. The display was smudged with dirt and grime from his day job so he wiped it against his pants. When he could see the numbers, he dialed 911. Now he had to call the police so they could locate the owner by the license tag. Pain in the ass, he swore. While he absently listened to the phone ringing on the other end, it crossed his mind that the girl who left the car might be in some kind of trouble. Hopefully, that was not the case. He had two daughters and the fact they were fast approaching adolescence was frightening to him. The dispatcher's voice brought him back to the task at hand and he relayed the request for a squad car.

****

Dee studied her shoulders in the bathroom mirror. Her skin was warm and sported a pink hue despite the sunscreen she had religiously applied earlier. She had just arrived home from spending the day at Lake Sammamish with some of her PLU friends whose parents lived in the Seattle area, too. Grabbing the aloe vera jar, she slathered it liberally anywhere her bikini had not covered to counter the mild sunburn. She completed the application quickly, as she was anxious to check her emails and see if Michael had made any more progress. Washing her hands, she slipped into a pair of shorts, threw on an oversized t-shirt for comfort and planted herself in front of the laptop on her bed.

The weeks of waiting for more information from Michael had been agonizing. Every day she struggled with whether or not she should tell Meredith about the pregnancy test in Annatha's bathroom. In addition, each passing day strengthened the possibility that Annatha did not have an abortion and was planning to keep the baby, with or without the father. Whatever choice she had made, Dee prayed that she was safe wherever she was. If Michael did not produce some data in the next day or two, she had decided she would have to break down and tell Meredith.

There were some problems early on with spyware removal

and the firewall on Annatha's laptop, but Dee had followed the geek's instructions and removed them. Then Meredith had turned off the laptop, presumably while rummaging through Annatha's room, although it didn't seem to register with her why her missing daughter's laptop wasn't closed. This caused problems for a while because Dee had gone back to her apartment dorm at PLU for two weeks after the Geek Squad picnic to help with orientation. A few days before, she had managed to return home and switched the laptop back on so Michael could resume his spying. Before the laptop was turned off, Michael had uncovered one chat session Annatha had with a male whose ID handle was *legaltenderguy*. They had agreed to meet at the Denny's by SeaTac the day Annatha disappeared. Dee assumed this was the father, but then the information dried up when the laptop was out of commission. Michael had searched *legaltenderguy's* profile but found everything in it was bogus. He even caught him chatting online one night but the IP address was a hotel in Boise. Dee asked him not to contact the mystery chatter until they had more information.

Meredith seemed to be in denial. When Dee asked her yesterday if she had called the police yet, she admitted she had. However, she called anonymously to find out what they would do in her case and they told her since the missing person was sixteen, they usually assumed they were a runaway unless there was evidence of foul play. Dee then asked if she had told her dad. Meredith disclosed she lied to him that Annatha was staying at her grandmother's for a while and of course, he didn't care one whit as long as she was out of his hair.

Dee adjusted the display screen because the setting sun was pouring through her window, blinding her ability to see it. She could have gotten up and closed the shades, but she wanted to check her email first. There it was, a message from Michael marked urgent. She opened it and gasped when she read it. It said simply, "CALL ME!!! She quickly dialed his cell number and he answered on the first ring.

"Hey Dee," he answered nonchalantly and she thought she heard a big slurping sound. "I think I found what you're looking for."

"Tell me," she demanded as the short hairs on the back of her neck started doing the wave. Another slurping sound followed. *My God,* she realized, *he's probably chugging a Monster beverage again.* That was all he drank at the picnic along with his computer buddies. Dee teased her dad because he inhaled energy drinks, too. She called them geek gasoline.

"Okay, here it is," he continued, "*legaltenderguy* and Annatha, who goes by *sassybrat18*, chatted on July second. He talked her into coming to his hotel, the Doubletree by SeaTac, and even sent her a cab. About three weeks later, Annatha contacted him in chat and asked him to meet her at the Denny's by SeaTac."

"What day did they meet?" Dee interrupted.

"I'm getting to that Dee," he chided. "It was the day you said she disappeared, July twenty-first."

"So they did meet on that day," Dee said aloud, mostly to herself.

"It would seem so."

"Did she say anything about being pregnant?"

"Annatha's pregnant?" Michael choked on his drink, his voice about two octaves higher.

Shit, Dee swore to herself. *That came out before there was time to stop it.* "Don't you breathe a word of this to anyone Michael," she said sternly.

"Not a problem," he promised. "That makes a big difference."

"No shit."

"No," he continued, "what I mean is this guy has gone to a lot of trouble to be anonymous and untraceable. The only times I've found him online he was at a hotel IP address. He doesn't want anyone to know who he is or where he's from. Most likely he's married and only chats when he's out of town, probably on business."

"Are you sure you're not on the police squad, too?" Dee chided him, but she had to admit what he said made perfect sense. Her mood quickly changed when the impact of his last remark hit her between the eyes. A married man with a lot to lose would do one of two things. Pay for an abortion or somehow make it all disappear.

"I watch *Missing* and *CSI*," he teased, "but more importantly, I stayed at a Holiday Inn Express."

"Very funny, dork," she said absently, but his attempt to lighten the conversation failed. Her mind was racing over a mental calendar she had conjured up to recall what was going on July second. *Oh my God*, she suddenly remembered. That was when her dad and Meredith went to Turneffe Lodge and she was asked to keep an eye on Annatha. She had decided to go to a party on Bainbridge Island because she never knew Annatha to socialize much. Plus her stepsister was a wreck from losing her cats and in a dark mood. She thought getting out of the house would give her some privacy, and she certainly didn't want to come off as an overbearing stepsister that didn't trust her. Not to mention the fact she felt guilty about what her Dad had done with the cats.

"This is all my fault," Dee groaned. She pushed the damp lake hair off of her face and played with her ear lobe nervously. It was a habit she had when she was feeling stressed.

"How the hell is it your fault?" Michael asked.

"I was supposed to be watching her, dammit." Dee cursed herself for failing to watch Annatha more closely. "My dad and Meredith were out of town."

"Bummer," was all Michael could manage. He heard the desperation in Dee's voice but couldn't find any words of solace at the moment. After an uncomfortable minute of silence, he asked, "Still not answering her cell?"

"No," Dee's voice quivered slightly now, "I call it every day at least once and I know Meredith is doing the same thing."

The torment Dee felt was palpable over the phone to Michael

and he wished he could be more help. "I'll keep trying to track this guy down," he said, "but I think it's time to call in the big dogs."

"I know," she said weakly. "First I have to tell Meredith."

"Good luck," he comforted her. "Let me know if there's anything else I can do."

"Thanks."

Dee disconnected her phone and then closed the laptop. She leaned back against her pillow and sank into it. If Annatha had resurfaced not pregnant, a good deal of drama would have been avoided. However, keeping the pregnancy test from Meredith had proven to be a bad idea and she was certain her stepmom would be furious, even though her motive had been good. Her brilliant plan backfired miserably and now four weeks had passed while she guarded her stepsister's secret. Getting pregnant by a married man had been a stupid blunder on Annatha's part and seemed very out of character for her stepsister, but she wouldn't have gone anywhere that night if Dee had been doing what she was asked. Her dad entrusted her with the task of watching Annatha while he was out of town and she had failed him. *Oh, what a tangled web we weave, when at first we do deceive*, she scolded herself. *Truer words were never spoken.*

Dee felt like crying, not only because she was responsible for affording her stepsister the opportunity to act out, but because she was afraid for the first time since Annatha's disappearance. It seemed less likely now that Annatha had resolved the situation with an abortion. If she had, she would be back home. The fact she was still missing filled Dee's head with so many ominous scenarios she had to turn them off so she could focus on her next step. It was time to tell Meredith and her dad then take the heat for being a miserable failure as a babysitter and withholding information about the pregnancy test.

****

Carlos waited patiently in the cart as the sun dropped below the horizon. A cool breeze had stirred just as the fiery orb dipped out of sight. He stretched his sore back again and wondered if riding around in the cart had been such a good idea.

The police woman was sitting in her squad car, entering the license plate numbers to get the registered owner. After printing out the information, she exited the vehicle and walked over to Carlos.

"Here it is," she said and handed Carlos the printout. "Brandon Reynolds is the registered owner. The address and phone number are on it."

"Thanks, Trudy."

She shrugged. "If you can't reach him by tomorrow, call us again so we can have it towed to the police lot and find out what's going on."

"You mean like foul play?" he asked.

"You watch too much TV," she winked.

"Me?" He pointed with both hands to his chest. "I don't have time to watch TV."

"Just call the number, Dick Tracy." She walked back to the squad car and drove away.

Carlos pulled his collar up to block the chilly night air as he drove back to the attendant station to call the number on the printout. He couldn't wipe the wide grin from his face, though. Trudy was cute for a police woman, but she was every bit as good at being a smartass as the male cops.

****

Downstairs was dark except for a dim light in the kitchen. Dee peeked inside and spotted Meredith sitting at the kitchen table, sipping on a martini. She noticed her stepmom drinking more every time she came home. Probably using it for mortar to build her wall of denial, she thought. It wasn't going to be strong enough to keep from tumbling down now. Glazed eyes greeted Dee when she approached the table and Meredith's head nodded slightly. Right before she grabbed the back of the chair to pull it out and sit down, the portable phone rang. It was sitting next to Meredith on the table. She picked it up and squinted at the caller ID display.

"It's some Park and Fly," she mumbled, "probably wanting to sell me something. Just let the answering machine pick up."

"No!" Dee protested a little too loudly and her stepmom's eyes widened. "I'll answer it." She didn't know why she was so anxious about this strange call, but her instincts told her it had something to do with Annatha.

"Hello?"

"Is this the residence of Brandon Reynolds?" a voice with a rich Mexican accent inquired.

"Yes it is, but he's asleep." Dee struggled to control her voice but felt her heart pounding like a bass drum. She glanced out the corner of her eye and saw Meredith was staring at her with a puzzled look.

"My name is Carlos and I work for Discount Park and Fly near SeaTac airport," the voice continued. "We have a Honda Civic here registered in his name that has been on the lot four weeks now and if it isn't picked up by tomorrow, it will be towed."

Jesus Christ, she thought, *what the hell was Annatha's car doing at a Park and Fly near the airport? Did she take a plane somewhere with this guy? Maybe she did run away after all. Maybe he wasn't married. Michael could have been wrong about that.* Her mind was racing out of control and she willed herself to calm down. *This could be a positive thing after all. At least something of Annatha's has finally surfaced.* She assured the attendant they would leave now to come pick it up.

When she hung up, she saw that the alcoholic glaze had been replaced by an alertness she had not seen in Meredith's eyes for weeks. *Well shit,* she swore silently, *here goes.*

"Annatha's car is at a Park and Fly near SeaTac and we're going to get it," she said quickly, before her stepmom had a chance to speak. "We need to get dressed and go now."

"What?" Meredith said shrilly. Her voice was a cross between terror and hope, and her eyes searched Dee's face for some kind of explanation for this sudden turn of events.

"I'll explain on the way," Dee said evenly, "but we need to get moving now."

Thirty minutes later they were driving across the I90 floating bridge over Lake Washington. Fortunately, the traffic was light this time of day heading toward downtown Seattle. Meredith was sipping on a Starbucks' Americano Dee had insisted she drink to sober her up for the news she was going to tell her.

"First of all," Dee began, "what is the real reason you haven't notified the police that Annatha is missing?"

Meredith shrugged and took a sip of the hot beverage gingerly. She winced as the liquid burned her lips and then her throat. "I just figured she ran away after your dad had her cats put to sleep. She hasn't contacted me because she wants to punish me with worry since I didn't stop him."

Dee felt only pity for her stepmom. The woman sitting in the front seat with her was only a pathetic shell, without enough backbone to take up for her daughter. Then she groveled in the role of victim, a victim of her husband and now her daughter. Her rationalizing was obviously camouflage for a deeper fear of how Dee's dad would react. *What makes a person turn out this way?* she wondered.

Taking a deep breath, she downed a generous swallow from her frappacino and then spilled the whole story to Meredith, starting with the episode in the bathroom when she found the pregnancy test and how she had hoped Annatha would have an abortion and be home within a few days. If no one was the wiser, a good deal of yelling and screaming would have been averted. When she didn't show up, she involved Michael and told her stepmom the information he had retrieved from her computer. Lastly, she relayed the information the attendant had given her over the phone. As she spoke, she noticed the tears coursing down Meredith's face as the flimsy wall of denial she had built came crashing down.

"I know you meant well," she finally managed in a voice choked with emotion, "but I'm her mother, Dee. Why didn't you tell me?"

"I see now it was a mistake not to do so," she answered, "and I'm so sorry I didn't tell you when I found the pregnancy test."

Meredith rode silently as they approached the ramp that led to I5 south towards SeaTac airport. Traffic was heavy despite the fact rush hour had ended hours ago. The air was clear tonight and a brightly lit Seattle skyline loomed in front of them, but the towering splendor blurred as tears of anger welled in her eyes. Inside she was boiling. Her stepdaughter had withheld vital information from her that would have given her a clue as to why Annatha vanished into thin air. *How dare she!* It was the kind of arrogant, know-it-all attitude her dad possessed in spades. She decided it wouldn't serve any useful purpose to scold Dee at this point. After all, it was somewhat noble of her to try and protect everyone from her father's wrath.

Besides, she had her hands full trying to unravel the mystery of why her daughter's car was at a Park and Fly near SeaTac. *Had she left the country with the father? Why hadn't she at least called? Did the fact she hadn't called mean something horrible had happened to her?* Her mind filled with tragic scenarios and she tried to drive them out but the coffee wasn't helping any. She no longer felt numb. Martini melancholia was a state she had drowned herself in over the past few weeks, but tonight she didn't have that option. This was real and she needed her faculties to deal with it. Another sobering fact was that Brandon would have to be told and he would most likely fly into one of his rages over Annatha's behavior and admonish her that he had tried to warn Meredith her daughter was a slut.

"What do we do now?" Meredith finally asked softly.

"We need to call the police and have them meet us there," she answered.

"Oh God," Meredith began to sob, "your dad is going kill me."

Dee didn't respond. She knew this was a big factor in why her stepmom had kept her daughter's disappearance quiet, which was the primary reason she had chosen not to disclose the pregnancy test. Despite the fact she loved her dad, she knew he was unfair with Annatha and blamed Meredith for her daughter's defiant behavior. Fear for her daughter's well-being as well as of her husband's rage put Meredith in a Catch-22 predicament. She had learned about this cerebral quandary in psych class her freshman year. It was thought to contribute to schizophrenia if a parent constantly did this to a genetically susceptible child due to the high level of anxiety it caused. Probably explained why her stepmom had been drinking so much lately--it was a simple case of self-medication.

Dee realized she could relieve some of the blame that would befall her stepmom by admitting to her dad she didn't supervise Annatha the night she got pregnant when they were on vacation. Also, she would take the rap for calling the police. Besides, Meredith seemed incapable of doing anything at the moment. She hoped her stepmom didn't think she was overstepping her bounds by notifying the authorities, but she was hoping to deflect her dad's wrath. Before she had a chance to reconsider, she opened her cell phone and entered 911. Hesitating for a moment, she took a deep breath and pressed send. The deed was done.

Meredith started to protest when she realized what Dee was doing, but sank back in her seat and continued drinking her coffee. Now Brandon couldn't hold her responsible for calling the police, and his princess would not incur the same vicious reaction he would almost certainly hurl at his wife.

Dee closed the phone after talking to the 911 dispatcher and turned off on the WA-154 exit west. "They're going to meet us there," she explained. Her stepmother's gaze was fixed on her with a look that communicated part gratitude and part terror. Nothing more was said until they reached the Park and Fly; Dee pulled in next to the attendant shack and they got out.

After she showed her identification to the attendant, he gave

Meredith the keys to Annatha's Civic. "Hold on one sec," he said and picked up a walkie-talkie. "Civic's here Carlos." A garbled reply blared from the speaker. "Carlos will be right with you," he smiled politely.

Within seconds, a golf cart rounded a candy apple red Hummer to their left and screeched to a stop in front of them. "Hop on, amigos," the leather-skinned driver with a healthy paunch said as he motioned for them to get in. The two women situated themselves and grabbed onto the flimsy roof struts for safety. In short order they were parked behind Annatha's Honda.

Meredith exited the cart first. Her hands were shaking as she fumbled with the keys before managing to open the driver's side door. The interior of the car was stale from sitting in the heat all day, but she detected an underlying yet distinct fragrance as she stuck her head inside. She drank in the aroma and closed her eyes. The familiar scent of her daughter's perfume released a gnawing guilt she had felt for weeks now because she hadn't contacted the police due to her fear of Brandon's reaction. Meredith fiercely shook off the unwelcome emotion and studied the front interior.

"The dispatcher told me we shouldn't touch anything," Dee said as she came up behind her and peered through the rear window at the back seat that was now illuminated by the dome light.

"Fuck that," Meredith swore and picked up the cell phone sitting in the cup holder. She disconnected the charger and turned to show Dee the phone. "This is why she hasn't returned our calls."

Dee had never heard her stepmother say the "F" word and despite the warning from the dispatcher not to handle anything, she was glad Meredith was finally showing some backbone. She watched quietly as Meredith frantically searched every inch of Annatha's car.

Headlights blazed against the Civic, and Dee turned to see a white police cruiser with a dark blue SeaTac decal running the full length of both sides. It pulled up behind the cart and stopped. She shaded her eyes until the blinding headlights were abruptly cut off. A few more seconds went by; Dee assumed the policeman was doing whatever they took so long to do before exiting their vehicle. Finally, a police woman appeared from the driver's side door and headed for the Civic. She was tall and lean, with dark brown hair that was fashioned in the usual utilitarian bun. When she drew closer, Dee could see she had a determined but pleasant face.

"I'm Officer Trudy Fuller," she greeted Dee and held out her hand.

Dee shook her hand and was not surprised at the firm grip. "I'm Dee Reynolds. I called 911," she said. *A Charlie's Angel,* she thought to herself. That's what her college friends called female police officers. *Cool, she might be a mom herself.*

Fuller glanced past Dee, studying Meredith, who was rummaging around in the back of the two door coupe with the driver's seat pulled forward. "That's not a good idea, ma'am," she chided loud enough to be heard and stepped around Dee. The woman ignored her and continued her frantic search.

Trudy sighed; it was obvious she was dealing with a distraught mother and the busywork helped her cope with the loss. No use picking a fight under these circumstances. She turned back to Dee, pen and notebook ready. "Just who is missing?" she asked.

"My stepsister," Dee replied vaguely, still watching Meredith in case she found anything.

"What is her full name?" Trudy persisted.

Dee turned and faced the female officer. "Oh, sorry," she apologized, "I'm just concerned about Meredith, my stepsister's mom," pointing at the Civic. "She's a little frazzled."

"Her name?" Trudy repeated the question, trying to focus the young woman standing in front of her.

"Annatha Mae Wolcott."

"Her age?"

"Sixteen."

"How long has she been missing?"

Dee's brow furrowed as she tried to remember the exact date Annatha disappeared. "About four weeks ago."

The officer's face betrayed her surprised response to Dee's answer. "Why haven't you reported this until now?"

Dee launched into a summary of events, beginning with the discovery that Annatha was pregnant after she had been missing only a few days. Then she revealed what Michael had discovered during his hackathon of Annatha's laptop, which led them to believe she was with the baby's father and most likely had simply run away. That was until they received the call from the Park & Fly that Annatha's car had been there four weeks. Now they were worried something had happened to her.

Trudy shook her head unconsciously while Dee relayed the story. "You should have reported this sooner, Ms. Reynolds," she scolded her when she was done.

"We know that now," Dee replied defiantly, "but it seemed very likely she was trying to work out what to do about her pregnancy and didn't want us to know anything."

Trudy ignored the rebuke and nodded at Meredith. "Excuse me, I need to speak to her mom now." She stepped closer to the car and tapped on the window. "Can you please come out now, ma'am? It's not a good idea to be rummaging around in there."

Meredith pulled back and struggled out of the car. All she had found was trash and junk on the floor board. She pushed the velour, cobalt blue sweatshirt hood off of her head, briefly straightened her rumpled hair and adjusted the matching bottoms. Her breath was labored from crawling out of the cramped Civic. "Why on earth not?" she asked the officer between gasps.

"Since your daughter is missing, this car will be going to the garage so that a forensics team can go over it." She patted her hand on the Civic's hard top. "This could contain crucial evidence."

Meredith squared herself in front of Officer Fuller. "I'm going to look in the trunk now," she flatly announced.

Trudy placed her hand firmly on the woman's shoulder. It

wasn't hard enough to be painful but communicated any further efforts to move would be met with resistance.

"Can you take your hand off of me, officer?" Meredith's eyes flashed with anger.

"I'm not the bad guy here, ma'am," Trudy squeezed her shoulder. "I know you are upset and I promise we'll look in the trunk in just a minute but first I need to get some more information."

Meredith hesitated. She felt the urge to bull her way past the woman standing between her and the Civic's trunk, but instead, took a deep breath and shrugged out of her grip. "Okay, you win," she surrendered, but her eyes were still ready to do battle. "What information do you need?"

Grateful no further confrontation was needed, Trudy's determined look softened and she altered the tone of her voice to a calmer level. "Let's start with your name, shall we?" she began.

"Meredith Reynolds," she replied and leaned back against the metal side of the Civic, still warm from sitting all day in the sun. The physical contact with her daughter's car was somehow comforting.

"Your stepdaughter," Trudy continued, "has filled me in on the details surrounding your daughter's disappearance, but I need your address, all phone contact numbers and a photograph if you have one."

Meredith looked at Dee. "You can give her the information while I get my purse."

Meredith went to her car and rifled through her purse. She produced her wallet and removed the only picture of Annatha she carried. It was her 10th grade school picture. There wasn't even the hint of a smile on her thin face. Funny, she thought, she hadn't noticed that before.

Trudy studied the woman as she walked back and handed her the photo. She was attractive and reasonably fit for a woman her age, but she recognized the thousand-yard stare in her sorrowful blue eyes. She took the photo, careful not to smudge the front, and attached it to her clipboard. A written description was scribbled on a writing pad from the picture and she returned the photo.

Meredith carefully replaced it in her wallet. "Can we please look in the trunk now?" she pleaded.

Trudy frowned but made no effort to dissuade her. She was obviously distraught and a reasonable argument was the last thing she would listen to. If it was her, she'd probably do the same thing.

"Hold on," she said grudgingly, "I'll open it."

She went straight to the squad car and returned with a pair of latex gloves. After donning them, she extended a gloved hand and Meredith surrendered the trunk key. Dee and Meredith gathered behind her to watch, the air around them thick with anticipation. Inserting the key, the officer turned it and felt the latch release as the trunk lid sprung open. Trudy quickly inspected the contents while the two relatives fanned out on either side of her. Luckily, there was no body and everyone breathed a sigh of relief. In fact, it was empty except for a spare tire, a fly fishing rod and a vest.

"What are you doing?" Carlos spoke up behind them. "You think there might be a body in there?"

Trudy bristled and turned and faced the attendant with an annoyed look. "Why would you ask a question like that?" she growled.

"I was the one who checked the girl in," he replied

Meredith wheeled and glared at Carlos. "Why didn't you tell me that before now?" she demanded.

Carlos shrugged. "You didn't ask me."

"She's been missing four weeks and that's your excuse?" Meredith shot back.

"Hold it," Fuller interjected, placed her hand on the angry mother's shoulder again and squeezed. "Let me ask the questions, okay?"

Meredith nodded but her eyes were wide, glaring at the Hispanic attendant.

"What's your name, sir?" The officer produced her notebook again.

"Carlos DeLaCruz," he replied warily. The intense stare from the girl's mother was a little unnerving.

"Okay Mr. DeLaCruz," Trudy instructed, "tell me everything you can remember about the day the girl left her car here."

"There's not a lot to tell officer," Carlos shrugged. "She said she would be back later that day to pick it up and walked to the entrance and got into a car. That's the last time I saw her."

"Got into a car with whom?" Meredith shrieked.

Ignoring the outburst, Trudy addressed the attendant. "Did you see the occupant of the car she got into?"

"The windows were tinted so I couldn't see very well," Carlos admitted, "but I think it was an older man."

Fuller held up her hand to thwart the anticipated barrage of questions the mother would surely fire at him. "One thing at a time," she admonished Meredith, then directed another question at the attendant. "Now, Carlos, could you tell the make and model of the car?"

Carlos had a pained expression on his face. "I'm sorry," he said shaking his head, "I didn't know it would be important. It looked like a Beemer or Audi or some other copycat foreign knockoff."

Not helpful. Trudy frowned. "No license plate, I presume?" she asked.

"No," Carlos replied. "I'm sorry, ma'am," he apologized to Meredith, "I have kids, too, and I wish I could help more."

Meredith waved him off absently. She was busy trying to process the information he had disclosed. Their suspicions that Annatha was with the baby's father were confirmed now. If only they knew who he was.

"Thank you for your help," Trudy offered the downcast attendant. She handed him one of her business cards. "If you can think of anything else that might be of use, please don't hesitate to contact me. " She wrote down his address and phone number, then closed her notepad.

"Mrs. Reynolds," she tried to sound reassuring, "it seems to me there is no evidence of foul play at this time, and believe me, that's good news."

"If you say so," Meredith grunted.

"My guess is since they met here, they must have been flying somewhere. And since she met him online, that could be anywhere."

"I doubt it," Carlos disagreed.

"And why is that?" Trudy inquired.

"They drove the opposite direction from the airport entrance," he pointed to the north with his right index finger.

The officer reopened her notepad and jotted down the attendant's last statement. It was like prying open a mummy's tomb to get anything out of this guy.

Meredith was deep in thought, hoping to make sense of the information thrust upon her that evening, so she missed this last observation by the attendant. She was attempting in vain to shut down the rush of dread her thoughts were conjuring up when a pain in her right hand interrupted them and she glanced down to see white knuckles still clutching the cell phone from the Civic. It was like a piece of her daughter that was all she had to hold on to. Flipping it open, she saw there were several missed calls from an unknown number. Those would be her calls, as their home number was unlisted, she realized. However, a strange number caught her eye as she scrolled down, that had the area code 303.

"Where is area code 303?" she looked up at Dee.

"Why?" Trudy asked.

"This is my daughter's cell phone and an incoming call has that area code." Meredith switched over to outgoing calls and saw the same number. "See, here it is in the outgoing calls, too." She held up the phone so the officer could see.

"That's Denver," Carlos piped up again.

They all turned and glared at him with exasperated expressions.

"My brother lives there," he admitted sheepishly.

Trudy shook her head. *This guy was a fountain of information but it trickled out slower than molasses in winter.*

"Mrs. Reynolds", she turned to Meredith, "you need to hand that over as evidence when you file your report. They can trace that number. I'll type up a quick report and send it to the detective who handles missing persons at the station." She nodded at the golf cart that transported them to Annatha's car. "You should get going now. Here's the address for SeaTac police headquarters; they'll be expecting you."

Dee felt like they were finally getting somewhere. First, the attendant revealed Annatha had driven away in a car with another man. Then Meredith discovered the missed cell phone calls from a Denver number. Less than an hour ago they didn't have a clue where her stepsister might be. Now they might be able to trace this guy who had gotten Annatha pregnant and hopefully he would know where she was. She prayed he had not done anything to harm her stepsister, but that was still an unknown--an unknown that hung like a heavy shroud over the darkening night.

"Good luck," Trudy held out her hand again and they shook. "It looks like this guy is traceable and you'll have your daughter back in no time."

"I want to believe that," Meredith said hopefully.

"Me too," Dee chimed in.

When they returned to Dee's car, Meredith selected the Denver number and pushed send. There was no answer, but the answering machine greeting announced she had reached Rocky Mountain Catering and asked her to leave a message. She hung up and told Dee.

"Catering?" Dee repeated. "That doesn't make any sense. And it was a woman's voice?"

"Yes," Meredith replied.

Curioser and curioser, Dee thought as she pulled out onto International Boulevard

****

Dee parked the Mercedes in front of the SeaTac city hall building, where the police station was located. It was a tall, three-story building with a white façade that was layered like a wedding cake with windows for icing. An array of floodlights made it a rather ominous structure at night. They marched quietly to the front door and received directions to the police offices from a security guard who guided them through a metal detector on the first floor. The officer on night duty buzzed the detective and ushered them to his office.

"He's expecting you," he gestured at wooden bench. "Have a seat and he'll be right with you."

"I'm not sitting on that," Meredith said flatly after he left.

Dee didn't blame her. No telling who or what had sat there before them. She glanced around at the empty desks with computer screen savers that displayed the SeaTac logo in a rolling arc. She had never been inside a police station in her life and didn't know what to expect, but this one seemed very tidy, not at all like the ones on television with stacks of files perched on desk corners ready to spill onto the floor. A door opened behind her, and the noise startled her. She wheeled around to see the detective who had stepped out of his office.

"Mrs. Reynolds," he said and extended his hand, "I'm Detective Knowles."

Meredith shook his hand limply but Dee returned it with her usual firm handshake. Knowles was middle-aged, thick but not fat, with an expansive balding head that was poorly masked with a thin comb-over. Reading glasses were perched on the end of his nose and the dark eyes behind them looked tired. He was holding a steaming mug of coffee with a Mariners' logo.

"Won't you come in," he gestured.

They went into his office and sat in the two chairs facing his desk.

"Officer Fuller called me and faxed a preliminary report," he began while perusing the printed copy in front of him. "It sounds like there is no evidence of foul play at this time. In fact, it looks to me like a runaway situation, and trust me, I see this a lot."

"I hope you're right," Meredith said warily.

"I know it's tempting to think the worst, Mrs. Reynolds," the detective peered at her over his glasses, "but this fax says we have some potential leads on this guy and he is the key to finding your daughter. Since I have Officer Fuller's report, the only things I need from you are a photo of Annatha and her cell phone so we can extract the data in it."

Meredith retrieved the items from her purse and pushed them across the desk towards the detective who placed them in a brown accordion file. She recounted what happened when she called the 303 area code number on the cell phone.

Knowles' considerable brow furrowed briefly at the information. "A catering company ..." his voice trailed off. After a moment of reflection, he looked squarely at the two women. "No matter, I'll get to the bottom of it," he promised, using his most reassuring tone.

Dee was beginning to think it wasn't going to be that easy. While driving to the police station from the Park and Fly she recalled a conversation with Annatha about abortions a few months ago. Dee couldn't remember how the subject came up, but she expressed her opinion it was a woman's right in certain circumstances, but didn't necessarily agree with using it as a form of birth control. Annatha was vehement that if she ever accidentally got pregnant, she would definitely have an abortion. She lectured her about the right to privacy every woman had and admonished Dee for being judgmental about the reasons some women had for terminating their pregnancies. It wasn't really an argument to begin with, but after her stepsister jumped her case, she backed off to avoid being drawn any further into a discussion about the touchy subject. In the end, they agreed to disagree and never spoke of it again. But the memory of this exchange convinced Dee that if there was any way Annatha could have had an abortion with this pregnancy she would have. Running off with the father she had a one-night stand with in a hotel met any criteria Dee could think of to define an accidental pregnancy. No matter how miserable Annatha was with her home life, the detective's conjecture she was a runaway simply didn't jive with the viewpoint she had voiced in their discussion. The only reason she would interact with the guy who got her pregnant was to get help having an abortion. Running away to have the baby seemed in direct contrast to her spoken beliefs.

"Detective," Dee decided to throw a wrench in his well-oiled thinking machine, "what if this guy is married and can't afford for his wife to find out he got a sixteen year old girl pregnant?"

Knowles took a sip of coffee and sat the mug down. He leaned back in his chair and placed his hands behind his head. "You're thinking he might have harmed Annatha?" he asked.

"Exactly."

"Mrs. Reynolds," he shifted slightly and turned his gaze to Meredith causing the chair to squeak. "Was Annatha happy at home?"

"No."

"Why not?"

"I'll answer that," Dee interrupted and lightly squeezed Meredith's arm. "My dad and Annatha do not get along because he is very hard on her. I'll give you a recent example. He punished Annatha by having her cats put to sleep, which I think is the reason she made the impulsive decision to meet this other man in the first place."

The detective didn't react to Dee's confession about her dad, but it wasn't because it didn't make his blood boil. He controlled the impulse to launch into a tirade about cruel parents because the poor mother didn't need that right now. Besides, it supported his impression about why the girl disappeared in the first place.

"That's why I don't subscribe to your fears about harm done," he removed his hands, picked up the folder and waved it above his head. "I get several of these a year, and they all start with an unhappy home life. Most of the time we find the missing person simply ran away and they never come back, or if they do come back, it's because they are fed up with living on their own." Knowles straightened in the chair and adjusted his glasses. "Look folks," his official voice changed to a more soothing tone, "I just don't want you to make yourself sick with worry when statistics and my gut say she has just run off with the guy who got her pregnant to rebel against an unhappy home life." The mother's head dropped and he noticed there were tear stains on her sweatshirt. "No offense, ma'am," he apologized.

"None taken," she said feebly.

"One more thing," Knowles added, "if you want, I can contact the media and have them run a story with her photograph. Someone might have seen her and call in with a tip. Before you answer," he raised a beefy hand, "we've had some luck with this in the past."

"No media!" Meredith said forcefully before she realized how it must have sounded. She continued in a more subdued tone. "No media for now, thank you. If I change my mind I'll let you know."

"Suit yourself," Knowles replied. It was time to end the interview. After goodbyes were exchanged, he watched them leave. He'd bet a month's pay the missing girl's mother was more scared of the ogre she was married to than if her daughter was safe. *What on earth could have possessed this guy to kill his stepdaughter's cats? That wasn't right. Made sense this girl took off,* he thought. He realized any further suggestions he made about posting pictures around SeaTac airport would probably have met the same strong response.

They exited the building and returned to Meredith's car.

"Now for the most difficult part," Meredith said glumly, "we have to tell your dad."

"I'll tell him with you," Dee said as she started the engine. "He won't act out as much if I'm there."

Meredith nodded gratefully. Dee had really come through for her. They had never been close, and it wasn't because she was jealous of her stepdaughter. But before Annatha's disappearance, she always seemed to keep their relationship at an arm's length, probably because she felt loyal to her mom. Also a product of divorced parents, Meredith understood this dilemma. Her dad remarried when she was fourteen and she hated her new stepmom. She gave the poor woman hell even though she didn't deserve it. Anyone her father brought home would have received the same treatment because it was an invasion of her rightful mother's position. It was a miracle they didn't drive her to the North Pole and leave her for dead.

Despite her desire to understand Annatha's behavior given her own experience, she couldn't help the resentment her daughter caused by inciting so much friction in her marriage to Brandon. He wasn't blameless, but he was used to adoration from his own daughter and had no clue how to deal with a rebellious adolescent. Meredith had chosen the part of spectator and let the two of them fight it out, but this passive role resulted in her daughter viewing her as weak and dependent. Maybe she was both of those, but she didn't want the stress of taking sides. Doing that would foster bad feelings from both of them. This way only Annatha despised her; besides, she was too old to get divorced, go back to work and try to find another relationship. She had hoped eventually things would work out or Annatha would go off to college and everything would be fine. Apparently, that wasn't meant to be. Now her daughter was missing, and she had no idea where she was or if she was safe. She closed her eyes and listened to the rhythmic thumping of the asphalt road against the car tires. It had been many years since she prayed, but it was time to start again.

CHAPTER SEVEN

Nine Weeks (9W0D)

Annatha stirred, opening her sleepy eyes in the dank, dark basement that had become her home. She tried to focus on the bedside table where she kept the bag of ginger root that was devoured each morning to stave off the persistent nausea she felt. The number of heaving episodes that forced her to slump unceremoniously against the toilet were down to about two a day now, but one was more than enough. She groped blindly for the lamp Wendy had placed on the makeshift night stand and remembered the nurse removed it after Annatha attempted to use it as a weapon. Now the only source of light nearby wasn't even a normal lamp fixture, just one of those cheap, portable gizmos you peeled off a paper strip on the back, revealing a gluey substance. It attached to whatever surface you wanted and activated by pushing the top down to turn it off and on. Her right hand finally found the smooth, plastic dome-shaped light and pressed it. Now she could see better. She grabbed the ginger root and chewed it vigorously; the taste caused her to salivate more but it definitely helped her nausea. Her face contorted from the bitter flavor as she rested her head on the pillow, staring blankly at the dimly lit ceiling. She couldn't help feeling uneasy about the bizarreness of her situation while she waited in the hushed stillness of the basement for the herb to soothe her queasy stomach.

A scratching noise interrupted the silence and she realized the kitten was using his litter box. Despite the weird feeling in her gut, it brought a smile to her face. Fortunately, he had been easy to potty train. Yesterday she had decided on a name for him, Alcatraz. It seemed fitting, given her current situation. "Come here, Taz," she cooed. She only used the kitten's nickname when Wendy wasn't around, but seized the opportunity to use his full name when the nurse brought her dinner last night. If it annoyed her captor, she didn't let on. A furry shape emerged from the shadows and bounded toward the bed. Just before he arrived, Taz leaped but only made it halfway up and fell in a heap to the floor.

Annatha laughed for the first time in days. "Taz the spaz," she giggled as she scooped the kitten up and onto the bed with her. She hugged him tightly and kissed his forehead several times. He stared up at her with loving blue eyes and reached out his paw to touch her face.

"Awww," she said and patted it gently, "you are such a sweet boy."

Gathering herself and the kitten, she sat on the side of the bed and looked around. Wendy left her breakfast early this morning and told her she had some errands to run. Their level of communication was still blunted, as the nurse relayed pertinent information and Annatha rarely spoke back. The only items she had requested thus far were some toys for Taz.

She had been too tired to get up and eat then, but her stomach grumbled impatiently and she knew the nausea would return if she didn't consume something soon, so she stumbled in the half-lit room and turned on the sun lamp. The tray was positioned in front of her recliner as usual, but there was a book sitting next to her plate. She sat down, placed Taz beside her and picked up the book. *What to Expect When You're Expecting* was the title. That bitch expected her to read this? "No fucking way," she cried aloud and angrily threw the book against the wall. After a few minutes, she managed to calm herself and began eating the fruit. God, she could use a Starbucks Americano, she groaned. Fat chance that psycho would ever bring her one.

After finishing her breakfast, she downed the glass of orange juice, gathered Taz again in her lap and sank back in the chair. She stroked the kitten absently and once again assessed her predicament. It was what she would imagine solitary confinement to be like in a maximum security prison. Wendy was like a seasoned prison guard who instituted every security measure possible to prevent an escape. Each time she opened the basement door, she scouted the stairs first. Annatha had discovered this the day before. She had crouched down on the second step so as not to be seen through the peephole in the door. Her plan was to trip or push the nurse down the stairs and run for her life. To her dismay, the door cracked slightly and a stern voice ordered her to go back down the stairs or she would be maced again. The one horrible experience she had with the noxious chemical and Wendy left her terrified at the prospect of feeling her face explode like that again, so she had reluctantly had reluctantly slinked back down, accompanied by a good deal of embarrassment.

Cut off from the outside world, her only lifeline was a deranged pro-lifer. It was a very unsettling thought for Annatha. This realization had led her to the scenario of what would happen to her if some tragedy befell Wendy. There was some food and water in the fridge, but it was doubtful she could stretch it for more than two weeks before she starved or died of dehydration.

The possibility of a rescue seemed remote, also. She wondered how her mom was dealing with her disappearance. Brandon was most likely being a dick, which wouldn't help matters. There was always the chance they would find her abandoned Civic at the Park & Fly, recover her cell phone and find Thomas's number on it. However, Thomas, despite all the grief this would cause him, would be unable to help with her current whereabouts since the last time he saw her was when she was dropped off at the clinic. And what a dead end the clinic would be. Wendy would admit she interviewed Annatha but would lie and say she had not seen her since. The guise the nurse had used to have Annatha sneak out to her car had been brilliant, she had to admit. No one at the clinic would have a clue what happened to her except the one person who would never divulge that information. A distant meowing noise brought her back to the present and she realized she had squeezed Taz a little too tightly with that last, grim thought.

"Sorry baby," she apologized and kissed his forehead tenderly. Despite the hopelessness she felt on one level, she held onto the remote chance that over time Wendy would make a mistake and she would be able to escape this dungeon.

The light over the stairs suddenly illuminated and she heard the deadbolt tumblers clicking. Seconds later, Wendy swung the door open, stepped inside and shut it firmly. Annatha watched as she made her way down the stairs and observed Wendy was carrying a metal suitcase when she reached the final step. The nurse cleared a spot on the bedside table and positioned the strange object carefully on the wood surface. She wordlessly flipped the latches and opened it.

"This is a portable ultrasound machine," Wendy explained in a matter-of-fact voice, as if she was giving a lecture. "It has an LCD screen here for viewing, and a keyboard for input and measurements. This thing is a transducer," she held up a plastic object that was about the thickness and size of three or four slices of bread. One side was straight where a rather substantial cable was attached in the middle, and the other surface was rounded. "It emits sound waves that help see the baby."

"What do you think you're going to do with that?" Annatha challenged. She placed Taz down in the chair and walked over to get a better look.

"I want to see how far along you are and confirm that the

baby is alive," Wendy answered, unperturbed by her captive's demeanor.

Just before she shouted "fuck you," Annatha stopped as she realized the importance of what the nurse had just said. *Confirm the baby was alive? That meant there was a possibility it wasn't.* Even though the nurse probably wouldn't let her go unscathed if the baby wasn't alive, it definitely meant her ordeal would be over. If the pregnancy was abnormal, she knew she would be in for the fight of her life to avoid whatever sinister plans the nurse had to dispose of her in that circumstance. Despite her initial reluctance to give Wendy her way, she decided it was worth a try to take a look, but she had to be ready to get that mace before the nurse did if all was not well.

"I'm not going to watch, though," she stated firmly.

"Fair enough," Wendy replied, "now lie down on your back please." Inside of her a sigh of relief escaped that Annatha had not made a scene and turned this into a fiasco. The Hydroxyzine pills tucked in her pocket for sedating the girl if she didn't cooperate would not be necessary after all.

"Pull your sweatpants down a little," she instructed her.

Annatha lowered the cotton pants and lifted her butt slightly to hold them in place.

Wendy took a bottle with aqua colored gel in it from the suitcase and squirted it liberally just above her pubic bone. It was cool against her skin and her abdominal muscles tensed reflexively.

"It will only feel cold for a minute," Wendy reassured her. She spread the gel over her skin with the transducer and felt the girl tense again. It wasn't that long ago she had a firm abdomen like that, she frowned. *Focus Wendy,* she admonished herself as she turned and flipped on the power to the ultrasound unit. It had a fully charged battery so she didn't need to plug it in.

Annatha turned her head away and began talking softly to Taz. The gel was tolerable now, as it had warmed up from her body heat.

Wendy ignored the girl's attempt to distract herself and began angling the transducer to find the pregnancy. Since she was so thin, there was no need to use a vaginal probe at this stage, even though the picture would have been clearer, and talking the girl into that would have been an even bigger hassle.

She stifled a gasp as the picture on the screen revealed the dark round shape of a pregnancy sac. Moving the transducer slightly, the white kidney bean shape of a fetus came into focus. Inside was a barely perceptible flutter caused by the tiny embryo's beating heart. Before the tears welled in her eyes that would make it difficult to see what she was doing, she struggled to block out the inevitable emotional reaction to seeing her child for the first time and willed herself to continue the exam. Forcing herself to complete one task at a time, she maneuvered the transducer until the entire fetal pole was visible and pressed the FREEZE key. The transducer was replaced back in the suitcase and she turned to face the keyboard.

"Finished?" Annatha asked as she turned to face her.

Before the nurse could answer, she saw the screen wasn't blank. A bean-shaped figure was barely perceptible but there it was, floating in the middle of a dark sac. Her first instinct was to turn away, but she was mesmerized by the tiny image of her baby's acoustic shadow. A weird sensation welled up from inside, and her throat felt like she had swallowed a cling free dryer sheet. *What the hell was that about?* she wondered silently and forced herself to turn away.

Wendy felt a guilty satisfaction the girl had seen it. Now maybe she wouldn't think of it as an appendage, and instead, realize it was a living, breathing organism that she had planned to kill.

Annatha kept her eyes closed until she was facing away from the screen again. When she opened them, Taz was staring at her curiously. She licked her lips, trying to find some moisture with no success. Her heart was pounding like a SWAT team about to knock down a drug dealer's door. She tried to calm her nerves and figure out what had caused this unexpected reaction.

At first she conjectured it was because the ultrasound image cemented the pregnancy was normal, and this smashed any hopes she had that this horrific ordeal could end today. She was forced to accept there was definitely a living baby, which meant her prison sentence had just been extended for several months. However, she would have anticipated rage or despair from this awareness. No, she continued her emotional inventory, there was something else going on. Replaying the event in her mind, it gradually became obvious what precipitated her internal panic. The inadvertent glance at her baby's shadow on the screen had awakened a peculiar sensation that resulted from an unreal perception the tiny creature was staring back at her. It was not an easy admission, because it bestowed a human quality to the life she had previously viewed as inanimate. Annatha struggled to understand the meaning of her unconscious reaction, but there was too much going on with the nurse pressing the hard probe against her pubic bone. She would have to deal with this later.

Watching the screen, unaware of the girl's quandary, Wendy selected the MEAS (Measure) key, and a small cross-shaped cursor appeared. Her forefinger found the smooth, rounded surface of the track ball and moved the cursor to the top of the baby's head. Pressing the SET key, another cursor appeared and she guided it to the tip of the rump. Satisfied, she selected the ENTER key and the measurement of 2.0 centimeters appeared on the left hand side of the screen. As with all ultrasound units, there was a menu to select what parameter one used to calculate gestational age. Wendy chose the CRL (Crown Rump Length) table and "8W6D" displayed on the screen underneath the measurement. By Annatha's LMP (Last Menstrual Period) she was nine weeks today so the ultrasound confirmed her dates, she observed with relief. The RECORD button was then selected and the unit printed a black and white picture of the screen shot with a faint whirring sound. Wendy removed the photo and placed it in her pocket.

"Are you finished yet?" Annatha said coldly. The creepiness of her unwelcome thoughts and this whole process was getting to her.

"Almost done," she said lightly. Wendy couldn't contain her excitement; this was amazing. She was the first person to see her baby. A prayer of thanks to her Maker was uttered in silence. Glancing at the girl, Wendy made a snap decision to goad her a bit. After all, if it weren't for her rescuing this poor fetus, it would be in a trash bin somewhere.

"The baby is alive and well," she declared in a cheerful voice. "Do you want to see it?"

Annatha felt a surge of rage erupt and was powerless to stop it. "Are you mental?" she cried. "Why the fuck would I want to see it? I was going to have an abortion, you selfish cow!"

Wendy was taken aback by the vileness of the girl's reply. She composed herself quickly. "No need to get nasty, Annatha," she scolded gently. "I'll just be another minute."

"Hurry up, goddammit," she mumbled. There was no need to be cooperative anymore since the news wasn't good for her. She was tempted to get up, but the thought of being maced again stopped her.

The transducer was placed on the girl's abdomen again and Wendy scanned the uterus one last time to make sure there was only one fetus before measuring the FHR (Fetal Heart Rate). *Thank God there's only one,* she sighed after the entire sac had been inspected. Managing a twin pregnancy and delivery would have been a much more daunting task. To measure the FHR she switched off the FREEZE button and changed the unit to real time again. The M-mode key was pressed and the screen split in two. On the left was the fetus, with the rapidly beating heart still visible. The right side of the screen was a vertical row of multiple straight lines until she placed the transducer directly over the heart and the lines transformed into waves. Freezing the screen again, Wendy measured the distance between two of the waves and hit ENTER. The baby's heart rate (FHR) was 161. *Normal,* she rejoiced inside.

Everything was just perfect so far, although she would have been surprised if things had not been given the amount of nausea the girl had. Her final act was to bring up the report page that showed Annatha's EDD (Estimated Due Date) as March twenty-first. This was only one day different than the calculated EDD by her LMP. Curbing her enthusiasm before Annatha's cooperative demeanor dried up, she removed the transducer and replaced it in the suitcase again. Making sure the screen's information was cleared before the unit was used again at the clinic, she cut the power switch off.

"All done," she announced. "Wait a sec and I'll get you a towel to wipe off the goop."

On her way to the bathroom, Wendy felt like she was floating on air. The ultrasound had gone very well and Annatha had been grudgingly cooperative. The pregnancy was viable and there were no signs of complications thus far, although the girl was only sixteen, which automatically placed her at some risk. She planned to repeat the sonogram at twenty weeks to locate the placenta and maybe determine the baby's gender. Accomplishing a second exam might prove to be a formidable obstacle, but she had plenty of time to work on the girl before then. She didn't foresee any problem persuading Annatha to have her fundus measured and blood pressure recorded every four weeks until she reached her twenty-eighth week, but convincing the girl to allow her to listen to the baby's heart beat during the exams would not be so easy. Bi-weekly checks would be necessary from that point until the last month, then weekly until she delivered. It was a typical standard of care regimen for normal pregnancies.

However, she wouldn't be able to perform two blood tests usually ordered. She had considered if they were necessary but came to the conclusion they weren't. The first was a screen for Spina Bifida and Down's syndrome drawn between fifteen and eighteen weeks. This would not be necessary as she would never consider terminating a pregnancy because the baby wasn't normal. The second was a screen for diabetes that required a sugar-loaded drink, followed an hour later by a serum sample to determine the level of glucose. She knew there was no history of diabetes mentioned in the questionnaire Annatha completed at the clinic and it was unlikely a skinny sixteen year old was at risk for this, anyway. It was fortunate these tests weren't required, because she had no idea how they would have been accomplished.

One final hurdle loomed menacingly in the distance, namely, a birth complication. She would have no backup and no alternative to a home delivery if things went wrong. From her L&D experience, Wendy knew ninety-plus percent of the time a birth could happen in a rice paddy with no problems. However, a small percentage had the potential for a catastrophic outcome, which was why she had been opposed to home births in the past. That bias had been swept away for practical reasons, but nagging doubts still plagued her when she imagined all the things that could go wrong. Shaking her head, Wendy brushed her fears aside as premature. This was no time for gloomy thoughts. It was arguably the happiest day of her life so far and nothing was going to ruin it. She scooped up a hand towel from under the sink, returned to the bed and handed it to Annatha.

"I'm going to return this unit to the clinic now," Wendy announced as she closed the suitcase. "You have some food in the fridge for lunch and I'll bring dinner down later."

Annatha didn't respond. She watched the nurse until the basement door was closed, fighting back tears. Once the door slammed shut, she surrendered and sobbed into her pillow. Taz climbed up on her head and snuggled into her hair. Unable to resist his comfort, she turned over and surprisingly, he licked the salty tears from her face.

"You are a lifesaver, kitty," she choked against the sobs. "I don't know what I'd do without you."

After a fleeting chance at freedom until Wendy documented

a normal pregnancy, the final door had been closed on her hopes to escape this hell-hole of a prison. *The crazy bitch has the baby she always wanted now, and nothing will stop her from keeping me locked up until it came out. There must be some way out of this,* she groaned and racked her brain for ideas. The scenario that she would be able to escape was discarded as so remote it was not worth wasting any time over. And this overzealous religious nut, who possessed a convoluted logic pattern that kidnapping was acceptable but abortion wasn't, would be very difficult to outmaneuver emotionally or intellectually.

"There must be some way I can end this, Taz," she cried and stroked the furry kitten, who was nestled against her. Disgusted by her weakness, she sat up and wiped her eyes, fighting the impatient sobs that threatened to escape. Taz was startled by the sudden movement and leapt off the bed. *What a scaredy cat,* she managed a weak smile. She considered briefly whether or not to go comfort him, but she had more important things to think about.

It was time to get a grip, she resolved. First, she had to figure out the weird emotional response at seeing her baby. If the nurse sensed any uncertainty about the decision Annatha made to have an abortion, it would be exploited mercilessly. Next, this whiny defeatist attitude had to be conquered. She couldn't allow herself to think like a victim. *No more crying,* she ordered sternly. It might cloud her judgment and blind her from recognizing a golden opportunity to outfox the nurse. Rational thinking would be her only chance to end this ordeal, she resolved. She vowed this would be her quest. A plot had to be devised then implemented without arousing suspicion. *It might take some time though,* she reminded herself glumly. No matter, she had all the time in the world.

****

A shaking sensation roused Dee from a deep sleep, and she moaned before turning over to see who it was. She was somewhat disoriented and struggled to figure out if she was at her PLU apartment or the home on Mercer Island. The hazy outline of the canopy above her confirmed she was in her bed at home. A blurry figure loomed over her and slowly came into focus as she wiped the sleep from her eyes. It was Meredith.

"Something wrong?" she croaked and then cleared her throat.

"Sorry to wake you," her stepmother apologized. "Your dad is downstairs on the couch right now but he's leaving in about an hour to play golf. Does your offer to tell him about Annatha together still stand?"

Dee sat up and straightened the T-shirt she wore to bed. *What an unpleasant task to face first thing after waking up,* she groaned silently. "Give me a minute," she waved Meredith out of the room, "I'll be right down."

After her stepmother left, Dee hurled back the comforter and made her way to the bathroom. She turned on the tap water and liberally splashed the cold liquid on her face. After drying off, she decided to brush her teeth to kill the disgusting taste in her mouth from morning breath. Standing in front of the mirror, she studied the face staring back at her. It looked drawn and there were dark circles under her puffy eyes. *Jesus, girl,* she thought, *you're looking a little rode hard.*

The past few weeks had been the most stressful situation she had encountered since her parents' divorce. This was probably worse, she decided, because there were so many unknowns and the whole thing seemed out of her control. Her noble attempt to resolve the situation covertly had been blown out of the water yesterday with the discovery of Annatha's abandoned car. Now it was time to face her dad and explain why he had been kept out of the loop. Despite his adoration for her, she still felt some anxiety about what she would say and how she would say it. But she had promised Meredith, and she never broke a promise. Throwing on some clothes, she left her room and headed down the stairs.

As she approached the family room, she could hear the TV

blaring; the surround sound subwoofer was pulsing with a steady beat that seemed to shake the whole house. Her dad was likely watching some action movie. When she entered the room her hunch was confirmed, as the movie *Predator* was playing on the large plasma screen. Her dad was sprawled out on the couch, wearing sweat pants and a T-shirt with a Microsoft logo. The couch was no match for his long frame and his bare feet were hanging over the arm rest. Meredith was perched in her Queen Ann chair as usual, sipping on a cup of coffee and pretending to read the newspaper. Brandon was so entranced with the movie he didn't see Dee when she entered the room.

Dee positioned herself near the couch and called out loudly enough to be heard. "Good morning, Dad."

Brandon saw his daughter, smiled broadly and grabbed the remote. He muted the sound and struggled to a sitting position. "Hey Dee," he said warmly and patted the couch next to him. "Have a seat."

Dee sat at the opposite end of the couch. She felt the distance would be useful when her dad erupted at the news she was about to give him. The crinkling sound of a newspaper being folded up signaled Meredith was also preparing for the worst.

"There's something we need to tell you, Dad," she began, surprised at how steady her voice sounded. She certainly didn't feel that way inside right now.

Brandon looked at her curiously. There was something about the way his daughter phrased the sentence that unleashed a feeling of dread. "What it is?"

Dee put the events together as best she could, deciding to leave out the part about Annatha being pregnant by an online encounter until the end since she knew it would elicit the strongest response. Her dad listened quietly, but a furrow creased his brow deeper and deeper as she spoke. From time to time he would glance at Meredith in an almost threatening way, as if annoyed she wasn't telling him this. When Dee finished, there was an uncomfortable silence while he seemed to assimilate the information from his daughter's lips. His right hand absently stroked the sparsely populated skin on his crown. It was a familiar habit Dee had witnessed in the past when he was trying to hold his temper. Finally, he set the remote on the couch and pressed it into the cushion deliberately.

"And why am I just now finding out about this?" Brandon asked evenly. His eyes betrayed the anger welling up inside.

"Because there's more to the story, Dad," Dee replied. "We're pretty sure she's pregnant."

Brandon's cheeks flushed and his eyes widened. In an effort to control the sudden rage that seized him, he stood up and paced fitfully around the large room. He wasn't entirely oblivious to a ploy the two of them had hatched to let Dee tell him the bad news. No wonder they disappeared together last night, he recalled. After a few minutes, he stopped in front of Meredith and glared at her.

"I told you she was a little whore, didn't I?"

His wife hung her head, unable to meet the intense stare from the intimidating figure who towered above her. Dee stood up, walked over and squeezed her father's beefy arm.

"Please sit down, Dad," she pleaded.

Her dad stared blankly ahead, and she could tell he wasn't really looking at her. She repeated her request and waited for him to respond. It took a few seconds but his eyes cleared and she could tell he finally understood the words she spoke. Thankfully, the tension that gripped his face relaxed and he complied, resuming his place on the couch.

"We need to talk about this calmly," Dee persisted. "We have information now that strongly suggests she has run off with the father of the baby. We didn't tell you after we found the pregnancy test when she disappeared because we were pretty sure she was off having an abortion and no one would have to know." She sat down next to her dad and took his hand, staring directly into his eyes. "You can be pretty intimidating, you know, and we didn't want to stress you out if Annatha handled the whole thing in a few days."

Brandon shrugged. His daughter was making a good case, but he was still angry at Annatha for bringing this chaos into his life.

"I guess this doesn't surprise me," he mumbled and then looked at Meredith. "She's been a rebellious little shit since the day I met her, and now she's given me the biggest 'fuck you' she could."

Meredith sat motionless, still unable to look up at her husband. Dee felt sorry for her and was irritated with her dad's reaction, although it was entirely predictable.

"Can't you put yourself in your wife's shoes for just a moment?" she asked her dad softly. "Imagine how you would feel if it was me instead of Annatha."

"You're not that stupid."

Dee sighed and let go of his hand. It was an exercise in futility to change the way her dad treated her stepmom or Annatha, and she wasn't going to try and smooth things over anymore. She had kept her promise to Meredith and told her dad. It was time to go.

"I'm going back to my apartment today," she suddenly announced and stood up to leave. She didn't want to be around for the next few days while he stewed, cursing Annatha and blaming Meredith.

"Honey," Brandon called after her. Dee stopped and looked at her dad, wondering what would be the next thing out of his mouth. "You've definitely got the CSI skills if you ever wanted a career in that, but it doesn't pay well." He winked.

"Whatever you say, Dad," she sighed and exited the room.

After it was just the two of them, Brandon looked at Meredith coldly. He silently rued the day he married her. Her daughter had been nothing but trouble, and his life would have been much simpler if he had just stayed single. Dee was obviously frustrated with him, but that would blow over. His mind turned to the unpleasant task ahead of having to deal with the police. Dee had not mentioned much about that aspect.

"So what's next?" He asked Meredith. "Does she get plastered all over Greta's Fox News channel program and milk cartons?"

Managing to finally meet his gaze, Meredith saw only contempt in his eyes. Despite the hell Bill's drinking had caused the last few years of their marriage, he had been a kind and decent man after sobering up. On the other hand, Brandon had been very charming when they first met and she had enjoyed being around him, but sober or not, he had turned out to be a consummate prick. All because Annatha didn't worship the ground he walked on. Her daughter's aversion to him and the acting out that followed had been like a tanker spilling its oil on a pristine beach. No matter how much she tried to clean up and restore its former luster, the damage had been done.

"No TV, newspaper or posters," she answered meekly. "I instructed the detective not to do anything like that without our permission."

"Thank God for that," he stated flatly. "I'm going to the country club." Secretly, he hoped Annatha had gotten married. His life would be more peaceful without the constant conflict between them. He honestly didn't think she was in any trouble, but if she was, she made her bed, now she could lie in it.

Meredith didn't tell him the detective wanted to come over some time in the next few days to interview them. Enough had been said for one day. She was relieved Brandon decided to leave, but she wished Dee wasn't going back to school. It would be lonely here and she couldn't tell any of her friends yet. If the news got out in their social circle Brandon would be furious. Never one for religion, she considered going to church the next day. At least it would be something to do instead of sitting around paralyzed with fear and worry. Thinking about it, prayer had never brought her the calm a dry martini could. Her bottle of gin would have to be the one who comforted her and provided companionship today. She justified it would be a well-deserved escape after what she had just been through. Mixing the drink that would take her away from all of this, one question kept circling her thoughts like a pesky fly. Why didn't Annatha call her?

Chapter Eight

Thirteen Weeks (13W0D)

Almost a month had passed since the SeaTac police were notified of Annatha's disappearance, and Meredith was beside herself with worry and frustration. The day after they spoke with Detective Knowles when the Civic was reported abandoned at the Park & Fly, he had a heart attack followed by major surgery and was out of commission for the time being. When she asked who was taking over, a Detective Gardner had apologized that they were currently short-staffed, as most of their manpower was committed to a missing five year old boy. Of course she had protested vehemently, asking why this child was more important than her daughter. The detective tried diplomatically to tell her they believed her daughter was a runaway and not an abduction, which placed her fairly low on their priority list, but he promised to forward the file to the State Patrol division for missing persons in hopes they would pursue some leads. To say this turn of events had been maddening was an understatement, she fumed silently as she made a pot of coffee.

Tonight, a State Patrol detective was coming over to "catch them up" on the investigation and conduct an interview with her and Brandon. She had tried in vain to convince her husband to call and complain about the lack of movement on her daughter's case but he just grunted and walked off. Dee was busy at PLU with soccer and her studies, but did manage to phone the State Patrol and demand some kind of action. In fact, her stepdaughter's protests had prompted this evening's visit by a detective and Meredith was grateful for that.

Other than Dee's support, she had no one to turn to with her churning emotions. The supply of gin was disappearing at an alarming rate, which did cause some concern, but she rationalized she would cut back when her nerves weren't so frazzled. The aroma of brewing coffee filled the kitchen, and Meredith sat down to finish her martini. Coffee would only get her keyed up, and that was the last thing she needed right now.

Brandon sauntered into the kitchen, dressed casually in a pair of jeans and a navy blue polo shirt. "I smell coffee," he said and grabbed a mug from the overhead cabinet.

She knew her spouse would be in shortly once the coffee's enticing odor reached him on the couch. He was the biggest caffeine junky she had ever seen. Meredith noticed he was barefoot as usual, but hoped he would slip on some sandals when the detective arrived.

"Do you want some apple pie?" she asked. "I have some leftovers in the fridge from this past weekend, too."

"Nah," he declined, "that detective's supposed to be here soon, and I don't have much of an appetite right now."

Just as he finished his reply, the doorbell sounded. Meredith glanced up at Brandon, who ignored it, so she got up and went to answer the door. A crisply dressed man in a gray pinstriped suit was standing on the porch with a folder tucked under his left arm. He was medium height, very thin and looked younger than she had expected. His dark brown hair was fashionably tussled and the styling gel cast a brassy reflection from the evening sun. A free right hand was extended and he flashed a polite smile.

"Mrs. Reynolds, I'm Detective Nathan Holloway from

the State Patrol." After a firm handshake, he produced his ID badge.

"Come in, please." Meredith motioned for him to enter.

She led him to the family room where Brandon was already perched on the sofa, drinking his coffee.

"This is my husband, Brandon Reynolds," she introduced them and they shook hands perfunctorily before Nathan helped himself to a seat on the leather recliner. "I have some fresh coffee if you're interested."

"That would be nice," he accepted, while trained eyes reflexively studied the expensive furnishings, artwork and large plasma screen TV with its state-of-the-art audio system. He returned his gaze to Meredith. "I take it black."

She left the room and returned shortly with a steaming mug of coffee. Neither Brandon nor Nathan had spoken a word while she was gone. "Here you go," she said and placed the cup on a coaster next to the recliner.

"Thanks," he said. He took a tentative sip of the hot liquid and set the mug down again. The folder was sitting on his lap. He opened it and began arranging the contents. "I'm sure you folks are anxious to find out where things stand with your daughter," he began, "so I'll get right to it."

"First of all," he reached in his coat pocket and withdrew Annatha's cell phone, "I want to let you know about the 303 area code number that was in her call records." He placed it on the table next to him. "I personally called the number, and it belongs to a Red Rock Catering in Denver. The owner denied any knowledge of Annatha or why their number would be in her call records."

"How can that be?" Meredith demanded. "Did anyone check them out?"

Holloway produced a sheet of paper before he replied. "As a matter of fact, we did. The Denver police department was very cooperative. They sent an officer to the residence and he faxed us this report." He leaned forward in the recliner and referred to the page in front of him. "The catering business is run by two women. Their names are Paula Davenport and Bridgette Lansing." He glanced up from the report. "Do either of these names mean anything to you?"

Meredith shook her head no and looked at Brandon, who just shrugged. "Never heard of them," he said.

"Well," Nathan continued, "we didn't think they were persons of interest in this case. They are a middle-aged lesbian couple and their background checks were clean except for one arrest for a political demonstration they were involved in several years ago."

Brandon snorted, which drew a glance from Holloway. "Don't be so sure, detective," he said sarcastically. "Annatha found a man online to have sex with and impregnate her; maybe she contacted them for some reason."

Nathan was surprised at his glibness. The mother was appropriately distraught in her demeanor, but the cocky stepdad seemed totally disconnected from any normal emotional reaction to Annatha's disappearance save sarcasm.

"Be that as it may," he said tactfully, "we have written it off as a wrong number dialed by the caterer since this area code begins with a three also."

"Just like that?" Meredith said incredulously. "That's your explanation for the number on my missing daughter's cell phone?"

"Sorry," he apologized, "I forgot one more piece of information." He scanned the report for a few seconds. "Here it is. Paula is from Washington State and admitted she sometimes messes up and dials 360 for the area code."

Meredith felt a hole in her gut was opening wider with each passing moment, and the hopes she had for finding her daughter were pouring out through it like a huge water main had burst. The one piece of information that she felt would lead them to her daughter had ended up being a dead end. Surely, there must be something useful they had uncovered.

"What else have you found out?" she asked tentatively.

Holloway described his efforts to review all of the Jane Doe reports that crossed his desk and determine if any matched Annatha's description. Also, any reports of remains that were found would be compared to Annatha's dental records. Finally, he had sent a missing person bulletin nationwide so that if her daughter was arrested, they would notify him.

"I have to be honest with you," Nathan stated grimly, "at this point it looks like your daughter has vanished into thin air."

Brandon shifted on the couch, gulped the last of his coffee and sat the mug on the table in front of him. "Look, detective," he began, "I know you have a job to do but my opinion is that you are wasting valuable resources when it's obvious to me she has simply run off with the father of her baby."

Nathan nodded, then looked at Meredith. "Do you agree with that?"

She did not, but didn't want to embarrass Brandon in front of the detective. "I don't know," she replied after a pause, "my husband may be right. Annatha made a stupid mistake getting pregnant, but she's not a stupid girl. I feel fairly certain she would have chosen to have an abortion, which is why I am so worried about her. It's just hard to believe she has decided to keep the baby and run off with some stranger. Besides, even if she did, why hasn't she contacted me by now?"

"Unless her intent is to punish you and piss me off," Brandon retorted.

Nathan was gaining some insight into the family dynamics during his brief interview with the Reynolds. The stepdad was obviously a prick to the girl and the mother was subdued, and it was doubtful she stood up for her daughter. The likelihood the girl had just run away seemed even more plausible now. He began organizing the folder pages and closed it on his lap.

"Any other questions?" Nathan's eyebrows lifted when he asked.

Meredith shook her head numbly.

"I think it's pretty obvious what's going on," Brandon said coldly and left to get another cup of coffee.

Holloway stood up and straightened his suit coat. "I'll be in touch," he said and followed Meredith to the door.

"Thanks for coming out," she said and offered her hand.

The detective shook it and placed his other hand over hers. "Don't take this the wrong way," he said quietly, "but if you want to come down to my office by yourself, feel free to do so."

Meredith acknowledged the offer with a nod, but did not reply. She watched him as he walked to the unmarked car sitting in their circular front driveway. The sun was beginning to duck behind the fir-lined hills on the other side of the lake. A soft pink glow was splashed across some scattered clouds on the horizon. She wondered silently how many more sunsets would pass before she learned what had happened to her daughter.

After returning to the family room, she headed straight for the bar to prepare a decanter of martinis for the evening. She fostered some concern with the increase in her drinking over the past few weeks that it might lead to the same alcoholism Annatha's father had fallen into. When she first met Bill, they enjoyed parties and his social drinking demonstrated no signs of becoming a problem. They married after he graduated from college and were so happy a few years later when she gave birth to twins, Annatha and Chloe. William had been such a good dad, pitching in to help her with the insurmountable task of bathing, feeding and changing the twins. The bottom had fallen out of their lives when Chloe died of SIDS at four months of age. Even though they still had Annatha, he took the death very hard but never wanted to talk about it. His drinking began to escalate to drown his grief. Meredith had tried to be understanding but years of this behavior had taken its toll. When Annatha reached the age of twelve, she finally filed for divorce. Sure she had used the affair with Brandon to leave, but their marriage had been in shambles for many years.

The thought of losing another daughter caused an

involuntary shudder. She quickly gulped a martini and poured another. Chloe's death had not crossed her mind for many years, but she could still picture the tiny coffin that held her precious baby being lowered into the ground at the graveside service. It was inconceivable that fate would take another child from her in this lifetime. Annatha had to turn up safe at some point. It didn't matter if she was pregnant or married. She could deal with either or both of them, as long as her daughter was alive and well. Mixing another decanter of martinis, she headed out to sit by the pool and drink in the balmy night air along with her gin. Brandon would be in a foul mood and she wasn't up to dealing with him right now.

****

Annatha secured the red string to its ball of yarn with a piece of tape, leaving about four feet free. She grabbed the ball and dangled it in front of her to get the kitten's attention. On cue, he shot around the recliner at full speed and lunged. Just before he reached the dancing string, she pulled it up and he tried in vain to acquire purchase on the thin carpet. He reminded her of the first time she tried ice skating and had to use the side of the rink to stop. Unable to halt his forward momentum, Taz slammed into the night stand.

"Taz the spaz," she smiled. She felt a slight chill and pulled on her hooded sweatshirt she had worn to meet Thomas. The only clothes she ever wore were a pair of loose-fitting sweatpants and a T-shirt that her captor supplied and washed weekly. The sweatshirt was comfy and the only thing she had contact with each day from her life before Wendy.

Today was the beginning of her second trimester according to the nurse when she brought her breakfast that morning. Annatha had been stunned to hear her pregnancy was one-third over. At least the nausea was gone and she had her energy back. The down side was being stuck in a padded cell with psycho nurse holding the keys. In addition, her boredom level was rising rapidly. If it weren't for Taz, she would be nothing but an MTV zombie by now. It was the only thing on television she could stomach. She missed watching the education channels and surfing on her laptop. The only other stations of interest were the cable news networks. Wendy didn't have a satellite package with local channels on the downstairs receiver, so Annatha watched CNN and FOX news for any stories about her disappearance. So far, Greta hadn't mentioned her name. Well, if it's not on TV, it must not be news, she would say out loud each time the half hour was up and no story about her was forthcoming. It was something her dad would say at times when an important story that interested him had not made it to the mainstream media yet.

The only light she used in the basement besides the flickering TV screen was the sun lamp over the recliner. Wendy had explained it simulated sunlight and would keep her from getting Seasonal Affective Dysphoric Disorder (SADD). It was tempting to reply, "Oh yeah you stupid bitch, if it weren't for that sun lamp, I'd be totally depressed, but you saved me with your kind gesture." Despite the overwhelming urge she had felt to blurt this out, Annatha had decided to remain cold and distant for now. Wendy didn't push her to talk, but it probably bugged her a little that the captive baby mamma wasn't warming up to her.

However, with more time awake now that the fatigue had resolved, some troubling thoughts began to worm their way into her brain. She absently tossed the ball of yarn while her mind wandered, then pulled it towards her when Taz would attack. He never tired of the game and it helped her pass the time. It was a rhythmic task she could do while mulling over an idea. The latest alarm to go off in her mind was the result of something that occurred to her while thinking of what plans the nurse had for her once the baby was born. Wendy was guilty of kidnapping her and once the baby was out, she would be guilty of kidnapping it, too. Letting Annatha go free would subject her to arrest and prosecution and she wouldn't get the baby, which would destroy her whole sordid scheme.

She's thought it through, Annatha realized. *There's no way she's going to let me walk out of here.* A chill that wasn't due to the damp basement air caused the hair on her arms to stand up. She swallowed hard and noticed her mouth had gone dry. Her sock was suddenly yanked on which diverted her attention and she looked down to see Taz was attacking the ball of yarn resting on her foot. His claw was caught in the sock. She reached down and removed the kitten's paw carefully and rested him on her lap. He wasn't interested in snuggling and jumped down from the bed. It didn't matter; her mind wasn't keen on entertaining him now, anyway. She was focused on what the hell she was going to do about getting out of there after the birth. The nurse's clever plan to capture a pregnant girl and hold her captive until she delivered a baby, then keep the newborn and raise it as her own was evidence enough there had to be an equally sinister plot lurking in that twisted mine to deal with her in the aftermath. Annatha had a sinking feeling it would include her demise.

Once again the possibility of an escape had to be considered. *There's just no way,* she groaned. Overpowering the nurse wasn't plausible, either. Wendy was bigger than her and looked pretty fit for her age. The only exercise Annatha got was when she went fishing or saddled her horse. A weapon of some kind was the only way she might be able to surprise and disable her. She had tried this before and was maced by the determined nurse, but had learned her lesson. Next time she wouldn't see her coming.

A towel rack from the bathroom could be removed and used as a club of sorts, but even if she was able to render her unconscious, there was still the issue of getting the basement door open. Wendy never brought the keys down with her, as the door had a keyless entry deadbolt on the basement side. She knew there was a four digit code because she counted the number of times the nurse depressed the keys before a chime sounded and the latch released. Following her up the stairs and striking at the exact moment the lock opened would be futile because Wendy always made sure Annatha was nowhere near the stairs before entering the code.

Without doing the exact calculation, she knew the number of combinations for a four-digit code were astronomical. In desperation a few days before, Annatha had made an attempt to guess the code, but after three tries it sounded an awful chime and refused to take any more entries. She had no way of knowing how long the "lock out" period would last before it accepted another attempt. The nurse made her believe she would have to reprogram the code if this happened, but she never saw her do it. Still, it was such a long shot she decided to abandon any future efforts to decipher it. A feeling of hopelessness engulfed her as dead end after dead end loomed before her, despite the constant struggle to reason her way out of this nightmare.

Teetering on the edge of despair, she failed to notice Taz had climbed into her lap and was purring. "I love you too, Tazzy." She scooped him up and gave him a kiss on his forehead. His presence had a way of raising her spirits even in her darker moments, like now.

The intensity of her attraction to the playful kitten had surprised even her. Annatha had been afraid she would never be able to love a cat again after what happened to Buster and Spanky. *Too late for that,* she smiled at him; he had stolen her heart but good. Every night he draped himself across the top of her head and they slept together. When he wanted some loving, as she called it, he would walk over to her and stretch out a paw. He didn't have a mean bone in his body. She could tussle with him and rough him up good but he never tried to bite her unless she rubbed his stomach. Then he attacked her hand ferociously, but when she whimpered and pretended to be hurt he immediately released his grip. He was such a sweet boy. Nothing on earth melted her heart the way cats did, she sighed. Through all the trials and heartaches with her parents' divorce, her dad's drinking, and her mom's remarriage to that asshole Brandon, she could always rely on her cats for unconditional love. They had been her best friends through thick and thin. She stroked Taz gently and felt his motor running.

After a few minutes, she set Taz on the comforter and dug between the mattress and box springs, producing her journal. One of the few times she had spoken to Wendy was to ask for some reading materials suitable for her age that didn't involve pregnancy, and a journal to help her pass the time. It had galled her to communicate in any way with her captor, but she was going stir-crazy with the television as her only form of entertainment. God, she missed her room and all the electronic toys in it. She grabbed a pen from the nightstand and scooted back just enough to sit cross-legged and opened the journal between her thighs. Putting her thoughts on paper always helped her organize them and see things more clearly. Actually, her dad had introduced her to this exercise. He began journaling in the treatment center and found it helpful for him, so he passed on the knowledge to her. Grudgingly, she had tried writing about her feelings towards Brandon and her Mom and it did seem to relieve some of the stress, but what she really needed was a punching bag.

One of her favorite books a few years back had been *The Diary of Anne Frank*. The day-to-day recording of her life in hiding from the Nazis in Amsterdam mesmerized Annatha and she had secretly sworn to be as brave in her life. At the time she had felt like a stowaway in her own home, sequestered in her room to avoid the dysfunction and chaos. And now, she paused and twirled the pen in her fingers, she was hidden away in a basement with a dreadful fate hanging over her. Like Anne, she was imprisoned, fearing for her life and praying the ordeal would soon be over. Hopefully, her fate would be different than the poor Jewish girl, who met her demise when finally captured by murderous Nazis.

She began writing and gently stroked Taz with her free hand. He was purring again. After a few sentences, she stuck the pen in her mouth and chewed thoughtfully while she read them over. The words on the page told a bleak story. *This is a fight for my life,* she had written. *As long as I am pregnant, no harm will come to me. However, after the baby is born, my life is worth nothing, and I will be unable to save myself if I can't come up with a way out of this.* Reading it over again, *as long as I am pregnant* stood out as if it was a neon sign. This was a key concept, she realized and resumed writing. Her thoughts were recorded feverishly now as she chronicled the two ways this pregnancy could end. The first, and Wendy's choice, was for her to deliver a healthy newborn. The second, clearly not Wendy's choice, was for her to somehow lose the baby. In either case, it was unlikely she would be allowed to return to her less than optimum life on Mercer Island.

A disturbing thought began to seethe in her gut and she stopped writing, since there was a good chance the nurse would be rude enough to read her diary. Maybe she couldn't figure a way out of this with either scenario, but why should Wendy get her way? She glanced down at her arms and saw a herd of goose bumps in response to her train of thought. She was creeping herself out, but she had to play it all the way through. Would she be able to end the pregnancy somehow? It would mean killing the baby. *You were going to do that anyway, genius*, she reminded herself. Doing in the baby might cause her to be injured too, but if she was going to die anyway, why not cause psycho nurse the biggest disappointment and pain of her life? Trouble was, she had no clue of how to go about it, and the only method that immediately came to mind was hanging herself. However, the thought of committing suicide like that repulsed her. Annatha mentally recoiled from the image of her limp, lifeless body swinging from a rope in the dimly lit basement. It was like a scene from her favorite Stephen King novel, *Pet Semetary*.

She shook off the grotesque mental picture and shut her diary. Looking around the room for some other option to explore that was less ghastly, she noticed the pregnancy book Wendy had left was still where she chunked it on the floor. Scrambling out of bed, Annatha scooped it up and began leafing through the pages until she saw a diagram that demonstrated the proper way to put on a seat belt. *Must be something here,* she thought. The narrative underneath the picture warned against placing the belt over the abdomen because an accident could cause blunt force trauma to the uterus and cause placental separation. "What the hell does that mean?" she wondered aloud. Scouring the index quickly, she found the pages that contained information about placental separation, or the medical term for it, placental abruption.

It was written plainly for the layperson, so Annatha had no problem understanding the concept. If the placenta was torn away from the uterus, the baby's blood supply would be interrupted and it would die within minutes. The mother's life was also in danger, as sometimes the blood loss could be massive; the clotting factors in the maternal blood stream were consumed by the process and that caused further internal hemorrhage and eventually death from shock. Why did the clotting factors disappear? Guess it doesn't matter, she decided, this placental abruption sounded like a foolproof plan. Causing blunt trauma to her uterus would be as simple as falling off the bed onto the floor. It would be difficult to resist breaking the fall with her hands, but if she landed solidly on her stomach, it just might work.

Wait a minute, she realized, *the uterus has to stick out enough for this to work.* She couldn't even tell she was pregnant yet, much less feel her uterus. Once again, she thumbed through the index and found a section on uterine size. There were more diagrams. Several arcing lines were drawn on an abdomen that indicated the approximate position of the top of a pregnant uterus at different weeks of gestation. Disappointed, she noted the uterus didn't even reach her belly button until twenty weeks, which was half way through the pregnancy. Returning to the section about seatbelts, she found a sentence that explained how the uterus became most vulnerable to trauma in the third trimester. "That's twenty-six weeks," she groaned.

She cursed herself for even being upset about how long she had to wait until her uterus was large enough to injure, when the overriding concern should be the fact she was thinking about killing herself! What the hell was wrong with her? This morbid shit felt awful and she was tired of it. Annatha felt confused as well as conflicted about her ruminations, so she shut the book hard and threw it on the bed. Exhausted from her mental voyage into self mutilation, she plopped down in the recliner. Her head was spinning with diagrams and medical terms. This was certainly a topic she had never dreamed of considering in her high school, Internet-chatting life. There had never been a more baffling dilemma laid at her feet before and she felt ill-equipped to solve it.

Taz leapt onto her lap and startled her. She picked him up and rubbed her nose on his soft tummy. Suddenly, a thought occurred to her as she buried her face deeper in the kitten's thick fur. Who would take care of Taz if she did away with herself? He let out a soft meow and she could feel it through her whole body. Tears welled in her eyes at the thought of leaving her precious companion with Wendy.

"Nobody could ever love you like I do," she choked and squeezed him tightly in her arms.

Now she was even more baffled. Thinking only of herself had led Annatha to entertain a rather gruesome plan to end her baby's life along with hers. She just couldn't leave Taz to that deranged bitch, she vowed and brushed the tears away with her shirt sleeve. If she really planned to go through with it, she would have to convince Wendy she didn't want him anymore and most likely he would be taken back to the animal shelter. At least there Taz would have a chance someone would take him who would care for him as she did. On the other hand, she shuddered, he could very well meet the same fate as Spanky and Buster.

Annatha gently put Taz back on the floor. Her feelings were a mixture of sadness overshadowed by sheer frustration. She gave in to the latter, raised both fists and pounded repeatedly on the recliner, screaming "Fuck!" each time they landed. Finally, she became exhausted and stared blankly at the TV screen, her hands burning in pain from the sudden outburst. She didn't care. The throbbing she felt was muted by the despair she felt over her inability to formulate a way out of this. It seemed every road she traveled down in her mind was a dead end, or so horrifying she wanted to turn back. Turn back to where? This was as good as it was going to get, she admitted bitterly, unless she figured out some way to defeat Florence Nightmare.

Chapter Nine

Thirteen Weeks, One Day (13W1D)

Wendy reached the bottom step and carefully padded across the floor with Annatha's breakfast tray. She never turned on any lights for her morning duties other than the one over the stairs. It had burned out a few times before she figured out a way to lengthen the cord and slip it through a small crack at the top of the basement door. This way she could switch it on and scout the stairway before venturing into the basement. The girl was always sleeping when she brought her breakfast down, and she tried to be quiet so as not to disturb her. The light in the room was enough to navigate to the recliner, where she left a plate of fresh fruit and removed the dirty one from dinner the night before.

    Wendy noticed the pregnancy book on the end of the bed and felt some satisfaction that the girl might be taking some interest in her situation. There were some dog eared pages and she stealthily removed the book from the comforter and opened it to the first marked page. She had to squint in the darkened room, but she could barely make out the print. A diagram of uterine sizes for each month of pregnancy--she smiled. This was a good sign. She leafed to the next marked page and her smile quickly changed to a frown. Why was the girl reading about placental abruption? Wendy glanced over at the still form under the blanket. Satisfied it was moving up and down with deep, slow, rhythmic respirations made by a sleeping body, she stepped back and moved softly towards the stairs so she could see better.

As she read on, she had to stifle a gasp as the meaning of the information became clear. This was talking about blunt trauma causing separation of the placenta and fetal demise. She put two and two together and realized the girl was only interested in how to cause her baby's death, and the diagram of uterine sizes was her way of finding out at what gestational age it could be accomplished by a traumatic injury.

There was always, of course, the consideration her caged subject would try to kill herself at some point. To that end, she had taken great pains to make the basement as safe as for a mental patient on suicide precautions. An electric razor had been chosen in place of razor blades. The basement ceiling had no beams to put a hanging rope over. Besides, she didn't keep any rope in the basement to begin with. She had the side stairway railing removed because a resourceful person could tie their clothes together and fashion a noose. The steps were lower than the railing and could pose a problem but she figured when all was said and done, they simply weren't high enough. Felt-tip pens were all that was available for writing so they couldn't be used to cut anything effectively. A hunger strike had always been a worry if the girl became desperate, but she had ways of force feeding her. However, it would require full body restraints and a tube passed into her stomach, something Wendy hoped to avoid. In addition, immobilizing her would increase the chances of a blood clot forming in her leg veins that could travel to the lungs resulting in cardiac arrest and death. She was already at more risk for a blood clot from the pregnancy itself. Then there would be bed sores to deal with too, not to mention the handling and disposing of other bodily functions.

Despite thinking through all these scenarios, and taking appropriate precautions, it would be impossible to stop the girl from taking a dive off the bed onto her abdomen and traumatizing the baby and herself, she realized glumly. She walked softly back to the bedside and stood over Annatha's sleeping shape. It was difficult to control the fear-driven rage she was feeling, and her body trembled slightly. *Maybe I should wake the girl up and threaten her,* she fumed. Threaten her with what? How could she make life worse than it already was? She noticed for the first time with her eyes becoming more accustomed to the dark, the kitten was perched on top of the girl's head. *That's it,* she thought, she could take away her kitten and tell her she was taking him back to the pound. *No,* she realized, thinking it through*, then she'd be really upset and definitely act out. Annatha had the power to end the baby's life if she so chose, and given she was about to have an abortion at the clinic, probably wouldn't give it a second thought.*

This is not a stupid child, Wendy, she admonished herself. She either reached the conclusion she would not be allowed to live once the baby was born, or she wanted to have retribution against her captor, no matter what the cost. One of the two issues could be turned around in her favor; the other was in the hands of God. Besides, regardless of which motive was driving the girl, it wouldn't be practical to restrain her the entire pregnancy so she wouldn't try to hurt herself or the baby. Somehow, Annatha had to be convinced Wendy had a plan that included her freedom after the birth. She had to come up with a plausible scenario that would allow the girl to live and then casually bring up the subject so she could put her mind at ease.

Of course, it would be a lie. After the baby was born, Wendy planned to do a reverse abortion. It was a term used when she was a labor and delivery nurse in Seattle. Whenever a particularly unfit mother presented in labor, the staff would joke the patient should have had a reverse abortion. In other words, the mother was aborted--killed--and the baby lived. *Very appropriate comparison here*, she thought.

That was her new task, she resolved, to persuade the girl there was no need to fear for her life. Then she wouldn't be so inclined to pursue what Wendy suspected was an all-out assault on her fetus. Even though Annatha's life had been interrupted and she was not allowed to terminate her pregnancy, why would she be angry that Wendy kept the baby she was planning to kill if she was ultimately allowed to go free? Satisfied she would succeed in her quest, Wendy laid the book back down on the comforter where she found it and left the room.

Annatha stirred and pulled the covers back. She had been secretly watching the nurse while she was reading the book. It wasn't hard to imagine she had been able to figure out why the pages were marked. The fact she didn't blow up and start yelling at her was somewhat of a mystery, but that might come later when she brought her dinner down. Turning over on her back, she stared at the bare sheetrock ceiling. She had memorized every pattern in the speckled tapestry above the bed. So now Wendy knew her little secret, she surmised, and pulled the covers tightly around her neck to keep out the bone chilling dampness in the stale air.

"Game on, you psycho bitch," she snarled out loud and her voice echoed eerily in the sparsely furnished room. "How does it feel not to have complete control of a situation?" She felt some satisfaction that today would not be as cheery for the nurse because she discovered her caged pet was plotting against her. Annatha suspected their relationship had just been transformed into a battle of wits.

CHAPTER TEN

Twenty Weeks, Six Days (20W6D)

Annatha awakened suddenly with an uneasy feeling. Something had happened in her sleep to arouse her but she wasn't sure what it could be. She glanced at her bedside clock and saw it was 6:50am. The sunlamp was on a timer but wouldn't activate until 8:30am so she could sleep in. Slowly, her eyes accommodated to the dark and a few seconds later she could see a little better. She listened intently and scanned the room to see if the nurse was there yet, but there was no unusual sound and no sign of her familiar silhouette. Besides, she never brought her breakfast before 7:00am. Puzzled, she wondered if a dream had woken her but couldn't remember if it had. Then suddenly she felt like her stomach flipped over. *What the hell was that? Gas? Maybe hunger?* It happened again, and this time it felt like a flock of butterflies were flapping their wings inside of her. She looked down at her swollen abdomen, half-expecting an alien to emerge.

"No way!" she cried as the reason for the strange sensation began to dawn on her. Was that her baby moving?

Annatha lay motionless, her entire being tuned in to the swollen mound where her flat tummy used to be. After a few moments of heightened anticipation, no further movement occurred. She exhaled loudly, unaware she had been holding her breath. Maybe she was mistaken about what caused the unfamiliar sensation. After all, she didn't really know what it felt like for a baby to move. Yet she had never experienced the internal fluttering that awakened her a few short minutes before. The only point of reference she could compare it to was when a fish tugged on her submerged nymph in a gentle riffle and she knew without a doubt it was a separate and distinct living creature pulling back against the monofilament line. *It had to be the baby*, she decided. No way could any of her internal organs cause such an alien stirring. Annatha resumed her vigil with renewed eagerness. As if on cue, the baby unleashed another burst of unmistakable quivering that surprised her so much she jumped and let out a shrill yelp.

Taz leapt off the bed, frightened by her unexpected outburst, but she ignored him. *This was amazing!* It was the weirdest feeling she had ever experienced, and remarkable all at the same time. She found it impossible to resist the urge to lie totally still with both hands pressed against her protruding abdomen and wait for the next movement. After a few long minutes of heightened anticipation, nothing further happened so she climbed out of bed and stood in the dark, her bare soles freezing against the icy cold carpet, but it didn't matter. She was struck by the awe and wonder that seized her now. It was easy to imagine her tiny baby wriggling furiously inside as if to say, "Hey, I'm in here." Life was insisting it be recognized, and she admired its tenacity. The novelty of her pregnancy milestone was unfortunately supplanted by a full bladder that demanded immediate relief, so she headed for the bathroom.

After peeing for what seemed like forever, she hovered on the frigid toilet seat and marveled at how differently she felt now. So far she had viewed the pregnancy as an inconvenience that resulted from a rebellious act, an inconvenience that needed to be removed. After that a circumstance of her own doing, and some really bad luck, had led to her kidnapping and imprisonment.

The subsequent months spent in isolation had been an exercise in reflection about the dire consequences that resulted from this unwanted life inside of her, not the life itself.

The insane nurse was a different story, she grimaced. Wendy was enamored with the life Annatha was carrying, to the point of being nauseating. She felt like a piece of hard candy with a gooey caramel center that Wendy couldn't wait to taste. Her prisoner was fed and watered simply to sustain the life growing inside of her and when it was time, Wendy would pluck it away like a ripe apple. Annatha was an aside, nothing more than a conduit for the nutrients that would sustain the baby. Needless to say, this had caused her to resent the object of the nurse's obsession, even to the point of wanting to do away with it despite the fact if it might require severely injuring herself in the process.

Afraid her butt cheeks would be frozen to the seat if she didn't get up, Annatha flushed the toilet and exited the bathroom, still blown away by the sudden change in her attitude. Sensing life inside of her for the first time had affected her in a way she wasn't prepared for. The flailing organism inside defined her as a mother. A mother! She suddenly grasped the full implications of the term. The harsh reality of being thrust into this role caused Annatha to wobble a bit, so she headed unsteadily to the recliner and sat down. Taz jumped in her lap and she stroked his back absently while she waited for her head to stop spinning from the rush of emotions that surged inside. Taking a few deep breaths, Annatha closed her eyes and mentally travelled back to a time before meeting Thomas. Her life was hell but at least she wasn't with child. The battles she waged with Brandon and her mother were trivial compared to this. It was futile to dwell on the past, she reminded herself, it was gone and the future wasn't here yet. Right now she had to come to terms with her maternal status even though she didn't want to. Sure, it was exciting to feel the baby move, but the ramifications of what that meant were very unpleasant. She had to put it all in perspective. Alone and imprisoned by a borderline nut case with almost no hope for escape, she was forced to deal with the depressing fact of being sixteen with an unplanned pregnancy she had no control over. It was a lot for a girl her age to deal with, and she wondered how long her sanity would hold out before she lost it and started screaming uncontrollably. She shuddered in the cold, damp basement and pulled the flannel blanket around her shoulders.

Annatha lifted her T-shirt, exposing her bare abdomen, and rested Taz on top, hoping he might feel something too. His furry coat kept the skin warm underneath. After a few minutes, she felt an almost imperceptible quiver. Taz sat up and looked at her belly curiously, with his head cocked.

"That's our baby, Tazzy," she cooed, marveling at how giddy it made her feel each time.

He looked at her curiously both ears standing at attention. Annatha remained silent, watching him bat her abdomen with his paw, trying to corral the strange creature. When his efforts failed, Taz began to lick the skin on her tummy with his coarse tongue. She laughed and ruffled his head.

"That tickles, you dork."

Annatha scooped him and snuggled him close. Her thoughts turned to her mother, wondering how she reacted the day she felt her and Chloe kick for the first time. Must be roomier for her baby than when she was crammed in the same space with her twin. They had to share the same tank. She had no real feelings of loss for her twin, as she died at four months of age. Her parents never spoke of her sister except one night when they were arguing and their rantings had become particularly nasty. Even though he was drunk as usual, her dad's voice wasn't slurred or thick when he launched a devastating verbal assault. It assumed a vicious tone she had never heard before then or since. He blamed her mother for not watching Chloe closely enough and letting her die. Her mother went berserk, screaming and crying at the same time. She told him she never wanted to see him again and the next day he was gone. Annatha mentally recoiled from the horrifying memory. A squeaky sound made her realize she was squeezing Taz a little too hard again.

"Sorry," she apologized and put him back on her belly.

Despite the dismal scene that had just played out in her mind, another flutter in her tummy flipped her mood on a dime. She wondered if her mother had felt the incredible awe she was feeling now, despite her dire situation. Did she imagine her babies jostling and playing together inside? How had she handled the realization she was truly a mother and all that meant? After all, she was married and the pregnancy had to be a joyful occurrence in her parents' lives. Wouldn't that have magnified her happiness a hundredfold? For the first time, Annatha viewed her mother in a totally different light. She too had experienced the uniqueness of a thriving organism that wrestled inside of her and the unconditional love that followed. The tragedy of losing one of her precious babies must have felt like someone had carved out a large piece of her heart. It was possible now for Annatha to understand why her mother never fully recovered from that experience. She longed to share this new awareness with her mom and hug her tightly. However, that moment would have to wait, perhaps forever.

Annatha stuffed the oversized nightshirt under her feet and curled up inside it. She withdrew her bare arms into the shirt to get them out of the cold air. Her hands scrubbed the cold skin on her thighs to produce friction and heat them up. The hair on her legs had been allowed to grow for some weeks now and she was a little grossed out that it felt like she was stroking a shag carpet. She was becoming a "greener," she groaned. No matter, it wasn't like she went out in public and at some point she would have a thick coat of fur to keep them warm. *That's a disgusting visual*, she frowned. However, her personal appearance was not something that had been of concern lately even though it was so important before her life had been turned upside down. The thought of doing anything other than cleaning her body in the shower repulsed her. How could she possibly put any effort into doing her hair or makeup when the only person who saw her was the psycho nurse?

A faint quiver interrupted her reverie and she glanced down at the swollen belly under her nightshirt. A planned pregnancy with a man she loved would be an entirely different circumstance, and the first stirrings of their precious baby would have been a joyful event. It saddened her to think this might be the only opportunity she would ever have to experience maternal feelings if she didn't figure a way out. The desolate basement that was her prison and the insane captor who planned to take her baby made certain this was anything but a joyful event.

Annatha realized the physical sensation of a living being inside of her had transformed her perception of this pregnancy in an instant, despite the dismal situation she was in. Given the knowledge she would never raise this baby, she had the choice to either cherish or reject it. A part of her wanted to deny the feelings unearthed when she felt her baby move for the first time. It was a defensive reaction, designed to avoid any emotional obstacles if she made the decision to end the pregnancy somehow. This might prove to be a daunting task because there was another side, awakened by her unborn child, that was fascinated by this morning's revelation. She was a mother carrying a living being that would forever be a part of her. *Flesh and blood,* she thought. The maternal gene inside of her was demanding to express itself, despite obvious misgivings about this horrific ordeal. It was a primal instinct that, if possessed, a human mother had no control over, and Annatha discovered she had it big time. She couldn't decide if it was a blessing or a curse, given her situation, but she felt powerless to stop it. The two perceptions were pitched in a fevered battle inside and she had no choice but to let them fight it out. One would emerge victorious and at this point she had no idea which one it would be.

The light over the stairs illuminated and she heard the familiar sound of deadbolts unlocking. The morning intrusions were usually unwelcome, but today she greeted it as a respite from the conundrum she was facing. Annatha turned and watched the nurse navigate down the steps with her food tray. It contained the usual plate of fruit, but today Wendy had placed a bagel on it.

No way was she going to mention the baby moving, she quickly decided. It would be nauseating to watch the nurse get all excited and happy. She did remember something she was going to ask, though, and waited for her to get closer.

"You're up early," Wendy greeted her cheerily.

Annatha cringed at the Magoo greeting. "Would it be possible to bring me a cup of coffee with my breakfast?" she asked as the tray was lowered in front of her.

"Coffee's not good for the baby," Wendy frowned.

Annatha moved the tray aside and walked over to the nightstand without a word. She retrieved the pregnancy book and brought it over to Wendy. Opening it to a marked page, she handed it to the nurse.

Wendy quickly scanned the underlined passage that stated caffeine had no adverse affects out of the first trimester if taken in moderation. Despite being corrected, she was glad the girl was reading something besides ways to kill the baby. That deserved a reward, she decided.

"Okay," she promised, "I'll bring you a cup tomorrow. Sugar or cream?"

"Black," Annatha said evenly, but inside she felt a triumphant glow even though she had only won a small skirmish. It wasn't much of a victory, but she couldn't help relishing it for a brief moment. She preferred an Americano from Starbucks but decided not to press her luck today.

"I see," Wendy chided, "a real coffee drinker."

Ignoring her, Annatha started eating her fruit. Gulping down a swallow of cold milk, she noticed out of the corner of her eye that Wendy had not started for the stairs, but instead was fidgeting with the book. She sat her fork down and without looking up, she asked impatiently, "What?"

"I'm going to Portland for Thanksgiving tomorrow, but I'll

bring you some leftovers. It won't be until late," she continued, "so I'll bring a frozen turkey dinner down tonight for you to cook in the microwave for lunch."

"Suit yourself," she replied flatly. Annatha tried never to look the nurse directly in the eye. It wasn't that she was scared to, it just creeped her out when she looked into the face of her kidnapper. Instead, she usually focused on the robe pocket where she knew the nurse kept her mace. It was a reminder not to jump up and start whaling on her when she felt like it. The robe moved and she saw Wendy had sat on the bed.

"Something else?" she asked and turned back to her food.

"Yes," Wendy answered carefully. "I want to do another ultrasound on Friday to make sure the baby is doing okay."

Annatha didn't reply. She really didn't want to fight about it. The idea of another conflict with the nurse didn't appeal to her, although, oddly enough, she'd have no problem bashing her head in if she thought she could open the basement door. Besides, things were different now weren't they? In fact, she felt a twinge of excitement at the prospect of actually seeing the movements she had begun to feel that morning.

The room was strangely quiet as Wendy waited for her reaction. The girl was chewing her food slowly but gave no indication of how she was taking the news. She half-expected her to lash out in anger and refuse to cooperate.

She knew she was making the nurse sweat a bit, Annatha thought smugly, but it gave her a modicum of satisfaction. Finally, she shrugged and said, "Whatever."

Wendy sighed, relieved at her response. "Thank you," she said gratefully. She stood up and retraced her steps, climbing the stairs with eager anticipation at the opportunity to view her baby again.

Annatha didn't watch, but she heard the familiar tones of the keypad entry and then the steel door slammed shut. The two deadbolts were latched and she heard the nurse's footsteps slowly disappear.

****

Wendy stepped out of the shower and toweled herself dry. She stood in front of the mirror while she slipped into her panties. Retrieving the newly purchased bra with padding to increase her bust size, she adjusted it and turned sideways to examine the effect. Pregnant women's breasts grew larger and she wanted to look the part. Her breasts were already a C cup and the padded bra made them look huge. Next, she hoisted the pregnancy tummy strap over her neck and secured the base with a belt around her midsection that fastened with Velcro. She had modified the one she bought online so she could add more gel to imitate the growth of a normal pregnant abdomen. The gel pack was inserted inside a zippered pouch that rounded out her tummy below the belly button so that she looked about twenty weeks along. When the device was situated to her satisfaction, Wendy stepped back to study the effect. It was perfect, she marveled. Pressing on her belly, she was surprised at how real it felt. If anyone bumped into her it had to feel authentic. She couldn't risk arousing suspicion, or her charade would fall apart.

Last month, she had finally broken the news to her coworkers that she was pregnant. Her story was that she went to a fertility clinic in Tacoma and had artificial insemination with donor sperm, and it finally worked on the third try. She told them she didn't want to say anything until after the amniocentesis to check the baby's chromosomes. Since she was over thirty-five this made sense and they accepted her explanation readily. They protested when she wouldn't tell them the sex, but she explained she didn't know herself, only that the tests were all normal.

They were also informed she was seeing a perinatologist in Tacoma since she had a high risk pregnancy. This was necessary because if she told them she was seeing a local obstetrician, one of them might know the staff and casually ask how she was doing. Despite HIPAA laws, offices still talked and she couldn't take the chance of being caught in a lie. It was one less problem to worry about. The story had worked like a charm. Her coworkers were happy for her and to celebrate, had taken her to lunch. Satisfied she had covered all the bases, she smiled at the unfamiliar figure staring back at her from the mirror. It reminded her of behind the scenes specials for movies that showed how the special effects artists transformed the actor step-by-step into a new creature.

She slipped into a white turtleneck and snugged it over the gel pouch. Fortunately, the days were cool now and it didn't seem out of place. Since she wore scrubs to work, it hid the strap from the maternity tummy that looped around her neck. The rest of her pregnant mom ensemble fit loosely and she cinched the string on her light blue scrub pants halfway up the curve in her abdomen. She turned sideways and admired herself again. The scrub top wasn't tucked in, and she purposely bought an extra long size so the pregnancy tummy wouldn't be exposed when she raised her arms above her head. "Nothing to chance" was her motto.

As the pregnancy progressed, she had larger sections of gel to insert so the size of her abdomen would mimic the gestational age. Even though she wasn't really pregnant, the device made her feel like she was, and that would do for now. Once the baby came, her role as a mother would be the genuine article, nothing fake about it.

Of course, she wouldn't wear this getup tomorrow when she visited her parents in Portland. After the baby was a few months old, she would simply tell them she adopted it. She didn't want her mother coming to Olympia to help with a newborn, for good reason. When Wendy informed her parents she was getting a divorce, her mother had insisted she was needed and stayed with her for a whole week. It was a nightmare. Instead of being helpful, her mother had driven her crazy by insisting she needed to "talk things out." All she wanted to do was sleep and cry. Dealing with a brand new baby would be difficult enough without her mom's special recipe for support. Its ingredients were a mixture of smothering, criticism and a dash of nosiness.

Wendy knew her mom all too well. She jumped at any

opportunity to help her children when she perceived they required her expertise. If things were going well she never visited. It was her way of worming into their business under the pretense of being a concerned parent. She especially thrived on crisis control, Wendy mused, and resumed brushing her hair. It was a role she had plenty of practice with since her younger brother had been in and out of prison the last few years on drug charges.

Enough negativity, she decided and brushed the train of thought away like an annoying bug. Leaning forward, she put the finishing touches on her makeup with her face only inches from the mirror. Her breath fogged the glass and she wiped it off with a tissue. A broad smile lit up her face as she stepped back and studied the end result. She was excited about her four day weekend, especially the ultrasound on Friday, when she would see her baby again and find out the sex.

****

Dee carefully packed her suitcase, resolved to avoid the temptation of hauling most of her winter clothes home for the Thanksgiving holiday break. She had a studio apartment in South Hall, a housing complex at the south edge of PLU (Pacific Lutheran University). This was her first year to qualify for residency at "The Hall" now that she was twenty. It was more expensive, but she had explained to her dad she was tired of traipsing to the library at night to study since the dorm parties or her chatty roommate always managed to keep the noise decibels at a level not conducive to concentrating. He had been all too happy to oblige her, not just so she could study in peace, but the safety factor was important too. Dee felt secure on campus, but she knew that throwing in the bit about walking alone in the dark would ensure her request to move would be granted.

Satisfied she had the essentials, she placed her knee on top of the bag and leaned hard against it so she could zip it closed. School and soccer kept her very busy, but she managed to keep in touch with Meredith on a regular basis. So far the news had not been promising. The Washington State Patrol had followed a few leads but each one had wound up a dead end. It was as if Annatha had vanished into thin air. Undaunted, Dee had done some online research on missing persons in her spare time and had come to the conclusion the FBI would be the best agency to involve in her stepsister's case. She vowed to bring it up, no matter how much resistance she met, during the long holiday weekend on Mercer Island.

One item had nagged her from the very beginning. The number on Annatha's cell phone that occupied her incoming and outgoing call record had not been fruitful when investigated by the police thus far, but she felt certain it was a vital clue. The explanation Meredith relayed to her from the State Patrol detective had not rung true. She didn't know why it didn't; it just seemed too coincidental to her that it was an incoming and outgoing call around the time her stepsister was meeting the man who got her pregnant. The police had come to the conclusion early on Annatha was a runaway and Dee felt this perception had put blinders on their subsequent investigation.

She took a deep breath, heaved the suitcase off of her bed and extended the handle. Her backpack was shouldered and she walked out onto the tiny porch, pulling her bag along behind her. Fumbling through her purse in front of the entry door, she located the keys and locked the deadbolt. She adjusted the hood to her raincoat, as it was drizzling steadily from a gloomy, gray curtain of clouds that moved lazily across the sky. Her car wasn't far and she hurried so her suitcase wouldn't get too wet. She quickly stowed it in the trunk and climbed inside the Accord, safe from the pesky rain. Shaking the hood off, she looked in the mirror and adjusted her rumpled hair.

As she steered her way out of the parking lot onto the main campus road, she couldn't help worrying about Annatha and what she was doing on this holiday weekend. Hardly a day went by that her thoughts didn't include her stepsister and where she might be, wondering if she was safe. Would she ever see her again?

It was now four months since Annatha had dropped off the face of the earth, and Dee was becoming more and more convinced foul play was a very plausible explanation for what had befallen her.

Dee waited patiently for the traffic light to turn green, her wipers slogging across her view every few seconds. She knew Annatha was an intelligent but troubled girl, all easily understood considering her past. The recent death of her father had been a huge blow to her happiness though she never talked about it with her. She suspected the combination of tragedies that befell her stepsister the past several months had clouded her judgment and resulted in the uncharacteristic acting out by having sex with a total stranger she met in online chat. Whatever the reason, she hoped the whole mess would be over soon and Annatha would return safely. Despite the fact they weren't close and she caused her dad so much stress, Dee didn't resent her. She had always hoped her stepsister's life would turn around after she was old enough to move out.

The light turned green and she eased the Accord right onto the ramp that led to I5 north. Her attention was focused on maneuvering the car into the busy traffic that flooded every freeway the day before Thanksgiving. The bumper to bumper standstill afforded her time to reflect some more. She loved her dad and preferred spending holidays and time away from school at his house. He was always loving and respectful to her. On the other hand, Dee's mother was becoming angrier and more bitter with each passing year, and it was too depressing to be around her for very long. She knew her dad could be a butt to Annatha and inside she felt badly about it, but to be fair, her stepsister could be a pill sometimes. This Thanksgiving would be sad and peaceful all at the same time, without the usual bickering between her Dad and Annatha. The peaceful part sounded nice but she felt guilty about even entertaining such a thought because of the reason for it.

The drizzle had turned into a steady downpour. Her wipers

picked up the cadence as they sensed the change. Dee focused intently on the hazy red lights of the car in front of her. She wondered what percentage of the drivers mired in this mess with her had begun their holiday drinking early and glanced at the cars around her warily. It reminded her of the phone conversations with Meredith lately. Her stepmother's speech was slurred, and sometimes her sentences were barely coherent. She wondered how her dad had been handling the stress of her stepmom's increased drinking. The atmosphere between them had to be strained, which was the main reason she had chosen not to visit on the weekends. In fact, she had not been home once since school started. Tacoma wasn't far from Mercer Island but she preferred hanging out with her friends when she had free time. Besides, her dad worked long hours even on weekends and Meredith would be too zoned to be much company. The other reason, she smiled, was a senior who was studying pre-law she had begun dating a month ago. He was flying home to Vermont to stay with his parents for Thanksgiving. In better times, Dee would have invited him to spend the weekend with her, but that invitation was on an indefinite hold.

The darkening sky produced a deluge of driving rain and Dee struggled to stay in her lane. Her only guide was the blurred, flickering red tail lights directly in front of her. It was horrible weather and she felt the same forecast would greet her when she arrived home. The promise of a traditional holiday dinner with her dad would be overshadowed this year by Annatha's disappearance. It would be a letdown, for sure, but she just had to deal with it. Her dad wouldn't bring it up, but she would miss her stepsister even though they had only spent three Thanksgivings together. It would be like a familiar fixture was missing.

As the traffic finally picked up to a decent cruising speed, Dee gunned the accelerator and vowed to use all four days of vacation to once again lend her efforts to finding Annatha: specifically, a trip to the FBI's regional office in Seattle.

Chapter Eleven

Twenty-two Weeks (22W0D)

Sitting in front of the TV, Annatha watched the Macy's Thanksgiving Day parade with Taz curled up in her lap. She closed her eyes and took a deep breath, imagining the familiar aroma of her mom's turkey, gravy, yams and dressing, prepared every year since she could remember. Annatha usually helped her, wanting to learn how to prepare the traditional dinner so she would know what to do when she had a family. A wave of homesickness grabbed her and she tried to fight it off. It helped that at least she wouldn't have to deal with Brandon, but he seemed rather tame compared to her new nemesis, the nurse warden.

She recalled the previous Thanksgiving. Due to a good deal of scotch, Brandon had been fairly decent to her. Later, they were watching a football game after dinner and she was sitting at the opposite end of the couch from him when she had a strange feeling she was being watched. Casting a furtive glance towards her stepdad, she noticed he was staring at her chest. When she looked down, she noticed her top was displaying some cleavage and her belly button. The fireplace had warmed the room so much she had shed her fleece top. It totally creeped her out and she quickly put the shirt back on and zipped it up all the way. He had never done anything weird around her before, but the look in his eyes had been all too familiar to her, although it was usually a guy at school or the mall, not her stepdad ogling her. She wrote it off to the liquor affecting him, as she never noticed it again.

Shaking off the unpleasant memory, Annatha stood up and began parading around the room, holding Taz above her head like a float. He was getting heavier, she noticed, but continued her march, singing how he was the most beautiful cat in the world at the top of her lungs. His expression appeared unmoved at the flattery, but his tail moved quickly back and forth, protesting the indignity of it all. Annatha finally sat down in the recliner again, winded from her activity. Damn, she frowned; she was in piss-poor physical shape.

The baby didn't move consistently, exhibiting only brief flurries of activity. It was difficult not to wonder if Wendy would be able to tell the sex of the baby when she had her sonogram tomorrow. She had never considered if she wanted boys or girls when she had children. Hell, she was only sixteen, it hadn't come up. Upon reflection Annatha decided she would like to have a little girl first. "No offense, Taz," she said aloud. It would be her chance to raise a female child in a better environment than she had experienced growing up. Not that it mattered, given her current predicament. The cold hard reality was the baby's gender was a moot point, as Wendy would be the mother. She found herself wondering what sex the crazy, religious nurse wanted the baby to be. It was morbid curiosity, but maybe this would be revealed tomorrow, too.

Annatha retrieved the frozen, pathetic excuse for a turkey dinner from the small refrigerator and put it in the microwave, setting the timer. As the loud whirring noise from the appliance filled the basement, she allowed her competing emotions about the pregnancy to surface again. A huge unknown was whether she had the nerve to execute a plan designed to kill her child. Until yesterday, her perception of getting rid of the baby had been akin to removing a hangnail, nothing more. She felt like her conscience had undergone a metamorphosis since feeling the baby move. It had taken on a life now, and wasn't simply an unwelcome appendage anymore. The idea that she could terminate its existence without remorse was much harder to swallow. To her dismay, the inanimate object had become animated. If she decided to willfully cause its death, such an act would change her role from mother to executioner. This realization sent a chill up her spine, and she felt every hair on her body stand up.

A sudden stabbing pain in her right side caused her to bend over and grab the edge of the microwave, almost pulling it off the counter. *What the hell was that?* It felt like someone had stabbed her just above the groin. She let go of the oven and slowly tried to straighten up, but before she was fully erect, her right side squeezed again like a vise grip and she groaned audibly. It reminded her of pregnant women in movies right before they lost their baby and she quickly shed her bottoms to check for bleeding. *Thank God,* she breathed a sigh of relief, her panties were dry. She fought to control the panic that threatened to spiral out of control as the pain crescendoed again. After a few more minutes of deep breathing to distract her mind from paging through horrifying scenarios, it vanished as quickly as it appeared and she discovered she was able to stand up straight again.

Her bible was retrieved since she could walk now and Annatha opened the pregnancy book to the second trimester and scanned the pages rapidly for anything about painful conditions. When she found round ligament pain, her anxiety level faded as she read the comforting text that described exactly what she had just endured. It was normal. *Damn*, she swore, *it didn't feel so normal.* If she were ever shot with a gun, she fully expected it would feel very similar. Satisfied she wasn't about to deliver the baby and her life wasn't in danger, she closed the book and placed it on top of the microwave.

The timer dinged three times and reminded her she had food ready. She removed the steaming dinner from the microwave and placed it on a tray. The plastic knife she was allowed to have only grazed the meat. As she pushed harder, the knife snapped and she threw the leftover stub across the room, releasing a barrage of four letter words. Now she would have to pick up the whole goddam thing to eat it.

While she waited for the food to cool, another aspect of killing the baby surfaced that she had not even considered before. Her mother told her she and Chloe were identical twins, much less common than fraternal twins. Annatha had done some research about twins and discovered she and Chloe had the exact same DNA. That meant, in a way, this baby also possessed part of Chloe as well. She rolled her eyes, gazed up at the low, stippled ceiling and cried out to no one in particular.

"Is there any other shit you want to dump on me to make this more difficult?"

It was a rhetorical question and she knew it, but it had to be asked. Maybe she should just stop thinking about it all together. It only made things worse. Somehow this didn't seem possible with all the boredom that surrounded her day after day. The only entertainment she had besides the TV was her overactive brain. If only she had a remote to shut it off.

Hunger pains gurgled in her tummy, a feeling she recognized as different than when the baby moved. She found some raw carrots and celery in the refrigerator and munched on them while she waited for the turkey to cool off enough to pick up with her bare hands. Crunching on a carrot stick, Annatha found her thoughts drifting again in the wrong direction. She wanted so badly to foil her captor's scheme that included imprisoning her for months, keeping the baby after it was born, then most likely killing her afterwards. Odd how the nurse felt justified murdering an adult but was rabid about anything to do with aborting a fetus. *Probably some biblical thing,* she reasoned, *an eye for an eye shit.* Still, there must be some way to defeat the nurse and preserve her life and the baby's. She closed her eyes tightly and wracked her brain, to no avail. It was hopeless. There was no other way to accomplish what she wanted without someone dying. The idea of committing suicide to end the baby's life had been an abhorrent concept to her, but Annatha felt she might be able to go through with it as a last resort just to piss of Wendy. Especially since she didn't see surviving the ordeal once the baby was born.

She poked the turkey breast and it didn't burn her finger, so she lifted it up and took a bite. It was actually pretty good. Annatha wolfed it down, along with the crusty dressing, and chased them both with a big gulp of cold water. It surprised her how much her appetite had increased in the past few weeks. Still, she had only gained eight pounds thus far. Satisfied, she settled back with Taz, who served nicely as a substitute for warm slippers on her feet.

It was too bad she couldn't turn back time, she frowned. Given the chance again, she felt certain she would still have an abortion, but the rest of her decisions would not be so rash. The life that stirred inside had provided a new perspective on her current pregnancy, but it would seem less personal if she were only a few weeks pregnant. *Or would it,* she wondered sleepily as she dozed off with a full stomach.

****

Meredith entered the lavishly appointed dining room with the turkey and placed the large platter near the center of the expansive, rich mahogany table. The sixteen pound bird had already been carved by Brandon, who was seated in his usual position at the end reserved for the man of the house. His dad was at the other end. Dee and Meredith were to sit together on one side, with Brandon's mother and aunt opposite them. The centerpiece was a rust-colored ceramic pot that contained a variety of freshly cut flowers. Scattered at the base were faux fall leaves and gourds to complement the harvest theme. A veritable feast was spread across the rest of the table, waiting for the signal to dig in. The mood was accented by classical music drifting softly from a Bose CD player.

Dee watched Meredith take her seat and noticed she was

already nursing her third martini. Her stepmother looked pale, and the noticeable weight loss since Annatha's disappearance made her clothes appear too large for her shrinking frame. The glazed, bloodshot eyes from the alcohol did not reflect any joy from the holiday with family, and even heavy doses of foundation could not hide the shadows under her eyes from lack of sleep. She looked like she had aged several years in the past few months, as the hours of worry etched their unforgiving sorrow across her face. Dee felt herself overwhelmed with an urge to hug Meredith and found it difficult to understand how her dad was acting like everything was just fine.

The meal was punctuated with small talk, most of it directed at Dee. Everyone wanted to know how school was going. When she revealed her new boyfriend, he became a target for many questions, especially from her dad. The most important one she already knew from long experience. Every boy she had ever dated, her dad's first question without fail was "What does his daddy do?" What significance this had escaped Dee but it was kind of a joke now. Yet her dad never missed his cue and seemed seriously interested in her answer each time. There was nothing to worry about with Jackson since his father was a small town banker and mayor, credentials she knew would impress her dad.

Although there was pumpkin and pecan pie waiting, no one volunteered to have a piece. They decided to have dessert later with coffee, when their digestive systems could fit more food. As was the tradition in the Reynolds family, each person at the table in turn had to express what they were most grateful for this Thanksgiving. The usual platitudes were uttered one by one. Even Meredith managed to recite her gratitude for having loved ones surround her with a grim smile. Dee was last. She had already decided that the absence of Annatha from any conversation she had heard thus far was borderline ridiculous. There was a great big elephant in the room as far as she was concerned, and she felt the need to point it out to everyone.

"I too am grateful I can spend this Thanksgiving with loved

ones," she began, studying the clueless faces watching her, "but I can't help missing Annatha and hope wherever she is, she's safe and knows we love her." She imagined the stony silence that followed her remark was similar to what it must sound like to be on the moon. The uncomfortable hush was finally broken when Meredith began to cry softly.

Brandon glared at his daughter. What the hell was she thinking? "Dee," he curbed his voice to hide his anger, but was unable to suppress a condescending tone, "I don't think that it's appropriate to bring up something so depressing at a time like this. Meredith is trying to put it aside and enjoy her Thanksgiving."

Dee felt her own flush of anger as it traveled from her toes to her cheeks. Her stepmom certainly didn't look like she had put anything aside. She decided not to be intimidated by how her dad would react; this was too important for Annatha.

"Dad," she replied evenly, "does Meredith look like she's enjoying anything today?"

"That's enough, Dee," he snapped.

"I disagree," she persisted, fighting the lump in her throat. "Frankly, I'm surprised no one seems to care about where she is, or what she might be going through."

Unexpectedly, she saw her grandparents nodding in agreement with her.

"We wanted to bring it up," her grandmother interjected. "We've been wondering why nothing more has been done."

Brandon shrugged. "We've reported it to the State Patrol, Mom," he said dismissively, "and they're pretty sure she's run off with the baby's father."

Emboldened by her grandparents' support, Dee continued to pursue her tack. "I've been doing research online, and it is very common for the police to brush off missing teens as runaways." She felt her dad's stare burning into her skin. "And what I've found out," she ignored his threatening look, "is that the FBI is the best agency to handle this sort of thing." Before she could be interrupted, Dee persisted. "I've known Annatha for about four years, and I believe it is inconsistent with her personality to be out of touch this long."

Despite feeling ganged up on, Brandon didn't waver. "Don't you think we've considered contacting the FBI?" he countered. "But Annatha is a rebellious girl and her mother and I believe she is punishing the both of us by keeping us in the dark."

"Dad," she said softly, "I know how much conflict there's been between you two, but I honestly believe one month, two at the most, would be plenty of time to torture anyone like this."

"She's making sense, Brandon," his father said sternly. "Maybe you should contact the FBI."

Visibly annoyed, Brandon shot back. "Annatha is our problem, Dad, not yours, and if we find out she's in trouble, we'll handle it."

The holiday spirit had evaporated into thin air. Tension was thick in the silence that followed Brandon's last remark, and brows deeply furrowed. Dee noticed her dad had the familiar look on his face that said the conversation was over, or there would be hell to pay. In all their years together, she had never contradicted him to this extent. Of course there were minor disagreements from time to time, but if he felt very strongly about something, she had learned it was not wise to cross him. He was tenacious, intelligent, and would ruthlessly take his opponent out at the knees in a few short seconds. Dee had witnessed this behavior many times with her mother. However, she felt so strongly about finding Annatha that she wasn't going to give in this time.

"Well," she announced to the table, "I've already scheduled an appointment at the FBI office in Seattle for tomorrow."

This time Brandon erupted. "Don't you have any feelings for anyone but yourself?" He shouted, clenching his fists. "Meredith is already upset enough, and if we go to the FBI, it's like we're admitting something bad has happened to Annatha."

Dee was shocked, and her gut was doing flip-flops. Her father had never raised his voice to her since she was a little girl, and then only if she had gotten into some pretty serious mischief.

Her hopes for a reasonable discussion about this were dashed with his outburst. However, she was unable or unwilling to back down now.

"I respect everyone at this table," her voice choked with emotion, still disturbed at her father's reaction, "but I'm thinking of Annatha and what she might be going through." She avoided looking at her Dad but continued. "If you guys don't want any part of it, that's okay, but I wanted to inform everyone, out of respect, since the FBI will want to interview family members."

Brandon's father stood up and walked over to his son's side. He squeezed one of the large fists resting on the table and rested his other hand on his shoulder. There was a familiar rage in his son's eyes, and he wanted to try and settle him down. Brandon pulled away from him and looked directly at his daughter.

"I forbid you to go to the FBI," he ordered.

Dee realized it was time to retreat. Her dad was irrational and out of control. She stood up and left the dining room, then climbed the stairs to her bedroom and shut the door. Saddened that the Thanksgiving dinner had been disrupted by her insistence on discussing Annatha's disappearance, she still felt she had done the right thing. How they could go on with their lives, blindly accepting the runaway theory without pursuing other avenues escaped her. The cell phone dead end was too neat, and she had a gut feeling the key to finding Annatha was right in front of them, if only they could find an agency to take an interest and launch a proper investigation.

Fighting tears, Dee retrieved her cell phone from the backpack. Dialing her boyfriend's number, she only got his voicemail. She managed to leave a cheery message wishing him a happy Thanksgiving and hung up. Sitting at her desk, she stared blankly at the steady rain that soaked the heavily weighted branches on the fir tree outside her window. Her reverie was interrupted by a soft knocking at her bedroom door. She knew it couldn't be her dad; he would just barge in unannounced.

"Come in," she called.

The door opened and Meredith stuck her head in. "I'll go with you tomorrow," she announced through thick lips and shut the door.

Dee was shocked. It was uncharacteristic for her stepmother to rock the boat, but she was rocking it hard with this decision. A faint admiration for Meredith surfaced again, similar to the evening they were at the Park and Fly. She must really be worried, Dee realized, or else she wouldn't have gone out on a limb like this. Lifting the laptop cover, she started the browser, quickly navigated to the Seattle FBI field office website and wrote down the number. She had been bluffing at dinner about calling, but she was definitely going to contact them first thing in the morning and make an appointment, if they had to call someone in from their holiday time off.

****

Wendy entered the basement with a plate of leftovers from her Thanksgiving dinner with family. She was still wearing her tan corduroy pants and olive green sweater over a cream colored tank top from the day's visit with her parents, but her trusty navy blue bath robe covered the outfit. It served a dual purpose of keeping her comfortable in the cold basement and housed her defensive weapon in its pocket. The plate had just been warmed in the microwave and the heat from it was beginning to bleed through the oven mitt onto her bare hand. She gingerly placed it on the food tray like she was playing a game of hot potato. Annatha was on the bed reading a magazine and never looked up until Wendy stepped back from the meal she deposited and removed the floral patterned mitt.

"How was your Thanksgiving?" Annatha inquired.

Wendy was surprised at the girl's interest in her day and eyed her curiously. "Just fine, thanks." Her hand instinctively cradled the mace in her robe pocket; something was amiss.

Annatha was sprawled out on her back in the bed, her legs bent at the knees. Her thick, auburn hair was unkempt and there was no sign of makeup on her pale face. She dropped the magazine and propped herself to a sitting position against the headboard.

"Well," she said sarcastically, staring her adversary directly in the eyes through a veil of overgrown bangs, "I had a great Thanksgiving alone in this hellhole without my family."

That's it, Wendy relaxed her grip, *she's trying to make me feel guilty.* Nice try, girly, but she wasn't going to bite. "From what you told me at the clinic," she retorted, "spending the holiday away from your family could be looked upon as a gift from me." She removed her right hand from the robe pocket and pinched it closed at the top, rubbing her thumb along the rough terry cloth fabric while she waited for a dicey comeback.

Shit, Annatha swore silently, *this bitch has ice in her veins; so much for that idea.* She had to admit, her reply wasn't far from the truth, although with all their failings, her family was looking pretty good right now. Truth be told, she really did miss her old mom, the pre-Brandon Mom. After the separation from her dad, she had her mom all to herself for a few months, until she married Brandon. Since then, there had been no sign of the woman she had known before.

Wendy shrugged off the girl's initial animosity and decided to show some sympathy. She sat down sideways at the foot of the bed, so as not to crowd the girl and make her feel threatened. Also, she always made sure to keep a safe distance in case she got any ideas about attacking her. Resisting the urge to be contrary, she took a deep breath and borrowed a lesson from her faith. It was a simple spiritual exercise where she considered Annatha to be a lost sinner, a sinner who could use some salvation.

"I know it's been hard for you with your parents splitting up and your stepdad treating you like dirt," she said softly, "but at some point, you have to take responsibility for your actions and stop blaming me and your family for all your troubles."

Annatha responded as most teens did to a lecture, with a distant stare in her eyes. Wendy recognized the blank look all too well. Most of the teens she interviewed at the clinic had the same reaction to her questions. The girl ignored her sympathetic gesture, wordlessly climbed out of bed and sat down in the recliner. She removed the aluminum foil wrapper from the plate and began picking at her food. Wendy sighed and stood up, resigned that failure would greet any attempts to approach this girl in a Christian spirit. As she turned to leave, Annatha called after her in an icy voice.

"So what consequences are you willing to pay for kidnapping me?"

The raw bluntness of the question surprised Wendy. Her behavior tonight was so uncharacteristic of the girl, who had been fairly docile since the second day of her captivity. *Must be the holiday and homesickness*, she guessed. Well, if she wanted to play the honesty game, it was time to lay her cards on the table.

"I have no consequences to pay in my Maker's eyes," Wendy wheeled around and replied evenly. "He rejoices that I have saved the life of one of His children. You, on the other hand, will have much to answer for when judgment day comes, for you were going to murder one of his chosen creatures."

Annatha sat down her fork. *That fucking does it,* she fumed. She swiveled the recliner around so that it faced the nurse.

"I don't accept your version of a vindictive God," her voice swelled with the tide of anger unleashed by the last statement directed at her. "I was doing what I thought was best for me and the baby. It would have been born into poverty, as would its children and so on." Struggling to keep her voice from spiraling into the rage zone, she gripped the arms of the chair firmly and continued. "I am too young to raise a child, and frankly, the baby's father is probably married. I made a stupid mistake," she admitted less abrasively, "but why make another one by bringing a child into my life and ruining any chance I would have of pursuing a career?" Before giving the nurse a chance to respond, she released her grip, stood up and took a few steps forward, squaring off only a few feet away from her captor. "And in case you haven't heard," she continued emphatically, "abortion is legal in the United States. I have a right to choose whether I have a baby or not!"

Wendy shook her head and fought the emotional reaction to the gauntlet the girl had just laid at her feet. Her impulse was to lash out at her and reap hellfire and damnation on her twisted soul, but that was not what the Master would do, she reminded herself, and overcame the urge. She released her clenched fists and took a deep breath.

"I've heard this same sad drivel for years now," she finally replied evenly, "but the holocaust of abortions in this country over the past thirty years is an abomination against God, and all of the lost souls that have been ripped from the safety of their mother's wombs will be there to greet their killers when Christ comes again to judge the living and the dead." Her voice changed to a more derisive tone. "You should consider the irony of the fact that you wouldn't be here if you had not planned to kill your unborn child."

Annatha realized she wasn't getting anywhere with this topic; she was just becoming more pissed off, and the simple fact was this nurse embraced fundamental Christianity and would never be dissuaded from her beliefs. However, she was curious about one aspect of Wendy's life that had occupied her thoughts during the long days alone in the basement. Folding her arms defiantly, she challenged the righteous figure before her. "So why do you work in an abortion clinic if you feel so strongly about it?"

Caught off guard by the sudden shift in the conversation, Wendy hesitated a few moments before answering. Her first instinct was to slap the smug look off the girl's face. "I wanted to work in a clinic that dealt with women who had unwanted pregnancies to show them another option than abortion," she admitted, managing to control her impulse.

"Why couldn't you have a baby of your own?"

Wendy eyed the girl carefully. *Should she repeat her trials and failed attempts to bear a child? Didn't she reveal all of this the morning she informed the girl she couldn't leave?* She realized the situation was so traumatic Annatha probably didn't remember much of what was said. Maybe it was time to go over it again so that the girl understood the motives that drove Wendy to such desperate measures. She made the decision to share again the story of her infertility and the loss of her marriage because of it. Her dream she had cherished for years to have a family and raise kids had been dashed by the endometriosis that covered her reproductive organs. The disease had ravaged her body so completely she had been forced to have her uterus and ovaries removed, and with their departure went any hopes she could have a baby naturally or with advanced reproductive technology.

"Why did you have a hysterectomy if it just caused you to be infertile?" Annatha inquired.

Wendy told her the pain had been too intense, and all other measures had failed. She had never revealed this to anyone before, but she told Annatha of the guilt she felt that she couldn't conquer the pain and keep her female organs long enough to have in vitro with donor sperm.

Annatha could hear the anguish in her voice when she relayed her story. Maybe this was a vulnerable moment she could capitalize on. She relaxed her defiant posture.

"Why don't you just adopt my baby?" she decided to try repeating her offer. "You could let me return home after I sign the papers and I won't tell anyone what happened."

Wendy recoiled. The girl was skillfully probing her weakness, and after she had just bared her soul! Her gaze hardened; she reflexively cinched the belt on her robe and dug her hands into the pockets.

"I considered adoption," she said coldly, "but there were too many unknowns. I had a member of my infertility support group in Seattle who adopted a baby, but the birth mother changed her mind after a few months and my friend had a nervous breakdown."

Dead end again, Annatha thought grimly. But before ending

the conversation, she wanted to get a few unknowns that had plagued her out of the way. The ultrasound was tomorrow and she needed some answers so she could be in the right frame of mind.

"I need to know what you plan to do when I go into labor."

Wendy shifted gears inside and unfolded her arms. No longer confronted, she was being asked a perfectly reasonable question. "I know how to deliver babies," she reassured her foe. "I have all the instruments and some pain medicine to give you so it doesn't hurt."

"So what if I have a complication and need to go to the hospital?" Annatha pressed her.

"That's not going to happen," she replied flatly.

"How can you be so sure?"

"God has brought your baby to me," Wendy stated. "He will not let any harm come to either one of you."

La la land, Annatha grimaced. *No use pursuing that any further.* Still, there was one more thing to clear up. "So what happens to me after the baby comes? You can't just let me walk out of here after what you've done."

Wendy was grateful the subject had finally been broached. She had been working on a story since she discovered the evidence that suggested the girl had considered ways to kill the baby.

"I was afraid you would think I would harm you," she began carefully as she eased onto the bed again, "but I want to reassure you I have no plans to do so. After the baby is born, I plan to leave the country. I will leave enough food and water for a week, and after I'm settled, I will call your parents and tell them where you are. The keys to the house and basement will be left in an envelope under my front porch mat."

Annatha studied the nurse's face and nibbled on her lower lip nervously. She appeared genuine, but she had managed to fool her into coming home with her from the clinic. That meant she was a skillful liar. However, it did stir a glimmer of hope deep down inside, as she wanted so much to believe it was true. On top of everything else to worry about, it would be nice not to feel like she was on death row.

Wendy examined the girl's face to see if her story had been accepted. There was no immediate verbal challenge, which meant at the very least she was considering it might be the truth. In a move to end the conversation before more questions were asked, she arose and suggested the girl eat her dinner before it got cold, then started up the stairs. She was emotionally exhausted from the conversation they had just engaged in, and Annatha's pointed question about her fate had required inspiration from her Maker to convince the girl she wasn't going to die. *Maybe she would abandon her plans to kill the baby now.* Wendy reminded herself this godless adolescent had no clue what God's true plan was for her as she entered the code on the keypad and shut the door firmly behind her.

Annatha sat back down in the recliner, swiveled it back around to face the tray of food and began eating. The stuffing was really good, better than her mom's. The turkey was a little dry from sitting out for so long during their talk, and the whipped cream on the pumpkin pie had melted completely. It looked like a bird had taken a big dump on it, but overall it was very tasty. For the first time in weeks, her stomach wasn't churning at the prospect of what would become of her after the baby was born. Wendy's plan had sounded reasonable. She probably felt some gratitude for what Annatha was enduring to give her a baby, and leaving the country was a good idea, as there would definitely be a manhunt for her once Annatha surfaced again. Besides, if the nurse followed the Ten Commandments, it was forbidden for her to kill another human being. *Even if it wasn't a defenseless fetus,* she mused. All in all, it made sense, so it wasn't hard to believe her life would be spared now that she had some time to mull over Wendy's response.

She pushed the tray to the side and raised the footrest on the recliner. Taz jumped in her lap after dutifully waiting until she had finished her dinner. Hugging him tightly, she said gleefully, "We're gonna be free in four months, Tazzy."

CHAPTER TWELVE

Twenty-two Weeks, Two Days (22W2D)

Dee and Meredith shoved through the glass doors and entered the building that housed the Seattle FBI office. Only a moment before, they were pushing their way up Third Avenue against a deluge belched out from gray flannel clouds hurried along by a powerful jet stream flow off the Pacific Ocean. The next moment they were in the calm, dry lobby, wiping their boots on a large mat that displayed the FBI seal. Neither one had bothered to pick up an umbrella before they left the house. Seasoned Northwesterners, they knew it would only become a sail in the howling wind that arrived early this morning. Meredith swept the hood from the royal blue Gortex rain jacket over her head, greatly improving her peripheral vision. She worked her hair some, disheveled from the restrictive hood, but it would have been drenched if not for the protection it afforded. Dee's shock of blonde hair was gathered in a ponytail and when she shed the hood, it was in fair shape, even though she really didn't care this morning. It always puzzled her how some people could maintain their vanity even in adversity.

Once again, they ran the gauntlet of a metal detector station after shaking off the rain as best they could. A plump, sullen

Asian security guard inspected their purses then grunted and directed them to the FBI's suite.

"He was kind of grumpy. I didn't think they celebrated Thanksgiving," Meredith mumbled as they walked away.

Dee shook her head. This was no time to enter into a discussion about ethnic stereotypes with her stepmom. They opened the suite's main door but no one was stationed at the reception desk. Just as the hydraulic door closed behind them, it swung open again and a woman shoved her back against it to keep it from closing again, as her hands were occupied with a large file box. Like Meredith and Dee, her knee-length rain jacket was soaked but the hood covered most of her face. She deposited the box on the reception desk, swept the hood back and shook her hair. Dee noted the woman was a little shorter than her, about five foot six, and athletic. Her wavy hair was dark brown and cropped fairly short in a kind of utilitarian length.

"I'm special agent Rachel Gray," she addressed the two women and smiled, then removed a glove to shake their hands.

Dee and Meredith introduced themselves and returned the handshake. The agent removed her coat and they were surprised to see she was wearing a brown fleece pullover with a cream colored turtleneck shirt underneath, and khaki colored jeans.

"I apologize for the casual wear but we're officially closed today and this seemed like the most appropriate attire for our lovely weather. You can put your jackets over there," she motioned towards a coat tree next to the door. "Please follow me."

The agent led them down a short hallway toting the box and pushed her office door open after deftly turning the knob despite having her hands full. She deposited her cargo and jacket on a matching credenza behind the lightly stained oak desk that displayed a sign with her name.

"Please sit down," she gestured and studied the two women as they slid into the upholstered cloth chairs facing her desk. The older woman named Meredith was obviously distraught. Despite excessive makeup used to hide the shadows under her troubled eyes, the mother's face had the lost, bewildered and terrified expression Rachel had seen so many times before in parents with missing children. The younger woman, Dee, seemed purposeful. The intensity of youth radiated from her, though the lines dug in between her eyebrows communicated she was very worried too. Rachel turned and retrieved a folder from the file drawer in the credenza, then sat down in the microfiber chair behind her desk and leaned forward. It was then she first realized her gun was prominently displayed in the shoulder holster after removing her jacket.

"Sorry," she grinned, "let's just take care of this." Storing it in her bottom desk drawer, she addressed the two women, who appeared more relaxed now that her weapon was stowed.

"I understand you have a missing child," Rachel began as she opened the file and pressed it twice to keep it open. "Why don't you start from the beginning and fill me in on when she disappeared and what's happened since then."

Dee liked the agent immediately. The remark about her clothing choice was real and self-effacing, qualities she admired. Most importantly, considering the gravity of their situation, her approach was direct and efficient, with no false reassurances or platitudes. Physically, the agent's large, hazel eyes were very observant, but also possessed a softness that put one at ease immediately. Dee guessed she was probably in her forties but appeared youthful, not to mention she was also mildly attractive; the few lines on her face seemed etched by experience rather than age.

Dee turned to Meredith and asked, "Want me to?"

Meredith nodded and Dee launched into a narrative that reviewed the events surrounding Annatha's disappearance, the cursory investigation done by her computer savvy friend, and the discovery of her stepsister's abandoned car at the Park and Ride where they found the cell phone number in the call records. She concluded with the findings of the State Patrol's investigation.

Rachel listened carefully and took some notes. The summation she just heard would need to be fleshed out, but it gave her a good place to start.

"Did the State Patrol follow up on the cell phone missed calls?"

Meredith spoke up. "They called the number and got a catering service in Denver."

"Did they check out the catering service?" Rachel inquired.

"The State Patrol hasn't done squat as far as I'm concerned," Dee replied, unable to conceal her disgust.

"In all fairness," Meredith interjected, "they sent a Denver policeman out to the residence and he confirmed it was a wrong number."

"So what do they think happened?" the agent asked.

"They think she's a runaway," Meredith replied.

Rachel tapped her pen thoughtfully on the legal pad in front of her. The age of the girl, the fact she was most likely pregnant and the computer data that indicated she met the father of her baby supported the State Patrol's conclusion, but there remained the annoying detail that Annatha seemed to have dropped off the face of the earth.

"Do you think she's a runaway?" Rachel directed her question at the mother.

Meredith sighed, unable to stop the tears that welled up quickly. "I want to believe she is," she swallowed hard to quell the choking sensation in her throat, "but I can't believe she hasn't let me know she's all right, wherever she is."

"Mrs. Reynolds," the agent measured her words carefully, "is there some reason at home that would make Annatha not want to contact you?" She noted the missing girl had a different last name than her mother.

Dee could see her stepmom was struggling not to cry. "I'll answer that," she said. "My dad and Annatha do not get along."

"How do you mean?" Rachel persisted.

Dee described the stormy relationship between the two and ended with her dad's cruel punishment of putting Annatha's cats to sleep. Rachel stifled a gasp at this last piece of information. It wouldn't surprise her if the kid got pregnant and ran off on purpose. The stepdad sounded like a real dickhead.

"Do you have the cell phone?" Rachel suppressed her impulse to comment on the stepdad's cruelty.

Meredith retrieved it from her purse and placed it on the desk. The agent gathered it up and wrote out a receipt for the item. "I'll get it back to you when I'm through with it."

Now for the unpleasant part, Rachel thought grimly. "I'm going to need hair samples from Annatha for DNA comparison, if you have some," she began, "and I'll need a copy of her dental records, along with a recent photograph." She paused for a moment to let this sink in then continued. "In addition, I want to interview your husband and any friends or relatives that were close to your daughter."

Dee felt hopeful. The agent appeared very competent and genuinely interested in finding her stepsister. Her dad was going to be pissed off that he had to be interrogated by the FBI, she realized, but it had to be done. There was still the matter of the cell phone number that nagged her from the moment it was found. It had to be important.

"What are you going to do about the call record on Annatha's cell phone?" Dee asked the agent.

Rachel responded without hesitation. "I'm going to visit the person who has the cell phone number in the call record and check them out more thoroughly. I believe the key to solving this case could very well be the number your stepsister called the day she disappeared. Also," she continued, "I want to interview the attendant at the Park and Fly again. Maybe there's something he saw that would be helpful even though he doesn't realize it."

Meredith was impressed with the agent's plan of action. Despite her misgivings about contacting the FBI because of Brandon's expected response, she was grateful Dee had arranged it. The hair sample and dental records request from the agent had sent a chill down her spine, but she knew it was necessary. There was still the matter of publicity she needed to clarify.

"No media," she blurted out.

Rachel looked at Meredith curiously. "What do you mean?"

"I can't allow you to publicize my daughter's disappearance at this time."

"Your husband?" The agent conjectured.

"Yes," Meredith replied, "he's convinced she ran off with the father of the baby, and he wants to avoid the media frenzy were this to go public."

"Fair enough," Rachel sighed, "but you'll have to consider it if I'm not getting anywhere in the next few weeks." *This guy must be a real ogre,* she thought, *although he might be dead right.* She had a teenage daughter and was well aware of how difficult they could be. Still, she couldn't imagine not doing everything humanly possible to find her if she ever disappeared.

Dee chimed in. "Here's my cell phone number if you need anything from me. I'm a student at PLU so I don't live at home."

"So what is your take on this, Dee?" The agent shifted her gaze to the younger woman. She had regurgitated the events about the disappearance of her stepsister in detail, a story that sounded like it had been told more than once. There was also the difficult frankness about her dad's mistreatment of Annatha. *Let's see if she has any other personal insights into this case.*

Dee was caught off guard a little by the agent's directness. "Well," she began slowly as she gathered her thoughts, "we weren't very close. She's very strong-willed but also withdrawn. She spends a lot of time alone in her room, and I don't think she has any close friends, male or female. I guess from some of the stuff that's happened to her growing up." Dee turned to Meredith. "No disrespect intended." Her stepmother shrugged it off. Addressing the agent again, she continued, "Her dad died this past year and I know it hit her really hard." She hesitated a moment, then went on. "I guess what I'm trying to say is I can see her making the mistake of getting pregnant on an impulse, to punish my Dad for putting her cats to sleep or whatever else he has done to her. But I also know Annatha to be very thoughtful, not flighty at all, and she believed strongly in abortion rights. So I can't see her making the decision to have the baby. She once told me she wanted to be a zoologist, and having a baby at her age would ruin that possibility." Smoothing her jeans absently with both hands, she looked up at the agent. "It just seems unlikely to me she wouldn't have had an abortion."

Rachel jotted down some notes while Dee spoke. Strong-willed, that certainly rang a bell with her being the mother of a teenage girl. The part about believing in abortion was very important; it made it less likely she would take off and marry the father.

"I appreciate your candor, Dee," she acknowledged.

Deep down, Rachel hoped, as she always did, that the girl would be found alive and well. The key was to keep an open mind and stay focused. Making assumptions before looking at all the evidence would only muddy the waters. The cell phone number was the first place to start, and she would get the records the State Patrol had to see if there was anything that hadn't been mentioned in this interview. She opened Outlook on her computer and checked her schedule.

"I can come over Monday evening to talk with your husband if that works for you," she shifted her gaze to the mother.

"Seven would be fine," Meredith acknowledged and handed over the school picture of Annatha she carried in her purse.

Rachel accepted the photo and glanced at it. At first, she couldn't believe her eyes. The girl in the picture bore a striking resemblance to her sister Ruth. It was weird, but she couldn't let it distract her from the task at hand. She placed the photo in Annatha's file and managed to block out the unpleasant memories stirred up like an agitated wasp's nest.

"If you could have a list of friends and relatives with phone numbers and addresses ready Monday evening that would really help," Rachel finished her laundry list of necessary information and stood to indicate the session was over. She would contact the State Patrol to send what they had before she left the office today and make sure the fax made it, but the investigation would begin in earnest on Monday. The two women followed her lead and stood up.

"Please find my daughter," Meredith pleaded.

Rachel took her hand. "I can't make any guarantees," she stared directly into the mother's eyes, "but I can promise you I'll use every resource available to the FBI to find her."

Meredith nodded gratefully. Dee shook the agent's hand and they left. Rachel watched with a heavy heart as the two women walked down the hallway. This case hit close to home for two reasons. First, her daughter Mazy was sixteen, too, and they didn't always get along. A few times she had threatened to leave when Rachel grounded her for breaking a rule. It was drama, to be sure, but drama that didn't result in anything concrete. This girl had taken it much further than that, and perhaps it had turned out badly for her.

Then there was the uncanny resemblance between the missing girl and her sister Ruth. Now that she was alone, Rachel didn't bother to suppress the memories this observation unleashed. Both had thick auburn hair, green eyes and delicate facial features. The coincidences didn't stop there. Her sister went for a secret abortion at age sixteen and confided in her before she left. Later that day a fateful phone call from the coroner's office informed her parents she had died of complications from an abortion. They were inconsolable. The investigation that followed painted a grim picture. Her sister had chosen a clinic that was under scrutiny by the Board of Quality Assurance for a higher than normal complication rate. Apparently, Ruth was inadvertently given a large dose of local anesthetic intravenously and her heart stopped. The clinic staff initiated CPR but the nurse giving the precordial compressions pushed in the wrong place with her hands and fractured several ribs. One of them pierced her sister's liver and she bled to death before the ambulance reached the hospital.

The fact she didn't go directly to her parents and warn them had haunted Rachel ever since. A sordid secret had killed her sister. If she had betrayed Ruth and told her parents, they would have been upset but likely would have taken her somewhere reputable for the termination. She was too afraid to ever mention her sister's confidence to them and decided to carry that burden alone.

A picture of Ruth and her on their bicycles sat on Rachel's desk top and she picked up the frame and gazed at it lovingly. Ruth had been a great older sister. She missed her terribly and each time the awful memory crossed her mind, it mercilessly gnawed on her heart. The therapist had told her repeatedly it wasn't her fault and that her sister alone bore the responsibility for her choices, but it never changed the way she felt. She wondered if Dee had any regrets about keeping her stepsister's pregnancy a secret for so many weeks. If she had gotten the ball rolling sooner…*Stop it,* she ordered. *'What ifs' are worth absolutely nothing and never brought anyone back.* Ruth stayed just as dead no matter how many times she replayed the dreadful story in her head, and as far as Dee was concerned, the same logic applied to her predicament with Annatha's disappearance. She replaced the frame, kissed the tip of her index finger and planted it on her sister's smiling face.

For obvious reasons, this case tugged on the web of guilt woven over the years since her sister's death. It had to be the similarities between the two. Their physical likeness, along with the fact both were sixteen and involved with seeking an abortion in secret, was eerie. It awakened a resolve deep inside her and she vowed to make a difference in Annatha's plight so that a tragic phone call wasn't the final chapter to this story. It wasn't atonement she sought. Instead, Rachel just hoped to make a difference and stop this secret from destroying lives, as she had witnessed with Ruth.

Time to turn off the board meeting in her head and get

back to work, she chided. Pecking out some commands on the keyboard, she checked the results on her monitor then dialed the number for the State Patrol.

****

Safely inside Meredith's Mercedes, the two women were quiet as Dee navigated the winding parking garage path that led to the toll booth. After the attendant was paid, Meredith turned to Dee and broke the silence.

"Thanks for contacting the FBI," she said earnestly. "I may never forgive myself for not doing it sooner."

Dee didn't respond right away. She had trouble understanding why this had not been done before, but it was water under the bridge now. Beating her stepmom up about it would be hurtful and wouldn't accomplish anything.

"Let's just focus on helping Agent Ward anyway we can," she consoled her. "No use crying over spilt milk."

They drove on in quiet reflection, the rhythmic beating of the windshield wipers the only sound inside the car. Both dreaded the reaction they would get from Brandon when they arrived home.

****

Wendy moved quickly across the parking lot to avoid getting drenched. Cold water splashed up from deep puddles and her socks were almost soaked by the time she made it to the front door. She didn't care; her mood was borderline ecstatic as she anticipated the ultrasound that was to be performed on Annatha when she got back home. Unlocking the door, she stepped inside, shed her raincoat and shook it out in the foyer, careful to avoid the slick spots that dotted the tile floor as she headed for the clinic suite. Once inside, she hurried to the sonogram room, shut the door and flipped on the light. No one was there as far as she could tell, since the office interior was dark, and it would be very unusual for any employees to be around on a holiday.

The ultrasound machine was fully charged, so she unplugged the power cord from the surge protector and packed it neatly along with the unit in the metal suitcase. She snapped the locks shut and donned her raincoat again. Picking up the suitcase, she headed out of the procedure room and was startled when she saw one of her coworkers, Traci Downing, rummaging through the drug sample closet.

Traci jumped and let out a small scream. When she recognized Wendy, her frightened look disappeared and she started laughing. "Jesus, woman," she gasped, "you scared the shit out of me."

Wendy hated Traci's foul mouth. Also, she was always unkempt and her fat body just amplified the contempt Wendy had for her lifestyle. She was a lesbian and appeared to be the male figure in the relationship. However, this was no time to mull over her coworker's sexual preference; she had some explaining to do, and quick. Fortunately, she had the presence of mind to attach her pregnancy tummy before leaving the house.

"Sorry," Wendy managed to apologize through gritted teeth.

"No problem," Traci replied, curiously eyeing the ultrasound suitcase in Wendy's grasp. "Are you going to look at your baby?" she asked. Before she had a chance to respond, Traci clapped her hands gleefully. "I want to see too," she cried. "Let's go to the procedure room and scan you here."

Wendy was disgusted. Even if she was really pregnant, she wouldn't want this woman to have any part of it. Swallowing her impulse to bolt out of the office, she smiled.

"It's not for me," she explained. "I have a neighbor who thinks her mare is pregnant and she wants me to confirm it for her."

"Oh," she sounded disappointed but her mood quickly changed. "I have some time, why don't you let me see it?"

Wendy shook her head. "I have had so many ultrasounds, I'm holding off on doing any recreationally so the baby isn't overexposed."

Traci seemed dejected. "Why all the ultrasounds? Are you having a problem?"

Wendy sighed and patiently explained. "I am high risk because of my age. Also, because this is an IUI pregnancy, I had several early on to make sure the baby was growing." Noticing the disappointed look on the medical assistant's face, she persisted. "I had an amniocentesis a few weeks ago and a Level Two ultrasound for fetal anomalies. It just seems wise to hold off doing anymore unless they're necessary."

Traci shrugged. She didn't know why Wendy was so paranoid about having numerous ultrasounds; patients had them all the time and there didn't seem to be any harmful effects as far as she knew. But the nurse seemed determined, so she decided to drop it.

"Can you really see a horse fetus with that machine?" she changed the subject.

"I've done it before." Wendy felt relieved Traci had bought her explanation.

"Don't get any horse poop on it," she winked.

"Okay," Wendy promised and strode out of the office, trying to appear casual. Once she was safely in the car, she waited for a minute to settle her nerves. That had been a little too close for comfort, she gulped. Fortunately, Traci had bought the pregnant mare story and didn't seem suspicious at all. Thank God it wasn't Rosie, the only coworker at the clinic who might be considered a friend. It would have been more difficult to shrug off her request since they had been to lunch a few times, and she had confided in her first about the pregnancy. She hardly ever interacted with Traci and had never been anywhere outside the office with her, which made it easier to blow her off. Shaking her head to focus on the task at hand, she started the car and shifted into reverse. She didn't want to be in the parking lot when Traci came out.

****

Thomas lit a cigar and plopped down on the king size bed in his hotel room. He had flown to Seattle for an emergency deposition the day after Thanksgiving. It had been a nightmare. The obstetrician he was deposing had a heart attack halfway through it and was taken away in an ambulance. He wasn't concerned about the doctor's health, just the fact his trip had been a monumental waste of time.

Shedding his dress suit, he had slipped into some sweat pants and a T-shirt shortly before devouring the room service dinner. A glass of scotch was perched on the nightstand next to the bed and he took a sip before drawing on the cigar again. He opened his laptop, logged in to the hotel wireless network and navigated to a Washington chat room. It was a ritual repeated many times since leaving Annatha at the abortion clinic in July. He felt badly about the whole thing and wanted to make sure she had the abortion. Unfortunately, he had not been able to find her online since dropping her at the clinic in Olympia.

More importantly, he wanted to be absolutely certain all the loose ends were tied up. It would be a disaster if the girl was still pregnant. He typed in a search for *sassybrat18* and puffed the cigar pensively when it displayed she was not online. *What the hell has happened to her?* he wondered. This was like a dog pulling on his trouser pants. It didn't hurt but it was sure as hell annoying. He felt like he had covered all his bases with the whole sordid affair. Even though he called her from his cell phone, it was trashed and the number removed from the firm's account by reporting it stolen. There was no way she could track him down, even if she had not gone through with the abortion. *Come to think of it, why the hell wouldn't she have gone through with it?* She seemed level-headed and mature for her age, never even hinting she would consider having the baby. Their interaction had been more along the lines of a business deal, no wailing or gnashing of teeth. He had every reason to believe when he drove away from the clinic Annatha was going to have an abortion. Still, there was the tugging on his pants leg, egged on by his inability to track her down online. Once again he typed in her chat ID and came up empty.

Shrugging off another dead end, Thomas decided to pursue something more akin to his sense of adventure. He chose chat room two and took the cigar from his mouth, tapping the ashes lightly into a hotel glass partly filled with water that sat on the night stand next to the scotch. The hot embers hissed angrily when they hit the water. He watched the mindless chatter in the cyber room absently as he inhaled the rich Cuban cigar.

Being away from home for the holiday wasn't a big deal, he admitted. His house was invaded by in-laws and the only way he could deal with it was to consume large amounts of alcohol. Also, he had taken refuge in his favorite recliner, watching whatever football game was on. He didn't care about the teams; he just wanted to look preoccupied. To top things off this year, Laurel had announced at Thanksgiving dinner she was pregnant again. He had been so busy he had almost forgotten about it. Despite feigning joy in front of the relatives after his wife's pronouncement, Thomas wasn't happy at all. It wasn't the money or added work another child would bring; Laurel handled their son just fine without him. The kicker was that another baby would be one more string tugging at him when he wanted to be gone. However, on the bright side, now she would agree to his having a vasectomy and there would be no more surprise pregnancies to deal with.

To make matters worse, his father-in-law, who was a career state worker in Nevada, had insisted on talking about how happy he was to learn he would have another grandchild. Any conversation with him was about as interesting as a bucket of hair, but Thomas had smiled and listened dutifully. He grabbed the bottle of scotch on the floor next to the bed and poured another drink. Downing the whole thing, he wiped his mouth with his shirt sleeve and placed the bedside phone next to him. He dialed home and waited until Laurel answered after four rings. She sounded frazzled. When he inquired what was wrong, she told him it was next to impossible for their son to calm down enough to take a nap since his grandfather had stuffed him full of pumpkin pie only an hour ago.

"And you want another one," he kidded, although inside he wondered how the hell she could want another child so soon. After a proper scolding about how he should be happy over the news, Laurel hung up.

During his wife's admonitions, Thomas had noticed a new chatter, who seemed playful, enter the room. He quickly opened her profile and saw she was a nineteen year old student, attractive and most importantly, single. Typing in his witty banter, Thomas subtly drew the new chatter into his cyber lair. Once he had her attention, he asked about what college she went to, how school was going, what her major was, and soon enough they were IM'ing each other in a private box. A triumphant smile appeared on his face as Thomas worked the young girl expertly. He had her now …

****

Annatha opened her eyes without moving. She was napping in the recliner when the basement door opened and a bright light flooded the stairs. It had been pitch-black in her dank, solitary prison cell of a room, except for the TV flickering, until this interruption. The sound of the nurse tromping down the stairs was a little louder, and she realized it had to be the ultrasound that was weighing her down more. It surprised her when a bolt of excitement shot through her body at the thought of seeing her baby for the first time. True, she had been anticipating it with some eagerness since Wendy told her she was doing one today, but the intensity of this reaction was more than she expected. Despite her enthusiasm, she turned the recliner nonchalantly to get a look at what the nurse was doing. Puzzled, she took a moment to solve what was wrong with the picture, but soon enough she noted the nurse wasn't wearing her robe for the first time since day one of her captivity. A fleeting thought crossed her mind that she might not have the mace with her this time.

Wendy was still a little frazzled from her encounter with Traci at the clinic, but she brushed it aside and resolved to fully enjoy the thrill she was about to witness. She walked over and turned on the bathroom light, grabbed a towel, then drew the door closed halfway to allow some illumination. The stair lights were then cut off and she walked over to the bed. By then, the girl was stirring in the recliner and Wendy began opening the suitcase. Before coming downstairs, she had the presence of mind, despite her impatience to see the baby as soon as possible, to shed the pregnancy tummy; it seemed like a bad idea to ever let the girl see her with it on.

"Ready when you are," Wendy announced as she tried to stem the tide of giddiness welling inside her.

Annatha moved slowly towards the bed; she yawned with a loud groan and stretched her arms as far as they could go. Her body felt a little cramped from falling asleep all crumpled in the cozy chair. When she brought her arms back down, her hands reflexively caressed the blooming pregnancy in her lower abdomen.

"Where do you want me?" she asked.

"Lie down on this side," Wendy pointed at the bed next to the night stand. She was pleased to see the girl acknowledging the baby she carried by stroking it. *Nurture it well while it's yours,* she thought. *I'll take over when it comes out.* The girl lay prone on top of the comforter, and Wendy noticed this time she didn't look away.

"Pull your top up above your belly button please," Wendy asked politely as she began pushing buttons on the ultrasound unit.

Annatha pulled her sweat top up, exposing the fleshy mound that arose from her thin, frail body. Wendy finished powering up the ultrasound and turned to see the girl had complied with her request. Grabbing the towel, she deftly tucked one end of it under the girl's sweat bottoms to avoid getting the slimy goo on her clothes. Next she took the conductive gel and squeezed a large dollop onto the girl's skin.

"Damn that's cold," Annatha flinched.

"Sorry," she apologized, "we usually have these in a warmer at the clinic." Next, she began to spread the gel over the girl's lower abdomen with the transducer, and her facial expression signaled a more intense reaction to the icy gel. "It'll warm up with your body heat in a sec," Wendy reassured her.

Annatha stared in wonder as the black and white images moved rapidly across the screen while the nurse moved the transducer expertly over the baby. After a few seconds, the probe stopped when an oval shaped object appeared. It was outlined by white lines and the center of it looked like the consistency of oatmeal with a few bubbles in it.

"That's the baby's head," Wendy informed her. She manipulated the image a bit more then pressed the freeze button. Using the cursors to measure the diameter, she dropped down to the OB table at the bottom and highlighted BPD. When she hit enter, the left side of the screen displayed "22 Weeks." *Perfect,* she thought. Next, she guided the probe until it was directly over the baby's heart. The individual chambers were pumping away and she felt mesmerized by their rhythmic motion. Forcing herself to continue the technical part of the exam, she switched the unit to M mode and the screen split in half. The left side still showed the beating heart, but the right side had several rows of lines drifting across the monitor in real time. A dotted line projected from the bottom of the screen like an anchor to guide her placement in order to position it directly over the moving heart. Once it was in the right spot, the lines changed to waves and when more than six evenly spaced waves displayed, Wendy hit the freeze button again. Measuring the distance between two waves, she highlighted FHR and hit enter. The left side showed the fetal heart rate was "147 bpm."

"That's the baby's heart rate," Wendy could barely contain

her excitement. "It's one-hundred forty seven beats a minute, which is normal."

Annatha was completely amazed at the sight of her unborn child. The undeniable evidence that a real human organism was growing inside of her was right in front of her face. Witnessing her baby's declaration of life with the beating of its tiny heart unleashed a surge of conflicting emotions as she remembered how badly she wanted to get rid of it a few months before. The memory of her initial plans for this pregnancy were in stark contrast to the current emotional bond she felt for this vital, living being that drew every ounce of maternal love from her soul as easily as drawing tap water from a faucet. The obvious dichotomy of these warring perceptions caused a surge of tears and the image blurred. She quickly wiped her eyes on the comforter and tried to focus again.

Despite her attention to the ultrasound exam and the baby, Wendy noticed the reaction of the girl out of the corner of her eye. *Wonder what you think of wanting to kill your baby now, you selfish brat,* she thought. Refocusing on the task at hand, she continued scanning the baby until she found one of the femurs. Even though she had no formal training in ultrasound imaging, Wendy had taken every opportunity to watch the sonogram technicians when she was a labor and delivery nurse, even practicing on the patients with the portable machine on the maternity unit whenever she could. She didn't recognize all of the anatomy, but she knew enough to do a cursory exam. Moving the probe slightly, she was able to freeze the picture with a good view of the baby's tiny thigh bone and measured the distance. Choosing FL on the OB table, the left side displayed "21.5 Weeks." Unfreezing the screen, she scanned the entire uterus, and to her relief the ground glass image of the placenta was at the fundus and wouldn't pose any problems in that position. Before she began her search for the baby's bladder so she could determine the sex, Wendy turned to ask the girl.

"Do you want to know what sex the baby is?"

Annatha hesitated. Part of her was dying to know the sex of the baby; she couldn't deny the emotional attraction that was forming as she watched the tiny human being who thrived inside of her. Yet she worried that if she found out the sex, it would cause her to obsess until it was born about what to name it, what kind of personality he or she would have and most importantly, the loss she would feel with the knowledge of her baby's gender. All of these reasons would only cause more pain and grief until it was born.

Wendy studied the girl and waited patiently. This was not the time to press her, despite the rising anticipation she felt. Everything was going well with the exam thus far. She couldn't have asked for more cooperation. Occupying herself, she adjusted the probe and in short order was able to visualize the bladder. *Open your legs, baby,* she begged silently.

Annatha made her decision. She wanted to experience everything about this pregnancy now that she had been forced to continue it. Sure, the nurse had promised she was not going to do away with her after the baby was born, but she couldn't be absolutely sure. Whether she survived or not, it would be a missed opportunity she could never take back.

"Yes," she finally declared and focused on the screen again, "I want to know."

Wendy paused before scanning between the thighs. She wanted more than anything to have a boy she could raise as a man who knew how to treat women right, how to be committed and dedicated to his wife no matter what obstacles might arise. Taking a deep breath, she moved the transducer down ever so slightly and was overjoyed to see the baby's thighs were spread and the undeniable shape of a scrotal sac with a protruding penis was as plain as day. Her eyes welled with tears and the image of the screen melted in front of her, so she fumbled blindly for a few moments on the keypad, found the freeze button and pressed it.

Annatha watched the nurse's reaction and wondered what it meant. She squinted her eyes to focus better and despite the fact she had never seen an ultrasound before today, the black and white picture on the screen looked very much like boy parts to her.

"It's a boy," Wendy finally said, her voice choked with emotion.

Staring at her the frozen image of her son's manhood, Annatha felt her heart drop like it had fallen off a cliff. The realization she was carrying a male child she would never know overwhelmed her. She would never experience what it was like to hold him, breast feed him, sing him to sleep, teach him to walk, talk, or play--all the things a mother does with her offspring. Only a few moments before, she had felt an irresistible maternal attraction to her unborn child. Now all she felt was abject sorrow and despair that this despicable woman was claiming her son as her own, and there seemed to be nothing she could do about it.

Wendy was still trying to compose herself, standing with the probe in one hand and dabbing a tissue to her eyes with the other. Suddenly, Annatha snatched the towel from her pants, wiped off the gel, threw the towel across the room and stormed over to the recliner and sat down. She realized the girl must have grabbed the remote, because the TV flickered on and an obnoxious rap video on MTV was blaring loudly from the speakers. In an instant, a wave of rage swept over her and Wendy struggled to suppress it. The exam wasn't over yet, even though she had the technical data she required. She wanted to spend some more time looking at the baby.

"Come back over here, young lady," she demanded, unable to completely control her anger. "I'm not through yet."

Turning to face her captor, Annatha was surprised at the menacing glare that greeted her. The wild look in the nurse's dark eyes was a little unnerving but she held her ground.

"No," she replied evenly, trying not to be intimidated by the figure looming by the bed. "You may be able to take my son from me after he's born, but as long as he's inside of me, he's mine, and I say I don't want to see any more."

Wendy worked hard to reign in her temper. The girl had turned back to the TV after her last statement and ignored her. She wasn't going to get away with this sudden claim on her baby without a response.

"If it had been up to you," Wendy replied sarcastically, "your baby would have ended up in a garbage dumpster behind the clinic, or flushed down a toilet."

Annatha felt her cheeks flush. The nurse was right but still, it pissed her off. Everything was different now. Since she had been forced to carry the pregnancy, she had felt her perception change drastically, especially today. Early on, it had only been an inconvenient, dirty deed that she needed to rid herself of. Now it had been transformed into a living, growing presence inside of her that was a son. He had her genes; he had Chloe's genes, too. That meant he was her possession and didn't belong to the insane nurse. Her maternal ownership of this baby vested her emotionally in a way she had never experienced before.

Annatha swallowed hard. "You don't understand how cruel what you're doing is," she managed to speak past the lump in her throat. "I've been forced to carry this unwanted pregnancy, and now it's far enough along that I can feel my baby and know I have a living person inside me, but you're going to take my son away from me, and you expect me to act like nothing's wrong?"

She started as a lump landed in her lap and she looked down to see it was only Taz; he had jumped up on her and began purring. Stroking his soft fur, she realized he had sensed the distress in her voice and was soothing her, not the other way around. *What a sweet boy,* she thought, and her mood softened a little.

Wendy was indignant. The girl was being such a brat! How dare she accuse her of being cruel? However, she feared her confrontational style and the girl's newly discovered maternal instincts were only strengthening Annatha's resolve to command the situation they were in. She took a deep breath. This was going to take a different, softer tack.

"Annatha," she said politely, mustering her sweetest voice,

"you've always had a living person inside of you since the moment of conception, now please come back to bed so we can look at your son some more." Acknowledging the girl's ownership of the baby might change her mind, she reasoned.

Without turning around, Annatha shot back. "You know, Wendy, you are so righteous about saving my baby, but you seem to have no reservations about kidnapping a person and holding them against their will. Also," she continued before the nurse could respond, "how do I know you're telling the truth about letting me live? For all I know, you are going to get rid of me after my son is born. Isn't that against one of your precious commandments?"

Wendy was taken aback by the girl's tiresome accusations. They'd had this discussion before. Why did she persist in bringing up what she perceived to be her sins, always turning the conversation away from the fact she wanted to kill her fetus? She was used to dealing with inane conversations with teenage girls at the clinic, but this was personal. Replacing the transducer in the suitcase, she walked over to where Annatha was sitting, because she was growing tired of talking to the back of her head. She placed her hands on her hips and stared directly at the girl, who was looking down at her cat.

"God forgives me," she measured her words carefully, "because He knows I am doing what is necessary to save a life. And if you want to accuse me of plotting to kill you, which I certainly am not, how is that any different than what you were planning to do to your own son?"

Annatha refused to look at the figure glowering at her in righteous indignation. She realized it was futile to continue the same weary argument with her. The claim she made that this was a God-like mission to save an unborn child was only a guise to have a baby of her own and bordered on psychotic. Her current dilemma brought back the memory of her father's drinking and her futile attempts to control it. Many nights she had begged him to stay home and spend some time with her, only to be disappointed when he headed off to the bars to feed his addiction. Alcoholism had control of his mind and nothing else mattered to him. Madness controlled Wendy's mind and nothing else mattered to her. She could offer a thousand arguments and every one would fall on deaf ears. If she was going to get out of this situation, words were not the vehicle; drastic action would be needed.

Wendy saw she was getting nowhere fast. At least she had the basic information she needed. The baby was appropriately grown for his gestational age, the placenta was implanted in a normal position, and most importantly, she now knew she was going to have a son. She refused to let this girl know she was getting the best of her, so she turned without saying anything else, returned to the ultrasound unit and began packing it up in the suitcase. Pushing the girl any more would be unsuccessful today, but she didn't have to return the ultrasound until Sunday; maybe Annatha would be in a more receptive mood tomorrow.

Reciting a silent prayer while she arranged the items in the suitcase, Wendy felt herself elevated spiritually. It was important to remember that the girl was a lost soul, driven by adolescent narcissism that would have resulted in her destroying her baby if Wendy had not intervened. Asking her to be unselfish enough to let her look at the baby a little longer was apparently asking too much. She locked the clasps, lifted the suitcase off the night stand and turned to Annatha.

"I'll bring your dinner later," she said, her voice devoid of emotion, and began walking towards the staircase.

Annatha could see the nurse's reflection in the TV screen. It suddenly occurred to her this might be a good time to try and take her down. One of her hands was occupied with the ultrasound unit and she wasn't wearing her robe with the mace in the right hand pocket. Maybe she didn't have it. The room was darkened more than usual and she had the element of surprise, since Wendy was probably sulking about not getting to see more of the baby.

Sliding out of the recliner quietly, Annatha ducked down and maneuvered around the side of the chair. It was obvious if she was going to go through with this, she had to make her move now. She darted across the room undetected and slammed into Wendy with every ounce of strength she could muster. The nurse went down hard under Annatha's driving tackle, and her head bounced off the floor with a sickening thud. Annatha heard the wind rush out of Wendy's lungs with a loud grunt. At the same time, the suitcase flew out of her hand and slid across the floor, crashing into the wall. Annatha untangled her body from the stunned woman beneath her, and ran up the staircase to the basement door.

"Tell me the code, you fucking bitch," she screamed between gasps, out of breath from her attack, "or I'm going to jump down and kill this baby!"

Her heart was pounding wildly and felt like it might break through her chest any minute. Surprised by her impulsive move, she realized there was no cohesive plan mapped out, but she was sick and tired of doing nothing. She stared in disbelief at the crumpled heap by the bottom of the stairs, and it occurred to her the nurse might be unconscious. Pitching her voice several decibels louder, she resumed shouting at the motionless form to elicit a response to her demand.

Wendy heard the girl yelling in a dark recess of her conscious mind like she was in a huge, empty warehouse and someone was calling her name from all the way across a vast room. It echoed around the periphery of her awareness because she was still stunned from the blow to her head. She tried to get up but her arms and legs felt like jello. The wind was knocked out of her and she struggled to breathe again. *What the hell just happened?* she wondered through a concussive fog. Wendy labored to catch her breath while the room slowly began to come into focus again. The girl's ranting grew louder and she was finally able to interpret the substance of the panicked shrieking. She was demanding the code to the basement door! After a few interminable minutes, she was able to bring herself to a sitting position and her respirations began to approach their normal rhythm. Her head started pounding like it was being beaten with an iron skillet. She squinted and looked up the stairs as the hazy puzzle pieces found their way together and formed a solid picture. The girl was perched precariously on the edge of the top step. *What was she planning to do?* Shifting her gaze, she checked to be sure the basement door wasn't open. *Of course it's not open,* she scolded herself, *get a grip.* The foolish teen wasn't going anywhere.

"I'm warning you for the last time," Annatha cried menacingly, "give me the code or I'm going to jump!"

Fully alert now, Wendy comprehended the gravity of the situation. The girl had knocked her down and if she didn't give her the code, she was going to traumatize the baby by jumping off the stairs. Digging in her pants pocket, she pulled out the small can of mace she had tucked away before coming to the basement. She struggled to her feet and wobbled a little but quickly got her bearings.

"It's no use, Annatha," she said, holding up the can of mace. "I'm not going to give you the code."

"Then I'm going to jump!" she threatened in a guttural tone that made the hair on Wendy's neck stand up.

"You don't want to hurt the baby …," but before she could finish the sentence, she saw the girl crouch down on the top step and realized in horror she was going through with her threat.

Wendy knew if she didn't react quickly this would end badly, so she sprinted towards the basement floor underneath the top step, holding out her arms to catch the girl just as Annatha dove off. She overshot her mark and the girl landed on top of her and the two women slammed into the floor in one tangled heap again. This time it was Annatha who had the wind knocked out of her, and Wendy managed to keep her head from striking the ground a second time. Squirming out from under the girl wasn't difficult as light as she was. Wendy stood up once she was free and looked down at the gasping figure beneath her. She wasn't the least bit concerned that the girl might be injured, only with the possibility the baby could have been. It probably wasn't enough of a blow to injure the fetus, since Wendy had been able to break her fall, but she knew the girl's abdomen had impacted her head before shoving the rest of her body to the ground like an accordion. There was a slight but very real chance she had succeeded in her attempt to damage the baby.

Wendy gathered the girl's limp body in her arms while she was still choking for air and carried her to the bed. She retrieved the suitcase and hooked up the ultrasound unit again. Pulling up Annatha's top, she deposited the gel on her skin. By the time the screen display powered up and Wendy turned around with the probe in her hand, the girl was wide-eyed and began swinging wildly at the transducer, pushing it away. The mace had been returned to her pocket after breaking Annatha's fall, but Wendy retrieved it without hesitation and sprayed it directly in the girl's face. Annatha cried out in pain and she began rubbing her eyes furiously as every orifice in her face struggled to douse the burning chemical with a rush of fluids. Wendy tried to apply the transducer again, but the girl blindly pushed it away.

"I will spray you again if you don't stop that," Wendy snapped and readied the mace.

This seemed to work, as Annatha stopped attacking the transducer and resumed her attempts to remove the stinging substance from her eyes using the bed sheet. Wendy quickly took advantage while the girl was distracted, replaced the probe on her abdomen and studied the screen. It wasn't easy to see what she wanted with the girl writhing in pain, but the dancing picture on the display confirmed the baby was still moving and his heart pumped steadily at a normal rate. She patiently guided the transducer over the heaving abdomen until she located the placenta and scanned for any signs of bleeding behind it. If a blow to the abdomen was strong enough it could separate the placenta from the uterus and the interruption in blood supply from the mother would kill the baby. Following the course of the placenta against the uterus, Wendy sighed in relief that no dark pools indicating a hemorrhage were between the two structures. This wasn't absolute proof that everything was okay. An early bleed might not show up now, and it could increase over time if severe enough, but Wendy knew from experience that the baby was well protected in its shock resistant hot tub and the likelihood of an abruption from the recent trauma was unlikely.

"The baby's fine," she announced and replaced the probe in its case.

Wendy lifted Annatha up by the arms and dragged her forcefully to the bathroom. She turned on the shower, stripped off the girl's clothes and shoved her inside.

"Now open your eyes and let the water wash them out," she ordered.

After a few minutes, Annatha felt the stinging subside a little. She was able to see fuzzy shapes through the tears that still streamed from her eyes. When she drew back the shower curtain, there was no sign of the nurse. She managed to towel herself dry and put her clothes back on even though she couldn't see much of anything clearly. As she padded tentatively across the floor, holding out her arms to keep from running into anything, she felt ridiculous about her failed attempt to escape, and even felt a little guilty about how close she had come to hurting her son. As Annatha neared the bed, she felt strong arms behind her guiding her onto the mattress and she collapsed limply in a sitting position.

Wendy studied the defeated figure before her. The girl's wet hair draped across her face like a wet mop and she sniffled continuously in vain as the river of snot pouring out of her nose resisted any attempts to contain it. Parting a few of the drenched strands of hair, she could see the blotched, fiery red streaks across the skin on her swollen face. She looked as pathetic as the surprise attack she had launched to no avail. Obviously, she didn't know who she was dealing with, she fumed. It's time she understood what she was up against if this behavior continued.

"I know you're in pain," she began firmly, "but I want you to listen to me very carefully. If you ever try something like that again, I'll put you in restraints the rest of your pregnancy."

There was no response; the girl hung her head and coughed with spasmodic wheezes. Wendy grabbed a bottled water from the fridge and squeezed Annatha's fingers around it.

"In case you don't understand the full impact of what restraints are," she continued in a stern voice, "it means you'll have to relieve your bodily functions in a smelly bedpan and you won't be able to watch TV because I'm not going to turn it on for you." Wendy paused to let the words sink in, then closed the suitcase again and started for the stairs.

Annatha still couldn't focus with the deluge of fluid flooding her eyes. Also, she felt a throbbing in her right hip, which meant she probably hit it on the floor when she jumped. Great, she cringed, now she was blind and would soon have a great big bruise on her butt. The metal basement door slammed shut and she jumped. She had heard it many times before, but tonight she felt like it was closing off the life she would have had with her unborn son forever. A feeling of helplessness consumed her as she sat all alone in her darkened prison cell. She couldn't help wondering how much worse this nightmare could get. The disastrous attempt to free herself had been brutally thwarted and it appeared she sustained the most wounds in the process. If she tried again, she faced the threat of being put in restraints for four months, which sounded barbaric. Needless to say, she would think long and hard before pulling something like that again.

Chapter Thirteen

Twenty-two Weeks, Five Days (22W5D)

Rachel carefully sipped her pumpkin spice latte from Starbucks as she glanced over her schedule for the day. She always looked forward to fall, when the popular coffee chain brought back this classic autumn beverage. It wasn't difficult to find one of the stores anywhere in Seattle; there were two on the city block where she worked. She once heard a comedian joke that you could walk across the entire city by just stepping on Starbucks' locations, an exaggeration to be sure, but still funny as hell. Thank God it was true. She shuddered as she remembered the bitter cold breeze funneling through the downtown streets on her walk from the coffee shop to the office.

The monsoon over the weekend had stopped just in time before the rivers north of the city crested and flooded low-lying farms. An arctic jet stream had blown away the moisture-laden clouds and replaced them with icy blue skies. Rachel removed the protective sleeve from her latte and cradled the cardboard cup with her hands, letting the heat from it warm them while she continued perusing her daily agenda. From the look of things, it appeared she would be able to get something accomplished, since today would not be as hectic as yesterday, with busywork such as a ton of emails to deal with after the long Thanksgiving holiday weekend.

As she worked on her morning dose of caffeine, her thoughts turned to the previous evening when she had met with Brandon and Meredith Reynolds at their home on Mercer Island. It was a very interesting interview to say the least. Brandon had been cordial to her but his voice displayed an underlying hostility towards Annatha when he spoke of her. He characterized her as a rebellious, spoiled brat who spent all of her spare time dreaming up ways to annoy him. This led to his attempts to draw boundaries for the girl with rules that she constantly broke, forcing him to punish her. When he was talking about consequences being good for teenagers, Rachel couldn't help but think about what the State Patrol detective had written in his report about the stepfather putting Annatha's cats to sleep as punishment for her MySpace profile pic.

What a cruel man, she recalled with disgust. *No kid deserved that kind of trauma for a stupid picture, unacceptable or not.* If there ever was a classic setup for a runaway teen scenario, Annatha's home situation was one. However, Rachel felt strongly the lack of any communication between the missing girl and her mother was unusual. It wasn't likely Brandon Reynolds would have insisted his stepdaughter come home if Annatha contacted her mom, or would threaten to hunt her down. Not only that, Meredith had been quiet and subservient, under the shadow of her domineering husband last night, so it was doubtful she would have overridden his wishes and demanded he take her truant daughter back. The girl surely knew this dynamic, yet she remained incognito either by her own choosing or an untoward event.

Even though Meredith's behavior was pathetic in Rachel's opinion, she understood it at some level. The multi-million dollar mansion Brandon provided for them in an upscale Seattle suburb would be hard to walk away from. In addition, her social stature and friends would change drastically if she were forced to fend for herself. These were all issues that could definitely affect an insecure woman who didn't have the self-respect to be her own person, no matter what the economic consequences. It wasn't her place, however, to judge the woman, she reminded herself.

The part of this case that really bugged her was why the mother had waited so long to contact the FBI, or to park on the State Patrol's front porch hounding the detectives to find her daughter. Rachel's frame of reference arose from how she would react if her sixteen year old daughter, Mazy, disappeared without a trace. Even if she thought Mazy had simply run away, she would never cease scouring the globe for her no matter how long it took, or how many toes she had to step on. The seemingly glib way Meredith had accepted the explanation that an all-out search for her daughter wasn't warranted because the State Patrol believed her to be a runaway escaped Rachel's maternal radar. It was disconcerting, to say the least, and difficult not to judge harshly.

Well, she reminded herself, *the mother has come forward now and asked for help. And it was her job to use all of the resources at her disposal to find her daughter. No stone would be left unturned.* With this last thought, she opened the file and looked at the list of phone numbers Meredith supplied her of relatives and a few friends. The only local relative was her grandmother in Snohomish County. A note in parentheses next to the name, Rose Wolcott, indicated she was Annatha's paternal grandmother. Rachel dialed the number and after two rings a woman answered.

"Hello Mrs. Wolcott," Rachel introduced herself, "this is Special Agent Rachel Ward from the FBI field office in Seattle."

She thought she heard a small gasp, followed by several moments of dead silence. *Oh my God,* she quickly realized, *the poor woman thinks something's happened to Annatha.*

"I don't have any information about your granddaughter Annatha," she quickly reassured her, "that's the reason I'm calling, to see if you've heard anything from her since she went missing a few months ago."

"Thanks for scaring the shit out of me, Special Agent Ward," the woman answered gruffly, "and no, I haven't heard from my granddaughter."

Point taken, Rachel grimaced. "So no emails, phone calls, faxes, snail mail, etc. since her disappearance?"

"Asked and answered," was the reply.

Tough broad, Rachel frowned, must have passed on some of those genes to her feisty granddaughter. Still, there was protocol to follow.

"I apologize if this offends you," she continued, "but we have our procedures. I'm required to inform you that withholding information from the FBI is a federal offense."

"Look, Agent Ward," her tone softened some, "there is no love lost between me and that jerk of a stepdad she has, and I don't understand why her mother puts up with him, but if I knew where Annatha was, I wouldn't be heartless enough not to tell Meredith, even if Annatha begged me not to."

"Fair enough," Rachel acknowledged, impressed with the woman's directness. "I'm not sure if it will help, but background from different perspectives can sometimes be useful in these cases. Learning everything I can about the missing person has paid off in the past, so if you don't mind, I'd like to schedule a time to come interview you in person."

After the grandmother agreed to cooperate in any way she could, Rachel hung up and typed in some notes from their conversation. Next, she glanced at her "to do" list and saw the next and what she believed to be the most important item: the issue of the call record on Annatha's cell phone. The State Patrol had faxed all their records after her interview with Dee and Meredith on Friday. The copied file was under the legal pad she was scribbling on while she was talking to Mrs. Wolcott. Retrieving it, she opened the manila folder and found the report dealing with their efforts to find the caller. She compared the number on the report to the number on Annatha's cell phone call record. They were an exact match. That left out an incorrectly transcribed number as the reason for the unexpected answer by a catering service. The State Patrol had instructed the Reynolds to deactivate Annatha's cell phone, so she couldn't place the call from the girl's cell. Dialing the number on her desk phone, Rachel sat back and waited while it rang.

"Red Rock Catering," a pleasant female voice on the other end announced.

Once again, Rachel introduced herself as a special agent for the FBI and asked if the woman or anyone at her establishment had any idea why their number would show up on a missing girl's cell phone call records.

"We've already told the detective from Washington as well as a Denver police officer that we have no idea," the voice responded with no attempt to hide her irritation.

"I understand," Rachel said in her most diplomatic tone, "but that's not the main reason I'm calling. I'm flying to Denver tonight, and tomorrow I'd like to interview in person everyone who has access to this phone number."

"What the hell for?" the woman snapped.

"Ma'am," Rachel decided to drop the polite tact and assume a firmer approach, "a young girl has been missing for several months now and the day she disappeared a call was received on her cell phone from your number." She paused for a moment, but when no further argument was made, continued. "This is more of a courtesy call, so I guess what I'm really asking is what would be a good time for you tomorrow?"

"Now that you put it that way," she replied bitterly, "9am would work best for us."

She checked to make sure she had the correct address for the catering company. "Thank you very much," Rachel said cheerfully, "I'll see you at nine tomorrow."

A face-to-face interview, no matter how much the caterer protested, would be essential, she had determined when the case was first presented to her last Friday. Rachel had a gut feeling something unknown as yet was likely to be discovered tomorrow.

Returning to her list, she picked up the phone again and called the Regional Computer Forensics Lab (RCFL) in Portland and asked them to send a Computer Analysis Response Team (CART) to the Reynolds' residence to pick up Annatha's laptop as soon as possible. The director agreed and promised to have something for her by next week, helpful or not. Finally, she called the Park & Fly and was in luck. Carlos Sandoval was working today and would arrive around 3pm. Typing an intranet message to her secretary, Rachel informed her she would be out of the office until Thursday and instructed her to fax a copy of Annatha's file to the RCFL in Portland. She planned to interview the parking attendant and then go directly from there to the terminal, where her flight to Denver would be leaving at 6pm.

There were notes in the file from an interview a uniformed officer had conducted with Carlos the evening Meredith and Dee had driven to the Park & Fly to retrieve Annatha's car. She read them carefully, but it seemed the parking attendant had not gotten a good look at the driver of the vehicle the girl left with. He was sure it was a rental but didn't know the exact make or model. A subpoena and search of all SeaTac rental car companies' records would be futile, she surmised from his statement since there was nothing specific to guide them. Despite the paucity of information the attendant offered, Rachel would use all of her training and skills to try and help him recall something that might be helpful. After all, he was the last known person to have seen Annatha before she disappeared without a trace.

Rachel glanced at her watch. The morning was winding down and she needed to pack her things, hit the gym, then grab a light lunch before heading to the airport. The challenge of this case provided an edge that she enjoyed. Solving mysteries was the love of her life and why she had been attracted to the FBI in the first place. Her work on missing person cases fed her deductive appetite despite the tragedies witnessed over the years. One final call was made to Stan Jackson, an old friend who was stationed in the Denver field office, to ask him to pick her up at the airport.

He was delighted to hear from her and insisted she stay at his home instead of a hotel. Rachel protested feebly, as she secretly wanted him to ask, since it would mean she could also use the trip to catch up with Stan and his wife Janet. After hanging up, she began to collect the items from her desk she would need for the overnight trip. The quest to find Annatha had begun in earnest today.

****

Wendy was finding it difficult to focus at work this morning. Her neck hurt from breaking the girl's leap off the stairs and the muscles in it were "as tight as Dick's hat band," her dad always said. Twisting her head back and forth, she could feel the spasms worsen each time she looked left. It was weird; the muscle would cramp and wrench her head down and to the left, making it hard to straighten back up. She had also discovered that touching any part of the right side of her body caused her to wince with pain, since every inch of it was sore from hitting the ground under Annatha's weight. She took a muscle relaxant from the sample closet after arriving at the clinic this morning but it wasn't helping much yet. A heating pad would feel good when she got home after work, but until then it was going to be difficult to avoid experiencing pain every time she used her neck. It helped some to rest her forehead against her hands, braced by her elbows on the desktop, but working from that position would be impossible. She felt like she'd been in a car accident. She groaned and opened her desk drawer to get some more Ibuprofen.

The basement brawl over the weekend had been unnerving to say the least, she recalled reluctantly. It had allowed Wendy to reinforce to the girl once and for all that she could not be beaten at this game. So that was good. However, it also taught her never to drop her guard around Annatha, a mistake she would never make again. Too much was at stake. At least the pregnancy was past the halfway point and the worst bump in the road thus far had been conquered. Wendy felt a chill on her ankles so she reached down and turned up the small heater under her desk, but the effort caused a shooting pain up the side of her neck. Her body jerked like an electrical shock had discharged through it, and she stifled the urge to scream. As she took slow, deep breaths, the throbbing sensation that replaced the initial feeling of being stabbed in the neck began to subside. She struggled to divert her focus to the soothing, warm air from the floor heater bathing her legs and managed to turn her thoughts to the situation at home again. Annatha had been quiet and sullen the rest of the weekend, refusing to acknowledge her existence when she brought the meals down. The cat and television were the only things that captured the girl's attention. No matter, she decided, this behavior was preferable to the angry debate and physical scuffle that marred the ultrasound exam on Friday. It would be foolish to think the girl could ever just accept her predicament, so she had vowed to play along with Annatha's resumption of the silent treatment. Sunday, she had returned the ultrasound unit to the clinic with the certainty that any further attempt to pursue that particular exam would be futile.

The computer chimed and jarred Wendy from her reverie. A message displayed on her screen that the next patient was ready. She sighed and acknowledged it with a key stroke. It had become increasingly difficult to listen to patients explain why they needed to get rid of their unwanted pregnancies. Before Annatha, she had been hoping to convince a patient to give up their baby and offer herself as the adoptive mother. Now that this motivation was moot, she had to force herself through each interview and often found herself biting her tongue. The change in interpersonal dynamic was obviously different now. For her part, the excitement she felt at finally having a baby on the way made it almost impossible to remain neutral. As far as the patients were concerned, they seemed uncomfortable and wriggled a little more in their chairs when they noticed Wendy was pregnant. No one ever acknowledged the fact or asked her any questions about how the pregnancy was going. That would be too painful, she knew, but it gave her some measure of satisfaction that the choice the nurse in front of them had made to have her baby caused the patients to squirm in their chair.

Fortunately, no problems had surfaced with her coworkers or physician boss. They had accepted her pregnancy and seemed happy for her. The encounter over the holiday weekend with Traci had been unexpected, but Wendy made of point of telling her yesterday the mare was pregnant. The medical assistant had only smiled and winked. Not knowing what this meant, Wendy dropped the subject and decided not to embellish the lie any further.

The final measure of success hinged on whether Annatha had an early complication with her pregnancy such as preterm labor or rupture of the membranes before thirty-six weeks. This would present a substantial dilemma for Wendy. Unable to take the girl to the hospital, she would be forced to let the premature infant live or die on its own. She tried not to dwell on this possibility and trusted in God that He would not allow this to happen.

Staring out the window, she could see the predicted cold front had arrived. The arctic wind was stripping the deciduous trees of their few remaining colorful fall decorations, sending the homeless leaves scurrying along, searching for a quiet resting place. Tall fir trees bowed in unison under the stronger gusts, and their graceful choreography reminded her of a ballet troupe. Stubborn, frosted tendrils spawned by the blustering wind reached through the smallest of spaces in the office window and touched her bare arms, sending waves of goose bumps up them. She pulled on her sweater and hugged it to her body while she continued to scrutinize her challenges.

Wendy had worked hard to carefully prepare for the most common complications that happened after the baby reached the thirty-sixth week of pregnancy, such as abnormal labor, pre-eclampsia (toxemia), and post-term pregnancy. Procuring the supplies she needed had been easy since she did the ordering for the office. Her refrigerator at home was stocked with drugs that might be necessary: pitocin in case Annatha's labor needed to be induced or augmented, and a vial of lidocaine for local anesthesia. In addition, IV fluids, tubing, angiocaths, syringes and needles for administering these medications were stored in a Rubbermaid container. The only drug she was still waiting on was magnesium sulfate in case Annatha developed high blood pressure with pre-eclampsia. She wanted to be sure no one else opened it so she had asked the supplier to put it to her attention. It was the only medication the clinic would have no need to keep in stock and was supposed to arrive any day. Besides the necessary drugs, Wendy had ordered a midwife delivery kit online and had all the instruments in her possession that would be necessary to deliver the baby at home.

Since it would make a big difference if she were around should Annatha have a complication after thirty-six weeks, Wendy planned to take her maternity leave at that time so she could be at home to intervene. Until then, if the girl experienced a problem, she would have to deal with it alone. She couldn't afford to give Annatha a way to contact her because she would certainly get in touch with someone else and ruin everything.

"You're cold, too," the receptionist, Summer, called from the doorway.

Wendy was surprised and then annoyed at the interruption. "What do you want, Summer?" she asked with poorly concealed irritation.

"I have a fax from Tacoma Perinatal of Jenny Staubach's medical records," she explained timidly. The nurse always seemed to intimidate her for some reason.

"Sorry," Wendy apologized, "just grouchy from a crick in my neck." She took the records from the receptionist and set them on her desk.

Summer hesitated for a minute. "Also," she continued reluctantly, "that patient is still waiting."

Wendy shot out of her chair and winced at the catch in her neck. "I forgot all about her," she blurted as she walked by a stunned Summer and headed for the chart holder by the door from the exam area to the waiting room. The clinic doctor was definitely not excited about his office nurse being pregnant, and Wendy didn't want to give him a reason to let her go before she took maternity leave. One of his pet peeves was making a patient wait, and she had violated that with her ruminating.

Summer watched her curiously as she gathered the patient's chart, swung open the waiting room door and called out the teenage girl's first name. *Never saw her move that fast before,* she shrugged and resumed her station at the reception desk.

The interview went quickly, without a long discussion of options to abortion, and Wendy sent the young woman back to the front to make her appointments. She then used the e-prescribe online portal to transmit a prescription to the girl's pharmacy of choice. Another twenty minutes and it was lunch time. The fax from Tacoma Perinatal was still sitting on her desk where she placed it. She leafed through the pages rapidly and found a letter to one of their referring doctors. Good, now she had a letterhead to copy. Retrieving the cover page, she put it with the letter and folded them together, then placed them in her bag. When it was time for her maternity leave, these would serve as templates for the forms she would fax with her disability statement. All she had to do was change the fax number on the letterhead to the FedEx store in Tacoma, where she would send it from so no one would be the wiser. It was doubtful the office manager would scrutinize them enough to be suspicious; her integrity was unquestioned at the clinic, but she wanted everything to appear official and aboveboard.

She planned to take at least three months off after the baby was born, but she wasn't going to tell the office manager. As far as she knew, Wendy was only taking the standard six week maternity leave. After three months, she hoped to come up with enough money to stay home with the baby for five years. There were some options she had, and the most likely candidate was the 401k settlement from her ex. It would carry penalties if she withdrew it now, but she was willing to pay them so she could be there every day with her son for as long as possible. *My son, she thought dreamily. Didn't think I'd ever use those words*, she smiled.

Wendy grabbed her bag and pulled out the sandwich she had made this morning, along with a small container of sliced fruit. She decided to eat her lunch at her desk, wanting to avoid Traci in the office lunch room. It was entirely possible her coworker would mention the weekend encounter at the clinic in front of the others. She didn't feel like dealing with that scenario today. Given a little more time, Traci would likely forget about the whole thing, anyway. A small shiver forced her to put the sweater on, as draping it over her shoulders wasn't enough to stem another wave of goose bumps on her arms.

Before taking her first bite, she wondered if leaving the clinic before her plan called for it at Annatha's thirty-sixth week was a possibility. Sick of what she perceived to be a slaughterhouse foreman's job, it felt overwhelming to imagine being in this position another fourteen weeks. The only thing that consistently stopped her from walking out the door for good was a distant cloud looming, and the cloud was shaped like a law enforcement badge. It seemed inevitable that somebody somewhere would locate the man she saw in the parking lot who dropped Annatha off at the clinic, and everyone there would be questioned. Her best chance to derail any investigation and throw them off the scent was if she was still at her desk. If she wasn't, the investigator or investigators would want to speak to her at home and that just wasn't going to happen. The clinic records would show she was the last one to speak to the girl and her story would cement an impenetrable wall between any well-meaning detective and Annatha. No, she affirmed once again, her mission from God was to remain at this station and confuse any attempts to find the mother of her child.

****

Rachel put Annatha's file back in her briefcase and pushed it under the seat in front of her in preparation for landing at Denver International Airport. She looked out the window at the rising landscape as the 757 continued its descent. Unfortunately, the parking attendant's recall had not improved any regarding what he witnessed when Annatha left her car there last July. Armed with her laptop, she had loaded several photos of foreign vehicles and asked Carlos to study them to see if any of them would jog his memory. When they failed to help him identify the car Annatha drove away in, Rachel had thanked him for his cooperation and left her card. The flight to Denver had departed on time and she was looking forward to seeing Stan. More important, though, was the interview with the catering establishment personnel the next day. It had to break the case, she prayed, otherwise she was back to square zero, not even as high as one. A loud whirring noise that announced the landing gear was being deployed interrupted her thoughts and she watched as the jet turned to enter the runway pattern. The airport buildings were visible out her window, brightly illuminated since it was night time. They always looked like a row of tents to her pitched out in the middle of nowhere like a band of nomads camped in the desert.

"Can I take that trash for you, ma'am?" the flight attendant asked.

Rachel nodded and produced the plastic drink cup. This trip had not been urgent enough to requisition a private jet, but she usually didn't mind flying coach. Fortunately, the gentleman next to her had napped the whole way and wasn't an armrest hog. She brushed off her pants, grabbed the sleeves on her business suit coat and tugged hard to fight the wrinkles they suffered on the trip. It didn't help much but no matter, looking fashionable was the furthest thing from her mind.

When Rachel emerged from the jet way, she spotted Stan standing at the counter flirting with the gate agents. He was hard to miss. The tall, stocky frame of the affable black agent she was stationed with in Seattle would be visible behind an eighteen wheeler. Still the same old Stan, she smiled.

The FBI agent interrupted his conversation with the attractive airline employee long enough to check the crowd of passengers disembarking at the gate. He spied Rachel and a wide grin welcomed her better than any words. His long strides reached her quickly and he put his beefy arms around her.

"How the hell are you, Rach?" he greeted her warmly.

Rachel felt like she had been swallowed by his sincere embrace and despite the size of his massive biceps, the pressure on her shoulders was more akin to a strong caress and she always welcomed it.

"Just great, Stan," she replied. They both stepped back and studied each other for a moment.

"You've lost weight, Stan," she teased and patted the part of his abdomen that was sporting a middle age bulge the last time she saw him.

"Been hitting the slopes more," he winked.

Stan transferred from Seattle to Denver because of his love for alpine skiing. He was disappointed in the type of snow the Northwest offered, and called it cascade concrete due to its thick, wet texture. Even though she had been sad to see him leave, she knew he would be happier in Colorado, where the ski resorts were plentiful and the snow well groomed powder in most places.

"Good for you," she grinned.

"Any checked bags?" he asked.

"Nope, just this one," she nodded at her carry-on.

"Let's go, then," he ordered.

They walked at a brisk pace through the terminal and exited at the arrival parking level; Stan led the way and Rachel brought up the rear. He was looking forward to working with his friend again and had nothing but admiration for her. She put herself through college and law school by working part time and grabbing loans where she could. Entering the FBI academy straight from law school, she had proved to be a tireless investigator, with steely logic as well as the ability to arrange a myriad of unrelated facts into a cohesive case. It was a talent only a select group of agents possessed. When they reached their destination, Stan hoisted Rachel's carry-on bag into the back seat of his Bureau Taurus and they both got in. A light snow was beginning to fall.

"Ah," Stan sighed as he watched the flakes drift onto the windshield, "nectar of the gods."

Rachel laughed. "You're a dork."

"That I am," he agreed and pulled into traffic. "So what's up with this case you're working on?"

She filled him in on the facts surrounding Annatha's disappearance and he listened quietly. One of the things she treasured most about Stan was his ability to stay silent and assimilate information rather than constantly interrupting to ask a question or critique an investigation. When she was finished, he was busy trying to change lanes, and after a few moments she couldn't stand it any longer.

"So what do you think?" she demanded.

Without hesitating, he replied, his eyes still glued to the road. "Sounds like a runaway to me."

Rachel punched his upper arm hard and Stan erupted with a deep, baritone laugh. The seat felt like it was vibrating under her, as if his voice was blaring from a sub-woofer in the car.

"I could always count on your amazing powers of deduction," she said wryly.

"Lighten up, Rach," he rubbed the spot where she landed the punch. "Just forget about this stuff until tomorrow. Janet's looking forward to feeding you when we get home, and extracting any gossip you might be inclined to divulge."

Stan's invitation for Rachel to spend the night at his home was a welcome respite. He and Janet were alone now that their kids were away at college, and they had extra rooms. It was unusual for her not to stay in a hotel room when she travelled, but her old friend's hospitality had been hard to resist. Besides, she missed his wife, too. They had taken tennis lessons together and became doubles partners in tournaments at the fitness club they belonged to. Rachel had not picked up a racket since she moved.

"As you wish," she teased.

After arriving at Stan's home, they sat around the dinner table and the two of them watched Rachel eat. She hadn't realized how famished she was and as always, Janet's cooking was delicious. While the dishes were being cleared, Rachel called Mazy to check in. When she walked into the den after hanging up, she was grateful to see Stan had started a fire; the plummeting temperature outside had chilled the inside of the house, too.

Janet produced two bottles of Chardonnay and they talked until midnight about old times. It was so comfortable being with them again. A crackling fire bathed the room with warmth and the reflected light danced across the walls. The snow shower was covering the lawn with a thick, white blanket that provided a perfect backdrop to the evening.

"You've been great company," Rachel stood up and felt a little woozy from the wine, "but I have an important interview tomorrow so I think I'll turn in." She looked at Janet. "That was a lovely meal."

Janet led her to the room she was staying in. The bed had been neatly turned down.

"Bathroom's through that door," she pointed. Taking a few steps forward she hugged Rachel tightly. "It was great to see you again."

"You too," she replied and hugged back.

Tucked inside the warm comforter, Rachel noticed the room was rotating a little bit like riding on a carousel. *Must be the wine,* she recognized the feeling. It always helped to shut her eyes tightly and think of something else. Within minutes, she was fast asleep.

Chapter Fourteen

Twenty-two weeks, Six Days (22W6D)

Rachel daubed a small amount of eye shadow on her left eyelid, examined the results and replaced the brush in its cartridge. She wasn't much on makeup but didn't particularly like the ashen, zombie look her face assumed without it. *Especially today,* she groaned as her pulsating temples reminded her of the several glasses of wine from the night before. Her eyes looked like Arkansas road maps and she hadn't remembered to bring any Visine. Maybe she could talk Stan into stopping for some. Positioning both forefingers, she tugged at the corners of her eyes. To her growing dismay, a few wrinkles had begun trenching their way across her skin, and when she stretched them out they disappeared and made her look five years younger. They were baby crow's feet to be sure, but all babies grew up to be adults. Growing older sucked, she frowned, but the alternative was worse.

As she began cleaning up her toiletry items to pack them, the smell of fresh coffee made its way into the bathroom like smoke through a keyhole, and she breathed it in deeply. Janet was a saint, she mused; she still made Stan breakfast every morning. How quaint was that! After depositing her luggage and handbag at the front door, Rachel followed the aroma of bacon and coffee to the kitchen, where Janet was busy scrambling a skillet full of eggs.

"Morning," she croaked. Shaking her head, Rachel cleared her throat. "I meant, morning," she repeated firmly as her voice recovered from the initial phlegmy greeting.

Janet laughed. "You don't drink often do you?"

Rachel shook her head. "No, I don't," she admitted. "That smells delicious, though."

"As I recall, you're not much of a breakfast person, are you?" Janet scooped the eggs onto a large platter. She took the skillet and tossed it in the sink. Turning on the faucet, she ran cold water over it and steam hissed angrily from the hot iron surface.

"Coffee with some kind of protein bar is all I usually have," Rachel replied, "but this morning I'll make an exception."

"You look like you could use some nourishment," Janet winked.

"My two favorite females," Stan boomed as he entered the kitchen, grinning from ear to ear.

"How is it you're so peppy this morning?" Rachel frowned.

"You've never been able to hold your liquor, Agent Gray," he chided. "Actually," he continued, "I'm in a good mood because I get to work with you again."

"That's all he's talked about the last few days," Janet sighed. "If I didn't know for a fact he wasn't into white chicks, I'd be worried."

Stan bellowed his deep, reverberating laugh, and Rachel found herself following his lead. She realized how much she had missed him. "Let's get cracking, Stanley," she ordered playfully, "we've got work to do.

They each dug in, while Janet watched with a satisfied smile on her face as they eagerly devoured the food. She never ate breakfast. Her taste buds didn't work until noon.

Rachel said her goodbye to Janet while Stan loaded her things in the car. Once they were settled, Stan entered the address of the catering company in his navigator. The female voice began issuing instructions.

"Okay LaFonda," Stan grinned and guided the sedan down the street as directed.

Rachel thought for a moment. Where had she heard that name before?

Noticing her puzzled expression, Stand chuckled. "It's from *Napoleon Dynamite,* genius," he said.

"Good call on the name," she smiled.

On the way, Rachel filled Stan in on Annatha's disappearance and the cell phone connection to the catering company. It was a thirty minute drive and at the behest of LaFonda, they turned down a residential street and stopped in front of a small frame home with yellow siding and a green shake roof. A wooden sign on the lawn bore the company name and logo, a drawing of the Red Rock formation near Denver.

"Must work out of their home," Stan observed as he put the sedan in park and switched off the engine.

"Let's do this," Rachel grabbed her briefcase and they headed to the front door. The sky was clear and a brisk wind cut through her charcoal gray woolen overcoat. She shivered and lifted the collar around her neck. The distant Rocky Mountains, draped by a shawl of fresh snow, framed the back of the house. She paused for a moment to admire the view while Stan forged ahead and rang the door bell.

The front door was opened by a tall, willowy woman with jet black, permed hair. Rachel guessed she was in her late thirties. She was wearing jeans and a cream-colored sweater. A thick canvas apron draped over the outfit sported so many food stains of different shapes and sizes it looked like a Jackson Pollack painting.

"I'm Special Agent Rachel Gray," she presented her ID," and this is …"

Stan interrupted her and said sternly, "I'm IRS field agent Stan Jackson."

"What is the meaning of this?" the surprised woman demanded, staring at Rachel. "You said this was an FBI matter."

Rachel suppressed the urge to burst out laughing. Stan always had a way of putting people he was interviewing off guard. "I'm sorry, ma'am," she apologized, "my partner has a warped sense of humor. He's not with the IRS."

"Paula Davenport," she smiled thinly, communicating the joke wasn't the least bit funny. "Won't you come in." She shot Stan a wary glance and he smiled and shrugged.

The two agents followed her and Rachel elbowed Stan. He grimaced but didn't make a sound. Almost immediately, a pleasant aroma greeted them.

"Something smells good," Stan leaned over and whispered in his partner's ear.

When they entered the kitchen, it was obvious the room had been remodeled to accommodate the catering business. There was a large butcher block counter in the middle of the room. A six burner stainless steel range with a griddle was atop two side by side ovens. A delicious smelling sauce was simmering in an oversized kettle on the range. Stan felt his mouth start to water.

A second woman, obviously Paula's associate, was placing a hefty metal tray covered with steaming meatballs on the counter. Her appearance was a stark contrast to the woman who greeted them at the door. About three inches shorter, she was stocky and had close cropped, bleached hair, and as many studs as her ears could hold. Rachel guessed she was in her mid-twenties.

"This is my partner, Bridgette Lansing," Paula introduced her. "Bridgette, these are Agents Gray and ..." she paused and looked at Stan, "I forgot your name."

Touché, he thought. "Special Agent Jackson." He ignored the dig and held out his hand.

Bridgette shed her padded oven mitts and shook their hands firmly. "Nice to meet you," she said.

Rachel sized up the two women. The Denver policeman had described them as a gay couple and that wasn't a far leap. Paula was the feminine one, and Bridgette was masculine, pretty typical in her experience when gay women coupled up. It was hard to imagine they were involved in Annatha's disappearance at first glance, but she had travelled a long way to settle this in person.

"Agent Jackson," Paula said sarcastically, "you seem to be eyeballing those meatballs. You don't look Italian."

Stan grinned sheepishly. "You're absolutely right, ma'am, no Italian in my lineage. I developed a taste for them when I was staking out the mob," he winked.

Paula grabbed a toothpick and handed it to Stan. "You can sample one if you like."

He wasted no time and stabbed one of the meatballs, deftly deposited the steaming morsel in his mouth, but it immediately re-opened with a loud gasp and he began breathing heavily.

"Oh," Paula smiled devilishly, "I should have told you they were hot." She handed the gasping agent a napkin and he emptied the contents of his mouth.

Rachel smiled despite her partner's obvious discomfort. She couldn't help but admire the blatant retaliation by the caterer. It served him right for being such a smartass at the door. Besides, they had just eaten a big breakfast. Where did he find the room?

After downing a glass of ice water produced by Bridgette, Stan dabbed his eyes with his coat sleeve. "Ms. Davenport," he said grimly, "are we even now?"

"If you say so," Paula winked and turned to Rachel. "So what's this all about, Agent Gray?"

They sat on the bar stools that flanked the end of the counter opposite the side near the ovens. Rachel removed a folder from her briefcase and produced a picture of Annatha, sliding it across the counter in front of the two women.

"Have either of you ever seen this girl?" she asked while she studied their reaction.

Paula shook her head and looked at Bridgette.

"I've never seen her before." Her business partner held the

picture up, examined it for a few seconds and then replaced it on the counter.

The fact that neither one of them pushed it back at her made Rachel believe them. When a person was hiding their recognition of a photo, they usually moved it away from them as quickly as possible. She retrieved the copy of Annatha's cell phone records.

"I know you were questioned by the Denver police a while back," she continued, "but I can't explain why your number is on the missing girl's cell phone records the day she disappeared."

"Are those the records?" Paula asked.

"Yes," Rachel replied, "the highlighted numbers are yours and occur twice within a short period of time."

"Can I look at it?"

Rachel handed the copy to the caterer and they waited in silence as she studied it carefully. Bridgette was looking at it, too, and they both had the same reaction simultaneously. They smiled knowingly at each other.

"Something you two want to share with us?" Stan asked.

Paula laid the page down on the counter. "Looks like you travelled a long way for nothing, Agent Gray," she said. "The dates you are referring to are a month before I acquired this cell number."

Rachel stifled the gasp that surged in her throat. She never liked to show emotion during an interview. *Jesus Christ,* she fumed, *the policeman never checked the dates!* Often the communication between law enforcement agencies left a lot to be desired, and this was one of those times.

"What exactly did the officer say when he came here?" she pressed the issue.

"He showed us a picture of some girl and asked if we knew her," Paula shrugged.

"And that was it?"

"I'm afraid so."

Which is why she came here in person, she reminded herself. *Look at it this way, Rachel, it paid off.*

"I'd like to take a look at your cell phone contract," she managed evenly.

Paula disappeared and returned a few moments later with the document that was dated August twenty-eighth, over a month after Annatha's disappearance.

"Can I have Agent Jackson make a copy of this and mail the original back to you?" she requested.

"Suit yourself," Paula replied, "just make sure I get the original back, Agent Jackson."

Stan flashed a wry grin. "I'll deliver it personally," he said. "It will give me a chance to napalm my mouth again."

Bridgette had returned to stirring the sauce and Stan saw her body shake with suppressed laughter. He wasn't sure if she was laughing at his retort or the joke her partner had played on him.

Rachel gathered the photo and phone records, replaced them in the folder and stashed it in her briefcase. She was done with the interview. It was time to leave and start chasing the real owner of the cell phone number.

"Thank you for your cooperation." She shook their hands perfunctorily and said, "We can show ourselves out."

When they were back in the car, Stan could see the familiar furrow in Rachel's brow that meant she was steaming mad. He didn't blame her; the dates would have been an easy thing to check and saved her the trip. However, he didn't mind since it had given him and Janet a chance to visit with her again. He decided to let her stew for a few minutes.

"Okay," he finally broke the silence, "I know that look Rachel. Spit it out, I can take it."

She put both hands on the dashboard and took a deep breath. "I don't know whether to be pissed or glad," she said in exasperation. "On the one hand, this case would have moved ahead a long time ago if that cop had done his job right, but on the other hand, it does bring a whole new person into the equation."

"Most likely the guy she drove away with at the airport?" Stan offered.

"Exactly." She removed her hands and cradled the briefcase. "This has to be the number of the mystery man the attendant saw Annatha get in a car with at the Park & Fly." She stared blankly out the car window as the neatly manicured lawns passed by. "It just has to be," she said fervently.

"Agreed," he nodded. "I guess you want me to drive you downtown so we can get the cell phone company to give us the name of the person who had this number on July twenty-fifth?"

Rachel was busy dialing the field office in Seattle on her cell phone. "Huh?" she asked absently.

Stan knew better than to continue; she was in the zone and wouldn't respond for the time being.

Rachel asked to speak to Jim Dalton and instructed him to call T-Mobile and have them fax over all contracts for the cell number on Annatha's phone to the Denver field office. Next, she told him she might be staying over in Denver if the records showed the owner was located nearby.

"Did you see the stack of files on my desk before you left?" Jim moaned.

"Make it so, number one," she said curtly and hung up.

"Damn Rachel," Stan chided her, "you look like you're on the Serengeti plains hunting prey."

"How's your mouth, Stanley?" she kidded.

"Shut up," he replied but his wide grin told her he wasn't serious. "That was one vindictive bitch," he shook his head.

Rachel laughed until she had tears in her eyes. It was a good release for the frustration she had felt upon finding out the caterers didn't even have the cell number when Annatha disappeared. At the same time, she could feel the adrenaline ramping up in her bloodstream, as it seemed she might have finally caught a break in her quest to find the missing girl.

****

Annatha was lying on the bed, absently leafing through a People magazine Wendy brought her as a peace offering after their fracas. Taz was fast asleep on her tummy. She was halfway reading the articles, but also thinking of names that she would have given her son if she had the chance. Masculine names appealed to her and she was drawn to either Michael or William, after her dad. However, her mischievous, rebellious nature conjured a name that she knew would annoy the shit out of Wendy. Given the opportunity, she would refer to the baby as Lucifer. It symbolized the pact Wendy had made with the devil to imprison her and steal this child. Sure, the nurse claimed that she was on a mission from God, but what little exposure she had to a concept of God, gleaned from her Dad after he sobered up, convinced her God had nothing to do with this.

Taz jumped and startled Annatha. He dove off of her abdomen and stood staring for a few moments at the mound in front of him as if he was expecting some creature to crawl out of it like in the movie *Alien*. She realized he must have felt the baby move. As if he was reacting to some primitive instinct, Taz went into pounce mode with his front legs bent at the knee, paws pressed against the comforter, and his back legs moving slightly back and forth as if an engine was idling. His ears were pointed straight ahead, sweeping back and forth like a radar dish. Annatha knew from experience Taz was so wound up he was like a slingshot pulled to its farthest reach. Stealthily edging her hand under the covers until it was behind the cat, she goosed him and he cart-wheeled off the bed in a backwards flip. A deep belly laugh wracked her body and she felt the tears streaming down her face. She hadn't laughed that hard in forever. Apologizing through gasps for air, she scooped up the frightened cat, who was trying his best to appear nonchalant about the whole thing, and sat down in the recliner. It was time for the TLC show *Maternity Ward*. The on-screen guide indicated they were going to show a birth today and she wanted to find out what she was going to be up against, despite her fervent wish that some other method could be used to extract this baby. A can opener like device for the uterus seemed like a better, less painful solution to her.

The program began with the introduction of the happy couple and how they went through in vitro to get pregnant. Luckily, she only had one baby since there was a greater risk of having a multiple pregnancy with this procedure. During the commercial, Annatha made a beeline to the fridge and grabbed a fresh, cold water bottle. When she returned to the recliner, Taz was meticulously cleaning himself. *He's recovered nicely from my scaring him half to death,* she smiled and fought the urge to burst out laughing again.

The next scene was in the delivery room, and the woman's face didn't appear so joyful or serene. She had belts around her abdomen that were connected to some kind of a monitor, and an IV was infusing medication that was supposed to induce her labor. Apparently, it worked well because her contractions began coming more often and were definitely more intense as evidenced by the pained expression on her face. The laboring mother was encouraged by her spousal coach to begin breathing away the discomfort. Weird, Annatha thought, how the husband described it as discomfort. He made it sound like his wife just had a pesky splinter. At first, she dutifully responded and initiated rapid "hee-hoo" breathing sounds in response to the cadence her husband set with rhythmic counting. Another commercial interrupted and when the program resumed, the contractions must have worsened, as the woman was "hee-hooing" very forcefully and the doting husband kept reminding her to follow his lead, whereupon his wife turned to him and screamed, "Your breath stinks; get out of my face!" The poor guy took a step back with a bewildered expression. His coaching debut wasn't going as expected. Annatha was focused on the woman's contorted face and sudden leap into madness. A cold shiver ran down her spine and she gulped a drink of water. She didn't do well with pain either, and the fact that her pain would be for nothing made it even more unbearable to think about.

After the outburst another commercial rescued the sinking Lamaze ship. When they returned, the woman was all smiles. An epidural had been initiated and the pain was gone. The husband seemed relieved and disappointed at the same time, now resigned to assuming the position of a fifth wheel in the whole process. *That's just fucking great*, Annatha fumed, *I won't have the option of an epidural.* There would be no hospital, no anesthesiologist, just the deranged nurse playing the role of labor god. She made a mental note to ask Wendy what she planned to do for her labor pains.

When the picture changed, Annatha sat up straight in the recliner and stared at the scene in front of her. The woman's legs were up in stirrups and her whole ass was hanging in the breeze for anyone to see. *Holy shit,* she gasped, *everything looked so swollen down there.* Next, a female doctor sat down and thankfully blocked this view for the time being. She looked like a catcher waiting for the next pitch. The order was given to start pushing and the nurse and husband each grabbed a leg, pulling them back until the knees almost touched the mother's chest. The patient held her breath and pushed down like she hadn't taken a crap in months, her face turning a weird purplish-red hue. After a few contractions, the camera angle changed and the vagina was exposed again. Annatha couldn't make out what the dark bulge was coming out of it until she recognized it was a shock of hair. *Jesus,* she felt her mouth dry up*, it was the baby's head!* The next round of pushing forced the bulge to grow but the head still wasn't out. Annatha couldn't believe it would fit without splitting the mother open from her butt to her boobs. She felt a cramp in her foot and realized her toes were curled so tightly the muscles on the bottom of her feet had locked up. Massaging her soles while she reluctantly witnessed the spectacle unfolding before her, she watched in amazement while the doctor stretched the skin around the baby's head. The nurse and husband rooted feverishly for the mother to push harder.

Suddenly, the bulge morphed into a cone-shaped head and the obstetrician began suctioning the nose and mouth with a bulb-shaped device. Next, she grabbed the head and pulled down, then up to deliver the shoulders. Annatha turned away, grossed out by the sight of the woman's vagina stretching to deliver the baby's body. When she managed to look again, the baby had been delivered and the doctor was clamping and cutting the umbilical cord. She announced they had a baby girl and placed the slimy newborn covered with some white, cheesy looking substance onto the mother's abdomen. The stunned parents were overjoyed and both of them began to cry. Annatha fumbled for the remote and quickly changed the channel to MTV. She didn't want to watch the happiest part of the birth, only the mechanics, and frankly, she had seen enough.

The reality series on MTV paled in comparison to what she had just witnessed. She had taken health classes in school, but never observed the actual birth of a baby until now. The subject had never crossed her mind. It seemed surreal to her that this was to be her fate in a few short months, without the technology or pain relief options. Her labor and delivery experience lay in the hands of a crazy nurse, and she had no idea if her captor had ever delivered a baby before. It seemed impossible to her she would be capable of surviving such a painful ordeal, much less pushing a baby out.

Annatha tried to focus on the silly antics of the characters on MTV's *Real Life* series, but it was in vain. Every time she closed her eyes, all she could see was the gruesome image of a dark bulge splitting the mother's vagina wide open. The idea that a human being would emerge from her own vagina was something she didn't want to consider right now. Plus, how anyone could ever have sex again after filleting their genitals like that haunted her, and she scrubbed the unwelcome thought away like a dirty stain. She cuddled her sleeping cat and tickled behind his ears with her fingers, trying to imagine a way she could endure her looming ordeal. Maybe she should ask Wendy to hit her with a hammer and when she woke up it would be all over. She shuddered involuntarily at the graphic birth scene that insisted on occupying her thoughts again and Taz stirred.

CHAPTER FIFTEEN

Twenty-three Weeks (23W0D)

Rachel awakened slowly to the sound of her cell phone alarm. She took a moment to orient herself to her surroundings. Then she remembered. Despite Stan's insistence that she stay with him another night, she had decided to check into the Marriott Residence Inn in downtown Denver. It wasn't that she didn't enjoy Stan and Janet's company. There were two reasons she elected to stay by herself. First, she didn't need another night of drinking and talking past midnight. Second, she wanted time to herself to prepare a strategy for her interview today.

The T-Mobile contracts showed a Denver law firm had been the contract holder of the cell number on Annatha's call records until July twenty-fifth, when the very same phone with that number was reported stolen. This seemed very convenient and suspicious to her. It was too late to call the law firm after receiving the information last night, but it would prove to her advantage, as she wanted to catch them off guard with an unannounced visit. The firm would have records of which associate had the cell phone number, as well as their travel records, to see who had been in Seattle on July twenty-fifth. Hopefully, he would be in town for her to interview. She allowed herself to consider the prospect that the person who knew where Annatha might be was within her grasp. A gnawing anticipation in her stomach signaled her instincts were communicating she was finally closing in on an answer to the mystery of Annatha's disappearance. However, years of experience had taught her not to get her hopes up too high. More than once a case she believed was close to being solved had vanished into thin air.

Willing herself out of bed, she turned on the night stand light and puttered into the bathroom, still only half awake. The change in time zone meant she was getting up an hour earlier than usual. In her youth she wouldn't have had any problem with such trivial changes, but that time was gone, she frowned. Shedding her panties, she stepped into the shower and turned the water up as hot as it would go. The warm water soaked her skin and she felt her brain brushing away the cobwebs from a deep sleep. When she stepped out of the shower, the mirror was painted with steam and she took a towel and wiped it several times so she could put on her makeup. She followed the same ritual every morning. The face paint went on while she was still naked, then her bra and panties were donned before drying her hair. Without a curling iron, her hair would be unruly and require a few strategically placed clippies to create a tight, professional female bun. Anyway, it really didn't matter today; she planned to be on her game no matter what her physical appearance was.

Once her face and hair were in order, she put on the same navy blue suit she wore the day before. She took the time to iron it the night before so it wouldn't be wrinkled. While she was pressing the suit, she called Mazy's dad, and he had been more than willing to keep their daughter another day. He was used to her uncertain schedule by now and was always there to help out. If only he had been more accommodating when they were married, she had wished briefly, but quickly brushed it off and focused on the task at hand.

Rachel gathered her briefcase, took one final look in the bathroom mirror and sighed. This would have to do. Getting off the elevator at the lobby, she stepped into the foyer and saw the bustling dining area to her left was full of businessmen and women having their complimentary breakfast. She spied the bulky figure of Stan Jackson sprawled out on the couch like he was in his living room at home, reading a newspaper. Raising her free hand, she waved until he saw her. The super-sized agent gathered himself, gave Rachel a big grin and stood up, stowing the paper on the couch.

"Sleep well?" he asked.

"Like a baby," she replied.

"Janet didn't make me breakfast," he complained. "Said I should eat with you."

"I just want a Starbucks latte," she explained. "I don't feel like eating anything yet."

Stan stared briefly at the dining area where the aroma of pancakes and coffee was drawing him like a moth to a flame. "Okay boss," he sighed longingly, "let's get some caffeine in you."

When they were settled in Stan's sedan, he punched in some navigator commands and found the nearest Starbucks. "Pretty nifty, eh?" he winked.

Rachel grinned weakly. She needed some coffee ASAP to complete her waking process. Luckily, it was only a few blocks away and Stan insisted on buying. She ordered a triple shot latte in the hopes of jump starting her cerebral engine more quickly.

Sipping the hot beverage gingerly, Rachel opened the folder from her briefcase while Stan devoured a cinnamon roll. It always puzzled her how he could eat so many carbs without getting a huge gut. True, he was a large man, but there didn't seem to be much fat on his massive frame.

"We need to go to the Estes Park law firm," she announced and gave him the address.

"No need to use LaFonda for this one," Stan garbled through chunks of dough. "It's only a few blocks away, near the Convention Center."

By the time they navigated through downtown rush hour traffic to the office building, Rachel had downed her beverage, and for the first time that morning, she felt alert. Stan parked along the curb and placed an FBI placard in the windshield. Once again, an icy breeze caused Rachel to bundle up her overcoat tighter, but this time there was no majestic vista to view. Only blocks of high-rise buildings surrounded them, jaggedly framing an overcast sky of gray, billowy clouds.

"Looks like snow today," Stan observed as they walked into the building.

Striding purposefully through the lobby, Rachel spotted the elevators and scanned the legend displaying the building's occupants. She found Estes Park law firm was on the twenty-fifth floor. *How ironic,* she thought to herself. *Annatha disappeared on July twenty-fifth.* The express elevator whisked them quickly to their destination and when they stepped out, they were standing in the law firm's lobby.

A large, semi-circular desk was directly in front of them. An older woman with wavy gray hair was sitting behind it with what appeared to be a Bluetooth device in her right ear. She continued her conversation with the caller while smiling warmly at them.

Rachel willed herself to be patient, casually studying the layout of the reception area. The richly upholstered waiting room chairs were neatly arranged against the wall and a centrally located glass-top table displayed a row of popular magazines. Her eyes wandered back to the busy receptionist and noticed a single doorway to the left of her desk. She surmised it was the main entrance to the rest of the office. Mundane exercises such as this were useful when it came to controlling nervous anticipation. Fifteen years in the FBI had given her ample time to learn how to douse her restless energy, and she mentally tamped it down like a blazing camp fire.

Stan, however, was a different story. After a few minutes of waiting, he removed his FBI badge and dangled it so the receptionist could see his credentials. Rachel elbowed him in the ribs but he just smiled and replaced the badge. However, his maneuver worked, as the receptionist's demeanor changed immediately and she placed the caller on hold.

"Can I help you?" she said cheerily.

Rachel and Stan introduced themselves and both produced their badges. "We'd like to speak to your managing partner," Rachel announced flatly, replacing her credentials in the briefcase.

"One moment," she responded and pushed a button on her phone. "Two FBI agents are here that want to speak to you, sir." Pressing the button a second time she looked at Rachel and said, "Mr. Burbank will be with you in a moment. Please have a seat."

The two agents settled in. Stan picked up a Sports Illustrated and began perusing it. Rachel was too preoccupied to read anything and just fidgeted with her briefcase. The receptionist became her entertainment, as she stayed very busy answering calls. After what seemed like an eternity but was probably only five minutes, the door opened and a crisply attired woman about forty motioned for them to follow her. She ushered them down a long hallway lined with office doors, nylons swishing together against beefy thighs. At the end of the corridor, she opened a door that led to a large office with wall-to-wall windows affording a spectacular view of downtown Denver. There was a large mahogany desk with a matching credenza behind it, adorned with family photos. Just to the left of the door was a sitting area with a couch and two leather chairs strategically divided by a coffee table.

"Please have a seat," the woman offered. "Mr. Burbank will be with you shortly."

They both chose the couch and Rachel immediately regretted it. Stan's huge frame claimed most of it and she huddled against the arm rest.

"Pretty fancy," Stan commented drily, looking around the office.

"Standard well-to-do law furniture, I'd say," Rachel agreed.

Only a few minutes passed before the door opened again. A

short, wiry man just a little taller than Rachel entered carrying a file box. He wore a pressed white shirt and dark gray tweed pants with a solid navy tie. Rachel noticed his matching coat was hung on an ornate antique brass rack in the corner by his desk. A shock of snow white hair devoured his narrow head and a pair of reading glasses perched precariously on the end of his nose. Deep blue eyes sized them up over the thick rims as he walked to his desk and placed the file box down on top of it.

"John Burbank," he offered his hand and the agents stood and introduced themselves. "Formality," he apologized, "but can I see your credentials?"

This guy looked kind of like a seventy year old Woody Allen with hair, Rachel thought as she and Stan produced their badges.

"Appreciate that," he nodded, "now please have a seat." After the three were settled, Burbank removed the glasses, crossed his legs and placed folded hands on top of them. He absently twirled the spectacles between two thin fingers. "Now, how can I help you?"

Rachel cleared her throat while she dug the folder out of her briefcase. "We are investigating a missing person and on the day of her disappearance, there were two calls in her phone records from somebody in your law firm." She retrieved the copy of Annatha's call records and handed it to Burbank. "The two calls are highlighted in yellow."

The attorney donned his glasses, adjusted them slightly and studied the copy. His face was stoic, as if this was an everyday occurrence. "Excuse me," he said politely and walked over to his desk, pressed a button and asked the person on the other end to step into his office. "I have someone who might be able to help," he explained as he turned to face them again and handed the page back to Rachel.

Within a few seconds, a woman entered the office and introduced herself as Marla. She was in her fifties, Rachel guessed.

Her body was a little pudgy for her height, and she had thick, cropped hair dyed light brown to cover any gray.

"Marla's our office manager," Burbank informed the agents.

Rachel wasted no time and produced the T-Mobile contract with the firm. "I need to know which one of your attorneys had this cell number."

Marla perused the page silently for a moment then a look of recognition gradually formed on her face. "This was Thomas's number, sir," she addressed Burbank. "The only reason I know this information off the top of my head is that it was reported stolen and I had to replace his iPhone, cancel the cell number and file a claim with our insurance company."

"Thomas who?" Rachel asked while she retrieved the contract.

"Thomas Loftin," Marla replied.

Burbank interrupted. "There you have it, Agent Gray," he declared, "it was stolen. The thief is the one who probably placed the calls."

Rachel turned and looked the smug attorney in the eye. "Not so fast, sir," she said evenly, "the calls have times on them, and the times these calls were made occurred before the phone was reported stolen."

Burbank's brow furrowed. It was unseemly anyone in their firm would be involved in a missing persons investigation, especially Thomas. He was a dedicated family man and did exemplary work. In fact, he was on track for a partnership.

"You said 'she,' Agent Gray." He appeared puzzled. "How old is she?"

"Sixteen," Stan interjected.

This information caused the color to drain from the older man's face, but he quickly regained his composure and walked back to his desk. "I'll see if Thomas is in," he announced with less bravado and pressed the intercom speaker button.

"Yo boss," a confident voice boomed.

Rachel felt the hair on her arms stand up and her pulse

quickened. The arrogant tone that blared from the intercom speaker made her even more eager to question this man. She was very good at deflating blowhards.

"I need you to come to my office immediately," Burbank ordered firmly.

"On my way," he answered without a hint of concern.

They didn't have to wait long, as Loftin soon strode through the door and glanced curiously at the agents when he entered. Not surprisingly, he was handsome, athletic, tanned and wore his hair rumpled in a youthful cut, Rachel noted. In fact, he was just as she imagined after hearing his voice. She also spied a gold wedding band on his left ring finger. *That would explain a lot,* she frowned.

Burbank introduced Thomas to the two agents. "They have a few questions for you," he informed the youthful attorney. Both handed Loftin their business cards.

Rachel stood and asked Thomas to have a seat. She wanted to be in a dominant position when she questioned him. Obviously, he didn't respect women much if he corresponded with and arranged a rendezvous with a sixteen year old girl in the context of a marital relationship. He assumed a relaxed pose in one of the leather chairs and she noticed his face never flinched, despite the fact two FBI agents were there for the sole purpose of questioning him.

Rachel produced a photo of Annatha and handed it to Loftin. "Have you ever seen this girl before, sir?" she asked.

Thomas took the photo and looked at it briefly, then handed it back. "No ma'am," he said confidently. "What's this all about, John?"

"Just answer their questions, Thomas," Burbank ordered. Staring at his boss with a curious frown for a moment, Loftin turned to face the female agent.

Rachel deliberately replaced the photo on the coffee table in front of the attorney. "Mr. Loftin," she said firmly, "please look at the photo again and carefully consider your response this time."

Thomas searched the agent's face for some clue as to what this was all about. His gut was churning as he looked a second time at a photo of the girl he had dropped at an abortion clinic in Olympia four months ago. Why would the FBI be involved in this mess? If John found out what went on during his business trips, he would be thrown out of the firm and Laurel would likely divorce him. *Get hold of yourself man,* he commanded, *they can't possibly have any hard evidence you ever met this girl.*

"Sorry," he said evenly and sat the picture down. "I can't help you."

Retrieving Annatha's cell phone records, Rachel placed them in front of Loftin.

"Your number is on her phone records, sir," she stated.

Thomas studied the highlighted sections on the page. They were his cell number, all right. He defiantly tossed the copy on the table and addressed Rachel.

"My phone was stolen that day, Agent Gray," he retorted, "now will you please tell me what this is all about?"

"Your cell company's records show these calls to Annatha Wolcott were made before you reported it stolen." She tapped the highlighted numbers with her index finger forcefully. "And," she continued, "they were made on the same day she went missing."

Thomas felt his stomach hit the floor. *Missing? Why the hell was she missing? She was fine when he dropped her off at the abortion clinic. Did something happen to her after the procedure?* He frantically tried to think of some way to get out of this without admitting in front of a senior partner that he got a sixteen year old girl pregnant then dropped her off at an abortion clinic with the money to cover her expenses. There must be another path around this persistent FBI agent that would deflect his involvement with her disappearance without John knowing any more than he had to. When nothing presented itself immediately as a viable alternative, he decided to pursue the theft of his phone.

"I know when I reported it stolen," he finally answered, "but I don't remember seeing it after my deposition that morning."

"Let me refresh your memory," Rachel placed his cell phone records in front of him. "You made a call to this firm an hour before the call to Annatha's phone."

"If you say so," he remained steadfast, "but I also went to the mall to do some shopping and could have left it on a store counter there. Some kid more than likely picked it up who knew the girl and called her."

"So that we're clear," Stan leaned forward from his position on the couch, presenting an intimidating figure. "On the one hand, you want us to believe that the person who stole your cell phone just happened to know this girl and called her?" He held up his mammoth hand to indicate he wasn't finished when Thomas opened his mouth to respond. "On the other hand, we have a call to the missing girl from your cell phone in black and white before you reported it stolen."

"Frankly, I don't care if you believe me or not," Thomas replied bitterly. "I'm a happily married man who was in Seattle for a deposition, and I don't have any idea who this girl is or why she is missing."

Rachel studied the attorney. Because he handed the photo back so quickly, she knew with certainty he recognized her. He didn't seem flustered or rattled, but that ability never predicted guilt in her experience. She had one more tactic that was certain to rattle her suspect.

"Do you have a laptop you take on your business trips, Mr. Loftin?"

"Sure," he replied, eyeing the agent warily, "why?"

"We know the missing girl met the man online who got her pregnant," Rachel unraveled her time bomb carefully. "Later, she corresponded with him again and set up a meeting the day she disappeared. If you had nothing to do with this, we won't find any evidence of it on your hard drive. We'll rule you out as a suspect, and you won't hear from us again about this matter."

Thomas glanced at John, who was staring at him with a very worried look on his face. Things had just gone from bad to worse.

There was a great deal of information a computer forensics team could extract from his computer that would compromise his out-of-town activities and likely get him fired. He couldn't let that happen.

"Hold on," he stood up and faced Rachel. "There is a lot of attorney-client information on my laptop and I don't want any computer forensics team rummaging around in it."

Stan smiled and produced his cell phone. He speed dialed the U.S. Attorney's office in Denver. Rachel had briefed one of the assistant DAs on the case last night and faxed over the evidence.

"Carl," his booming voice filled the room. "This is about the Annatha Wolcott case we discussed last evening. I need a search warrant for any electronic devices used by a Thomas Loftin at the Estes Park law firm regarding online recreation, and any personal electronic devices in his possession." He read the business address from Burbank's card, hung up and turned to Rachel. "He said we'll have it within an hour."

"Don't worry, Mr. Loftin," Rachel assured him, "the warrant doesn't include any business client information. They won't have the authority to examine anything else."

Thomas experienced a desperation he had never known. If the internet chat data was discovered, especially the IM's with the missing girl, his career at the firm was history. He felt certain there was no evidence tying him to her disappearance since he last saw her at the abortion clinic alive and well, but the propriety of his actions would be unseemly and the consequences devastating. *Oh God*, he remembered, *Laurel's pregnant again.* If his sexual escapades were uncovered, it was over between them and the divorce would be messy. *Hell hath no fury like a woman scorned*, he recalled from his family law days. There must be something he could do to save his position at the firm, not to mention his marriage. An idea surfaced from the morass of despair that gripped him, and he decided to pursue it.

"John," he turned to his boss, his voice slightly rattled now, "I need someone in the firm to file a motion to block any warrant that would jeopardize privileged attorney-client information."

Burbank hesitated, sizing up his junior partner's demeanor. His initial gut reaction had been total faith in the integrity and decency of this man, but Thomas's insistence that the FBI be prevented from looking at his laptop seemed guilty on the face of it. He had travelled to Seattle and was there the day the girl disappeared, and his cell phone number was on the call records from her phone. It was prudent of the FBI to pursue Thomas as a suspect. Surely, if he were innocent of any wrongdoing, he would agree to let them extract the data and clear him. It was a dead certainty he was interested in what information was gleaned from Thomas's laptop, so he would know without a shred of doubt if his junior associate was leading some kind of double life. However, he had to admit the point about the attorney-client information was a valid argument, although it could also be construed as desperate.

"Everyone please leave," Burbank said in a commanding voice. "I want to talk to the agents in private."

Thomas shook his head. He recognized the boss's tone and knew it would be futile to refuse. Marla and Loftin filed out of the room silently.

Stan stood up and followed them to the door. "I'll just keep an eye on the young lawyer." He paused and winked slyly. "Wouldn't want any evidence to disappear."

Once they were alone, Burbank gestured for Rachel to sit again. She complied.

"Can you give me any more details about what you have found out that makes you think Thomas is involved?" he asked. This time his demeanor was one of concern, and his cobalt eyes purposeful.

Rachel lied they had Annatha's laptop examined by a forensics team and found she had chatted with and arranged two meetings with a man who went by the handle of *legaltenderguy*. This seemed very consistent with a name a lawyer would choose. Even though it had been uncovered by a hacker and not an FBI CART team, she felt certain they would find the same information.

"Now, Mr. Burbank," Rachel said evenly, "Annatha Wolcott turned up pregnant a few weeks after meeting with *legaltenderguy*, and arranged a second meeting with him, ostensibly to inform him she was pregnant." She paused for a moment to let this information sink in. "The same day of the second meeting, Thomas Loftin's cell phone calls her and she calls him back." Just to make sure her case was convincing, she decided to embellish a bit. "We have a witness at a Park & Fly lot near SeaTac airport who checked in Annatha Wolcott's Honda and saw her leave in a foreign car with a man. I can obtain rental car records from Mr. Loftin's trip, find the car he rented and show a photo to the attendant. More than likely he will identify it as the car the girl left in the day she went missing."

Burbank's face softened. "I've known Tommy since he attended law school. He even clerked for me. I've witnessed every indication that he has high moral standards." He smiled ruefully. "Sure, he's cocky and abrasive, but it serves him well with what he does day to day. He's a damn fine litigator."

Rachel listened respectfully, allowing the attorney a chance to come to a decision without further input from her.

When she didn't respond, Burbank walked over to the massive windows and gazed at the skyline that dwarfed his office view. His shoulders slumped when the painful decision was finally made.

"Despite my affection and respect for Thomas," he turned to face the agent with a pained expression, "considering the information you just disclosed, I have no choice but to place him on administrative leave until your investigation of his involvement, if any, is complete."

Rachel thanked Burbank for his assessment, but realistically, he had no choice given the circumstances.

"I'll ask the U.S. Attorney handling the case to keep you up to speed," she promised.

Burbank walked over behind his executive chair, placed

both hands on top and looked at her sternly. "Pardon me if I don't thank you for forcing me to make one of the most difficult decisions of my long life."

"It may be difficult sir," she replied, "but it's the right one."

He waved off her response. "Follow me," he ordered and they left the office together.

As they made their way down the hallway to Loftin's office, there were small groups of people watching and Rachel could hear whispering as they walked by. Burbank seemed oblivious. She could tell when they reached their destination as Stan was parked at the doorway, his arms crossed, looking very much like a sentry. They entered Loftin's office and he was sitting at his desk, nervously tapping a pencil on a legal pad in front of him.

Thomas looked up hopefully as his longtime mentor and the pesky FBI agent walked in. The large black agent named Jackson had made sure he couldn't do anything while he waited, treating him like he was a criminal plotting to destroy evidence. He eagerly waited for John to say something, as he felt fairly certain he would back him up with blocking the warrant. After all, they had been together for many years and he couldn't imagine his boss would believe anything the agents said. Even with John's support, he had quite a mountain to climb yet to put this all behind him. When he saw the face of his senior partner, drawn and resigned at the same time, his heart sunk.

Burbank lifted his pants leg, sat on the desk corner closest to Thomas and stared directly into his pleading gaze.

"From what Agent Gray tells me, Thomas," he began, "there is circumstantial and some direct evidence that links you to this missing girl." He paused and sighed, then placed his hand on Loftin's shoulder. "I'm sorry, but I have no choice but to put you on administrative leave with pay until their investigation of your involvement is over. I'd strongly advise you to contact Foster Davis as soon as possible. He's an excellent criminal attorney and a friend of mine."

Burbank removed his hand and slid off the desk, then walked

to the doorway and turned. "Leave your company phone, office key and laptop; we'll give you thirty minutes to get your things together." He gestured at the agents. "They'll let you know if they need anything further today, but I'd like you to respect my wish that you not contact me until this mess is settled."

Rachel was impressed. Burbank had a lot of dignity and was tough when circumstances demanded. He was direct but not spiteful, despite the alleged seedy facts he had learned about his protégé today.

"Mr. Loftin," she stated flatly, "we are in the process of obtaining search warrants for your business electronics as well as the ones at your residence. You might want to phone your wife and warn her someone from the Denver field office will be there in about an hour." He didn't look at her and seemed distracted. Not surprising, she thought. "I want to request that you come to the Denver field office at 3pm today for questioning. If you don't," she threatened, "we will be forced to seek a warrant for your arrest."

Thomas sunk in his chair, still withered by John's words. He couldn't believe this was happening to him, he groaned, and all for a piece of teen ass! The only criminal act he had committed was statutory rape, but currently there was no victim to press charges. Unfortunately, the fact he didn't break the law was moot. His out–of–town adventures would more than likely be uncovered on his laptop, and he would have to struggle to maintain his position at the firm. Even if he could, his stature would be destroyed and he would be relegated to some lowly job. All of that paled in comparison to Laurel's reaction when he told her the FBI was searching their home due to his alleged involvement with a young girl's disappearance in Washington State. He winced at the thought of her hurt expression that was sure to follow the news. Very likely he would be ordered to leave their home, unable to see his son or be there during her pregnancy. *Jesus,* he put his head in his hands*, could things get any worse?*

Slowly, he stood up and began putting some personal items

from his desk into his briefcase. He could feel the accusing glare from Agent Gray. She suspected he had something to do with her missing person, but for now he couldn't tell her the truth. In order to maintain some semblance of his former reputation, he had to persist in the off chance his laptop would not reveal anything incriminating. If it did, he would have to come clean. He would make the call to Foster Davis when he got home, away from prying ears. Placing his key and cell phone on the desk top, he closed the briefcase and walked to the side of the desk. He started to say something to John, but decided against it. The senior partner was staring at him with a sorrowful gaze, and he couldn't bear to look him in the eye.

Instead, he turned to Rachel. "I'll call you about the interview after I've had a chance to talk with my attorney," he said evenly, brushed past her through the door way and disappeared quickly down the corridor.

Rachel addressed Burbank. "Please secure this office by locking it and don't allow anyone in here until the CART team arrives."

He nodded and turned to Marla, who was hovering in the hallway. "Make sure that's done, will you?"

"Yes sir," she replied. She retrieved the key from Thomas's desk top and locked the door.

"Can we have a moment of your time?" Rachel asked the office manager.

She looked at Burbank, who nodded. "Sure," she agreed.

Stan followed directly behind Marla, and Rachel brought up the rear. They entered another office that was distinctly more feminine, with flowers and plants strategically placed. The furniture was more austere, definitely not as posh as the senior partner's. Also, Rachel noted, no panoramic view.

"What can I help you with?" Marla asked as she sat behind her desk.

"We need a copy of the expense report from Mr. Loftin's trip to Seattle that coincides with the July twenty-fifth date," Rachel requested.

"May I ask why?" she said as she typed in some commands on her computer keyboard.

"We need to know the rental car agency Mr. Loftin used so we can ascertain the type of vehicle he was driving," Stan interjected.

"I'll provide you with a copy, but I can tell you Mr. Loftin always used Avis and he always rented a BMW 520i," she replied. As she typed in a few more commands, her laser printer whirred to life and produced the documents within a few seconds. "Here it is."

Rachel wished her secretary was that efficient. She took the papers from Marla and studied them. Without looking up, she asked, "Did you ever notice anything odd in Mr. Loftin's expense reports?"

The office manager shook her head. "Mr. Loftin has always acted professional around me and his expense reports were thorough and detailed." She paused. "I don't mean to be contrary, but I think you have the wrong guy."

"We'll see," Rachel smiled. "Thank you for your help, Marla, and if you think of anything else that might be helpful, please don't hesitate to call me." She handed her a business card and they left.

Stan was quiet until they were back in the car. He turned to Rachel and asked her what Burbank had said to her. She told him the attorney just wanted more information before deciding what to do about Loftin and repeated the list of evidence she had disclosed.

"You're kinda sneaky sometimes, Agent Gray," he smiled broadly. His face turned more serious. "Do you think this guy actually harmed the girl?" he asked.

Rachel pondered Stan's question for a few moments. She hadn't actually thought much about what Loftin might have done to Annatha. Her entire focus had been on finding the person on the other end of the calls to the girl's phone, which would logically lead her to what happened. However, she had failed to seriously entertain the last part of this equation up until now, and Stan's point was valid.

She let out a long sigh and shrugged. "I don't know, Stan," she admitted. "Burbank seems to think he's a stand-up guy, but we've heard that before."

"Ain't that the truth," he agreed.

"I know one thing for sure," she continued, "Loftin knows more than he's telling us. He's gambling we don't find anything on his laptop."

"Like a little boy whistling in the dark," Stan offered as he pulled into traffic.

"Exactly," she said, "but he doesn't know we're likely to get an ID on his rent car from Carlos at the Park & Fly. I'm saving that bit of information for this afternoon if he continues to stonewall us."

"You're a tough bird, Rachel," Stan shook his head. "Hope I never get on your bad side." He produced his cell phone and informed the listener to have a U.S. attorney available when they arrived so they could obtain their search warrants and get to work.

"You've always been on my bad side, you dork," she smiled, then began making notes of the interview with Burbank and Loftin. It was very likely the search warrants for the attorney's electronic devices would uncover his online trysts with Annatha, destroying his assertion the cell phone calls were not from him but some mysterious thief. Then they could really put the squeeze on this guy.

****

Thomas entered the semicircular drive in front of his five thousand square foot antique brick home on Sixth Avenue, an upscale Denver neighborhood. He had worked hard for the money to pay for it, and Laurel had done a superb job of accessorizing the interior. It was their dream house, but right now Thomas felt like he was in the middle of a nightmare. He stopped his silver BMW roadster behind Laurel's burgundy Lexus station wagon parked in the drive. *Good,* he thought, *she's home.* Better to prepare his wife before the FBI arrived, as opposed to her driving up to a house with federal agents poking about inside. A story had been brewing in his mind all the way home to explain his predicament in a way that would keep her from tossing him out on the street. Despite the fact his chosen career demanded he be very good at the art of persuasion, he knew this would be the most difficult test he had ever faced. It was no easy task trying to conjure something reasonable that explained what he was doing with a sixteen year old girl on a business trip, but he had hopes the explanation devised during the trip home would fly. He put his key in the deadbolt lock and opened one of the double entry doors and stepped inside. *Here goes,* he sighed.

Thomas called his wife's name and she appeared soon after at the top of their richly stained wood staircase that curved gracefully up to the second floor.

"Thomas," she sounded surprised and her voice echoed in the large foyer. "What are you doing home so early? Is anything wrong?"

"I'm coming up," he replied. "We need to talk."

When he reached the top of the stairs, he noticed his wife looked pale. It was hard to tell if she was pregnancy sick or worried by his unannounced early arrival. Thomas kissed her on the forehead and took her hand, then led her to a sitting area that opened off their bedroom. He sat down on the lavender floral French country style loveseat, still grasping her hand, and she followed suit. Gazing directly into her eyes, he could see the total look of bewilderment at his strange behavior. It was time to start.

"Laurel," he began, "the FBI came to the firm today as part of a missing girl investigation." There was a barely perceptible gasp from his wife and he quickly continued. "Her cell phone records showed my number as a received call and her number was on my phone records, too."

Laurel let go of his hand and inched away from him. Her face had gone from pale to ashen in an instant. Thomas let the disturbing information settle and made no attempt to take her hand again.

"I know it sounds bad, honey, but let me explain," he pleaded. His wife nodded numbly, so he pressed on. Thomas described being bored and surfing online chat rooms to pass the time. A young girl instant messaged him and asked if he was an attorney since his chat ID was *legaltenderguy*. When he replied yes, she told him she was pregnant and wanted to know what her rights were regarding the father. He felt sorry for her because she was scared. Her parents were Catholic and would never approve of an abortion, but she didn't want to be stuck with raising a baby at age sixteen. She was young and naïve and wanted to know if she could legally force the father to pay for an abortion, and asked if he would help her.

"She seemed so desperate, babe," he lied, "and I had a few hours before my flight, so I offered to loan her the money for the abortion. I know it was wrong, but for some reason I felt sorry for her."

"Altruism isn't your strong suit, Thomas," Laurel said icily. Her expression had changed from shock to skepticism.

"I know," he replied sheepishly, fully aware of her sarcasm, "but it gets worse. She talked me into meeting her at SeaTac airport and I drove her to an abortion clinic that was able to work her in for an appointment." He proceeded to tell her the clinic was in Olympia, a city seventy miles south of Seattle. Since he had to make his flight, he just dropped her off and gave her enough money for the abortion and a ride on an airport shuttle back to SeaTac.

"The FBI is sending a computer forensics team to the house within the hour," he continued. "They are going to take my computer. Since my number was on her cell phone the day she went missing, they suspect I had something to do with it." Thomas lifted Laurel's downcast chin and her skin felt moist. When she met his gaze, he could see the tears welled in her sorrowful brown eyes were streaming down her face.

"Laurel," he looked directly at her, "I swear that's the last time I ever saw her." He knew she was struggling with his story, but this was no time to waver. Even if the partially true tale wasn't convincing, he had to be.

At this point Laurel began to sob uncontrollably. Even in her anguish, she did not seek comfort in her husband's arms. Instead, she leaned forward and buried her head in her hands.

"Why is Mommy crying?" a tiny voice asked, and they both turned to see their three year old son Nicholas standing at the entrance to the small alcove. They realized her sobs had awakened him from a nap.

"Mommy's okay, baby," Laurel managed a weak smile and held out her arms. Nicholas ran over and jumped in her lap. She held him tightly and choked back the sobs as best she could. Swallowing hard, she looked at Thomas, her face wrought with pain.

"Why did you feel the need to go to a chat room?" she managed to control her crying long enough to get the question out. "Why didn't you call me and talk?"

Thomas shook his head. "I didn't want to bother you," he replied. "You have Nicholas to deal with and it was just a way to unwind and break the monotony of being alone." He knew she felt humiliated by his admission and wouldn't understand, but this was no time to act desperate. "It was only for a few minutes, then I would get bored and do something else."

Laurel placed Nicholas on the floor. "You go downstairs and watch TV," she ordered. "I'll be down to fix you a snack in a few minutes." The toddler seemed satisfied all was well and made a beeline out of their bedroom. She fixed a stern stare on her husband after Nicholas left.

"You better be telling me the truth, Thomas," she managed

through involuntary sobs, "and the truth is even difficult for me to accept. I don't know what the hell possessed you to take a total stranger to have an abortion and give her the money for it, but if I find out you had anything else to do with this child being pregnant, I won't be around for emotional support when you lose your job. In fact, I will file for divorce." As she finished, the sobbing jag returned with a vengeance.

Thomas slid over and took his distraught wife in his arms, squeezing her tightly. Her body stiffened in his grasp. *She's really pissed,* he thought grimly.

Laurel found no solace in her husband's embrace. She frantically worked his story over in her head and tried very hard to believe he had nothing to do with the girl's baby or disappearance. They had been together many years and she felt like she knew the man she married inside and out. It was difficult to imagine he would harm anyone, yet the fact he admitted to meeting a sixteen year old girl, regardless of the reason, seemed very suspicious. The FBI's involvement was even more disturbing, but at least she would know if he was being truthful after their investigation. Despite her need to trust her husband, she didn't want to be blindsided. She felt emotional walls forming all around her in a defensive reaction, to distance herself from Thomas in case he had been involved in something more than he was telling her. It just seemed so incongruous to her he would reach out and help this girl. A girl he met online! Maybe she was missing something here. She was confused, humiliated, pissed off and scared for her future all at the same time. It was overwhelming.

Thomas released his wife and stood up. He wanted to appear confident yet sympathetic.

"I know this is hard for you," he said softly, "but once they clear me from this nightmare, I swear I'll make it up to you." Unable to tolerate the intensity of this toxic atmosphere any further, he excused himself and went downstairs to have some scotch.

Laurel was relieved when he left. She was fighting the urge

to pound on Thomas with her fists. They both had a lot to lose if this ended badly. Before this thought invited another rush of tears, she stifled a sob, wiped her eyes with both hands, and resolved to prepare her son's snack to keep busy. It was a dead certainty her life would be in turmoil until this crisis was resolved one way or another.

****

Rachel was sifting through her notes. She sat at a long, hard-top table with metal legs in the interview room at the FBI field office in Denver. The CART team had procured Loftin's laptop and home computer. Currently, their lead tech was diligently working on extracting data. She hoped they had something soon that would supply her with even more ammunition when the attorney arrived for their meeting. One of the agents told her Loftin had a 20 inch monitor at home with a souped up graphics card in his PC that indicated he was an avid gamer in his off time.

Ten minutes before the scheduled interview with Loftin, she called Mazy's dad from Stan's desk to update him on yet another change in plans. He reassured her that he never minded spending more time with their daughter and not to worry. Expressing her gratitude, she informed her ex-husband, Phil, an important meeting was about to start and that she would call Mazy later that night. He kidded her that it wasn't fair she was off skiing in Colorado while he had to deal with the unrelenting Seattle rainfall. Rachel had just laughed, told him to quit whining and hung up.

They remained tentative friends only because she had chosen not to torture Phil for his marital infidelities. No small task, but she did it for their daughter's sake. It served no purpose to shoot her ex in the face with a blow torch like she dreamed of doing in weaker moments. *That's weird,* she frowned. It had been some time since she entertained vengeful thoughts towards Phil. *It had to be this case and that snake Loftin lying out his ass about doing a sixteen year old girl behind his wife's back.* The memories of her personal betrayal, though distant as a thunderstorm on the horizon, still possessed the energy to move in and cause destruction.

The door to the interview room opened and Rachel mentally reeled in her emotions before she looked up to see who it was. Stan, Loftin and she presumed Loftin's attorney entered. She had asked the assistant U.S. Attorney to stand by but she didn't need him for the questioning. He had gratefully accepted her suggestion since he had a mound of paperwork on his desk to deal with.

"Foster Davis," the unidentified party introduced himself and extended his hand. He was rotund and looked to be in his late fifties, with a clean-shaven head and sharp green eyes. His navy blue Armani suit reflected he was also very successful.

Rachel returned his handshake. "Special Agent Rachel Gray," she said. "Please sit down."

"Before we start," Davis announced, "I want it to go on the record that my client is here of his own free will and wants to cooperate fully in this matter."

"So noted," Rachel responded.

Thomas didn't shake the agent's hand. His were clammy. As time had gone by he found himself becoming more unnerved at this whole situation. The talk with Laurel had gone badly; he could see the suspicion in her eyes lurking behind the obvious devastation. Even if he cleared away the myriad of potential sink holes for him in this muddied field of consequences, it became obvious his main focus had to be the successful removal of himself as a suspect in Annatha's disappearance. This singular truth provided a tiny sliver of dry land that would save him from being drowned by criminal charges, but it was insufficient refuge to prevent his life from being washed away if the other misdeeds were uncovered on his laptop. Divulging any one of them on purpose would have to be forced on him by solid evidence. His career and marriage were on the line--in other words, everything.

Rachel arranged the documents in front of her. She asked

Davis if his client agreed to be videotaped. He looked at Loftin, who nodded his approval. Stan excused himself and left. He was an excellent interviewer but Rachel had asked him not to be present as she felt Loftin might feel cockier with only a woman for an adversary. This attitude could prove to be a liability for the sexist attorney; besides, Stan was an intimidating figure and this factor worked better with less educated suspects. She told him she would call him if she needed a "closer." He had just laughed and raised his middle finger in a mock salute.

Just as she began to ask her first question, Stan reappeared at the door and motioned for her to come outside. "Stop the video," she ordered. She closed her laptop and briefcase, excused herself then left the room. Stan was waiting in the hallway with a gangly young man in his twenties. He had a thick folder cradled under his right arm.

"This is Stu," Stan introduced them. "He's the CART agent who has been working on Loftin's laptop data." He nodded for the eager techy to begin.

"The Logicube 5000 sees all," Stu declared confidently and opened the folder. "After we transferred the data from Loftin's laptop, we did a word search for chat rooms and hit the mother lode." Rifling through the pages, he pulled out several in the middle that were earmarked. "There are tons of entries that look like chat handles to me," he nodded at the documents. "We don't have any of the text fleshed out yet, but I thought you might recognize some of these. I highlighted the ones that appear to be chat ID's for you."

Rachel took the pages from Stu and focused on the highlighted words. *Bingo,* she smiled grimly*, there it was, sassybrat18, the ID Annatha used.*

"Do you have any dates for these entries?" she asked.

Stu shook his head. "Not confirmed, but we should have more by tomorrow. By the way," he continued, "your guy looks like he goes by the handle *legaltenderguy.*"

"We know," she said. "Good work, Stu; keep in touch."

"Will do," he agreed.

"If Annatha's chat ID is still on the laptop, the text will be too," Rachel told Stan. "This means he's lying his ass off, just like we thought."

"Sic 'em," Stan grinned and their fists touched like baseball players greeting a home run hitter at the plate.

Rachel reentered the room. As she walked back to her chair, she noticed the table top was moist where Loftin was sitting. It was satisfying to see the arrogant prick was nervous. She took her seat and opened the briefcase again, placing the pages Stu gave her beside it. Next, she motioned for the video to restart.

"Before I ask any questions," she began and looked directly at Loftin, "I want to save you any embarrassment by letting you know why we are so interested in you regarding the disappearance of Annatha Wolcott."

Rachel didn't need to look at her notes. She launched into an itemized list of evidence that linked Loftin to the girl. First, there were his cell phone records at a date and time they believed it to be in his possession despite his claims it was stolen. The same day the girl disappeared, he was on a business trip and staying at a hotel near SeaTac airport, only blocks from the Park & Fly where Annatha's abandoned car was discovered. A parking attendant at the lot saw the girl get into a car. His description of that car was consistent with a BMW 520i, the same vehicle Loftin had rented for his trip.

"Finally, this is some preliminary data from your laptop," she waved the pages Stu had supplied her in the air and then dropped them somewhat dramatically on the table. "And the chat ID Annatha Wolcott used, *sassybrat18*, has been found more than once on your hard drive thus far. It's just a matter of time before the CART team elucidates the contents of any text messages to this ID." Rachel inserted the copies in her folder, slowly closed it and leaned forward, her eyes conveying only contempt for her suspect. "Now, you initially denied ever seeing Annatha when I asked you earlier today, but I would urge you to reconsider your answer and tell me everything you know about what happened with her that day because frankly, things don't look too good for you right now."

Thomas hung his head and pondered his next step. His last hope that the laptop would not sink him was gone. Everything else could be argued and deflected with lies, but not forensic evidence. Sure, it could be challenged but that would be a whole other mess in court, complete with the potential for even more shame and humiliation.

Davis read his client's facial expression and asked if they could have a moment alone. Thomas waved him off and looked at the agent with a mixture of defiance and resignation. He could no longer save himself from the firm or his wife finding out about his unseemly Internet activity. The story he told Laurel would be blown out of the water once the text messages were decoded, but he sure as shit didn't have anything to do with the girl outside of getting her pregnant and driving her to the abortion clinic. Still, he realized with bitter satisfaction, she wasn't there to refute any watered-down version he disclosed about their relationship.

Rachel waited patiently as the attorney struggled with his inner demons. She knew he was guilty, but to what extent wasn't clear as yet, and she suspected he would continue to lie, but it would be foolish for him to persist with the claim he had never met the girl.

Thomas took a deep breath. He grudgingly admitted to the agent he had lied because of the fallout it would have on his job and marriage. Yes, he had chatted with Annatha online and they had agreed to meet at his hotel. However, after he discovered her age, he didn't have sex with her. They only talked in the lobby for a few hours and then she left. A few weeks later she IM'd him again and asked to meet a second time. She said she was in some kind of trouble, so he agreed. They met at a Denny's near SeaTac and that's when she told him she was pregnant. The baby's father was denying ever having sex with her and she was scared to death how her parents would react if they found out. When he asked her why she contacted him, she told him she knew he was a lawyer and had money, so she wanted to ask for a loan to have an abortion. If she tried to get help from any other family members, they would tell her parents, so she had nowhere else to turn. He agreed to help her but insisted he drive her to the clinic to be sure that's what she was using the money for. They found an abortion clinic that could see her and he stopped at an ATM on the way to withdraw the money in cash.

Rachel jotted down a note to herself to check his cell phone records for a clinic number and confirm he withdrew cash from his bank account that day.

Thomas continued. He relayed that the only clinic able to see her that day was in Olympia. Annatha didn't want to have the abortion in Seattle on the off chance someone would see her, so they had tried Tacoma first but had no luck. He dropped her off at the clinic in Olympia and gave her enough cash for the abortion and to catch a shuttle back to the airport so she could retrieve her car from the Park & Fly where they left it.

Listening carefully, Rachel realized everything the attorney had told them was consistent with the evidence they currently had against him, and he was smart enough not to have it contradicted by the chat messages waiting to be fleshed out by the CART team. However, she believed the part about not having sex was bullshit. He was probably the father, which is why the girl asked him for help. Without Annatha, his story could not be disproven, and she knew he knew that, too.

"Do you recall the name of the clinic, Mr. Loftin?" she asked.

"No, I don't," he replied, "but I might recognize it if I saw it in a phone book. Or you can get the number from my cell phone records."

"You bet we will," she said evenly. "Now if you'll excuse me, I'll be right back." She took the printout of Loftin's cell phone records and exited the room. Stan was still waiting outside.

"He's admitted to seeing the girl, and says he drove her to an abortion clinic and it was the last time he saw her," she said. "I need you to bring me a laptop connected to the office wireless Internet so I can do a reverse lookup from his phone records to get the name of the abortion clinic."

"Okay sarge," Stan gave her a mock salute. "By the way, thought you might want to know there is a woman in our waiting room I'm pretty sure is Loftin's wife, because no one else has an appointment now."

"Get the laptop and I'll meet you back in the interview room," she ordered.

Rachel went directly to the waiting room. When she arrived, she saw a very attractive woman sitting in the corner with a look on her face that only belonged to women living in a hell thrust upon them by a wayward spouse. It had to be Loftin's wife. Why in the world he found it necessary to have sex with a teenage girl was beyond her; this woman was gorgeous. However, external appearances were no measure of a relationship, she reminded herself. She walked over to the woman and introduced herself.

"Mrs. Loftin?"

The woman acknowledged she was Loftin's wife with a mixture of bewilderment and anger.

"You're the one accusing my husband of a crime?" she demanded more so than questioned.

Rachel fought the urge to tell Loftin's wife what a sleazeball her husband was to avoid the inevitable blindside that was looming. *Best not get mixed up in that drama,* she warned herself.

"I'm Agent Gray and I'm truly sorry for the disruption in your life," she apologized, "but we have to investigate every lead in cases like this."

Laurel nodded weakly. "How strong a suspect is he?" she pleaded.

Rachel could almost feel the pain in the woman's eyes. "I don't know how much your husband has told you, but he had contact with the girl on the day she went missing, Mrs. Loftin. That's all I know at the present time."

She handed the attorney's wife her card. It was obvious she had been crying, as her eyes were puffy, red, and underscored by dark, crescent-shaped shadows from inner torment.

"Call me anytime if you need to talk," she said and excused herself.

Rachel returned to the interview room. Stan was typing in commands on the laptop. He turned the screen so she could see the display. It was a reverse lookup that revealed the clinic name from the phone number. She wrote down the business name, Olympia Women's Choice, along with the address and phone number from the screen.

"Mr. Loftin," she said after recording the information, "would you be willing to take a polygraph relating to the disappearance of Annatha Wolcott?"

Davis interjected. "I'd like a moment alone with my client." This time Loftin didn't object.

Rachel agreed and stopped the video before she and Stan left. Once outside, she gave Stan a summary of Loftin's remarks.

"He's lying about the sex," Stan declared. "I doubt he's going to take a polygraph since the only person who can refute his statement is missing."

"Agreed," Rachel nodded, "so we're going to have to get our hands on that rental car ASAP and sweep it for evidence."

Her cell phone ring tone sounded and Rachel answered it. Jim Dalton was on the other end from the Seattle field office and informed her they had impounded the rental car and it was on its way to the garage for a forensics team to examine. She thanked him and told him she'd be flying back tonight. The clinic in Olympia was of primary interest now, and she wanted to drive down tomorrow and see what she could find out.

After she hung up, the door opened and Foster Davis gestured for them to come back in. She told Stan he could accompany her and he performed an exaggerated, ceremonious bow. Once again, she found it necessary to plant her elbow in his side. After they were seated, Davis walked over to Loftin and placed a hand on his shoulder.

"My client is willing to take a polygraph that is limited to questions about Annatha Wolcott's disappearance or her current whereabouts," he announced. "You have presented no evidence that suggests foul play involving Mr. Loftin, which means you have no grounds to arrest him at this time. That's our offer, take it or leave it."

Stan glanced at his partner, who was staring intently at Loftin. She badly wanted to catch him lying about getting the girl pregnant. It was so obvious Annatha contacted him again because he *was* the father. However, his willingness to take the polygraph regarding his knowledge about the girl's current location could only mean he honestly didn't know where she was. And if that were true, she was still no closer to finding Annatha. But at least she'd rule out Loftin having any involvement in the girl's disappearance. This begged the question that if he didn't, who did?

"Agreed," she finally responded.

Stan told Davis he would call him tomorrow to arrange the polygraph at a convenient time for everyone. They followed Loftin and Davis down the hallway. Rachel wanted to see the interaction between the attorney and his wife.

Stan grabbed her arm. "You really think this guy can be caught lying on a polygraph?" he whispered.

"The table top where he was sitting was wet from his clammy hands," she replied softly. "If he's not being truthful, the test will know."

When they reached the waiting room, Loftin was walking towards his wife. She seemed relieved he wasn't handcuffed. He reached out his hand and she took it. They left the office without a word.

Stan turned to Rachel. "I think I just threw up in my mouth a little."

She managed a thin smile, but she knew all too well the hell Loftin's wife was about to endure. The emotions that accompanied a betrayal of marital trust were all too familiar, although she had admitted after intensive soul-searching it wasn't entirely Phil's fault. She kept long hours and brought work home with her. Because of her ambition, she didn't pay much attention to their relationship, so he had sought comfort and validation elsewhere. The dissolution of her family as a result of his affair was traumatic and it seemed like the fallout never ended, as holidays and birthdays were divided legally between the two of them. They tried to make things as normal as possible for Mazy, but they didn't live together anymore, and that made all the difference. Mrs. Loftin's hell would prove to be much worse. Her husband had chosen to have sex with a teenage girl, maybe girls, and the blow to her pride as well as the creepiness of it would be catastrophic.

Stan nudged her. "Don't you have a plane to catch?"

Shaken from her grim memories, Rachel mentally sealed the old wounds and replied. "Yes, let's get going."

On the drive to Denver International, she asked Stan to make sure he set up the polygraph sometime in the next few days. She wanted to find out once and for all if Loftin had any knowledge of Annatha's fate. Then she phoned Meredith to update her on the investigation. She assured her they were making progress but had no definitive answer as to her daughter's whereabouts yet. There was a faint sound of ice tinkling in the background while they were talking. Rachel recalled the girl's mother was drinking the night she came over for her interview. It wasn't unthinkable she might turn to some self-medication if Mazy went missing, she admitted.

"Do you think this attorney knows where Annatha is?" Meredith asked in a slurred voice.

Rachel told her the polygraph could be helpful, and they needed to examine the rental car with a forensics team before she would know the answer to that question. A stifled sob followed the last statement, and Rachel realized the thought of finding Annatha's blood or other evidence of her demise in the rental car probably frightened the woman. She quickly reassured Meredith they had no evidence that anything bad had happened to her daughter, and the possibility she simply ran away was still on the table. Before hanging up, she warned Meredith not to contact the attorney until after their investigation of him was complete. Not that it mattered; she was probably too drunk to remember his name anyway.

"That was the mom?" Stan asked after she hung up.

"Yep," she answered, "she's a spineless jellyfish of a mother, but that doesn't mean she's not sick with worry."

Stan pulled along the departing flights curbside drop off and put the car in park. "Keep in touch," he grinned. Rachel leaned over, kissed him on the cheek and opened the door.

"Get the polygraph, Jackson," she smiled, slung her carry-on over her shoulder and waved goodbye.

****

Meredith hung up and groped her way to the bar. Her eyes were blurred from crying, but she had to get another drink. Locating the martini shaker like a blind man would, she poured the rest of it in her glass by feel. She grabbed a cocktail napkin from the dispenser and wiped her eyes. *That was better*. Returning to the kitchen table, she sat down and sipped on her drink. The sense of grief she felt was overwhelming. First there had been the assumption Annatha had run off with the father of the baby after finding out she was pregnant. Now the FBI agent had informed her this lawyer was probably the father but didn't know where she was, and worse, he was the one who drove her to an abortion clinic in Olympia. It caused her heart to hurt as she imagined how scared her daughter must have been to resort to such drastic action instead of coming to her. She wondered why Annatha had not believed in her enough to know it didn't matter if Brandon reacted badly, she still would have helped her. Sure, he would have thrown a tantrum and said a lot of mean things, even threatened to kick Annatha out of their home, but after a few days, Meredith knew she could have reasoned with him enough to get his cooperation to pay for an abortion. Instead, Annatha had made the decision as a sixteen year old girl to avoid a catastrophic family scene and strike out on her own to deal with the problem.

Her mind wandered through an alcoholic fog. She dipped an olive in her martini and rolled it against her tongue. After all, she had to admit, the fact her daughter didn't confide in her was tragic but predictable. A harsh awareness burned through her inebriated haze and for the first time, she shouldered the blame for not insisting Brandon treat her daughter better. She chastised herself for viewing Annatha as a burden, blaming her for rifts that upset her relationship with Brandon. It was no secret that Annatha was willful and rebellious, qualities she inherited from her father, but after all, she was still a child trying to find her way.

Meredith knew she didn't have gumption, as her mother used to call it. The only time she ever stood up to Bill, Annatha's father, was when she had Brandon to fall back on. She had been so hopeful that getting her daughter away from a raging alcoholic dad would improve her life. Brandon seemed so good with his daughter Dee, she felt certain he and Annatha could forge a relationship if he invested only half the effort with her. Then Bill, that sonafabitch, got sober shortly after she left him. He became the father Annatha had always needed through working the steps of his AA program. This didn't sit well with Brandon, who reacted jealously to their close relationship and made it worse by cracking mean remarks about Annatha's dad in front of her. It was only because he felt hurt that he had not been allowed to assume the role of her father. Sure, it was immature and petty, but that was Brandon.

Once she realized Annatha was not going to come around and grow to love her new stepdad, Meredith focused on providing material things to counter the shabby treatment her daughter received. Unable to stand up to Brandon and fight for Annatha, she had decided to abdicate her role of providing their daughter with emotional support to Bill, who seemed capable after his recovery from alcoholism. It was a cowardly thing to do, but she had felt helpless and vulnerable. The standard of living Brandon provided her was intoxicating and she had no desire to strike out on her own at this late date. However, her patience with her husband's nasty behavior had worn very thin during the current ordeal. She knew her drinking had escalated exponentially, not only because Annatha was missing, but also because if she didn't, she might slap the shit out of Brandon after one of his biting remarks, and that would be that.

These ruminations fueled by martinis were magnifying her guilt and she didn't like it. Meredith downed the rest of her drink and got up to mix another batch. She was going to have to take a sleeping pill so she could knock herself out completely. The emotional pain she was feeling was intense and unwelcome. After pouring another glass, she decided to call Dee before she was too out of it and let her know what was going on. She felt driven to share the agent's news with someone who cared, and her husband, sprawled out on the couch watching TV, was definitely not that someone.

Meredith speed-dialed Dee's cell phone and after a few rings she answered. She managed to relay most of the information from Agent Gray, but it was not in a clear or cohesive fashion.

"When is the polygraph, Meredith?" Dee asked when she finished.

"I think Agent Gray said sometime in the next few days," she replied groggily. "She said she was going to question the employees at the abortion clinic in Olympia tomorrow."

Dee thanked Meredith for calling and hung up. *Good God,* she thought, *the woman's drunk again.* However, the news she provided her was hopeful, and it was vindication for her decision to contact the FBI. Also, it proved she had been right about the cell phone records. They had turned out to be the key. Her elation at being dead right about Annatha not being a runaway and the cell records was short-lived. The FBI had found the person who called Annatha on the day she disappeared, but they still didn't know where she was. It would have been better if she was shacked up with the lawyer somewhere, but that was not the case. This raised an ugly possibility. An attorney with an impeccable professional reputation and a family would have a substantial motive to get rid of his dirty secret rather than be discovered. She feared now more than ever something awful had happened to her stepsister. Tomorrow, she would phone Agent Gray and find out what, if any, information her drunken stepmother had omitted.

She tried to focus on the page in her International Marketing textbook, but the words were just jumbled symbols with no meaning. Her thoughts were elsewhere, wrapped around a mystery that was as yet unsolved: the fate of her stepsister.

****

Laurel was brushing her hair. Thomas was already in bed, reading the newspaper. She had noticed he was more like his old self after the meeting with the FBI. On the drive there, his brow was furrowed and he seemed sullen, preoccupied, but since they had returned home, he played with Nicholas and was extra sweet to her. Not that this dampened her suspicions, but if the FBI had a case against him, she felt like they would have arrested him today. Everything hinged on the polygraph Thomas told her he was going to take sometime soon. If he passed it, at least she knew he wasn't lying to her about only meeting the girl to take her for an abortion. He had reassured her he would probably be back at work within the week. "So you can resume chatting online during the trips out of town," she had responded sarcastically. He apologized profusely and promised it had only been a silly pastime and he would find other things to do. She repeated her invitation that he could always call her and he heartily agreed.

This was far from over, she frowned. Her feelings had been hurt, and her trust level was as thin as a spider web, since there was still the distinct possibility her husband wasn't being completely truthful. She would find out soon enough. *Jesus,* she cringed as she caught a glimpse of her face in the mirror, *when were these swollen eyes going to look normal again?*

Thomas watched Laurel over the top of the newspaper. He knew she was struggling with all the information that had been heaped on her today. Even though she was hurt and suspicious, he knew time would heal this wound after the FBI cleared him of having anything to do with the girl's disappearance. The text messages would be embarrassing, but Davis had told him no one needed to know anything other than the FBI's final determination. This would allow him to tell John and Laurel that he had been cleared and they would be none the wiser. The whole mess would be behind them soon and he could rebuild trust over time.

The one thing he had not considered yet was once he went back to work, would he continue playing his out of town games? It was something he very much enjoyed. There was the thrill of the hunt, followed by snaring his unwitting prey, and the final sexual act that completed his conquest. *All good stuff,* he sighed. If it was to continue, he would have to devise a foolproof security apparatus to protect him from ever being discovered again. Maybe a personal laptop he kept in a safety deposit box, that he only used during the trips out of town. He could hide it in his car and replace it the first chance he got after returning home. This would keep his business laptop clean of any incriminating data. He suddenly realized his mind had slipped back into his sexual obsession so effortlessly it surprised even him. It was time to switch gears. *First things first,* he resolved. He needed to focus all of his attention on getting his ass out of this sling.

"Are they going to find porn on your laptop, Thomas?" Laurel interrupted his thoughts. She had walked over to their bed from the bathroom without him noticing. Her hands were kneading moisturizer lotion into her soft skin.

"No honey," he reassured her. He knew he deserved that but

wanted to tell her to shut the fuck up and go to sleep. Instead, he said sweetly. "Look babe, I know you're pissed because I destroyed your faith in me, but you'll see, I'll be cleared in a few days and I swear I'll do everything in my power to earn your trust back."

"I hope so," she said grimly.

Laurel climbed into bed and pretended to read a magazine. Her stomach felt like a washing machine gyrating wildly on spin cycle with a missing leg. At the same time it protested the emptiness caused by a lack of food. She had not eaten anything since Thomas told her his cockamamie story, and the burning acid reflux punished her throat in defiance. *Why did this have to hurt so much?* The anger boiling inside her would surface from time to time and replace the pain with a trembling rage. It was maddening. Goddammit, she cursed silently, she was a CPA and had given all that up to raise his children. Not that she minded; it was a choice she had made of her own volition, but she would not be played a fool if this ended badly. Final judgment about her husband's integrity loomed ahead and she didn't want to be naïve, so she would maintain a skeptical heart to avoid being destroyed completely. The fact that she had another child on the way raised the stakes exponentially. However, she would wait and see how this played out, but the possibility of not continuing the pregnancy had already entered her mind. If infidelity was involved, Thomas would not be told about these thoughts, or if she decided to terminate it. She vowed to call Agent Gray next week and find out what the laptop data had revealed. Thomas couldn't be trusted to tell her what they discovered, of that she was certain.

Thomas wished he could read his wife's thoughts. She wasn't screaming and yelling at him. That would have been preferable to these quiet spells she repeatedly lapsed into. *What was she plotting? Don't be so paranoid*, he admonished himself, *she's probably just giving you the silent treatment. That's more her style anyway.* Besides, their family was very important to her and he felt she would decide in favor of keeping it together when all was said and done.

Laurel shut the magazine and closed her eyes. She couldn't concentrate, anyway. It was doubtful she would be able to sleep and she didn't know what to do to pass the time through the long night ahead. She wanted to know what secrets Thomas had not revealed to her yet. *Was it too much to ask to know the truth about the man she had been married to for seven years, the father of her son and as-yet unborn child? No matter,* she decided, *there was no use trying to guess his innermost thoughts.* The geeks who came that day and whisked his computer away would be able to open that window for her and she would learn once and for all what her husband's true colors were.

Chapter Sixteen

Twenty-three Weeks, One Day (23W1D)

Annatha lounged lazily in the recliner, scrolling through the on-screen satellite TV guide for something to watch while the sun lamp bathed her in its warm glow. However, her thoughts were elsewhere. This was December fourth, her dad's birthday. He would have been forty-seven. Last year he died a week after he celebrated his forty-sixth. It wasn't much of a celebration, since he was dying. She spent the last week of his life by her dad's side in his rented townhouse. He had arranged for hospice care because he told her he didn't want to die in a cold, sterile hospital room. Annatha shuddered at the memory of his skin that had turned a pasty, golden yellow color due to his terminal liver failure. When she looked into his sunken eyes, his pupils were stained yellow too, but more like the color of scrambled eggs. His breath reeked of a horrible odor, and he scratched at his body constantly. The hospice nurse had informed her it was due to a high concentration of the chemical in his blood that caused jaundice. What made it worse was he drifted in and out of dementia because his failed liver couldn't detoxify proteins in his body any longer. When he started hallucinating, the nurse would give him Lactulose, a drug that helped clear the toxins in his gut, but it caused him to have explosive diarrhea. Each time he soiled himself, the stench was so unbearable she had to retreat to the bathroom and vomit. It was a horrible way to die, and she cried often but always alone. She couldn't bear to have him see her like that, even if his mind wasn't clear.

Before he lost his mental faculties, they had been able to talk about her life and what she wanted. She told him her most important goal was to finish high school and get out of the house. He admonished her that life was lived one day at a time, because today was all one had, shitty or not. It was a concept he had learned in AA. He told her of the "when I's." Loosely translated, it was the axiom that "when I do this I'll be happy, or when I get that I'll be happy." Meanwhile, life just passed one by. Intellectually she understood the wisdom of it, but she didn't feel it in her soul the way he did.

Every single day she lived in that home with Brandon was hell. It wasn't that he went out of his way to bother her, but their dynamic was pathetic. When she arrived home from school she went straight to her room. Her mother was seldom around because she was off doing upper class housewife duties. After Brandon came home, she made a special point of staying holed up in her fortress until dinner time. They all ate together at Brandon's insistence. Why, she never knew, as it was like eating with corpses. He devoured his food quickly and quietly, only speaking if he had some biting criticism to hurl at her. If Dee happened to be visiting, he would converse with his daughter, but ignored everyone else. Her mother, whom she had shared many talkative mealtimes with before moving in with Brandon, always sat meekly like a deaf mute. After the thrilling dinner experience, she retreated again to her room and only surfaced to get a snack or something to drink. She had her own TV, laptop, cell phone and stereo so she was pretty self-sufficient. Sure, she had a comfortable living and lots of toys to amuse her, but she might as well have had rocks for parents. On second thought, she viewed Brandon more like a junkyard dog. He guarded everything outside her room when she was home, and if she came out for something, he barked at her like she was trespassing.

Annatha half expected to cry at the thought of facing her dad's first birthday since his death, but that had not happened. She had noticed herself become increasingly numb to emotions since the abduction. It was the result of a gradual desensitizing program she had embarked on to help deal with the forced captivity. The only events in her current situation that broke through this hard shell were Taz and when she felt the baby move. Despite the fact she knew it was futile to have any part of her vested in the unborn child, when he moved it was impossible not to react. The nurse could chastise her all she wanted for planning to abort her child, but once she felt him stir inside her and saw his life on the sonogram display, she had never felt more bonded to another human being in her life. Sure, she had made that stupid attempt to end the pregnancy by leaping off the stairway in a moment of rage, but it was clumsily conceived out of desperation. All she wanted now was for her son to be born healthy. Knowing he would be taken from her, she still managed to tender this unselfish wish.

If her dad was still alive, it wouldn't have changed her decision to have an abortion, but she would have gone to him with the problem. *Wait a minute,* she stopped herself. Would she really have gone to him with such a shameful secret? No matter how close she felt to him, would she have been willing to admit she "did it" with an older guy she met online? She recalled since her dad got sober, he had been more accepting and seemed more serene, too. Despite the humiliation she would have suffered by revealing her impulsive actions to him, it was very likely she would have eventually told him. And any judgments would have been cast aside so he could assist her in the process of making a decision, her decision. In this fantasy scenario, everything would have been different. He would have driven her to the abortion clinic and kept the information from her mom and Brandon. Then she would never have had to deal with this psycho nurse.

It always galled her to remember how vulnerable and naïve she had been the day she presented to have an abortion, and Wendy had recognized it immediately. Annatha felt her fists clench tightly, and she looked down to see they had blanched a pale white color. She never liked being taken advantage of, but she had fallen right into Wendy's trap, and she hated the weakness that caused her to be caught off guard. She stopped herself short of further recriminations. *Get your own foot off your own neck, Annatha,* she chided herself. It was something her dad always told her. He said people were often their own worst critics. His favorite expression was that we were all spiritual beings in a human condition, so we shouldn't be surprised when we acted like flawed humans.

Despite his spiritual beliefs, her dad steered clear of any religions. He had been raised Catholic, and often said he was also a recovering Catholic. One of his favorite sayings was that religious people sought spirituality to stay out of hell, and alcoholics sought spirituality because they had been there. Annatha had thought of that phrase often as she watched her dad's illness put him through a living hell. She knew he was referring to the hell alcoholics go through with their disease and its effect on their lives, but his liver failure had tormented him with a hell she had never witnessed before. Her strong, intelligent, vibrant father had been reduced to a weakened, demented shell of a man from the sickness that wracked his frail body. Even though she wanted more than anything for him to remain alive for her, she had felt a peaceful transformation engulf her after he died and his suffering was finally over.

Wendy couldn't hold a candle to her dad's spirituality with her psycho religious fervor. Her rationale for abducting Annatha and stealing her baby was ludicrous. Annatha had done a paper in school about the Spanish Inquisition, so she knew there was precedent for torturing and killing people in the name of God.

Since the fiasco on the day after Thanksgiving, the two had hardly spoken. She remained silent and withdrawn when the nurse was in the basement. Once she left, Annatha had developed a routine to combat the endless boredom. She found a fitness show on TV and exercised to it every morning at 9am. It was low impact aerobics, and she had read those were okay during pregnancy. Some of the routines called for her to lie on her stomach, so she skipped those. Her belly protruded so much now it would have been like lying on a volleyball, and she was pretty sure the baby would protest. The muscles in her arms and legs were sore the first week, as she had never done any formal exercise. However, she could feel the growing firmness in her calves and thighs. Her arms had more definition, too. She hadn't been in this good a shape since she was a child and rode her bicycle everywhere.

After the half hour of fitness, a yoga program came on. At first, she had just watched the different poses and listened to the narrator describe their meaning. Upon further reflection, she realized it would be beneficial for her and her unborn son to do something to manage the stress she was under. It was awkward at first, and Taz climbed on her while she was trying to hold a pose like she was one of those carpeted cat trees. However, with time she had learned many of the positions by heart and whenever she felt stressed, a few minutes of yoga would smooth things out. Her desire to be fit and stress-free so as to improve the chances of having a healthy baby was foreign to her. She seldom thought of anyone but herself. The only other person she recalled putting before her own selfish needs was her dad during the last week of his life.

Before he had gotten sober, she was pissed at her dad for not putting down the bottle because he loved *her* so much. It wasn't much different after he went through treatment, as she was jealous other people were better suited to help him stay sober. Her father had suggested in a commanding voice that she read *The Big Book* of Alcoholics Anonymous. She had grudgingly followed his firm request. Most of what she read seemed foreign to her, but she did understand after reading it that love, intelligence and horrible consequences had no effect on the practicing alcoholic. They suffered from a disease of the body and soul. Her father had urged her to attend Alateen meetings to learn about spirituality, but she always came up with excuses why she couldn't. It wasn't that she didn't believe in it, she had faith because she saw what a profound effect it had on her dad. She had more important things to do. *Yeah, right.*

Suddenly it occurred to her. "That's it," she said aloud, "faith." The exercise and yoga were helping her pass the time, but she still felt something was missing that could help her endure this ordeal. Her dad had used it to get through many rough situations and prayed daily until his mind no longer functioned. In fact, he had made her promise before he died that she would pray every day to be more tolerant of Brandon. He even had the nerve to suggest she pray for twelve days in a row for Brandon to be happy. She had told him she was incapable of doing it. He then suggested she pray for the willingness to pray twelve days for his happiness. It all sounded pretty convoluted to her and she had failed to fulfill her promise. Not out of disrespect; she just couldn't resist the urge to gouge out Brandon's eyes every time she saw him. Besides, she simply couldn't imagine how all the prayers in the world or a blessing from the pope had the power to remove the hatred she felt for her stepfather.

However, today her memory of her dad was so strong she could almost feel him in the basement with her. She longed to smell his aftershave lotion and hold him in her arms again. Since this wasn't possible, the least she could do was honor his memory and make an attempt to embark on her own spiritual quest. Right now she was in a pretty hopeless situation and was up for trying anything that might bring her some relief. She got out of the recliner and walked over to the bed. Hesitating, she looked over at Taz and said, "Here goes nothing, kitty."

Dropping to her knees, she folded her hands reverently on the comforter and raised her eyes towards the ceiling. She prayed silently, "God, whoever or whatever you are, please help me in my time of need." It was more a cry for help, but she hoped somewhere some being would hear it and reach out to help her. She vowed to repeat the prayer every day when she awoke, and at night before she went to sleep. Suddenly, the tears she had anticipated began to flow when she realized if there was some way her dad was watching, he would be pleased.

****

Wendy finished her final follow-up call of the day. She always performed this task last. The day after a procedure, she was charged with phoning patients to see how they were doing. An entry was then made in the electronic record to document the information. She shifted in her chair; the pregnancy tummy was bugging her and she needed to adjust her position. It was kind of annoying, but it was all part of the process. Next week she would add some more padding to match her supposed gestational age. The one thing she hadn't anticipated was the nursing pads she was forced to wear because her breasts had started to leak from the medication she was taking to stimulate breast milk production. She longed for the time when she would have this bonding experience with her son. Besides, if this were a natural pregnancy she would be facing the same if not more discomfort, and she just looked at it as a challenge from the Savior to test her resolve. She glanced at the computer screen clock; it was almost time to go home. Releasing a contented sigh, she typed in the data from the last phone call.

"Wendy," the receptionist's voice called over her intercom. The sudden interruption startled her.

"Yes," she answered abruptly. *It was too late to see another patient, what could that dimwit want?*

"An FBI agent is here and wants to speak to you about a missing girl who was seen at our clinic."

At first, she felt her mouth go dry and her heart sped up dramatically. She took a deep breath and struggled to compose herself. It was almost inevitable this would happen since she had seen someone drop the girl off, but so much time had gone by, she was caught off guard by the sudden intrusion into her well-laid plans. *Speaking of tests from the Savior,* she thought grimly.

"I'll be right there," she managed to respond calmly.

Rachel was sitting alone in the waiting room, jotting down some notes on a legal pad that sat atop her briefcase. She had already questioned the receptionist, who recognized Annatha from the photo, confirmed she was there on July twenty-fifth for an abortion consult, and witnessed her exit the clinic after the visit. She was unable to provide any further information about what happened after Annatha left the office, so Rachel had thanked her and asked to speak to the nurse Annatha saw. She looked up as the door leading to the back office opened and a tall, fairly attractive woman stuck her head out.

"I'm Wendy," she announced, "please come on back."

Rachel followed the nurse into her office. She noticed right away the woman was pregnant, and appeared to be only a few years younger than her. She also noted there was a window that overlooked the parking lot. After introducing herself, she sat down and the nurse followed suit.

Wendy turned her computer screen so the agent couldn't see it. "Sorry," she apologized, "HIPAA rules."

"No problem," she smiled.

First, the agent asked Wendy her vital statistics: full name, date of birth, home address and phone numbers. At first she hesitated, then apologized again for the privacy streak she possessed and rattled off the answers while Agent Gray wrote them down.

"So when are you due?" Rachel looked up after making her last entry.

"March," she smiled broadly. "I can't wait."

"I have a sixteen year old daughter and I can't remember anything about my pregnancy that didn't hurt," she joked to put the nurse at ease.

"This is my first," Wendy admitted, "and it took a lot of work and money to get this one. I couldn't be happier."

Rachel noticed the nurse wasn't wearing a ring. Maybe she took it off at work.

"Okay," she opened her briefcase, "let's get down to business. As your receptionist told you, I'm here investigating the disappearance of Annatha Wolcott, who was seen at this clinic the day she vanished into thin air." Rachel produced the photo she had and handed it to the nurse.

Wendy studied the picture. The girl wasn't smiling and she seemed younger in the photo. Also, her hair was a bit longer.

"Do you recognize her?" Rachel asked. As was her custom, she noted the reaction of the nurse to the photo, but couldn't see any change in her expression.

Wendy stared hard at the photo, wondering how she should respond. It didn't seem to matter either way, as it was months ago the girl was at the clinic.

"I don't know," she finally answered, "I see so many girls here." Then an idea occurred to her like a sudden inspiration from above.

"Wait a minute." She placed the photo on her desk and began typing in commands. Annatha's electronic record appeared on the screen. She feigned studying it intently, glancing back and forth between the display and the photo. After repeating the charade a few times she turned to the agent.

"I remember her now," she admitted.

"Why is that?" Rachel asked.

"Well," Wendy lied, "I recall her visit because she asked me when she could travel. I told her within forty-eight hours if she had an abortion procedure, but if she took misoprostol and mifepristone the bleeding could last between nine and sixteen days and it would be best for her not to travel until it was done."

"Excuse me," Rachel was confused, "but I'm not familiar with those medications."

"Those are drugs we use to induce abortions," she replied.

Rachel asked her to repeat them and provide their correct spelling. The nurse complied and she wrote them down.

"Sorry for the interruption," the agent smiled. "Please continue."

Wendy shrugged her off. "I asked her if she was going on vacation since she mentioned travel, and she told me she wasn't going back home. Her stepdad was cruel to her and her mother didn't care. She said she had some money and was planning to leave the state so they couldn't find her." The agent was writing furiously as she talked and she felt the divine brainstorm continue to flow. "When I asked her where she was going, the girl clammed up. I guess she thought I might tell her folks. Apparently she didn't know it was against the law for me to divulge any information she gave me."

"Did she make another appointment?" Rachel inquired. If she had, that would be a significant bit of information.

Wendy wondered why the agent didn't check on this with the receptionist. However, she would suggest it before the agent left. "Annatha decided to take the medications that induce abortion. Here," she swung the screen around so the agent could view it. "I guess it's all right for me to show you this."

Rachel leaned forward and saw the cursor underneath the entry that both medications were dispensed on July twenty-fifth at 4:52 pm. Still, the nurse had not answered the question.

"And here," Wendy continued as if she read the agent's mind, "you can see I recommended a follow-up appointment in four weeks. If she didn't make one I wouldn't know because that's done at the front desk. You can ask our receptionist if there is a record of it before you leave." She had made sure to cover all her bases after Annatha's appointment for just such an occasion. *Thank God for that.*

"Okay," Rachel glanced at her notes. "Our investigation has located the man who drove Annatha here the day of her abortion. He claims that he didn't stay for her appointment and it was the last time he saw her."

Wendy nodded. "She was alone."

"So you confirm the receptionist's statement," Rachel said aloud as she noted it. "Actually, it surprised me your receptionist recognized Annatha's photo, but she told me she has a knack for faces and also recalled she was your last appointment of the day."

"It's in the computer, too," Wendy smiled thinly. *A dimwit with a photographic memory,* she thought, *lovely.*

Rachel pointed at the window overlooking the parking lot. "You have a good view of who comes and goes," she observed. "Did you see Annatha arrive with anyone or leave the clinic?"

"I keep my blinds closed until my last patient leaves," Wendy replied, "for privacy reasons."

Makes sense, but the girl was her last patient, Rachel thought. "Were they open after she left your office?"

"Sorry, I don't look out much because I'm charting my phone calls," Wendy stonewalled her, "so I didn't see her leave."

"No need to apologize," Rachel smiled. "Now, is there anything else you remember, anything at all, even if it doesn't seem pertinent?"

Wendy manufactured an expression of deep thought and glanced at the computer screen, as if studying her notes. After a minute, she shook her head no. "Sorry," she said, "nothing comes to mind."

"Let me ask you this," Rachel continued, "is it common for patients to disappear and their parents show up looking for them?"

"Very rare," Wendy answered. "In fact, this is the only case I'm aware of. I mean, I assume it's her parents who reported her missing."

"One more question," she noted, ignoring the nurse's self-correction and methodically leafing through her notes.

Wendy squirmed in her chair. The pregnancy tummy was digging into her pubic bone and her nipples felt chilled from the moisture caused by the discharge, despite wearing the nursing pads. This agent was very thorough, she thought, but overall she felt things were going well. Hopefully, this was the final question.

"Here it is," Rachel announced. "How far along was Annatha when you interviewed her?"

Wendy moved the cursor and clicked on the Summary tab. "She was about six weeks."

"So when would that make her due date?"

"It looks like March twenty-fourth," she replied.

Rachel stopped writing. She looked up at Wendy. *This was a weird coincidence.* "So she was due the same month as you?"

Her question caught Wendy off guard. How would she respond? *Just go with it,* she told herself, *you're doing fine so far.*

"I admit it was awkward for me to talk with a patient who wanted to terminate her pregnancy when she was the same number of weeks pregnant I was." This statement triggered another piece of information she could divulge that would solidify her credibility. "I'm pretty sure," she continued, "that's another reason I remembered her."

Rachel nodded. "Don't you run into that issue every day with your clients now that you're pregnant yourself?"

Darn it, Wendy fumed inside, *why is she getting so personal?* Maybe this was a tactic to size her up a bit more. "I look at it this way, Agent Gray," she responded evenly, "for some women, getting pregnant is a catastrophe. The joy of having a baby isn't shared by everyone. Some women don't have the option to carry a pregnancy and abortion is their only choice."

"So you believe in abortion, Wendy," she personalized her question, "just not for you?"

"I work here, don't I?" she replied icily.

Kinda touchy, Rachel thought, *but the observation wasn't really pertinent.* "Sorry," she apologized, "I guess I asked one too many questions."

Wendy forced a smile and waved off the apology. Rachel supplied her with a business card and thanked her for her time and cooperation. She asked her to call if Annatha showed up again, or if she thought of anything that slipped her mind today. Wendy agreed politely. They shook hands, and Rachel stood up and walked to the door.

"Agent Gray?" Wendy stopped her.

Rachel turned around. "Yes?"

"You have a sixteen year old daughter?"

She nodded.

"What would you do if she got pregnant?" The agent had saddled her with some tough questions, so she figured turnabout was fair play.

Rachel paused for a moment. "I'd take her to get an abortion," she answered thoughtfully.

"That easy?"

She studied the nurse's face for a second then replied. "Yes, that easy."

"Thanks for your candor," Wendy said and turned back to her computer keyboard. *Another heathen,* she gritted her teeth.

Kind of an odd duck, Rachel thought but shrugged it off. When she opened the door to the waiting room, her cell phone rang and she answered. It was Stan. After a good deal of wrangling, Loftin's polygraph had been scheduled for the following Monday. She knew better than to argue the point because she believed Stan had done everything in his legal power to get it done sooner. Her friend was dogged and persistent; she couldn't have done any better. A muffled curse escaped her lips after she hung up. Now she had to go the whole weekend before she knew if the investigation would focus entirely on Loftin. After speaking to the nurse, it seemed more likely her suspect was hiding something. Annatha had disclosed she was leaving the state. *Where would she have gotten the money? It had to be Loftin.* The importance of the polygraph had just been multiplied a thousand-fold. She was pretty sure the results of the test would be reliable if positive or negative, but it would be a nightmare if they were inconclusive.

She looked down at her legal pad and leafed through her

notes, trying to make sure she had written everything down. Only two employees at the clinic had interacted with Annatha. The information provided by the nurse sure seemed to indicate the girl was planning to leave town. The unanswered questions were where to and with whom? She had obtained Annatha's bank records and no money had been withdrawn. There was a CD with several thousand dollars in it that her dad left her in his will, but it was untouched since it couldn't be withdrawn until her eighteenth birthday. She might turn up something when Loftin's account records from the twenty-fifth were secured to confirm he had only withdrawn five hundred dollars. The medications couldn't be that expensive, but she would check with the receptionist to see what her bill had been. Annatha might have had enough money left over to secure transportation somewhere. She made a note to check the local bus and train passenger lists for the last week of July.

Lost in thought, she heard a woman clear her throat. The receptionist was standing at the entrance to the clinic.

"I need to lock up, ma'am," she said impatiently.

"Sorry," Rachel smiled, "I need you to look up a few more things, if you don't mind."

The girl sighed and went back to her station at the reception desk. She plopped down unceremoniously and glared at Rachel.

"Can you look up how much Annatha's bill was that day?" she ignored the receptionist's reaction. She was used to annoying people.

"I've already turned off my computer," she shrugged, as if that would relieve her from providing any further information.

"I'd appreciate it immensely if you would turn it back on for me; it will just take a few seconds."

"Whatever," she replied and pushed out her bottom lip, displaying the metal stud like an exclamation point for her pouting expression.

Rachel waited patiently, amused at the young woman's

immature behavior. She lied, too, as the computer wasn't turned off after all. It was just set on hibernation.

"I don't see any charges," she informed the agent.

"Why is that?"

"If a patient decides not to have an abortion, we usually don't charge for just talking to them about their options."

So Annatha would have the whole five hundred dollars to use for getting the hell out of Dodge, she determined.

"One more thing," Rachel knew her subject was fit to be tied at her persistence. "Do you show any return appointments for Annatha Wolcott?"

A click of the mouse was followed by a resounding, "No."

"Well, if she did make an appointment and didn't show up," Rachel continued, "would you delete it?"

"Not at this clinic. If a patient doesn't show up, we change their appointment type to DNKA."

"DNKA?"

"Did not keep appointment," she replied sarcastically, as if everyone knew the meaning of the acronym.

"So," Rachel was curious, "as far as you can tell, Annatha never made another appointment."

"Not with me."

"Well, who else would she have made it with?"

"Wendy."

Rachel was surprised. Didn't the nurse tell her she didn't make appointments?

"Is Wendy still here?"

She sighed and dialed the nurse's extension. No one answered.

"She's gone," she replied and raised a pierced eyebrow, as if daring her to ask another question.

Rachel thanked her and walked quickly to the building exit, hoping to catch the nurse before she left. It was raining hard and she pulled the raincoat hood over her head and sloshed through the puddles in the parking lot, turning her body back and forth to see past the blinders formed by the hood in order to locate the nurse. She had no luck. There was no sign of her and no cars were pulling out. *Guess she wanted to get home,* Rachel decided. Groping for the car door handle, she dove inside to get out of the downpour. She laid her briefcase on the passenger seat and shed the dripping wet hood.

Sitting for a moment while sheets of rain pounded against the car in waves caused by blistering gusts of wind, she tried to focus through the deafening roar from the storm beast attacking the earth around her. Even though it was difficult to hear herself think, the upside was the din drowned out any stray thoughts that might have distracted her. Nothing she gleaned from the interviews brought her any closer to finding the girl. Wendy Malloy's recounting of Annatha's plans to get the hell out of Dodge was one place to start, but it was another needle in a haystack, she sighed. However, there was one tiny contradiction that tugged at her curiosity like a dog pulling on her pant leg. She found it kind of odd the nurse told her she didn't make appointments when the receptionist said she did. The fact Annatha didn't make another appointment wasn't inconsistent with her plans to leave the state, but why did the nurse lead her to believe she could not have scheduled it? Even though it was a small incongruity, the devil was in the details and it needed to be pursued. She would call the nurse at the clinic tomorrow and find out why her statement and the receptionist's were at odds. No reason to bother her at home. *It was probably much ado about nothing anyway,* she thought as she started the car. She speed dialed home and told Mazy she was picking up Chinese food for dinner.

****

Wendy absently listened to the rhythmic sound of the windshield wipers as she drove home. She wasn't paying much attention to the road. Right now she was navigating on instinct. Her mind was miles away as the full gravity of what she was doing appeared at the clinic today in the form of Special Agent Rachel Gray. It was ironic the person the FBI agent was looking for so desperately was only inches away from her today. This realization thrilled her in a weird way. The female agent seemed very intent on finding Annatha, which made it all the more delicious she had deflected any suspicions of her involvement so handily, although why would there be any suspicions about her at all? She was simply a nurse at the clinic Annatha had visited the day she disappeared. All Agent Gray had discovered today was another dead end, thanks to her quick thinking and foolproof story. The hapless agent would have to get used to dead ends since she was never going to find the girl. Wendy had seen to that. The drive home passed quickly as she replayed the interview in her head; basking in how clueless Agent Gray had been about the involvement in her missing person case by the nurse sitting right in front of her.

Once inside, she began busying herself in the kitchen preparing dinner. She watched the news as the microwave heated up the food she had retrieved from the freezer where she stored her prepared meals. Even though the FBI was investigating the girl's disappearance, none of the news channels had anything about it. *Must be her parents' wish*, she conjectured.

She loaded Annatha's dinner tray and walked to the basement door. Peering through the peephole, she was satisfied the girl wasn't lying in wait. She unlocked the deadbolt, balancing the tray on her hip, and shoved the door open. As she walked down the stairs, she noticed the girl was watching TV, as usual, with the cat sitting on her lap. And as usual, she didn't turn around to acknowledge her. Wendy walked over, placed the food on the TV tray and stepped back, staring down at the girl.

Annatha felt her gaze and wondered why she didn't just leave like she usually did. Finally, when she realized she wasn't going anywhere, Annatha turned around and dropped her fork when she discovered an obvious protrusion from Wendy's abdomen. The nurse was wearing something under her clothes that made her look pregnant!

Wendy saw the girl glaring at her stomach and winced. She

had been so preoccupied about the encounter with Agent Gray, she had simply forgotten to remove the annoying device.

"Well," she quickly spoke to deflect the girl's curiosity with her pregnancy tummy, "you have parents who love you after all, child."

Annatha recoiled at the nurse referring to her as "child"; then realized she had used it in a statement about her parents. *What the hell was she talking about?* She refused to respond and instead waited quietly for her to explain.

"The FBI came by the clinic today," she said smugly, "so apparently you've been reported missing, although I must say they took their sweet time to do it."

Annatha looked up at Wendy, who towered over her, though not in a threatening way. More like a queen addressing a lowly subject. She stood triumphantly with her arms crossed, although she looked a little silly with the fake pregnancy getup.

"Did they say how they knew I came to your clinic?" she asked.

"They somehow found the guy who dropped you off," Wendy replied.

Annatha gasped audibly. Somehow they had located Thomas! Did they discover the chat IM's on her laptop? Wait, she remembered, he called her cell number and she called him back. They probably found her car where she left the cell phone and retrieved his number from it. She never asked Thomas if he was married, and understandably, he didn't say anything about having a family. However, if he did, he was probably going through hell right now. It dawned on her the FBI would consider him a suspect, since she disappeared the same day he drove her to the clinic. If he was married, it sure gave the FBI a motive for why he would want to get rid of her. She didn't feel sorry for him. He was a player, and if he had a wife, that made him an asshole, too. He deserved the wrath of God from his wife if he was married, but he didn't deserve to be a suspect in her disappearance. After all, he had given her the money and left her at the clinic, expecting the problem he caused would be resolved. All she wished for him was humiliation, not an arrest or a trial. That should be the fate of the psycho bitch standing over her with a stupid grin on her face wearing that ridiculous outfit.

"I told the FBI I haven't seen you since you left the clinic," Wendy interrupted her train of thought.

Annatha suddenly realized why the nurse had her duck down in the car. No one had seen her leave with Wendy! She groaned. Salvation had been so close today, but that was as close as it would get. There was absolutely no reason they would suspect her captor. She was too clever. It was as if someone had boarded up the well she was trapped in, unable to hear her screams before closing off any hope for escape.

Wendy knew she had dashed any dreams the girl had that an investigation would find her. It was time to try and cheer her up a little. "Look," she said soothingly, "I know you're pretty upset right now, but just think how happy you'll be when I call your parents and they come get you."

Annatha was seething. *How dare this bitch try to comfort me!* Despite the horrible news that the nurse had seen to it no investigative roads would lead to her, there was still something else going on. It was buried in the last statement the nurse made about making the "rescue" call after the baby was born. *Something stinks in the petunias,* she recalled her dad saying when he couldn't reconcile an issue. Then she suddenly realized the source of her consternation. Why was Wendy pretending to be pregnant with that ridiculous costume? If she was leaving the country after her baby was born, what would cause her to fake a pregnancy?

"Yeah," she said coldly, "that makes sense. You're going to free me after you leave the country, but for some reason you have to pretend you're pregnant around people who will never see you again."

She's a little too smart sometimes, Wendy grimaced. On the bright side, her son would inherit that sharp mind. However, she needed to come up with something that would convince the girl she had every intention of letting her go. If she didn't, the restraints might become a necessity. As in the past, inspiration was like a button, ready for her to press it and create a completely false but believable story.

"Okay, I didn't lie to you about setting you free," she admitted and faked exasperation, "but my situation has changed at work. A few weeks ago I found out my clinic has a short term disability policy that covers maternity leave. That allows me to collect a lot more money than just using sick and vacation time. So I decided to lie and tell them I'm pregnant. The padding is to make it look real. Besides, I can stay home now your last month and get paid for it." She allowed this to sink in, although she wasn't sure Annatha had any idea about disability or paid time off in a job situation.

"My new plan is to wait until two weeks after you deliver, take the baby up to the office and work for one day. That way I can qualify for my disability pay." The girl was staring at her, dumbfounded, so she decided to press on. "I know you're disappointed and so am I, but I need all the money I can get since I can't stay and sell my home if I'm out of the country."

Annatha was upset with the abrupt change in plans, but she also felt conflicted. She wanted so badly to believe the nurse was going to spare her life when this ordeal was over, but now she was changing the rules in the middle of the game. Could she be trusted? She didn't know enough about disability or sick leave and all that crap to know if what she was telling her was bullshit or not. It had been the small light at the end of a very long, dark tunnel to imagine finally getting out of this hell hole a week after she delivered her son, but now another seven days had been added on for a reason that didn't make any sense to her.

"Why two weeks?" she finally asked the nurse bitterly.

Wendy ignored the biting tone in the girl's question. "They won't expect me to be up and around after only a week. Two is more believable."

Annatha felt her blood boiling. She couldn't resist the urge to strike back at the nurse who basked in holding all the cards.

"You'll get Lucifer after he's born," she smiled sarcastically, "but he's mine every day until then."

Wendy gasped. "Why on earth are you calling my baby that name?"

"Exactly," she replied defiantly.

The nurse's eyes flashed angrily and her face flushed a crimson color. Annatha recoiled, as she had never seen her exhibit this level of rage before.

"Don't you ever use that name around me again," she shrieked.

She knew it was probably in her best interest to back off goading the nurse, but it wasn't in her nature to do so. Once she sunk the knife in a person she loathed, she couldn't resist the urge to twist it a few times just to see them squirm.

"I just figured since you're doing the devil's work," she continued, glaring at her captor, "it seemed like the most appropriate name to me."

Wendy's gaze hardened even more. When she spoke, her voice was more controlled, but unbridled rage boiled just beneath the surface.

"You need to consider very carefully how far you want to push me, girl," she threatened. "When you go into labor I have medication here that can ease your pain considerably." She stepped forward and pointed at Annatha menacingly. "You keep this bratty, immature crap up with me and you won't get a single drop of pain relief."

Wendy back-pedaled a few steps as she realized how close she was, and distracted by her rage. The girl's adrenaline was flowing and she might launch another attack. When a safe distance had been reestablished, she continued, "So the next time you think about hurting me, just remember how much I can let you hurt." She wheeled around and hurried out of the basement before she said something she would regret later.

Annatha felt only defiance coursing through her veins. That bitch had all the control, but she sure as hell wasn't going to censor her words. Threatening her with pain during labor was like throwing down a gauntlet. It only motivated her to read the chapter in the pregnancy book about natural means of relieving pain in labor. She recalled seeing something about a Lamaze method. This would be her mission in life over the next few months. She would learn how to Lamaze away the pain or whatever it was called, then the nurse wouldn't have anything to hold over her head. It was important to her that she maintain some semblance of independence, and she would take any steps to accomplish this. Wendy would just have to live with her rebelliousness and stinging remarks. She knew the nurse wouldn't do anything physical to hurt her for as long as she carried the baby.

Annatha grabbed Taz and calmed herself by stroking his thick fur. She willed her thoughts in a different direction and focused on how her mother might be coping. The fact the FBI was now involved meant her mom had notified them her daughter was missing. She cringed at how much grief she must be getting from Brandon. He probably raised hell when she contacted the FBI, since he would never have lifted a finger to find her. The resentful side of her wasn't sorry her mom was suffering. It served her right for not sticking up for her against Brandon. Now she was paying the price. However, what bothered her most about her mother was why it took so long to notify the police she had a missing child. It was a painful question to ask and almost smacked of abandonment and even though it wasn't technically true, it sure felt pretty close. She derailed her thoughts from the unpleasant emotional track this was leading down and willed herself to think of something else.

Another twist was that her abduction was certainly affecting more lives than her family now that Thomas was involved. It was useless to speculate on the degree to which this was messing with his life. Besides, his status was the least of her worries now. She had to accept the fact the FBI would never find her before the baby came. She was certain the nurse had acted appropriately clueless during her questioning today and most likely sent them on a wild goose chase. *Too bad people like Wendy didn't have "crazy bitch" tattooed on their forehead. It would certainly make the FBI's job easier.*

She despaired as her heart slowly sank beneath the surface of her dashed hopes. It seemed impossible she would be found in time to prevent Wendy from taking her baby. A nagging thought reared its ugly head that she might not be found at all.

Chapter Seventeen

Twenty-three Weeks, Five Days (23W5D)

Rachel glanced up when she heard a light knocking on her office door. It was Jim Dalton.

"Come on in," she waved at him and watched as he entered the room. He was a solid, stocky ex-Marine with wavy blonde hair and always wore a permanent furrow above the bridge of his wide nose. Intensity was a way of life for him. She liked Jim, but preferred limited contact to avoid getting sucked into his gung ho vortex.

The furrow deepened. "Got the forensics report from Loftin's rental car," he declared in a serious tone and laid a thick folder on the desk in front of Rachel.

"This looks like a lot of reading Jim," she sighed. "What's the bottom line?"

"Simply put, they found nothing that suggested foul play," he shook his head. "Most of it catalogs all the evidence they took out of it; seems it was vacuumed between rentals, but rather shabbily."

Bet Jim's car is so spotless it could qualify as a mobile surgical suite, Rachel mused. "So no blood or tissue?"

"Nope," he replied.

Rachel felt relieved. No one had scrubbed it clean, and if there was any blood or tissue the forensics team would likely have found it. At least this eliminated two possibilities. The first was that Annatha had been harmed outside the car then transported in it. The second was that she was attacked in the car and dropped somewhere else. This didn't completely rule out that Annatha had been the victim of foul play, but if she had, the rental car wasn't in the mix. She noticed Jim was still in the room.

"Anything else?" she raised an eyebrow.

The agent excused himself and left. Rachel was impatiently waiting for Stan's phone call about the polygraph. Now that it was Monday, the test should be completed soon. With a clean bill of health on the rental car, she didn't have any evidence to seek an arrest warrant for Loftin. If he flunked the polygraph she would move heaven and earth to find some physical evidence the lawyer was involved with Annatha's fate, whatever it was.

She swore under her breath and grabbed the stack of messages on her desk. No point twiddling her thumbs when she could get some things done. She saw the one on top was from Dee Reynolds, logged in Friday. Rachel glanced at her watch; it was 8:30am. Maybe she wasn't in class yet. She dialed the number on the message. After a few rings, Dee answered.

"It's Rachel Gray," she identified herself.

Dee asked her to hold on a sec, she was in a history lecture and wanted to go out in the hall.

"I can call back at a more convenient time, Dee," she said.

"No," she begged, "please don't hang up."

Rachel waited and Dee finally told her to go ahead.

"You called me, Dee," she replied.

"I'm an idiot," the girl apologized, "sorry about that. I called because I spoke to Meredith and it wasn't clear exactly what you told her, so I wanted to find out from you what's been going on."

Rachel repeated the same information she had given Meredith

last week. When she was finished she said. "I'm sorry, Dee, but I still don't have a clue where Annatha is."

"You think it's the lawyer though, right?" Dee asked excitedly. "I mean, he admitted to meeting Annatha and driving her to the abortion clinic. He has to be the one who got her pregnant. Wouldn't that make him a suspect in her disappearance?"

"Slow down, Dee," Rachel admonished her. "He's taking a polygraph this morning," she continued, "but at the request of his attorney, we can't ask if he got Annatha pregnant, only if he knows where she is."

Her secretary's voice sounded over the intercom to advise her Stan was on line two. Rachel told Dee she had to put her on hold and pressed line two. "It's me, Stan."

"He passed with flying colors Rach," he stated glumly. "Loftin had nothing to do with the girl's disappearance and he has no idea where she is, according to the polygraph results."

She thanked him and told him she was on the phone with Annatha's stepsister. He told her to call him back later and hung up. Rachel waited a few seconds to overcome the disappointment she felt at Stan's news before resuming her conversation with Dee. It seemed that once again, she had played the right cards but lost the hand.

"I'm back," she announced. She went on to tell Dee the phone call was from an agent in Denver. Loftin had passed the polygraph. The phone was silent for a few seconds before Dee responded.

"So where do you go from here?" she finally asked.

"I just received the news myself," Rachel offered, "so I have to go over everything again, but I'll keep in touch."

"Please find Annatha," Dee pleaded.

"I'm on it," she promised and hung up.

Rachel opened the folder that contained the RCFL (Regional Computer Forensics Lab) report from Denver. It contained all the Internet activity data from Loftin's office laptop and home PC that had been extracted using the Logicube 5000. Maybe there was something she missed. The home PC had been devoid of any online chat, but his business laptop was a different story. Using a printout listing Loftin's business travel for comparison, she had matched every instance of his online chatting from the laptop to dates he was out of town. The IP addresses were all hotel servers. *Smart attorney,* she thought, *in case he pissed some girl off who was a hacker or knew one, she couldn't track him to a specific room number to acquire his personal information and blackmail him.* In addition, his online profile was bogus, to cement his anonymity.

However, the text from his chatting was most unflattering. Loftin's modus operandi was to lure girls between the ages of sixteen and nineteen from the chat room into an instant message (IM) box. Each time, his victim had been complaining about parents or an ex-boyfriend in the chat room. Once he had them alone, he would be very empathetic and supportive of their plight. After gaining their trust by not hitting on them right away, he eventually suggested they meet for a drink in his hotel lobby. To Rachel's surprise and chagrin, over half of the girls agreed to his offer. Some of the time they drove themselves, but other times he paid for a cab to bring them. She wondered what percentage of his prey found themselves in his hotel room later. So far there had been no repeat correspondence between Loftin and a girl he met for drinks except Annatha. Maybe they were too embarrassed or more likely, he was too smart to shit in the same hole twice, which begged the question why he met Annatha a second time.

Her secretary's voice over the intercom interrupted again. "A Laurel Loftin is on line three for you."

Rachel cringed. She was holding information that if disclosed, would end the Loftins' marriage and badly. Well, she had instructed Mrs. Loftin she could call any time so it was her own fault. Taking a deep breath, she picked up the receiver and identified herself.

"Do you have the forensics report from my husband's laptop yet?" Laurel asked in a strained voice.

"I received it this morning," she replied.

Laurel asked her if she heard Thomas had passed the polygraph and Rachel admitted she had.

"Are they hard for people to beat?"

"The polygraph?"

"Yes."

"Yes, Mrs. Loftin," she replied, "they are hard to beat but it has been done. In your husband's case, the polygraph given to him was very limited at the insistence of his attorney."

"What do you mean?"

Rachel patiently explained the conditions imposed by Loftin and Foster Davis.

"So you didn't ask him about why he took the girl to an abortion clinic?" Laurel asked frantically.

"That wasn't part of the agreement," she explained.

There was a long pause at the other end of the line. Rachel wondered what was going through her mind. She fought the urge to tell the woman her husband was a philandering pervert and the best thing to do was leave his ass as soon as possible.

"Can I see the laptop report?" she finally asked. The tone of her voice was different now. It contained no emotion as if she was requesting a recipe.

Rachel explained that she could send the report regarding their home PC, but the laptop belonged to the firm, which meant the data obtained from it was their property, too, and Laurel would need permission to see it.

"Is it worth my time to look at the PC report?"

"That's up to you, Mrs. Loftin," she said.

"What about the laptop?"

Rachel purposely didn't answer right away, hoping she could read the meaning of her silence. Just when she was about to reply, Laurel interrupted.

"I have my answer," she stated flatly, "thank you for that."

"I didn't answer you," she protested.

Laurel ignored her and asked if she would fax a copy of the laptop report to Marla at the firm right away. Rachel agreed.

"I'll call you back with the number," she promised.

"I have it," Rachel replied. The line went dead. *You've done it now*, she thought. Loftin's wife was most likely putting on her war paint and preparing for battle.

****

Laurel sat at the kitchen island absently tapping the portable phone on the butcher block counter top. "That asshole!" she swore aloud. Thomas had been walking on air since he arrived home after passing the polygraph. She had felt relieved, too, and for the first time entertained the hope her husband had not impregnated a sixteen year old girl. However, she had decided to delay her half-hearted celebration until after she spoke with Agent Gray about the laptop data. Now she was informed the polygraph only focused on if Thomas knew where the missing girl was. He led her to believe they had confirmed the entire bullshit story he fed her. Apparently, he was of the opinion the law firm wasn't going to examine his laptop data, because he was meeting with John Burbank tomorrow to talk about when he could resume his work at the firm. Agent Gray's hesitation when asked about the advisability of her reading the report was an unspoken communication there was damaging information on it that didn't have to do with the missing girl. Thomas had taken their son to the movies, so she had some time before he returned home. Everything hinged on talking Marla into letting her see that report.

Last Christmas at the firm's office party, she had spent a good deal of time with the office manager. Marla seemed upset and when Laurel asked her why, she poured out her sorrows. She had suspected her husband of improper Internet activity so she loaded a key logger on their computer. When she read the email reports she found out he had been surfing porn sites regularly, and even more disturbing, had paid women to strip for him on cam. Never suspecting she would face anything so horrible, Laurel had comforted her and provided a willing shoulder for her to cry on.

She felt fairly certain if the report showed Thomas was engaged in seedy activity on the Internet, Marla would find some way to let her see it. Dialing the firm's number, she asked for Marla and was connected right away.

"Marla," she began, "it's Laurel."

"How are you holding up, honey?" she asked.

"Not too well," she admitted.

"Why? Thomas passed the polygraph," Marla said encouragingly.

Laurel explained the limited content of the polygraph and told her the FBI field office in Seattle was faxing a copy of the computer forensics report on Thomas's laptop to the firm.

"I don't know for sure, Marla," she continued, "the agent wouldn't tell me anything since the laptop belongs to the firm, but her manner seemed to communicate there was something weird on it I should know about."

"I'll look it over," she agreed, "and if there's anything you need to know, I'll tell you. I don't care what they do to me."

Marla's tone had changed drastically. She had been upbeat and sympathetic towards Thomas initially, but now she sounded like she was on a mission. Laurel knew then she had hit a nerve. If there was anything that smacked of her husband cheating on her, virtually or in real life, Marla would let her know. Satisfied she had accomplished her goal, she thanked the office manager and hung up.

****

Thomas pulled into the driveway. Nicholas was fast asleep in his car seat. The Disney movie had been boring, but his son had thoroughly enjoyed it. He was beginning to feel his life winding its way back to normalcy, although he had to admit there was still a lot of work to do on his relationship with Laurel. Climbing out of the roadster, he stood for a minute to watch the snow falling softly on his front lawn. There was a blanket of two to three inches already and no sign of letting up. He always enjoyed the peacefulness that accompanied a snowfall, as if a thick cloak had been draped around the earth to muffle any ambient sounds.

He gathered his sleeping son and walked carefully to the front door on the slippery sidewalk. The frozen precipitation climbed over the sides of his loafers and he winced as it turned into a frigid liquid on his socks. He stepped inside the towering entrance door and slammed it shut with his elbow. Stomping his feet on the foyer mat, he was surprised to see Laurel's mother step out of the living room. She was holding a small suitcase.

"Sophie," he said with a puzzled look, "what are you doing here?"

Nicholas was awake now and recognized his grandmother through sleepy eyes. He came to life and shrieked with delight, so Thomas deposited him on the floor. The toddler ran headlong to where she was standing and latched onto a leg.

His mother-in-law fixed a withering look at him, and Thomas didn't know how to react.

"Nicholas is spending the night with me," she informed him coldly. Changing her demeanor abruptly she took her grandson's hand. "You ready to go to grandma's house?" she asked sweetly.

The boy jumped up and down as they opened the front door and left. Thomas just stood there, bewildered at Sophie's sudden appearance and odd behavior. *What the hell was going on?* Then he had a hopeful thought. *Maybe Laurel had a celebration planned since he passed the polygraph and wanted them to be alone.* This possibility was quickly dashed when he saw Laurel appear at the top of the stairway and slowly walk down with a pained expression on her face. When she reached him, he could see her eyes were red and swollen from crying again. Immediately, his guts wrenched sideways and he felt unsteady.

"We need to talk," Laurel said evenly and went to the living room, where she sat down on their overstuffed, floral sofa. She turned on a lamp to provide some light and waited.

Thomas followed numbly and positioned himself next to her.

He gazed into her eyes that were now cold and distant. "What's wrong, honey?"

Laurel's voice was flat and devoid of any affection. She informed Thomas she phoned Agent Gray and was told of the polygraph rules that limited the questions he was asked. The agent wouldn't disclose any of the information in the report about the data from his laptop, but it was faxed to the firm. A friend, who would remain nameless, looked at the report and disclosed the pertinent items to her.

"I know about all the online chatting and IM's to girls, Thomas. Girls you lured to your hotel for drinks. I'm not stupid," she said bitterly, "I know you had sex with most of them if they were brazen enough to meet a man they just met online." Laurel took a deep breath to will her voice to remain calm and continued. "And I know all of this was done when you were supposedly on business trips."

Thomas felt like he was being grilled by a prosecutor laying out the evidence against him in a case that couldn't be won. His earlier elation after the polygraph was now replaced with utter and complete despair. He leaned forward and put his head in his hands and, for the first time since this whole mess started, felt tears of anger and sorrow welling in his eyes. He wanted to get his hands on the person at the firm who had broken company policy to disclose privileged information, but this thought was quickly replaced by the realization John Burbank, his boss, also had access to the laptop forensics report. Despite the fact he was cleared of any involvement in the girl's disappearance, he was guilty as hell of philandering with teenagers on company business trips. The meeting tomorrow with the firm's managing partner was supposed to be about his return to work, but now it would more than likely turn into a discussion about the terms of his resignation. Worse still was that Laurel had knowledge of everything now and there was no way he could dig himself out of this calamity. He had juggled all the aspects of this mess for days now and suddenly the carefully arranged props had come crashing down in a muddled frenzy. How could he have been so ignorant?

He looked up at Laurel through blurred eyes. "I'm sorry," he apologized weakly. "They meant nothing to me. I was lonely and just wanted companionship."

"Shut up!" she screamed and at the same time struggled to keep from crying again. "I gave up my career for our family, Thomas, and I spent many lonely nights while you were away on *business*. The only thing that got me through those nights was the fact I thought you were working hard for our future."

She paused and choked back a sob. It was important to finish the speech she had prepared after Marla had reluctantly disclosed the damaging information. "You have betrayed my trust in the worst possible way. And if fucking around on me wasn't bad enough, you had to pick teenage girls, Thomas. Teenage girls! I can never forgive you for that."

Thomas recoiled as he knew the next words that would come from her mouth. He wasn't disappointed.

"I want you out of this house and out of my life!" she demanded.

He pleaded with her to think about their son and unborn child.

Laurel fixed her gaze on the pathetic excuse for a husband next to her and said coldly, "I'm not having your baby, Thomas." She paused. "Maybe you can drive me to the abortion clinic and hope I disappear, too."

She started to get up but Thomas grabbed her arm. "I'll get help, Laurel," he pleaded, "don't do this."

"Stop it," she cried and wrestled out of his grasp. "I could never believe another word out of your mouth, and I choose not to be married to someone I can't trust." Laurel walked over to the wrought iron coat rack by the entry doors. "I'm going to my mother's for a few hours," she announced shrilly and donned her parka. "When I get back I want you out of here. You can arrange to get the rest of your things later." She grabbed her purse and left.

Thomas was devastated. It was painfully obvious Laurel no longer felt any semblance of love for him. His family was gone, including his unborn child. His job was gone, too. He had never felt so vulnerable or uncertain about what the future held for him.

****

Rachel hung up the phone after speaking to Meredith Reynolds. She had given her an update on the polygraph and rent car forensics. Meredith was grateful and relieved that nothing had been found in the car. She felt badly that she had to tell the girl's mother they were currently at a dead end. All of the leads had led nowhere in terms of locating her daughter. Meredith had pressed her to reveal her opinion on whether she thought Annatha was a runaway after all. She had begged off the question and told her she was keeping an open mind. The important thing to remember was that there was still no evidence of foul play. She didn't tell Meredith, but she considered the lack of evidence might be because the girl's body had not yet been discovered. Rachel hoped for her mother's sake that Annatha had run away, like she told the nurse at the clinic, and nothing bad had happened to her.

She again broached the subject of going public. Since they were currently stymied in their efforts to locate her daughter, it might prove helpful to broadcast her picture on television and put posters up around the clinic in case anyone had seen her. Meredith did not dismiss this option out of hand. She informed Rachel she didn't want Brandon to be blindsided while he was watching the news tonight. Meredith okayed her to go ahead with the preparations and she would call tomorrow and give her the green light. No press at our house, she warned her and Rachel agreed to withhold information about their names and where they lived.

She called her secretary and rattled off instructions for a press release and to prepare a photo for the major networks in Seattle. Satisfied this might open a door in an otherwise baffling case, she perused her legal pad to see what was next on the list. *Oh yeah,* she remembered when she saw her scribbled notes, *the nurse.*

Rachel dialed the clinic and asked to speak to Wendy Malloy. A few seconds later the nurse identified herself.

"It's Agent Gray, Wendy," she said.

Wendy balked. Why was the FBI agent calling her back? She shook off the feeling of dread quickly. "How can I help you?" she willed herself to ask pleasantly.

Rachel told her of the dilemma she had after speaking to the receptionist who told her Wendy did make return appointments. "I know it's a small matter," she apologized, "but I just wanted to clear it up."

That idiot, Wendy cursed silently. She felt certain yesterday after the interview she had totally deflected any interest in her regarding the missing girl. Now Summer had disclosed a piece of information that contradicted what she told the agent. It didn't make her guilty, but it suggested she was a liar.

"I don't understand," she finally managed through gritted teeth. "What does this have to do with your investigation?"

"I know," the agent replied, "it's a small matter, but I'm a stickler for clearing up any contradictions in statements I receive."

Wendy searched for a response that would satisfy the agent on the other end of the line. Inspiration had not failed her yet. Once again, her God shoveled a brilliant cover into her mind.

"I guess I misspoke," she apologized. "I do make some appointments, but I specifically told Annatha to make hers at the front." She paused and when there was no reply, continued, "The front receptionist doesn't know the method to my madness, but I rarely make a return appointment for patients who take medication for terminations."

"Why is that?" Rachel was curious.

"My notes are more detailed in those types of patients and I have to log the medications into our EMR system," she replied, "so I would delay the patient's visit if they had to wait for me to finish before making their return appointment."

"Makes sense," Rachel agreed. "Thank you again, Ms. Malloy."

"No problem."

Rachel hung up and recorded the nurse's response. That loose end was tied up now, she thought with satisfaction. She opened Annatha's file again and leafed through the documents. *Let's go over this one more time,* she resolved. *The clinic was the last place anyone saw or spoke to the girl. Thomas was off the hook after the polygraph as a suspect, but he was probably in the middle of a shit storm right now.* Following her line of reasoning a step further, she noted that the nurse was the last person to talk with Annatha, and she claimed she didn't have a clue where she was. The nurse was an unusual character in her opinion, but it didn't matter unless she was withholding information Annatha had given her about where she planned to go. Tapping her pen on the legal pad a few times, she tossed it down, leaned back in her chair and forcefully rubbed her eyes, as if somehow she could grind an idea through the orbital sockets into her gray matter. Was she missing something? Obviously she was, or she wouldn't be sitting there with an empty box of physical evidence.

It was time to go work out, she decided, this was getting her nowhere. She needed to let off some of the frustrating steam that was building inside her like a boiling teapot. Rachel grabbed her gym bag and headed for the office building exit. She hoped the TV spots and posters might beat the bushes enough for something to jump out because right now, all of the leads that had seemed so promising a week ago were as dry as the Sahara desert.

Chapter Eighteen

Twenty-six Weeks, One Day (26W1D)

The baby was getting bigger by the day it seemed, and the increase in size was accompanied by more intense kicks. Annatha liked to play a game with Taz now that involved her son, too. She would place the cat on her swollen tummy and watch his reaction when the baby kicked. At first he had flailed madly and scurried off under the bed, but after a week or so, he would crouch down and watch the undulation as if he was stalking prey in the wild. From time to time, Taz would swat at a wave of clothing pushed out by the baby. The cool thing was that her baby sensed a stimulus in reaction to his movement, and when the cat pummeled her tummy, he would react by using her insides as a punching bag, like he was fighting off an intruder.

It was only a week or so until Christmas and the basement was colder than usual. Her internal thermostat had been reset by the pregnancy, which kept her warmer than normal, but today was different. The Weather Channel said it was going to snow in Olympia, but she would never see it. She had clothed herself with two pairs of socks, doubled up on pants and shirts, then pulled on the same hoody she wore to the clinic. It was her only outerwear garment. Even though her tummy was padded pretty well by the extra clothing, Taz was still able to detect movement underneath the thick blanket of garments.

Wendy showed up with a small Christmas tree, and Annatha ignored her. She tossed some clean sheets on the bed and looked at the girl. It was annoying to always talk to the back of her head, but things actually went smoother when she was given the silent treatment.

"Do you want me to bring you some lights and decorations for the tree?" she asked.

Annatha didn't acknowledge her presence, but kept playing with Taz.

"Annatha," Wendy insisted.

She sighed dramatically. "I don't feel very festive given my situation," she answered, "so no, I don't want to decorate the stupid tree."

Wendy shrugged. "Suit yourself." She sat the tree down in a corner near the fridge and quietly left the basement.

The naked tree reminded Annatha of Dr. Seuss's *The Grinch Who Stole Christmas*, after the Grinch had removed all of the Who's Christmas tree decorations. It looked barren and forlorn standing all alone in the corner. *There's a good name for a new book,* she thought*, The Grinch Who Stole My Baby.* The basement door opened unexpectedly and she spun the recliner sideways. *What the hell does she want now?*

Wendy marched to the tree with a cardboard box in hand. She set it on the floor and began removing the pieces of a Nativity scene. After they were lined up neatly side by side, she knelt down and arranged them carefully.

"There," she stood up and admired her handiwork. "It doesn't matter if the tree is decorated. What's most important is that we remember *Christ*mas is about the birth of the *Christ* child." Satisfied she had made her point, Wendy exited the basement again.

Annatha was boiling. She was sick to death of the nurse's pompous religious sayings. Not to mention the way she cherry-picked which of the Ten Commandments she chose to obey. Never brought up in a formal church environment, Annatha couldn't recite the commandments by heart, but she knew there was language in them that forbade killing, stealing, and cheating. It would be a cold day in hell before she ever set foot in a church if people like Wendy attended. *What a fucking hypocrite.* Her fanaticism about abortion being akin to murder contradicted the fact she totally ignored the coveting your neighbor's goods part.

She had never even considered religious laws or the moral implications of abortion when she made her decision after discovering the pregnancy. Despite the raging political debates over the morality of abortion, she had never engaged in any discussions about it save for the one time she and Dee had talked about it briefly. Beyond that, she had no interest in it. There was something in her history book about *Roe vs. Wade* back in 1976, but that was long before she was born. The matter was closed as far as she was concerned. Every woman had the right to control what happened to her body. She didn't understand the objections of people who fought against legal abortion. It wasn't like there was a separate and distinct human being involved. At least that's what she believed before seeing and feeling her son move. Now it was a little more confusing. A growing dilemma challenged her previous concept of when a fetus should be considered a legal person. True, he was still more a part of her body than a separate being, but she viewed him as a distinct organism now after feeling his movements and viewing the ultrasound. It was completely foreign to her for such deep debates to wage inside, and her life prior to the pregnancy suddenly appeared shallow and meaningless.

Before the abduction, her world revolved around going to school, playing online games, chatting, listening to music and texting with the few friends she felt were worthy of her time. Nothing else mattered. When she looked at it from her current predicament, it all seemed very shallow. All she and her friends ever talked or texted about was boys, what girls they were dating, who was cheating on who, and the girls they classified as sluts because they slept around with anyone.

During her Emo days, there were depressing conversations with her melancholy clique about parents and how perverted they were to worship the almighty dollar, all the while playing songs in the background by *My Chemical Romance*. Her dad disapproved of the Emo culture and tried to explain how whiny she and her friends sounded. His point was that she was living in the problem, not the solution. At first she brushed off his disapproval, deciding he was a clueless adult who didn't understand their plight. Unfortunately, his words stuck in her head and over time she began to listen more closely to what her like-minded friends and their music were saying. In time, she grudgingly admitted her dad was right after all, they were whiny. Most of them had privileged lives, yet they chose to complain and be depressed rather than see the opportunities they had if they would just shut their mouths and open their eyes against the thick makeup heaped on them. Disillusioned, she gathered her sinister wardrobe in a bag and took it to Goodwill with her grateful mother. Afterwards, they went on a shopping spree and she replaced her midnight black attire with more preppy, colorful outfits.

Shedding her depressive ways, she focused again on school to make sure she passed all her courses. The non-Emo cliques didn't appeal to her either, so she pretty much kept to herself except for a few girls who seemed to fit the outcast role, too. There were guys who took an interest in her after she shifted to a more chic look, and even asked her out, but she thought high school boys were the most immature creatures on the face of the earth. Boys in general seemed to regress after the age of twelve. She recalled the one party at Sammamish Lake when she camped overnight with some friends. A group of jocks crashed their party with several bottles of liquor. Not one to avoid experimenting, she drank enough to puke and pass out, but not before one of the more aggressive soccer players had his way with her. The next morning she had felt only shame, but it had been replaced a few days later with anger. She was smart enough to go to Planned Parenthood and get tested for STD's and also asked for Plan B treatment along with a birth control pill prescription. Fortunately, the tests were negative. Brief consideration was given to contacting the police but humiliation and shame stopped her from coming forward with an accusation of rape.

In fact, she didn't tell anyone about it, but the "date rapist" found it necessary to spread it around the school. After that, she was taunted and ridiculed in the hallways, which caused her to withdraw even more into a protective emotional cocoon. It didn't ruin her life by any means. She knew it wasn't her fault, but the reaction of her classmates at school cemented her disgust with their shallowness and underlying cruel nature. They weren't worth her time or effort to strike back. Instead, she vowed to finish high school wrapped in a protective shell and get the hell away from them and Brandon.

It didn't matter what happened after this was accomplished, because she wasn't sure what she was going to do after graduation. If her dad was still alive, she was certain he would be pushing her to pursue a college degree. Assuming she survived this mess, she wondered if two years from now when she finished high school, the motivation to achieve something with her life would be there. Her mom never mentioned college or asked her what long term goals she had. She guessed her mother's secret to success was to marry a wealthy man. Not a lofty goal, but hey, it had worked for her. Money had never seduced her the way it did her mom, but then again, she wasn't on her own struggling to make ends meet. When she lived with her parents before the divorce, they had a modest home but didn't have unlimited income to buy her whatever she wanted. Still, she had everything she needed and more.

Brandon and her Mom were perfect examples that money didn't buy happiness. He was probably the catalyst that tossed her into the Emo pit because despite making a six figure income, he was unhappy and made it his mission in life to bring her down any chance he got. Her dad admonished her when she confided this fact to him that she was letting Brandon live rent-free in her head. This she could understand, but it escaped her how she could go about evicting him. The praying thing was her Dad's answer, and she had recently been attempting it daily with some relief, but no burning bush as yet. She realized sitting alone in her personal prison cell that living in the problem was the very thing that had landed her in this basement and she bore the responsibility for her actions.

Yet it had been so hard not to react when Brandon put her two precious cats to sleep, all over a stupid MySpace photo. She had never experienced that kind of blind rage before. It caused her to act out with no thought of what consequences she might face. All she could think of was to find something to do that would drive him up the wall. She planned to tell him about having sex with Thomas the next time he ragged on her. Despite the swift and severe rebuke that would surely have followed, the satisfaction at watching him go through a meltdown would have been worth it.

Annatha put Taz down and went to the fridge to get a snack of celery and carrots. She munched absently as she watched TV, pausing often to chase the bland food with a swig of water. Her eyes wandered over to the corner where Wendy had left the tree and Nativity scene. It looked so forlorn and desperate, an overwhelming rush of sadness coursed through her soul. She had never spent a Christmas without her mom around, and despite her faults, she always made it a special time for Annatha. Every December, they picked out a movie to watch each week from a list of their favorites: *Miracle On 34th Street, Scrooged,* and *Christmas Vacation.* When she was a little girl, the list had been much different, but more enchanting: *Rudolph the Red Nosed Reindeer, Frosty The Snowman, The Grinch Who Stole Christmas* and *The Little Drummer Boy.* They would park themselves on the sofa in their flannel pajamas, cover their legs with a warm wool blanket and pig out on caramel popcorn and the red and green peanut M&M's. Annatha wiped a tear from her eye. She wasn't usually a sentimental person, but she had never been in a situation where she wasn't at home for Christmas. It sucked to feel so much emptiness.

An advertisement on TV interrupted the holiday memories, causing her to sit bolt upright in the recliner while her son protested the sudden change in position. It was a beer commercial with a scantily clad blonde leaning against a sixty-eight Mustang convertible surrounded by swarthy males. "Cherry Blue," she suddenly exclaimed aloud. In her self-absorbed confinement, it had totally slipped her mind she was supposed to receive her Dad's precious Cherry Blue for Christmas. She spewed forth a litany of four letter words that reverberated in the sparsely furnished basement. The one possession willed to her that she most prized was her Dad's car and she wasn't going to be there to claim it. *That fucking sucks,* she swore under her breath. What else was this bitch going to take from her?

Despite the seething rage she felt, Annatha managed to consider what effect her disappearance was having on her Nana. After all, she was the one who was given the final say on when to bequeath the prized Mustang to her granddaughter. *Poor Nana,* she groaned. *First her son dies and then less than a year later her granddaughter goes missing.* She was a tough old broad, but everyone had their breaking point. For her sake more than anyone else, Annatha hoped she was ultimately set free so her grandmother wouldn't suffer another loss.

The frustration she felt was interrupted by a rather violent kick underneath the ribs on her right side. As if she couldn't feel any worse emotionally, this caused her to wonder what kind of Christmas holidays her son would experience. Wendy would more than likely brainwash him that Santa Claus was a pagan belief and they would spend the whole day on their knees in prayer. If she survived to see more Christmas holidays, Annatha knew she would always wonder about her baby and what he was doing that day. The feeling of loss this thought created, along with the disappointment over Cherry Blue, caused the dam to break and she began to sob softly while she squeezed Taz against her moist face.

****

Wendy poured herself a glass of red wine and padded over to the sofa. After she settled in, she pointed the remote at her TV and pressed the power button. It sprang to life and as usual was on the CBN (Christian Broadcasting Network) channel. She thought for a moment. It had been over a week since she watched the local network news reports. She was curious if there was anything about Annatha yet so she changed the channel to KOMO news in Seattle. Taking a sip of wine, she propped her feet up on the coffee table and wiggled her toes in the fur lined slippers.

A female reporter was standing outside a local mall prattling on about the merchants' complaint that this was a slow year due to the economy. Then she shifted to a warning by the mall security staff that theft was up and provided safety tips on keeping packages safe. She'd never had anything stolen from the church parking lot, Wendy mused. They should talk about that. The TV screen now showed the entire news team. The anchor woman was Asian and she announced the FBI had requested they broadcast a photograph of a missing girl who was last seen at the following address on July twenty-fifth. The clinic's address, an FBI contact number, and a photograph of Annatha replaced the anchor woman on the screen. It was the same picture Agent Ward had shown her at the clinic and "Annatha Wolcott" was displayed under the photo. The text information faded out and Annatha's photo was enlarged. Wendy sat her glass of wine down. She couldn't fight the knot that was forming in her stomach as she stared at the picture of the girl who was in her basement. Seeing an official newscast about something she was intimately involved in was unnerving. It had been her little secret until now. Sure, the FBI agent's visit let her know law enforcement had become involved, but the public announcement of Annatha's disappearance broadcast on a local TV network seemed to drive home the seriousness of her actions in a whole new way.

Wendy took a deep breath and picked up the Bible sitting on the end table next to her. It opened to Psalm 23 and she read it aloud. She always felt comfort from this passage and could feel its soothing effect almost immediately. The knot in her stomach mercifully faded. Replacing the Bible, she finished her glass of wine and got up to pour another one. The news had gone on to another topic when she returned so she switched off the TV. It was disturbing to her that she had felt fear at all. Her faith was supposed to banish all fears. She chided herself for the momentary lapse in devotion to her Maker. Her Lord and Savior would always be there for her. He would protect her and keep her and her new son safe. Satisfied her soul had been recharged, she took a sip of wine and got up to add another log to the woodstove. The dry timber crackled as the dancing flames lapped around it. She closed the door and adjusted the ventilation slightly to release more of the heated air.

When she returned to the sofa, she downed the last of her wine and basked in the warm sensation it left in her stomach. She wondered if there was any chance someone had seen Annatha get in her car at the clinic. The parking lot was empty of patients and the staff was still inside, but there were cars driving on the main road in front of the building. It wasn't likely a passing motorist would have seen her well enough in the blink of an eye to recognize the photo on TV. She felt secure that this attempt to find the girl would fail, too. The vessel that carried her unborn child was safely locked away in her basement. She would have her son and the girl would stay missing forever. God would see to that.

Chapter Nineteen

Thirty Weeks and One Day (30W1D)

Wendy guided her car into the spot she always managed to secure at the clinic parking lot. In front of her was a street light pole with a badly tattered poster holding on for dear life that displayed Annatha's picture and contact information. The hard Northwest winter rains and blustering winds had beaten it up pretty good. She found it was slowly dissolving a little more each day; it was as if the girl's chances of being found were falling apart with it. It had been a month since the TV news station had first broadcast Annatha's photo, and all had been quiet on the home front. No calls or visits from the FBI agent, which meant they had struck out trying to locate someone who had seen the girl, at least not getting into her car. If some crackpot had phoned in and given information she didn't care, since it wouldn't lead to her.

The short walk to the clinic entrance was becoming more difficult as Wendy added more gel to her pregnancy tummy. It wasn't like blowing up an inner tube with air. The gel was heavy and threw her weight forward, making it more difficult to walk upright, and her lower back felt it. When she didn't think anyone was watching, she braced her hand against her lumbar spine to provide some support and minimize the stress. She opened the back entrance to the clinic and headed for the break room to stow her rain jacket.

"My, aren't we showing," Traci called from an exam room she was stocking as Wendy walked down the hall. She just patted her tummy, smiled thinly and continued.

When she reached her desk, she shoved her purse in the back of the bottom drawer and turned on her computer display. She logged in to the EMR program and double clicked the schedule icon. Her daily appointments appeared and she perused them while she sipped on her Starbucks decaf latte. This morning she had two interviews, but it wasn't unusual to have a work-in or two. Later this afternoon, she would assist Dr. Garner with two surgical terminations and a patient who probably needed a D&C. Wendy had spoken with her yesterday. The woman was still bleeding two weeks after taking the abortion pills so she more than likely needed to have her uterus evacuated with a suction catheter.

Wendy was certain she would face no retribution for her part in the procedures come judgment day. Her only responsibility was monitoring the patient's blood pressure, pulse and oxygen saturation. She would be praised for her efforts to steer young women away from having an abortion. No sin was being committed by her. After all, her task was simply to ensure their physical state remained stable while they underwent the operation. Dr. Garner was the one who would be called to task when it came time to meet his Maker. Even though she abhorred the murderous procedures he performed, she grudgingly admired Dr. Garner's expertise. The patients felt almost nothing and it took him very little time to complete the abortion. Her one solace was that she would never meet this doctor in the afterlife. He was headed for a different place than her. It went without saying the patients would inevitably join their abortion doctor in the bowels of hell.

Summer announced over the intercom her first patient was ready. Wendy still held a grudge against the receptionist for contradicting her to Agent Gray, even though she had satisfied the agent it was a misunderstanding. She took a large sip from her coffee mug and waddled to the back office door. The patient's billing slip was removed from the smoke gray wall rack. She perused the form quickly, opened the door and announced the woman's first name to the waiting room. To her dismay a young woman who couldn't have been more than twenty stood up and began toting a toddler alongside her. She wore low-cut bell bottom jeans and a short tank top that exposed pasty white rolls of fat. Actually, it was an understatement to refer to the spectacle as toting; in fact, the exasperated mother was dragging the child, who was kicking and screaming, across the carpet. The other patients looked on with a mixture of annoyance and horror. Wendy hurried her into the hallway and shut the door.

"I'm sorry," she apologized firmly, "but I can't do a thorough interview if you have a disruptive child in the room." She expected her to argue that she could calm the child down. That was the usual response. Instead, she admitted the day care wouldn't take him because he was sick. When Wendy glanced down at the toddler's face, it was smeared with snot and his grimy face was flushed. *Good Lord,* she realized*, he has a fever! Great call,* she muttered under her breath*, bring your sick child to a gynecologist's office and infect everyone in the waiting room as well as the staff.*

"How far along are you?" she asked, stepping back a few steps.

"Two months, I think."

"I'm pregnant, ma'am," Wendy declared, "it's not safe for me to be around sick children. I'm sorry, but you'll have to reschedule.

The distraught patient nodded weakly. Wendy ushered her back to the waiting room and handed the billing slip to Summer through the checkout window. "Please reschedule her," she requested and pivoted to return to her office and get far away from the diseased child as quickly as possible. In her haste, Wendy failed to notice the little boy had broken loose from his mother's grasp and was standing right behind her. When she took her first step she felt her legs contact a small object and she attempted in vain to retreat. The momentum caused by the heavy gel pouches propelled her forward and desperate arms flailed as she hurtled towards the floor. She landed with a loud thud on the padding and air escaped from her lungs in one long whoosh. Gasping for breath, she groped at the gel pouch to make sure it was still in the right place. Fortunately, it hadn't moved an inch as far as she could tell. After a very long minute, her breathing normalized and she struggled to a sitting position. She knew better than to jump up right away, since she had just had the wind knocked out of her.

The young woman was apologizing profusely and the toddler was screaming like someone had just stomped on him. Wendy knew she hadn't hurt him because she landed on the floor. He was just frightened and probably worried he was in trouble. When she looked up to see if she could reach the edge of the counter at the checkout window to pull herself up, she was greeted by a horrified expression on Summer's face. Wendy knew the receptionist had just witnessed her fall full force on what she thought was a pregnant abdomen. It was time to get up. Grabbing the side of the counter, she hoisted herself up and waved off the patient's apology. Before she could stop the dismayed receptionist, she had darted past her and was heading down the hall towards one of the closed exam rooms. Within moments, Dr. Garner emerged with a worried look on his face, followed closely by Traci and Summer. Wendy quickly ducked into her office and began studying her computer screen as if nothing was wrong. *That didn't just happen,* she groaned.

Dr. Garner strode into her office, still looking very concerned.

"Are you all right, Wendy?" he asked.

"I'm fine," she smiled. "I broke my fall with my hands."

"That's not what I saw," Summer exclaimed from behind the doctor.

Traci emerged from behind Dr. Garner and Wendy instinctively placed her hands over the gel pouch. "The baby is moving and I don't feel any pain," she reassured them. "From your position, you couldn't see me break the fall," she corrected the receptionist.

"I'm not calling you a liar or nothing," Summer disagreed, "but it sounded like you hit your stomach pretty hard."

Dimwit, Wendy fumed. How many times was this idiot going to undermine what she was trying to accomplish?

"Wendy," Dr. Garner said firmly, "you will not return to this office until you go to L&D at St. Pete's and let them monitor you for four hours to be sure you didn't cause an abruption." When she protested, he held up his hand. "I want a doctor's release," he ordered, "is that clear?"

"I'll drive her, Dr. Garner," Traci offered.

"Very well," he agreed.

Wendy was in full panic mode now. If she went to L&D to be monitored, her charade would come to a bitter end. It could also induce someone, probably the dimwit, to notify the FBI agent that she was pretending to be pregnant. Faking a pregnancy would indicate she was capable of a huge lie, and she might be lying about other things. That's a stretch, she had to admit, but her frantic mind was whirling with paranoid thoughts. She turned her attention to how she was going to get out of this looming disaster. Her boss wasn't backing down. She shrugged, gathered her purse and followed Traci to her car.

They drove the few blocks to Providence St. Peter Hospital's Emergency Room entrance. Traci prattled incessantly about the complications from abdominal trauma and how this was the best thing to do. Wendy was silent until the car stopped.

"You go find a parking place while I check in," she said while exiting the car. Thankfully, Traci agreed and Wendy strode quickly through the entry doors. She knew the hospital pretty well and continued at a brisk walk down shiny linoleum corridors until she reached a side exit at the other end of the building. Fortunately, she spotted a security guard sitting in his car and she talked him into taking her back to the clinic, lying that her car had broken down. He could see she was pregnant and felt sorry for her. Within minutes, she was back at the clinic's parking lot. She thanked the guard and watched him as he turned onto the main road and headed back to the hospital. Quickly opening her car door, she slid inside, started the ignition and sped out of the parking lot. The relief she felt at dodging this particular bullet was beyond description. What initially seemed like an impossible situation had once again been swept away by her Savior. She whispered a prayer of thanks as she drove away and wondered how Traci was going to react. That would present another challenge to overcome. She had to concoct a story that would satisfy her coworkers and boss that a better option had occurred to her and she acted on it. Their acceptance of her explanation wasn't critical when she thought about it, because her narrow escape from being exposed as a fraud and kidnapper trumped everything else.

****

Traci walked into the admitting area and scanned the waiting room for her coworker. Wendy was nowhere to be seen. *They probably took her directly to L&D after she told them what happened,* she surmised. She walked over to the admitting desk and asked the clerk if a Wendy Malloy had checked in.

"What is your relation to the patient?" she asked.

Traci explained she wasn't a relative, but a coworker who had driven her to the hospital after an accident at the office.

"I'm sorry, ma'am," she smiled, "but I can't release that information."

"I don't want any medical information," Traci persisted, "I just want to know if she checked in."

"Again," the clerk informed her, "I can't release that information."

Traci swore inaudibly. She decided to go to the Family Birth Center, where Wendy and the baby would be monitored, to see if she could find out something there. Pushing through the double doors, she made her way to a large semicircular desk. Two clerks and what appeared to be a nurse were laughing about something. When they saw her standing there, the mirthful chatter ceased and one of them asked if she could help her.

Traci donned her sweetest smile and asked if a Wendy Malloy had been admitted. The clerk hesitated and Traci immediately launched into a description of Wendy and how she was seven months pregnant and fell on her abdomen really hard at work.

"I can tell you no one has checked in with that complaint today," the clerk informed her.

Traci was puzzled. "Maybe she just checked in and she isn't in your computer yet," she offered.

"No one gets past me, ma'am," she said proudly. "Maybe your friend went to Capital Medical Center."

"I drove her here," Traci declared. *This was becoming a little strange*, she thought. *Where in the hell was Wendy?*

"Did you check with admitting?"

"Yes."

"Perhaps she stopped at a restroom," the clerk speculated. "Why don't you have a seat in the reception area on the other side of the double doors and wait for her? She should be here shortly if you just dropped her off."

Traci grudgingly pushed through the double doors again, shed her jacket and plopped down in one of the vinyl-covered chairs that lined the wall. Now she was worried. *What had happened to Wendy?* Hopefully, she would show up soon. After a half hour of watching people come and go through the Birth Center entry doors, she decided something was wrong and returned to her car. When she arrived at the clinic parking lot, she noticed Wendy's car was gone. She went inside and asked Summer if she had seen the nurse. The receptionist shook her head and admitted she had not.

"Why," she asked. "What happened?"

Traci ignored her, not out of rudeness, but she was very upset.

She immediately went back to tell Dr. Garner Wendy had simply disappeared at the hospital and her car was gone.

****

Wendy clicked on the scanner icon and it whirred to life. She was scanning a work release form she had copied at the office that bore the letterhead of a Tacoma perinatologist. It was in a patient's medical records and crossed her desk last month. She had quickly realized it would come in handy later when she needed to forge a disability statement from a doctor.

The document was simply a template with handwriting in the appropriate fields. She took some white-out from her desk and carefully erased the filled in portion. Next, she checked the box that released her to work without restrictions, substituted her name, and wrote down tomorrow's date. The perinatologist's signature was at the bottom, which provided the authenticity she required. She scanned it in to make a copy and admired her work. More alterations would be necessary when she presented her pregnancy disability paperwork, but this was good practice, as well as reassuring that it could be done.

A sigh escaped her as she placed the document in her purse. On the way home, she had been blessed with another inspirational story. She would apologize profusely to Dr. Garner and Traci, but she would inform them she only trusted her perinatologist in Tacoma. Also, if anything was wrong, she wanted to be at Tacoma General (TG) where they had a Level Three nursery since she was only thirty weeks pregnant. St. Peter's only had a Level Two nursery and she would have been forced to endure a transfer to TG, or worse, if her baby had been in distress and an emergency C/Section needed, his level of prematurity bought him an automatic ticket to TG in a helicopter or ambulance. She had hitched a ride back to the clinic, so that part wouldn't be a lie. Not wanting Traci to make the long drive to Tacoma since she would have been unavailable to assist Dr. Garner, she decided to drive herself since she felt fine. The only reason she drove to TG was Dr. Garner's insistence that she had to have a doctor's note to return to work. She didn't feel any pain or contractions, and the baby was moving throughout the trip up. It seemed silly to waste the time of an L&D nurse, but she had promised to be checked. The monitor at TG didn't show any contractions and the baby had a nicely reactive strip.

The phone rang next to her and Wendy jumped. Her caller ID showed it was the clinic so she didn't answer. She needed to be unavailable for a few more hours to play out her story. Ignoring the persistent rings, she left her room and went to the kitchen to get a glass of water. When she sat on the sofa, she sipped the cool liquid slowly and pondered the close call she had just managed to thwart. It was Murphy's Law in action, she guessed. Yet once again God had shown her the way out. It seemed to be a foolproof story to her. Dr. Garner and Traci might think it was foolhardy, but they would see the logic in it when they realized she was an emotional pregnant woman bonded to her obstetrician, and only wanted to have a NICU available for her premature baby if something went wrong.

The narrow escape made Wendy realize for the first time her situation was more fragile than she had imagined. If she were incapacitated and unable to function, her fake pregnancy would be discovered. Also, a prolonged hospitalization would mean Annatha would run out of food and water in a few short days. Conjuring a worst-case scenario, Wendy shuddered at the thought of her unborn son starving to death with his mother. It had never occurred to her how vulnerable she was, and in turn, the same vulnerability could spell doom for Annatha and her baby. She vowed to be more careful, especially when driving. This same caution would be manifested when she finally had responsibility for her son. She would make sure he was properly nurtured and resolved to safeguard him with every inch of her being.

The room was chilly and she realized the ice water wasn't helping any. She went over to the woodstove and lit a fire starter brick. When it was engulfed in flames, she began adding logs from the bag she used to tote them in from the woodshed. She warmed herself for a few minutes before closing the iron door on the antique stove. *That's better,* she thought, returned to the sofa and cozied an afghan around her legs. The room began to heat up and her eyes felt heavy. She drifted into a daydream about the events of the day, and an image of the patient dragging her sick child across the waiting room reared its ugly head. Her son would never be taken anywhere in that condition except to his pediatrician's, she vowed. Discipline wrapped in love was the key. Teaching a child proper manners was something she felt strongly about, and she believed many parents were sorely lacking in this necessary and often difficult task.

She willed the unpleasant scene from the clinic away and replaced it with a serene vision of strolling along the Puget Sound beach at Burfoot Park, collecting shells with her son while a warm summer breeze caressed them. This scene faded to a merry-go-round at the Thurston County Fair, where her child was shrieking with delight as she held him safely atop a richly adorned plastic steed. Images continued to drift through her partially conscious mind. They would plant seeds in the garden together, and she would laugh when he chased her chickens around the yard. What really gave her pleasure was imagining the first time she would show him off at church. Her fellow congregants knew she was pregnant and would gladly share in her joyful blessing. It would be her mission to raise him as a good Christian boy. She would never tell him about his heathen mother and how close his life had come to being snuffed out by her evil narcissism. He would only know how precious his life was to the mother who fed him, clothed him and provided spiritual nourishment. She would see to that ... her body twitched slightly before she drifted off to sleep.

Chapter Twenty

Thirty-two Weeks, Four Days (32W4D)

It was the beginning of February and Annatha felt as big as a house. She was finding it more and more difficult to perform the low impact aerobics. Her balance was off and she felt more short of breath. Even the yoga poses were awkward and she was unable to hold them as long. She modified both routines to accomplish as much as her body would allow, but the drastic change in her center of gravity caused by the added bulk to her midriff limited her valiant efforts. During the yoga TV program, she found herself returning to "center," the cross-legged pose one assumed when a position was too difficult, more and more often. Despite the physical hardships her pregnancy imposed, the mere act of attempting these activities was helping to keep her sane. It was quite comical to her when she hoisted herself off the floor after a routine was finished. She felt like she was boating a big fish.

Wendy recently bought her another maternity bra when she noticed the bulge from her growing breasts hanging over the top of the one she had. Annatha had named them her quad boobs. Another weird transformation was her nipples. They had been a rosy pink hue but now had darkened some to a light caramel shade. She wondered if they would ever be their original color again. Lifting her shirt, she was disconcerted by the thin brown line that ran from beneath her breast bone all the way down to her pubic hair. It was darker now than it had been only a week ago. Pesky hairs were growing out of the section that dove below her belly button. The way she discovered them was standing in front of the mirror in the bathroom, where she was able to see underneath the growing mound that normally blocked the lower half of her body from view. Jagged, lightning bolt shaped red lines had split the skin where her hip bones met her abdomen. They were very unattractive and itched like crazy. She knew from her reading the stretch marks would fade, but she would wear these maternal scars forever.

A few hours of her endless days were spent standing in front of the mirror, carefully inspecting the misshapen figure that stared back at her. All of these changes were listed in great detail in the pregnancy book, so she wasn't shocked when they appeared. It still bothered her that the physical transformation of this previously pristine body was all for nothing. If one had to endure nature's merciless assault on the pregnant body, it might be easier to face if there was a reward when the ordeal was over.

Annatha struggled out of the recliner to get a bottled water from the fridge. She waddled clumsily now and felt like she knew what it was going to be like at age eighty. Everything was sore; her feet, ankles, hips, back and even her hands. It was almost impossible to sleep through the night when everything went numb and began aching. Not to mention the constant trips to pee. She couldn't imagine her petite body was capable of anymore added weight, especially since it was already protesting loudly with seven weeks to go.

When she settled back in the recliner and gulped the cool liquid, Taz jumped in her lap. He was a full grown male cat now and Wendy had recently taken him to the vet to get fixed so he wouldn't spray in the basement. The inactivity was making him fat and she cringed when his full weight landed on her thighs.

"We're both getting huge, Taz," she announced. He purred

and she stroked his engine to keep the soothing vibration on her legs going.

It was hard to imagine the baby could grow another three to four pounds between now and her due date. She didn't know how much more stress her poor body could take. Her weight gain had been tightly controlled by the nurse. She only supplied her with protein and vegetables. Breakfast time was the only occasion she would bring fruit. Her explanation was that too many excess pounds might cause her to have a big baby. The last time she climbed on the scales, she had only put on fifteen pounds so far. Wendy was pleased. Again, she stressed the importance of keeping the baby's weight down to minimize complications during the birth process. Annatha tried to block any thoughts about what it was going to be like when she went into labor. She knew the nurse would make sure the baby was born in this basement, no matter what went wrong. This dreadful knowledge was another contributing factor to her bouts with insomnia.

Annatha also realized the external remodeling that had occurred was only a part of her personal renovation during the long months of confinement in the lonely basement. The empty days and constant stress forced upon her had resulted in much reflection. She understood now what her dad had been talking about when he would suggest she adopt an "attitude of gratitude." Prior to this experience, she had chosen a victim mindset and felt sorry for herself in reaction to the unhappy home life with Brandon. This had caused her to block any consideration of the positive things in her life. In reality, she was young, healthy and relatively free to do what she wanted in the outside world. Even school didn't seem so bad now and she wished she was sitting in a boring history class instead of inside desolation cave. The unwanted flirting by a dorky guy would have been a welcome break from this prison, she frowned.

In addition, a dramatic internal awakening had been kindled by the growing life inside of her. So self-absorbed in the past, now her thoughts and feelings were constantly tuned in to the precious creature she carried, who would not exist without her. He was totally dependent on her. This new responsibility she felt was frightening and thrilling all at the same time. Often these thoughts would lead to the inevitable fact she would never hold her baby or put him to her breast to feed, never rock him to sleep at night while singing a sweet lullaby. The sadness such reflection spawned was undesirable to be sure, but the fact this baby had become the most important thing in her world was ample proof her inner consciousness had been elevated to a whole new plane. She knew in her heart, difficult though it was to admit, this process had made her a better person than she was before. It was a feeling of redemption. Not the old-time religion variety, but a spiritual salvation of sorts.

She felt like Wendy had soured her on any future encounters with religious people. Lately, the nurse had insisted on reading to the baby from the Bible every evening for thirty minutes. She claimed the fetus could hear her voice and wanted him to recognize it after his birth. Annatha wanted very badly to put a finger in either ear and chant "la la la la," but decided to resist the urge. Her decision had been motivated by the nurse's threat that if Annatha didn't cooperate, she'd remove all the satellite channels except the Christian ones. With seven weeks to go in her pregnancy, and two more afterwards, such a punishment seemed like a fate worse than death.

For what it was worth, Annatha talked to her baby throughout the day. It was like having another person to chat with, one who never answered back verbally. Sometimes she thought a particularly strong kick might have been a sign of disapproval to a comment she had made. She doubted it on a realistic level, but it was fun to pretend. Besides, she wanted her son to know his real mother's voice. She fantasized at times about tracking down Wendy some day in the future and recovering her stolen child. It didn't hold much promise, Annatha realized, but it was a vengeful pleasure she rewarded herself with to imagine the look on Wendy's face if such an event occurred.

****

Dee walked into her dad's house from the garage entrance and flipped on a light. It was dark and quiet downstairs, but she knew Meredith and her father were home because both of their cars were in the garage. She made her way up the stairs and set the small travel bag on her bed. The decision to visit had been motivated by the past few times she had spoken to her stepmother on the phone. She was stoned on martinis and tranquilizers, and Dee was worried sick. When she glanced down the hallway, she noticed a thin ray of light under the door to her dad's office. *Good,* she steeled herself, *he's by himself.* She passed the master bedroom on her way and heard Meredith snoring loudly. Unconscious again, she frowned. She knocked on the office door lightly and opened it.

Brandon turned and his expression was one of disgust until he recognized it was his daughter and not the drunken sot he was married to.

"Dee!" he exclaimed with a wide grin.

"Hi Dad," she smiled and walked over to where he was sitting in front of his computer. The usual can of Red Bull was perched next to him, she noted.

Brandon lumbered out of his chair and gave his daughter a warm hug. "What the heck are you doing home?" he asked. "Did I miss a voicemail or something?"

"No, Dad," she released her grip and took a seat across the desk from him. "I just wanted to see how you were doing."

He stared at his daughter with a puzzled look. "Something you couldn't talk about on the phone?" When she didn't reply, he put his feet up on the desk. "I've been doing all right. Work mostly, and hacking around the golf course when it isn't raining too hard."

"Any news about Annatha?" she ventured.

Brandon just shook his head, and Dee knew he didn't want to pursue the topic any further because he removed his feet from the desk top and began pecking on his keyboard absently. She girded herself before continuing. The real purpose of this visit had nothing to do with her stepsister.

"Are you going to get Meredith some help?" she challenged him.

He stopped typing. His shoulders slumped and he gazed at his daughter with sorrowful eyes. "She's beyond help," he gestured in exasperation. "Her drinking is out of control and she's passed out half the time. She doesn't leave the house anymore and when I run into one of our friends, they ask me how she's doing because they haven't seen her in months."

Dee leaned forward. "Dad," she began earnestly, "there are treatment centers for people who have Meredith's problem." She purposely avoided using the word alcoholic, remembering his vicious attacks on Annatha about her father and his drinking.

Brandon shrugged but didn't respond.

"We need to do an intervention, Dad," she continued. "I've checked into it and my friend Jade's mother just got out of treatment and is doing much better. She gave me the name of the interventionist they used."

Brandon shook his head in defeat. "You've got such a big heart, honey," he smiled wanly. "You didn't get it from me or your mother."

"Like hell I didn't," she declared. "I've seen it, even though you like to keep it hidden. Now show me your big heart and let's call this interventionist." She gazed intently at her father. "Meredith is going downhill fast, and it doesn't look like we're ever going to hear from Annatha again. I know she has plenty of reasons to be sad and try to drown her pain. The thought of losing a child is incomprehensible to me, but Meredith is destroying herself and I'm afraid she's going to take you down with her."

Brandon sighed. His daughter was right. Annatha's disappearance had caused a cloud of despair to descend upon his home. He never let on to anyone, but he secretly felt guilty for putting her cats to sleep, since it was likely the event that triggered her rebellious behavior and drove his stepdaughter away. His remorse wasn't so much for the loss of his stepdaughter, but for the effect it was having on his wife. Deep down, he still cared for Meredith, and she was sinking into a morass of gin and pills.

He looked at his daughter in admiration. She had become a mature, compassionate young woman. His heart swelled with pride. "Okay," he promised. "Give me the guy's number and I'll call him first thing tomorrow, and I'll let you know what we decide."

Dee stood up and walked to her father's side. She leaned over and kissed him on the forehead. It was obvious this was a tremendous strain on him, as his face was drawn with worry.

"Goodnight Dad," she said.

"Goodnight honey," he squeezed her arm.

She left the office without another word and started down the hallway. There was no sound from the master bedroom. She wondered if Meredith was awake so she tiptoed to the bed. Her stepmother was sprawled out on her stomach and there was a large spot of drool on her pillow. Dee was shocked at how her face looked like she had aged a hundred years since the last time she saw her. Impulsively, she leaned over and kissed her stepmother on the forehead. The stench of gin and unwashed clothes made her recoil. Meredith stirred after she kissed her, but then rolled over and resumed snoring. Dee left quietly and changed into her warm flannel pajamas. She was satisfied the ball was rolling now and if it meant coming home more often, she vowed to support her dad through the hard times ahead. *And Meredith too,* she reminded herself as she snuggled under the warm comforter.

Chapter Twenty-One

Thirty-three Weeks (33W0D)

Rachel closed the file in front of her. Her brain was fried. She leaned back and rubbed her eyes vigorously, trying to erase the glaze formed by the monotony of her task. She had just finished the paperwork for a mail fraud case involving a postal worker in Renton. Her investigative skills had been put to the test, but a trap she sprung on the unsuspecting employee had worked beautifully and she had all the evidence needed for a conviction. Tomorrow she would turn it over to the U.S. Attorney's office.

Mazy was bugging her to go to a high school football game, but she was mentally fatigued and just wanted to go home and relax. A glass of wine and a hot bubble bath sounded like heaven. It would have to wait. She knew it was important not let her work interfere with raising her daughter. That mistake had cost her a marriage, and she didn't want her daughter to end up on a shrink's couch somewhere in the future complaining about her emotionally distant mother.

It was time to leave, so Rachel began clearing the top of her desk and instinctively straightened the framed photograph of Ruth. It never ceased to amaze her how much Annatha Wolcott resembled her sister. Months had drifted by without any news about the missing girl's case, until a troubling revelation by Annatha's grandmother had shot a rather large hole in the runaway theory. Grabbing her briefcase, she switched off the lights and navigated through the dimly lit hallway, aided by a red exit sign.

When she reached the sidewalk in front of the FBI building, it was raining as usual. Rachel switched on the wipers as she exited the parking garage and pulled onto Madison Avenue. Traffic was heavy and she blinked as the annoying glare of headlights multiplied tenfold as they fanned out against the blurred veil of precipitation. She switched on the defogger, hoping it would help some. It didn't. Muttering swear words, she continued on and despite the need for concentrating on the road, her mind wandered again to Annatha and the surprise phone call from Rose Wolcott around the beginning of January. She asked Rachel if she was ever going to interview her. Puzzled, Rachel had explained another field agent was given that assignment but reported she never called him back. Rose informed her she was waiting for her to call. When Rachel inquired as to whether she had any new information, the insistent grandmother admitted she did. One week later Rachel took a short hiatus from her mail fraud case and made the long trip to Rose's Snohomish County mini-ranch.

Rose had been very talkative. She was convinced her granddaughter was not free to come home or she would have by now. When Rachel asked her how she could be so certain, Rose had led the agent around the side of her barn where a large tarp was draped over an automobile. Removing the cover, she stepped aside and waited while Rachel admired the metallic blue Mustang convertible. Rose explained to the clueless agent the importance of showing her the car.

"Annatha's dad called her Cherry Blue," Rachel recalled Rose's words and the way she had lovingly stroked the hood. "He gave her to Annatha before he died and I promised her she could have her at Christmas." Rose had paused for a moment and Rachel saw the tears forming in her sorrowful eyes. "I know that girl would have moved heaven and earth to get back here and take Cherry Blue. She meant everything to her."

Rachel left Rose and Cherry Blue with the conviction Annatha's grandmother made a very good case for why the girl might be in some kind of danger. It was hard to imagine a teenager who adored her father would not return to claim such a valuable inheritance, not only because the car was in mint condition and a classic, but more importantly, because it was her father's pride and joy. If Annatha wanted to remain estranged from her family, she likely would have contacted her grandmother to arrange a secret meeting or clandestine visit to her home. Rose might have demanded certain conditions before turning over the car, like making Annatha promise to contact her Mom and let her know she was all right, but the fact there was no word at all from her granddaughter with the promise of Cherry Blue seemed to suggest the missing girl might not be in a position to contact anyone.

A blaring horn snapped Rachel from her thoughts, and she looked up to see the light was green. Glancing in the rear view mirror, she saw the driver behind gesticulating angrily as he gave her the one-finger salute. She gunned the accelerator and ignored the angry motorist riding her tail. It was tempting to slam on her brakes and cause him to crash into her car and get a ticket for it. However, the determined clouds were dumping buckets of rain from the dark sky and she had no desire to venture out of her car unless it was absolutely necessary. Her fantasy would end up causing her a lot of inconvenience and a trip to the body shop, besides; she had more important things to deal with. The enraged driver zoomed past her on the left and sprayed her windshield with a fresh dose of street water. Rachel sighed and slowed down until she could see again. Turning left down the freeway access road, she resumed her introspection.

Even though the information Rose possessed didn't put her any closer to knowing Annatha's fate, it caused an aspect of the case to be illuminated like sunshine marching across an emerald green meadow as dark storm clouds receded. If the girl was not a runaway, a possibility that seemed less likely now, that meant another explanation for her disappearance would have to be found. It felt like she was on a scavenger hunt with no rules. Revisiting Annatha's disappearance could end up an exercise in futility again, but she felt driven to try one more time. It wasn't just the new perspective gleaned from her visit with the grandmother that fueled this rebirth in motivation. There was something else. Her memory of Ruth's tragic end was a big part of it. The similarities between her and Annatha were like a subconscious melody that struck a chord deep inside and harmonized her determination. It was mesmerizing and she couldn't turn it off even if she tried. Besides, she didn't want to. If she was able to rescue a teenage girl from suffering for a secret pregnancy, the demons might leave at long last.

Now there was nothing else demanding her immediate attention, so it was time to pick up the shovel and start digging again. Ignoring the foul weather conditions, she formulated a plan while she drove. She would start with Loftin. His denial of any knowledge of the girl's whereabouts, backed up by the polygraph, did not dissuade her from checking the attorney out one more time. He was a skillful liar and maybe he had taken some medication to help him beat the lie detector test.

A few weeks after her last phone conversation with Laurel, Loftin had phoned her and unleashed a tongue lashing for ruining his life. Rachel had listened patiently until he finished, then admonished the brash attorney with "you reap what you sow." His response had been for her to "fuck off" right before he slammed the phone down. Out of curiosity, she phoned Burbank and asked him about Loftin's status. The senior partner informed her Thomas had been asked to resign. The last he heard, his protégé had secured a position in the public defender's office, but he knew Loftin was applying at other law firms, as they had called for references. He expressed regret at Loftin's unseemly behavior, and noted again what a good litigator and moneymaker he had been for their firm. Rachel responded it sounded like good riddance to her. Burbank had turned cold and said he was busy.

She had no illusions about interviewing Loftin again. He would most likely be hostile and she doubted he would change his story, but time and circumstances had a way of breaking the toughest adversary. His life had been destroyed and the perception that she was the destroyer ensured she would not be well received, but she had to try. Maybe he had undergone a catharsis and decided to take some responsibility for his actions. Stranger things had happened, she mused. She made a mental note to make sure she brought Stan along. It was doubtful Loftin would try anything physical, but her fellow agent's size would make certain he didn't. There were no doubts she could handle herself in any situation, but a tincture of Stan would prevent an incident altogether.

First she would drive down to the clinic in Olympia again and interview everyone who worked there this time. It was the point where the trail ended, and it might be her only chance to pick up the scent again. Hopefully that nurse still worked there. *What was her name?* She searched her memory banks. *Oh yeah,* she recalled, *Wendy.* She was pregnant and with luck wouldn't be on maternity leave yet. Racking her brain, she tried to recall the month she was due. It was March. The same month Annatha was due if she was still pregnant. That was a weird coincidence, or perhaps it meant nothing. She pulled into the driveway of her townhome and turned off the car. It was time to shut off her brain, too, and be mentally present for her waiting daughter.

CHAPTER TWENTY-TWO

Thirty-Four Weeks (34W0D)

Brandon forged ahead through the weekend traffic. The rain had let up last night and the days of dreary cloud cover had given way to a blazing sun. He felt like a groundhog that had surfaced after a long winter and saw the sun for the first time in months. It always seemed brighter and more obtrusive when the dark, gray curtain finally parted. Yet towering stands of dark fir were now brightly lit, shining like an emerald forest. In the distance, Mt. Rainier's majestic, sloping face was drenched with snow that glistened against the backdrop of a deep blue sky. It was a shame his mood was just the opposite of the natural wonder displayed by a sunny Pacific Northwest day. He was doing everything in his power to ignore his wife. She had been pleading nonstop since they left the house.

After finding Meredith passed out in her own vomit, the gravity of her problem had been driven home and he called the number Dee gave him. The intervention had been last night and it proved to be one of the most difficult trials of his life. It was pitiful to listen while Meredith made excuses and minimized her drinking. He had been advised what to expect, and his wife followed the script almost exactly, as the interventionist had predicted at their meeting. Dee had been helpful, calmly informing Meredith of the effect her disease had on her. She empathized with her pain, but didn't back down in her assertion that her stepmother needed professional help.

His wife was sobbing uncontrollably. Brandon glanced in the rearview mirror and noticed Dee had tears streaming down her face. He cracked the window and felt some relief as brisk, cold air flooded over his face. Revived a bit, he reached over and squeezed his wife's shoulder gently.

"It's going to be fine, honey," he tried to console her. "I'll visit you as often as they let me."

"You don't love me anymore," she cried bitterly. "You're going to divorce me while I'm in treatment, aren't you?"

He looked at Dee again, who was staring back at him in the mirror. She nodded at Meredith as if to say, "Tell her you love her, Dad."

"That's just not true," he said in his most reassuring voice. "I do love you and I'm not going to divorce you."

Thankfully, they arrived at the treatment center, and another scene occurred that Brandon had been warned about. He was trying to pull Meredith out of the car, but she latched on to the door handle and wouldn't let go. After several minutes of pleading with her and making promises, he finally let go and stepped back. Brute force was not going to work here, he realized. There was one thing he was pretty sure would get his wife's attention and convince her to cooperate.

"If you don't go to treatment, Meredith," he said firmly, "I will divorce you."

He heard Dee gasp behind him. His wife stopped struggling and looked at him with glazed eyes; the next second her expression changed to abject fear. The gamble worked and she climbed out of the car and straightened her hair.

"Satisfied?" she said sarcastically. "You're getting rid of me."

"Are you kidding?" he shot back. "This is the last place on earth I want to be. I've put up with your drinking much longer than I should have. Satisfied? How can I be satisfied when I'm taking my wife to an addiction clinic?"

Dee realized she was holding her breath and exhaled forcefully. She had never seen her Dad like this before. He was using a brutal emotional tactic, but she knew it was out of sheer desperation. Most importantly, Meredith had been scared shitless with his last remark and finally surrendered. The three of them walked in silence to the front door of the treatment center, Meredith clutching Brandon's arm tightly. Fortunately, her theatrics were over.

The admission clerk supplied the forms needed to check Meredith in. A woman approached them and introduced herself as a nurse, but Dee thought she looked more like a person who worked behind a perfume counter at Nordstrom. She had a warm smile, though, and her manner eased the palpable tension a tiny bit.

"Come with me, Meredith." She held out her hand. "Your husband can fill out the paperwork; you and I need to talk."

Meredith rose numbly and accompanied the nurse through a set of double doors. She swiped a pass card to open them, which precipitated a loud buzzing noise as the locking system disarmed, and Dee realized Meredith wasn't coming back through them until they said she could. A few minutes later, her dad finished the admissions process and they returned to his car.

Brandon was deep in thought. The snowball from hell slowly gathering mass over the past few months had finally smashed into his world. It would not be fatal, he vowed. He and Meredith would rebuild their lives. Somehow he had to help his wife get past the loss of her daughter. It would have been easier to do if she were gone as in dead gone. Still, he was willing to seek help from a professional to learn tools that could help him deal with the uncertain grief; uncertain because the reason for it wasn't defined as yet. It was a nebulous "maybe this and maybe that" kind of grief, the kind that easily crushed strong wills and reduced them to a rummy pulp.

Dee knew better than to make conversation by the expression on her dad's face. She also knew how hard it had been for him to admit *his* wife was defective and in bad need of repair, not only because it reflected on his choice of a mate, but she felt deep down he had to own some of the responsibility for his stepdaughter's disappearance. She leaned against the passenger door and rested her forehead on the window. The glass was cold and hard but she didn't care. It was better for her to look away so she couldn't see the lost look in her dad's tearstained eyes anymore. The sight of her distraught father was very unnerving, even at this age. It was a fairly common occurrence with her mom, so it didn't have the same effect when she had a meltdown. Her paternal monolith had been shaken to its very foundation, which did not cause any change in her feelings for him, but it resulted in the revelation that he possessed a fragile side just like everyone else. She would always see him differently now, but in a good way.

Brandon fumbled in his pocket and retrieved his sunglasses. The brilliant glare caused him to squint and when it struck his eyes the already-present tears flowed more freely and the whole world blurred. It made it almost impossible to see the road. He headed east over the I90 floating bridge towards Mercer Island and home. Once again nature produced a beautiful scene as the lake shimmered like thousands of tiny lights and white caps danced along, choreographed by a brisk breeze. He silently wondered when such sights would bring him joy again. Things had to change, he hoped. Shit had been piling up on his plate for some time now and it had to slow down so he could start removing what was already there. The bright star in his life at the moment was Dee. She had been a huge help through all of this. He glanced over and saw she was staring out the window. It was a sign of respect and maturity that she had remained silent. She was very good at giving him space when he needed it. Her avocation should have been a bear handler since she did pretty well handling him, he smiled grimly.

"Thanks Dee," he said softly and touched her arm.

"No problem, Dad," she turned and smiled.

For the first time, Brandon actually experienced some of the pain his wife must have felt at the loss of her daughter. If she loved Annatha half as much as he loved his daughter, who lit up his life with her smile, the pain had to be unbearable. Shame overwhelmed him at the memories of how badly he had treated Meredith's daughter. Annatha was her flesh and blood, but he had treated her like a pariah. It was unlikely he would ever get the chance to make it up to her. His stepdaughter seemed to be gone for good. However, he resolved to seek other avenues to make it right. His wife deserved no less.

****

Standing in the doorway to take in the full impact of the finished nursery, Wendy felt flushed with joy. Everything was arranged just perfectly. In the far corner was the richly stained pine convertible crib and right across from it, a changing table that matched the crib. On the side of the room near the doorway, a small dresser she painted a pastel yellow and stamped turtles on was positioned in the middle of the wall and a plush upholstered rocker recliner fit nicely in the corner. She liked the look of wooden rockers but they weren't very comfortable, and she planned to spend a good deal of time rocking her son. They would fall asleep together in the chair. She walked over and stroked the headrest, dreaming of the times she would nurse him and sing him sweet lullabies.

Next she admired the smooth walls, painted the same pastel yellow as the dresser with her very own hands. *It was a labor of love,* she smiled. Glancing up, she followed the paper border where the wall met the ceiling. It had sunshine yellow background and contained all the primary colors including bright green turtles. As a girl she had a pet pond turtle, but it was a muddy brown color with a leopard pattern on its reptilian skin. Her mother begged her to let it go but she named it Mortimer and once that was done, she couldn't part with it. The bold green turtles on the wall were vastly different than her Mortimer but it didn't matter. She wanted that part of her life in this room with her son.

Wendy felt like she was standing in front of a shrine. It paid homage to the years of sacrifice and suffering she had endured to create this special place for the child she longed for. There was a strong sense she was on hallowed ground. None of this would have been possible without her undying faith in Jesus Christ. He had provided the vessel that held her son and allowed her to save his life. It was no coincidence all of this happened the way it did. She firmly believed it was a miracle.

The sun was high in the sky now and shone like a spotlight on the nursery through the window next to the crib. She took a few steps towards the crib and noticed there were shadows cast by the mobile. It was purchased from a Christian store online and contained biblical characters. There were tiny stuffed figures of Noah, Moses, David, John the Baptist and Jesus. She tapped it gently and the shadows danced on the sheets below it. The image of her son trying to grab it with his tiny hands caused a warm glow of happiness to engulf her. Running her palm along the padded bumper that matched the quilted comforter folded neatly on the railing, Wendy's heart was full. This was the culmination of her dreams: a child of her own to love and cherish for the rest of her life. All of the obstacles still waiting to be overcome melted away and she basked in the powerful moment of peace and serenity that flooded her senses. She closed her eyes and allowed it to wash over her with its divine calmness.

After a few minutes, she opened her eyes and found she had to squint at the dazzling sunlight pouring through the window. She pulled the drapes closed and waited for her pupils to adjust. Able to focus again, she turned around and surveyed the changing table's contents. The top drawer contained the cloth diapers she planned to use. There was no way she was putting synthetic material against her son's soft bottom. She was more than willing to clean them out instead of just tossing them in the trash. It also was a "green" way to do things since she was recycling instead of adding to the pile of garbage at the city dump. The top of the table had a shelf that was lined with a container for the diaper pins, baby lotion, Vaseline and powder. Wendy picked up the lotion and squirted some on her palm. She caressed the lotion into her skin and then smothered her face in her hands. The sweet aroma of a newborn baby filled her senses and she drank it in fully. There was no more enticing fragrance in all the world, she thought dreamily. Soon enough the body of her newborn son would be bathed in the lotion and she would inhale it hungrily as she hugged his naked skin against her own.

Enough fantasizing, she sighed. It was so uplifting to be in the room she hated to leave but it wasn't good to stay too long. She liked to mete out small visits like this to whet her maternal appetite for when the real experience arrived at long last. Returning to the entrance, she glanced back for one last look around. Satisfied everything was ready for her son's arrival, she closed the door and walked down the hallway past the basement door. She wondered if she would ever look at it the same way again once this was over. It would forever be a window to the vestibule where her son's wayward mother was forced into giving him life and then giving him up. That aspect of her mission stirred a tincture of sadness inside her for Annatha, but when she reminded herself what the girl had originally planned for her son, it vanished as quickly as it came.

Chapter Twenty-Three

Thirty-four Weeks, Four Days (34W4D)

Wendy was standing over the kitchen table checking the inventory of medical supplies spread out in front of her. It was only a little more than a week before she began her maternity leave. The forged medical disability form had worked like a charm. No one questioned its authenticity. She hadn't expected any problems with it, since they had accepted the form she provided from the Tacoma perinatologist's office after the nasty spill she took a few weeks ago.

Traci was understandably upset about being abandoned at the hospital, but Wendy didn't really care. Dr. Garner had forced her to listen to a lecture about how foolhardy it was to drive herself thirty miles in her condition, but in the end had accepted her explanation. Fortunately, he hadn't mentioned the episode again. Once her maternity leave started, she would be at home almost every minute of the day. This would help allay her fear that the girl would go into premature labor while she was at work.

She had to be sure she possessed the needed supplies before she no longer had access to the clinic's stock. Opening the tackle box, she removed the medications stored there and compared them to the list she was holding. She checked them off one by one. There were four vials of pitocin, one vial of Nubain, two vials of methergine, and eight misoprostol tablets. Two IV bags of magnesium sulfate (MgSO4) she mixed herself were stored in the refrigerator in case the girl developed toxemia. The pitocin was necessary in case Annatha's labor needed to be induced or augmented and to contract the uterus after the placenta delivered. In case the pitocin wasn't effective, she had the methergine to provide even more stimulation to the uterus. Misoprostol was used to ripen an unfavorable cervix, but it wasn't being used much before she left L&D at UW. It was also reserved for instances when the uterus failed to respond to pitocin and methergine, and was administered rectally to keep a patient from undergoing an emergency hysterectomy, which would be necessary to save her from bleeding to death. It had occurred to her that allowing Annatha to hemorrhage uncontrollably would accomplish her final task, but the thought of cleaning up all that blood wasn't appealing. Wendy also knew that the girl would beg her to save her life, because she had heard those very words before from patients when they began to go into shock and realized something was terribly wrong. She had decided to avoid that scene if at all possible. The Nubain would be reserved for pain relief as a last resort. She didn't want her son to be born sleepy from repeated doses of a narcotic. The last medication on her list was local anesthetic. For that she had chosen three multi-dose vials of 1% xylocaine. She checked it off and carefully replaced the vials.

Next, she examined the compartment where she stored what she called her Kevorkian drugs. There was a large vial of Versed, a strong sedative that would be used to put Annatha to sleep when the time came to end her life. The substance that would stop the girl's heart was potassium chloride. All of the medications in her tackle box were ones used at the office, except the potassium chloride and magnesium sulfate. She had ordered them and squirreled both away before anyone noticed. The office manager paid the bills, but she doubted the woman had a clue what drugs were used at the clinic.

It didn't matter much, anyway, since she wasn't going back to work there despite what she had told Annatha. She would give notice two weeks before her maternity leave was up. Her days of working where abortions were performed would thankfully come to an end. The house and car were paid off, so she only needed enough money for living expenses. The only loose end she hadn't worked out yet was child care when she did look for a new job, but there was still plenty of time before she would need it. Her savings would be enough to allow her to take six months off after the baby was born. She had decided to apply at the two hospitals in Olympia for PRN duty in labor and delivery when she did return to work, but this time it would be totally different being around new mothers and babies since she would have her own son. The pain endured when she last cared for laboring women was a living hell. *No more,* she rejoiced and continued with her inventory.

Wendy counted the syringes and various needle sizes, then replaced them. Next she checked the number of alcohol wipes and betadine prep sticks. *Should be enough,* she decided. Everything was neatly packed in the tackle box again, and it was closed. She slid the plastic tote tray filled with supplies in front of her to inspect the contents. There were four 1000cc IV bags of Ringer's Lactate, an electrolyte solution she would administer during Annatha's labor. They felt cold, so she made a mental note to warm them first when the time came. Lengths of IV tubing, wrapped in sterile packs, were checked off, as well as the four angiocaths. These were inserted into the vein, and she had acquired extras in case she missed the first time. The IV tubing would be attached to the angiocath then pierced through a rubber nipple in the bag of Ringer's, allowing the fluid to flow through the apparatus into the vein.

The tote tray was set aside on the kitchen counter and she turned her attention to the instruments. She planned to take them to the office this weekend when no one was around so she could run them through the autoclave and wrap the whole collection in a sterile pack. All the necessary tools had been purchased online at midwifery websites. Lining them up neatly on the table, she referred to her list again. She had two pairs of scissors, one to cut the umbilical cord that had plastic handles and the other, straight Mayo scissors, in case an episiotomy or more extensive surgery was necessary. There were two hemostats, a bulb syringe and two plastic umbilical cord clamps in case she dropped one. A Kiwi vacuum device, pediatric Ambu bag and a fetal Doppler had been purchased on eBay. The Kiwi would be used to assist Annatha in delivering the baby if she was unable or unwilling to push him out after she was completely dilated. She had never used one but had witnessed many deliveries where an obstetrician attached the suction cup to a baby's head and pulled it out. It bothered her when she thought of using it on her son, but as long as she kept the pressure reading in the green band, it would not be dangerous. Hopefully, it wouldn't be needed.

A needle driver and tissue forceps were checked off as well as two packs of suture in case Annatha suffered a deep laceration during the birth and was bleeding a lot. The final item on her list was a scalpel. Wendy cringed at the thought of using this instrument. It would mean the labor had gone terribly wrong. If the girl wouldn't dilate, the baby's head wouldn't descend, or her son's heartbeat showed signs of distress, she would be forced to perform a C/Section. She had assisted with this procedure many times and felt certain she could get the baby out, but anesthesia would be a real problem. The local would only numb the skin so she might have to resort to giving the girl a large dose of intravenous Versed to keep her still, which meant she had to get her son out quickly, before the tranquilizer drug affected him. It was a scenario she dreaded, but to be unprepared for this contingency would be worse.

She gathered the instruments and returned them to the box they were stored in, then replaced everything in the bedroom closet again. Satisfied all was in order, she poured herself a glass of wine and stretched out on the couch. The woodstove sounded like popcorn was cooking so she sighed, got up and opened the door to arrange the logs better. When she returned to lounge on the sofa again, she mentally reviewed her plan to dispose of Annatha's body after the lethal injection was administered.

She had decided a stand of trees at the back of her three acres would provide cover from her neighbors and the road. The ancient cedars would form a fitting burial shroud for the girl's final resting place. An old Ford tractor with a backhoe, purchased from the previous owners when she bought the house, would be used to dig the grave. When it was dark, she would wrap the girl's body and cart her to the cedar grove in a wheelbarrow. She didn't want to start the tractor at night for fear of disturbing the neighbors, who might find it necessary to investigate where the annoying sound was coming from. So she would fill in the grave with her backhoe behind a dense fir curtain as soon as it was daytime. The chances of it being discovered were nil since she planned on living there the rest of her life.

It seemed only fitting that the birth mother's final resting place would be close by so she could witness her child being raised by the mother who truly loved him. The irony of the girl meeting the same fate she had planned for her unborn child did not escape Wendy. She was finally going to do a "reverse abortion" that she and her L&D coworkers had jokingly wished for at times when their patient had seemed most unfit to be a mother. It was gallows humor, to be sure, but this time it was for real.

Wendy rolled the wine around in her glass absently. She felt a sense of satisfaction. Her job as God's messenger had been difficult at times and the biggest test was yet to come, but she felt prepared. Annatha would have to deal with her Maker after she passed on. She wondered how the girl would explain her plan to destroy the living creature she possessed. It didn't faze Wendy that she was also ending a life. What it came down to in her mind was the Old Testament teaching of "an eye for an eye." God was using her to save one life at the expense of another. The difference was that the unborn child had no choice in the matter, but his mother did. That was the reason she had to be punished.

Her brain shifted gears and the thought occurred to her that after all these years she would finally have her *own* child by the end of next month. She consumed more wine but it wasn't helping curtail the excitement this realization aroused the way she hoped it would. Wendy inhaled a deep breath, let it out slowly and began to pray. Her adrenaline was not dissuaded to leave so easily, but eventually dissipated and at last her mind settled down. God was doing for her what she could not do for herself. She took another sip of wine and turned on the TV.

****

Annatha was sitting on the bed with her sweat bottoms rolled up above her knees. She was pressing down on the skin over her calves. It dented from the pressure but took a long time to fill in again. She noticed her feet were swelling a few days ago and her toes looked like tiny sausages. Now it had crept up to her knees. It was also affecting her hands. Her fingers were swollen and she had spent almost an hour with her right hand in the refrigerator this morning, trying to reduce the swelling so she could remove the emerald birthstone ring her father had given her. After applying a healthy dose of saliva, she managed to pry the ring off of her pudgy blue finger. She decided not to try and wear it again until after the baby was born so she placed it in the nightstand drawer next to her bed. The birthstone had reminded her she would be seventeen in May. It was hard to believe it was almost two years since her Dad gave her the ring. She knew he couldn't afford it, as he had just sobered up and started a new job, but he chided her not to worry about the money and insisted she keep it. Whatever it cost him at the time, it was priceless now.

She held up her hand and thought the fingers looked less swollen as the day passed, but she dismissed the urge to put the ring back on. Frostbite was painful and she had flirted with it after holding her hand in the icy fridge that long. Annatha stood up and went to look at herself in the bathroom mirror once again. She lifted her tank top and studied the swollen mass that used to be her abdomen. Her belly button was sunken and looked like a meteor crater. There were a few more stretch marks over her hips, which elicited a pronounced frown. The maternity bra was the least sexy thing she had ever seen, but she was forced to wear it twenty-four hours a day now or her upper back hurt from the strain of her heavy boobs. She also read that if the enlarging breasts were not supported, the ligaments that held them up would stretch and they would become saggy. That alone was motivation to keep it on. Leaning forward, she noticed for the first time that her nose even looked bigger. It was always a source of pride with her that it was so petite and had a slight upturn like her mom. No more. Now she looked like Miss Piggy. She wondered if her body would ever look the same again.

Disgusted with the ghastly creature she had become, Annatha turned to leave the bathroom and doubled over as a knife-like pain shot down her left groin. As if to add insult to injury, her baby wriggled and she felt like someone was twisting a knife in her vagina. She breathed rapidly and slowly straightened up. If she hadn't read about this in the pregnancy book, the pains would have scared the shit out of her. Lifting her basketball-sized tummy with both hands, she hoped the baby would change position and relieve her from the stabbing pain. Instead, he kicked in protest and the knife twisted again. Annatha cursed loudly in response to the movement, but she had to admire her son's rebellious personality. *He must get that from his mother,* she winced, while she pointed an accusing finger at herself in the mirror.

She waddled to the recliner and felt the sharp pain flash through her groin each time her left leg moved. When she flopped down clumsily in the chair, she noticed she was still breathing hard. *What's up with that?* she wondered. Before she had time to contemplate this observation any further, an abdominal cramp similar to the ones she experienced with her periods replaced the pain in her groin. She rested her hands on her tummy and pushed. It felt rock hard. Maybe she was having one of those Braxton-Hicks contractions she had read about in the book. "This just keeps getting better," she moaned.

Taz jumped on the recliner arm and carefully made his way to the only spot he felt comfortable. He had found a perch between her breasts and swollen abdomen, but it was shrinking fast. Kneading her skin a few times to display affection, he curled up and began to purr. The baby must have kicked him, because he lifted a paw and swatted at her tummy a few times. It didn't occur to him that this would only cause the baby to kick more. Right on cue, she watched as her son fought back, causing waves in her skin like someone pushing on a balloon from the inside. Taz scolded his nemesis with a deep growl, then darted under the bed. Annatha chuckled but was cut short by another sharp jab in her pelvis.

She leaned forward and situated the TV tray in front of her so she could elevate her feet on it. The recliner's footrest was broken, and the nurse didn't seem to think it was important. It pulled out fine, but when she put weight on it, the whole thing collapsed with a loud thud. The TV tray worked okay, and she used it often to try and get the swelling in her feet to go down. Reading in the pregnancy book, she had found that some degree of edema was normal in pregnancy, but now it was spreading. She wondered if it was a sign she was developing high blood pressure. The book called it pre-eclampsia or toxemia. It was more common in first pregnancies and teenagers, and was thought to be inherited. In fact, she had read twins were a risk factor for developing toxemia. Her mother wasn't around to ask. The scary thing was that the condition could be very dangerous for the mother and her baby. Wendy was taking her blood pressure every week now and the last reading a few days ago must have been normal because she didn't say anything about it, but the swelling had worsened dramatically since then.

This morning, when she first noticed her pitting calves, she had searched for the topic in her book. It said the cure was delivery, but if the baby was too premature, the mother could be watched carefully with lab tests and fetal monitoring. A urine protein test was mentioned, but Wendy had never asked her to pee in a cup to check it. Sometimes, she had read further, it became so severe the baby had to be delivered regardless of its gestational age. It also said that the most advanced manifestation of it was known as eclampsia. This was when the mother had seizures and could result in a chemical pneumonia if the mother aspirated her own vomit. It could even result in maternal death. She wished she had ignored the swelling and never read the section on high blood pressure in pregnancy. All it had accomplished was to cause even more trepidation for her plight. She knew no matter how ill she became, the nurse would try to manage any complication in the basement, and that thought frightened her even more.

Annatha didn't want to die during childbirth. She wanted to survive and go on to have children of her own someday, when the time was right. Her recent experience had opened her heart to this future possibility. She wanted desperately to survive this ordeal so she could rebuild her life in a whole new way. Her selfishness and all the character flaws it created were unproductive and a silly waste of time and energy. The consequences she now suffered from her decision to meet with Thomas were palpable and convinced her she needed to think things through before she impulsively struck back at someone in anger. Before, all the preaching and advice from her dad and mom had fallen on deaf ears. They had seemed like mere scare tactics. The reality of how devastating her behavior could be had been a cruel but effective lesson. If she had gone through with the abortion and never met Wendy, nothing would have been learned. She felt that in her heart, despite the looming danger she faced by placing herself in such a predicament.

Survival for now, and emotional rebirth after she returned home were her primary goals. First she had to walk through another painful consequence, the labor and birth of her son.

However, over the last several weeks she had developed a steely resolve to overcome this final hurdle before freedom was returned. Wendy would have her baby, she grudgingly admitted, but she would have her life back and a chance to make it better.

CHAPTER TWENTY-FOUR

Thirty-five Weeks, Five Days (35W5D)

Wendy stood over her replacement as she studied the computer screen while the nurse navigated poorly through the clinic's electronic medical records program. She was much younger than Wendy but weighed a good bit more. Blonde hair, limping from a perm some weeks before from the looks of it, was bleached too white and her dark roots looked more like dirt from where she stood. Wendy couldn't tell if it had been washed lately. As if her physical appearance wasn't off-putting enough, she had the personality of a bucket of spinach.

"No Gwen," she said through gritted teeth, "that's not the screen you select patients from." It was so hard not to push her off the chair and do it herself. The nurse wasn't retarded, but she wasn't the shiniest floor in the hospital either. Wendy had very little patience for training, especially since she instinctively disliked her replacement. Swallowing the words she wanted to say, she showed her for the fifth time how to pull up her daily schedule so a patient could be selected and their record opened.

Summer appeared in the doorway. "Excuse me, Wendy," she interrupted.

Great, she thought, *now I'm in the company of a retard and a dimwit.* "What do you want, Summer?" she scowled.

The receptionist shrugged off the sullen glare from Wendy. She was used to it. "Just thought you might want to know that FBI agent is coming back today to interview us again."

Wendy's annoyed frown quickly changed to concern. "Did she say why?"

"Nope," she replied. "I didn't talk to her. Robin told me to inform everyone--said Agent Gray would be using her office and interviewing all of the clinic staff this time." Summer paused for a response but saw the nurse was ignoring her now, so she left.

This was odd. Wendy felt a twinge of panic as questions began pouring into her brain. *What reason could the agent have to return to the clinic after all this time? And why was she using the clinic manager's office? No one else had interacted with Annatha that day, so what would be the purpose of talking to them?* She was so distracted she didn't hear Gwen ask her a question.

"Wendy!"

The sound of her name half-shouted not more than a foot away reeled her back to the present situation. She shook her head and looked at Gwen with a puzzled look.

"Why is the FBI coming here?" She sounded alarmed.

Wendy shrugged off the question. "It's not important," she said and ordered her to take a break. She needed some time to think. The blonde nurse needed no encouragement; she grabbed a large bag of chips from her tote bag and headed for the break room. Wendy sat down hard in her office chair. The cushion was hot from that obese woman's big ass, she realized. It was too warm, so she stood up and paced around while she tried to make sense out of the agent's return to the clinic.

"Hello there, Wendy."

She wheeled around at the familiar voice of Rachel Gray. The FBI agent was smartly dressed in an olive green suit. Their eyes locked and Wendy forced a smile.

"Nice to see you again, Agent Gray."

"See you in a few minutes," Rachel announced, then followed the receptionist to Robin Kelly's office. She introduced herself and displayed her badge. The office manager shook her hand firmly and asked her to have a seat.

"I understood from our phone conversation," Robin began as Rachel settled into the chair, "that you want to conduct interviews of our entire office staff, including Dr. Garner."

"That's correct," she nodded, "and I apologize for kicking you out of your office while I'm here, but I want to speak to each one privately."

Robin paused and appeared to be considering if she should ask her next question. After a brief hesitation she blurted out her concern. "Is there anything I should know about an employee here?"

Rachel smiled disarmingly. "Not that I know of," she replied. "This is the last place a missing girl was seen and I'm working the case. No one's heard from her since that day, so I thought I'd give it another shot."

Robin breathed a sigh of relief. "Who is your first victim?" she joked.

"I'd like to talk to Wendy Malloy first," Rachel requested, referring to her notes to find the nurse's full name.

"I'll get her for you," she offered and invited the agent to let her know if she needed anything before she made her exit.

Shortly after the office manager disappeared, Wendy appeared at the doorway.

"Please come in, Wendy," Rachel smiled and carefully studied the nurse's face as she took her seat, but it revealed nothing. She looked very pregnant now but didn't appear as uncomfortable as she remembered being at that stage of pregnancy. Armed with her notes from their first interview as well as the subsequent phone conversation, Rachel glanced over them briefly before she began.

"How's the pregnancy going?" she asked.

Wendy ignored the question. "Have you found the girl?" she inquired.

Rachel shook her head. "No, I haven't."

"Sorry," Wendy apologized. "I was curious. To answer your question, it's going fine. My last day here is Friday. I'm going on maternity leave."

"Glad to hear it." Rachel shifted in her chair. "Where are you going to deliver?"

"Tacoma General," she replied. "I'm seeing a perinatologist there who specializes in high risk patients." She noticed the concerned expression on the agent's face. "It's nothing serious," she reassured her. "It's because of my age and how much trouble I had getting pregnant."

Rachel nodded. "The reason I'm talking to you again is because we have no leads on the girl as yet and this was the last place she was seen. Have you thought of anything Annatha said that might be a clue as to where she was running to?"

Wendy responded quickly that nothing had come to mind. "How are her parents taking it?" she inquired.

"Why do you ask?" Rachel looked puzzled.

"Well she went on for quite a while about how cruel her stepdad was, killing her cats, and how her mother never stood up to him." She paused to select the right words. "I didn't really buy all that. Most kids blame their parents for everything. I just wanted to know if I was right. You know, that they really loved her and she was exaggerating."

The nurse sure remembered a lot from her conversation with Annatha after all these months, Rachel observed. "Her mom's taking it very hard, as you would expect," she replied.

Wendy shrugged. "Well," she offered, "she was a very unhappy girl when I talked to her and there's no telling where she went after leaving here."

Leaning forward, Rachel stared directly into the nurse's eyes. It was time to push her as far as she could, even if it meant being unpleasant. She told her she knew Annatha confided in her and maybe she felt sorry for her, so sorry that she might be protecting Annatha from her parents. If this was the case, her loyalty to the girl was causing a great deal of pain and suffering for her mother. Since she knew Wendy lived alone, it would be easy for her to hide the girl for months and no one would be the wiser. It was understandable, given Annatha's wretched home life, that Wendy might have promised to support her during the pregnancy, but as well-meaning as her intentions might have been they could be clouding her judgment. The nurse stared steadily throughout Rachel's attempt to verbally shake the bushes and see if anything fell out.

"If you know something," she concluded, "please tell me. Hiding the girl from her parents or withholding information regarding her whereabouts at her request are not felony offenses. You probably wouldn't face any charges from her folks if you came clean now."

Wendy remained expressionless. She fought hard to suppress her surprise at how close the agent was to the truth. It was obvious she viewed her as the most likely person to know where Annatha was. That or she was fishing really hard. No matter, Agent Gray would just have to accept the fact that when she pulled her hook out of the water it would be empty.

"I wish I could help you," she replied indignantly. "I'm going to be a mother soon, so I have an idea how painful this must be for her mom, but to suggest that I had anything to do with her disappearance, or that I have knowledge of where she might be now, is way off base, Agent Gray."

Rachel leaned back. Maybe she deserved that, she admitted. Still, there was something not quite right she couldn't put her finger on as yet. Loftin's version had been confirmed by a polygraph. She wished she had the same latitude with the nurse. *That's an idea,* she suddenly decided. *It wouldn't hurt to ask and see her response.*

"I apologize if I came on a little strong," she offered. "It's just that I can't quite put this thing together. The last person she spoke to was you and we have nothing to go on after that."

"Apology accepted," Wendy relaxed her defensive pose. "I'm not trying to be difficult. If there was something I could do to help you find her, I would."

The nurse had inadvertently opened the door for her next request. Rachel scribbled some notes on her legal pad to appear nonchalant. Without looking up, she asked, "Would you be willing to take a polygraph?"

Wendy felt like she did as a child when a roller coaster plunged headlong down a steep incline. Her heart was in her throat and her hands were suddenly clammy. She didn't know how to respond. Obviously, she couldn't take the test and risk being discovered, but refusing to take it would make the agent suspicious that she had something to hide. Inspiration was needed and she begged for help silently.

"I have to decline," she replied carefully as an idea how to get out of this mess crystallized. "I took one for a nursing job in Seattle that was designed to screen for drug use. I failed it, even though I have never used drugs that weren't prescribed for me. The examiner told me some people were just too nervous for polygraph tests to be reliable, and I was one of them."

Rachel studied the nurse. There was some truth to what she was saying, but it seemed very convenient given the circumstances.

Wendy felt her heart returning to her chest. Her bogus story had materialized out of nowhere. *Well, not exactly out of nowhere*, she thought. Her Maker had once again saved her from a tricky situation. She decided to distract the agent from the subject of her taking a polygraph.

"Agent Gray," she said with empathy in her voice, "can I give you some advice?"

Rachel was caught off guard at this question. "Go ahead," she gestured.

"I have been at this job for about a year now. Most of the young girls I've dealt with were flaky and irresponsible. At first

I was shocked, but then it became so commonplace that I'm not surprised anymore. Trying to make sense out of Annatha's behavior is impossible and ultimately futile. It will drive you crazy, trust me, I know. I realize you're just doing your job and you seem like you are really dedicated to finding her. But--and this part is my advice--it is unlikely you will find her unless she wants to be found. Even though she might not be smart, the girls I've talked to like her are very clever and resourceful. She will call her mother if and when she's every ready to return home. Whether or not she will bring a baby with her is anybody's guess."

Rachel had listened reluctantly. The nurse was obviously trying to change the subject. Her refusal to take a polygraph was accompanied by a reasonable explanation, but she still had not decided whether she bought the nurse's excuse. But she had to admit, her opinion of the patients she saw was illuminating.

"So you don't feel sorry for the girls who come here?" she observed.

Wendy recognized the agent had just fired a personal shot across her bow. She decided to back-pedal away from any further personal comments.

"I don't have an opinion about their troubles one way or the other."

"Yet you can remember everything Annatha told you?"

Score one for the FBI agent, Wendy admitted silently. "Recalling clinical history is different from having an opinion about their social circumstances," she replied drily. "Feelings have no place in this business." Her tone changed and she managed a smile. "I save my feelings for my animals and vegetable garden."

"And your baby," Rachel noted.

Wendy blushed. "Of course."

Rachel needed more information without arousing suspicion, so she decided to delve into her personal life. Maybe she could find something to pursue there. Mentioning the baby gave her an opening.

"How did you get pregnant, if it's not too personal?" she inquired.

"Not at all," she replied. She was glad the agent had not returned to the polygraph test and didn't mind another line of questioning. "I had Intrauterine Insemination with donor sperm at a fertility clinic in Seattle."

"Not the same doctor who will deliver you?"

"No. They are different specialties. Infertility docs don't deliver babies; they just make them," she winked.

Rachel rubbed her eyes. She was getting nowhere. The nurse was either telling the truth or she had pulled off a brilliant job of stonewalling. It was time to move on.

"Thank you for your time." She stood to indicate the interview was over. "I'll contact you if I have any further questions."

"I hope you find her, Agent Gray," Wendy offered. She was gloating at how effectively she had shut every door the agent had tried to open. Once again, she felt satisfied any suspicions had been allayed. She left the office and returned to her mundane task of training the new nurse.

Robin poked her head in after she saw Wendy leave. "Dr. Garner is available for a few minutes. You better catch him now before he has another patient."

Rachel agreed and Dr. Garner entered the office a few moments later. He was a handsome man who looked to be in his fifties. It appeared he worked out, too, because he looked very trim in his scrubs. His cropped brown hair was obviously colored, as there was no sign of gray. Intense blue eyes studied the agent curiously as Rachel began her interview.

She started by providing him with a summary of Annatha's visit at the clinic and the fact she had gone missing right after. He listened carefully and when she was finished, apologized that he had never seen the girl. Rachel revealed her frustration that Wendy was the last person to speak to Annatha and even admitted the girl told her she was running away. Yet she steadfastly insisted she had no idea where the girl was. She asked Dr. Garner point-blank if he thought Wendy might be protecting the girl. The doctor admitted he didn't know anything about his nurse's personal life and would not venture an opinion regarding her question. All he knew was that she was efficient, reliable and her skills were superb. He was sad to see her go on maternity leave, and she would be sorely missed.

After the doctor left, Rachel asked Robin if Wendy had any friends at the clinic. The office manager offered that the nurse was a very private person. Every so often the girls would go to happy hour but Wendy never attended. She wasn't aware of any friends Wendy had at the clinic. The only employee who might come close to being described as a friend was Traci. Rachel asked to speak to her next. Traci entered the office a few minutes after she spoke to Robin. The medical assistant was the opposite of her tall, willowy coworker. She was about the same age, but was short, pudgy and very animated. Rachel liked her immediately.

Traci denied any contact with Annatha, too. Next Rachel asked if she knew Wendy very well. The medical assistant was curious why she was asking questions about her coworker. Rachel explained it was a formality since she was the last person who spoke to the girl before she disappeared. Traci seemed satisfied with her answer and described Wendy in much the same way as Robin and Dr. Garner. However, she revealed two items that had not been disclosed in her previous interviews. First, she complained Wendy never let anyone touch her pregnant tummy. It wasn't pathologic, just odd in her opinion. Secondly, the nurse was so independent she had risked her baby's life after a fall over a month ago. This piqued Rachel's curiosity and she asked her to elaborate more about the second observation. Traci relayed the whole story of Wendy's fall and how she ditched her at the hospital then drove herself to Tacoma General so she could be monitored there. Rachel asked the medical assistant why a pregnant woman would need to be evaluated after falling on the floor. Traci explained that a blow to the abdomen could cause the placenta to separate. If it was a large enough separation, the baby's blood supply would be cut off and it would die. The mother's life was also in danger, since the separation caused an internal hemorrhage.

Rachel was stunned. She asked Traci if she knew why Wendy would take such a chance. She seemed less concerned than the agent and informed her Wendy had been an L&D nurse so she knew the signs of an abruption. When everything seemed fine, she felt safe to make the thirty minute drive alone. Rachel asked her how the nurse could be so sure. Traci admitted that was what concerned Dr. Garner when she relayed to him that Wendy had fallen. He told her there might not be any signs at first, which was why it was so important to be monitored. If the uterus was contracting, it could indicate an early separation. In fact, Dr. Garner had ordered Wendy to be monitored and threatened her not to come back to work without a note from a physician.

"Let me get this straight," Rachel leaned forward. "A skilled L&D nurse took a chance that she had an early separation of her placenta and instead of being monitored down the street, chose to drive thirty minutes to Tacoma."

"Sounds kinda foolish when you put it like that," Traci admitted. "It could have bled on the way and killed her and the baby before she got there."

This didn't make sense. Wendy was a seasoned L&D nurse who had probably witnessed placental separation after a seemingly harmless accident. Why would she chance it, especially since this had to be considered a premium pregnancy? She could throw a rock and hit the hospital from the clinic parking lot. Driving thirty minutes instead of one seemed more than foolish as Traci had put it. But what did it say about Wendy? Maybe the medical assistant had more information that could shed some light.

"Did she bring a note?"

"Yes."

"Was Dr. Garner upset with her?"

"Very."

Rachel asked her what explanation Wendy gave when she

returned the next day. Traci rattled off the reasons the nurse had given about feeling safer where there was a NICU to care for her baby if something was wrong. It made some sense to Dr. Garner, but he still admonished her for taking the risk. Rachel admired the amazing rationalizations the nurse came up with. She had witnessed a few today. Still, perhaps she could find out more.

"Have you noticed anything else you felt wasn't quite right that you witnessed Wendy do?" she pressed the MA.

Traci pondered the question for a few moments. "There was one thing."

"Go ahead."

The MA recounted the episode when she ran into Wendy on a weekend. Her coworker was walking out of the office with their portable ultrasound equipment. When she asked her if she was taking it home to look at her baby, the nurse denied it and said she had a neighbor who wanted to see if her mare was pregnant. She asked Wendy if she could see the baby, but she refused for some reason she couldn't remember and left.

Rachel knew Wendy could have been telling the truth, but again, it might have been an outright fabrication to deflect further questions. However, she had a friend who bred horses and she had once witnessed a vet performing an ultrasound on one of her brood mares. Without further information, it was impossible to judge the veracity of the nurse's explanation, but it definitely could be correct. Besides, Wendy's neighbor could save a few bucks if she knew what she was doing. A farm call by a vet with an ultrasound wasn't cheap and scanning the mare for a neighbor would require her to take the equipment off premises. Therefore she couldn't dismiss the excuse as an outright lie. She glanced at the MA, who was applying a coat of lip gloss.

"Anything else?" she asked.

Traci shook her head no and stuffed the tube of lip gloss in a side pocket of her scrub top.

Rachel thanked her and the MA left. She wondered if she would tell Wendy about her questioning. Not that it mattered.

Maybe she was barking up the wrong tree. On the other hand, there were lots of little things that kept the nurse on her radar screen. First there was refusing to go to the local hospital and risking the long drive to Tacoma alone. Then there was begging off submitting to a polygraph. A third odd tidbit was secreting the ultrasound equipment on a weekend when she didn't expect anyone to be around. Each one examined alone didn't mean much, but when she put them all together, it smelled like something stank in the petunias. What exactly caused the odor still remained a mystery, but she would pursue it until she found the source.

Next to be questioned was Summer. Rachel had a less than optimum experience with the Goth receptionist the first go-round and wasn't expecting anything different this time. As she walked in and sat down, it was obvious there were even more piercings on her lips now. It wasn't clear how she managed to keep from getting bits of food stuck in the studs. Rachel shrugged off her instinctive bias towards persons who decorated their bodies with sharp metal objects for attention, and focused on the task at hand.

Another review of Annatha's visit to the clinic in July was carried out, with no new information. Rachel sat back thoughtfully, wondering how best to approach the receptionist with her next statement. Summer was fidgeting with her hair and appeared bored with the whole process.

"So," she said nonchalantly while pretending to scribble some notes, "I'm interested in any impressions you have of Wendy Malloy."

"You think she had something to do with this girl you're looking for?" Summer's eyes suddenly gleamed through the overdone jet black eyeliner and thick mascara.

Surprised at the girl's reaction, Rachel didn't show it and maintained a steady gaze. "Do you?"

Summer shrugged. "I don't know. She's moody and rude to me. I know she thinks I'm an idiot." She met the agent's firm stare for a moment before she continued. "I really don't know anything about her other than what I see at the office, so it wouldn't be right for me to make a guess about that."

Fair enough, Rachel thought. She launched into her usual explanation of why the question was being asked about Wendy. Summer nodded but remained silent.

"One more thing and then I'll let you get back to work," Rachel continued and repeated the same question she posed to Traci regarding any oddities in the nurse's behavior.

"Hell yes," she replied immediately.

"Go on," Rachel encouraged her.

"Well," Summer began earnestly, "there was this one patient who was here to have her third abortion with us. We call them frequent flyers," she winked, and her eyebrow piercings dipped when her eyelid closed. "Anyway, she came in for her appointment and begged to see anyone but that bitch of a nurse Wendy."

"Why was that?"

"She claimed the last time she was here Wendy pressured her to have an adoption and even mentioned herself as someone who would be interested." Summer seemed pleased she was dissing the nurse she despised. "I told her it wasn't possible; Wendy was the only one at the clinic who did the interviews, so she left and said she would go somewhere else."

"How long ago was this?" Rachel asked casually. *This is pretty goddam interesting,* she thought.

"Gee, I'm not sure, but it was before that girl you're looking for came in."

"Anymore complaints about Wendy since then?"

"Nope," she declared.

Rachel pursued the line of questioning further. She determined the receptionist did not report the incident to Dr. Garner, as Wendy would claim she was lying, and as far as the doctor was concerned, his nurse did no wrong.

It was an isolated incident and it wouldn't be right to jump to the conclusion Wendy Malloy was actively seeking to adopt a baby from one of the clinic patients without having all the facts. However, if it was true, it painted a kind of desperation on the embattled nurse who had such a hard luck story when it came to conceiving a child. All of that was moot now that she was pregnant. *At least that's what she says,* Rachel noted. It was tempting to march up the hallway and barge into Wendy's office to raise her shirt and confirm she was really pregnant. *Not a good idea, Rachel*, she admonished. If she embarrassed herself and the FBI it was entirely possible she would be transferred to a remote station in Alaska and spend the rest of her time with the agency counting caribou. There was no need to rush into anything for now. Careful investigation and working the evidence was the safest, most effective method. However, it did raise her level of suspicion enough that further digging into the nurse's past had become a priority.

After she dismissed Summer, Rachel completed the rest of her interviews. Robin stuck her head in and told her she had some errands to run. She thanked the office manager for her help and said she would be leaving soon. After Robin disappeared, Rachel stared at the filing cabinet across from the desk. A label identified one of the drawers as "Employee Files." She got up and shut the door. When she reached the filing cabinet she tugged on the handle but it was locked. She noticed a key hole on the top, right side of the cabinet. *It must unlock all of the file drawers,* she deduced. Retracing her steps to the desk, she opened the top drawer and found a key that appeared to be a match for the lock. She grabbed it and returned to the cabinet, inserted the key and turned the lock. The drawer designated "Employee Files" opened easily. Quickly rifling through the hanging folders, she found the tab marked "M." Wendy's was the only file in the folder. She opened it and scanned the documents inside. A disability form for the nurse's maternity leave was on top. Rachel took the folder to Robin's desk and set it down. She straightened the legal pad in front of her and wrote down the name and address of the doctor who signed the release form. Shuffling through the papers, she located Wendy's resume. It contained her previous employers, and she recorded all of them. She realized she had probably crossed a legal line that forbade a search like this without a warrant, but she was desperate to probe into Wendy's life and see if something turned up that would define the nurse as an upstanding citizen or not. If this information somehow led her to Annatha, any potential criminal charges against the nurse could be dismissed because of this transgression, but at least the girl would be found and returned to her mother. Rachel replaced the file, locked the oak wood cabinet and replaced the key in Robin's desk drawer exactly where she had found it.

She made a point of letting Summer know she was done before leaving through the clinic front door. Once she was settled in the car, she debated whether she should use the data secreted from the office manager's private employee files. On previous occasions, her zeal had caused her to overreach her authority and she paid dearly, both personally and professionally. However, there was a young girl's life at stake here. She launched into a logical argument with her "by the book" conscience and began listing reasons why she should use the ill-gotten data.

First and very important was the fact Wendy was the last one who saw Annatha before she disappeared without a trace. Not incriminating but very coincidental. Second, Traci's story about Wendy's accident and refusal to be evaluated a mere block away could be construed the nurse was hiding something. Third and most enlightening was Summer's recollection about the patient who asserted Wendy wanted to adopt her baby. It didn't make sense if she was actively being treated for infertility, and in fact, successfully treated if indeed she was truly pregnant. All together the separate facts contained not one shred of physical evidence. The flip side of this record could easily contain a tune that carried a very innocent explanation for each item listed in her mental inventory. However, her gut was telling her this rock needed to be turned over and its slimy underbelly examined thoroughly.

After several minutes of careful consideration, she knew it was the right thing to do, despite her reservations. The file's contents would be used and damn the consequences. Wendy was the last person who saw Annatha, and either she knew something she wasn't telling her or she didn't. There was only one way to find out: examine the scattered, tiny pieces of her life and see how they fit together, much like solving a jigsaw puzzle. Once the entire picture fell into place, her hope was that some clue would be formed by a fusion of the loosely related whole. This was the only way she knew how to confirm or refute her suspicions once and for all. It was a long shot, she admitted, a hunch. But sometimes a hunch was all one had to go on, and she had a strong intuition Wendy might be cleverly scrambling the pieces of the puzzle.

Rachel gunned the accelerator and merged with the interstate traffic. She had a long drive home, but it would give her ample time to formulate a new game plan.

CHAPTER TWENTY-FIVE

Thirty-seven Weeks (37W0D)

Wendy did a double-take when she saw Annatha resting in the recliner with her feet propped on the TV tray. The girl's face was puffy and she couldn't tell where her calves ended and her ankles began, or cankles, as they were jokingly referred to when she worked on the L&D unit. She sat the lunch tray down on the bed and retrieved an automatic blood pressure cuff from her robe pocket, trying to conceal the worried expression on her face. Last week she had noted a minor bump in the girl's blood pressure but brushed it off as a fluke. Now she wished she had kept a closer eye on it.

"I need to take you blood pressure before you eat," she said nonchalantly. Annatha just shrugged and held out her arm. Wendy wrapped the device around the girl's frail wrist and was surprised to see how swollen her fingers were. The cuff purred as it inflated then gradually released the air in halting spurts. When it was finished, the display read 147/95. *That's not good,* she frowned.

"Come over to the bed and lie on your left side."

Annatha turned with a puzzled look on her face. "Is something wrong?" she asked.

"Your blood pressure is a little elevated," she replied evenly. "If it comes down on your side, I'll know it's nothing to worry about at this point."

The girl complied and Wendy repeated the reading. It didn't respond to the girl's position change enough to satisfy her. This wasn't looking good, she fretted.

"I'll be right back," she said and scurried up the stairs to her bedroom closet. The box containing medical supplies was retrieved and placed on her desk. She located the urine test strips container as well as a specimen cup and deposited them in her robe pocket. The dipstick test for protein would let her know if the girl's rise in blood pressure was a sign of toxemia. She hurried back to the basement.

"Pee in this," she held up a small cup. "I need to run a test on your urine."

Annatha could hear the concern in Wendy's voice and followed her instructions without a word. She left the specimen on the counter and watched the nurse as she disappeared into the bathroom.

Wendy held the transparent cup up and noted the urine's color. It was a deep amber hue, which meant it was very concentrated. Not a good sign. She dipped the test strip into the specimen, kept it submerged for a few seconds, then pulled it out. The indicator had turned a dark green. Comparing it to the jar's label, which contained a legend for the results, she identified the color as 4+ protein. She dropped the strip into the toilet and flushed it along with the urine. This was disconcerting to say the least. In a few moments, the girl's pregnancy had catapulted into a high risk category. She had severe pre-eclampsia! Without collecting a twenty-four hour urine, it was impossible to confirm the diagnosis. A spot urine was a snapshot of kidney function, but a total protein over twenty-four hours was more accurate. In fact, in a hospital setting, a whole series of lab tests would be ordered for someone in Annatha's condition to check the function of various organs that were commonly affected by toxemia; a blood count to check the number of platelets, liver enzymes, and serum creatinine with a uric acid level for kidney function. She lacked the resources to do any of these. The girl could be in grave danger and Wendy was flying blind. The only good thing was that she was thirty-seven weeks so the baby would almost certainly have mature lungs, especially with the stress of toxemia, and the cure was delivery of the baby.

A clinical intervention was critical now, she told herself, so get a grip. The girl had to be induced. First she needed to check Annatha's cervix to see if it was ripening. Hopefully the induction would not be starting from scratch with an unfavorable cervix. She dreaded the thought of convincing the girl to cooperate with a forced labor induction, but she had no choice.

Annatha waited nervously while the nurse checked her urine. When Wendy emerged from the bathroom, it wasn't hard to read the look of concern on her face. She felt her knees go weak.

"You have toxemia, Annatha," she had a more professional ring to her voice. It was a natural reaction that gutted any emotion so that she could be objective in her decisions. This time it wasn't working very well. She had a great deal vested in the outcome.

"What are you going to do?" Annatha asked, her voice trembling slightly.

"I'll explain everything when I get back. I have to get some supplies and I want you to have your bottoms off when I return."

"What for?"

"Please, Annatha," she begged, "just do as I ask."

Annatha persisted. "Shouldn't you take me to a hospital?"

"I have all the tools necessary to deal with this complication," she insisted. "Please, just do as I say. I'll be right back." Not wanting to continue the debate, she turned and left the basement again.

Annatha was petrified. She had suspected something wasn't right when her swelling suddenly increased. This morning when she studied herself in the bathroom mirror, she was shocked at what she saw. She looked like the Pillsbury dough boy. The thing that really frightened her was that the nurse would never let her leave the basement, which meant her and the baby's lives were in the hands of her unstable captor. It was pointless to resist, though, she realized. The deck was stacked against her having any say in what was about to transpire. Wendy had informed her she had been a labor nurse in a large Seattle hospital and possessed a great deal of experience, but she had no confidence in her abilities. All she had witnessed was her obsession with the baby and religion. The fact the nurse had kept her locked up in a basement for almost seven months now communicated one thing only. Her life meant nothing. It would be tossed aside as easily as a piece of chewed gum if it meant saving the baby. She grudgingly shed her sweatpants and underwear right before Wendy appeared on the stairs, and modestly slid under the comforter.

Wendy was relieved to see the girl had followed her directions. Removing the sterile gloves and lubricant pack from her robe pocket, she peeled open the wrapping and pulled a glove over her right hand. With her left hand, she held the lube pack up to her mouth and tore the top off with her teeth. Squirting a liberal dollop of the slimy substance on her gloved index and middle fingers, she asked the girl to move to the far right side of the bed. She walked around and when she arrived by the girl's side, she grabbed the comforter and exposed the girl's bottom half.

"Now lift up your legs and drop your knees to the side in a frog leg position," she instructed her.

Annatha was caught off guard by the sudden exposure of her naked vagina. The dank basement air felt icy on her bare skin.

"Try to relax; now you're going to feel some pressure."

Pressure hell, she cringed as the cold gloved fingers entered her vagina. It felt like she was cramming her whole hand inside and she inhaled a muffled scream.

"You're only making it worse by tensing up," Wendy chided. "Take some slow, deep breaths and I'll be done in a sec."

Annatha closed her eyes and called upon the yoga breathing

exercises to help her cope with this unwelcome invasion of her privacy. It helped a little, but everything felt so tender down there it was hard to concentrate.

Wendy frowned. The girl's cervix was firm, thick and closed. She could feel the lower uterine segment ballooned out over the hard cervical nub. The baby's head filled it completely, but it was sitting atop a locked gate. The axis of the cervix pointed towards the rectum, another unfavorable sign. This process was going to take a long time, she realized with growing trepidation. Removing the glove, she tossed it in the trash can, along with the wrapper and empty lube packet.

Annatha quickly pulled up the covers to recover her lost dignity and waited for the verdict. The nurse wordlessly moved the comforter aside just far enough to expose her right leg and sat on the edge of the bed. First, she tested the edema more clinically and dimpled the puffy skin over her calf. It didn't come back out; 4+ edema. Next, she grabbed the leg under her knee and pushed down on the ankle to bend it.

"Let your leg go loose," she commanded. Tapping on the patella to determine how brisk the girl's reflexes were, Wendy almost jumped when Annatha's lower leg immediately flew up like it had been shot out of a cannon. She grabbed her right foot under the toes and pulled it towards her knee. It reacted with a few involuntary beats like she was tapping her toes. *Clonus*, she winced. This abnormal neurologic response she had just witnessed indicated the girl could be on the verge of a seizure.

"What are you doing?" Annatha pleaded.

"Give me a minute," she grumbled and dug the fetal Doppler out of her pocket. She applied a small dose of lube to the girl's swollen abdomen and pressed the transducer against the skin just below her belly button. The baby's heartbeat was strong. It sounded like a galloping horse. Wendy timed the beats against her second hand and after fifteen seconds the rate was thirty-five, which translated to 140 bpm (beats per minute). She felt relieved the baby had a steady, normal rate although she longed for a fetal monitor to perform a Non-Stress Test (NST) to document a reassuring pattern. However, high tech instruments were never in the equation, she reminded herself and replaced the Doppler. Wendy remained seated on the edge of the bed. It was time to tell the girl what was happening and how she planned to treat her condition.

"You have toxemia," she began. "Do you know what that is?"

Annatha nodded.

"Good," she continued. "You have the severe kind and judging by your brisk reflexes, you could have a seizure, which would endanger your life as well as the baby's."

Annatha's jaw dropped. It was worse than she had feared.

"The only cure for your condition is delivery of the baby," she hurried after seeing the girl's frightened expression. "That means I need to induce your labor. I have pitocin, a drug that stimulates contractions, and a lot of experience doing inductions so I don't want you to worry about that. Unfortunately, your cervix isn't dilated or effaced so this is going to be a very long labor."

"Do you have anything for seizures?" Annatha couldn't disguise the alarm in her voice. The labor wasn't scaring the crap out of her as much as flopping around, foaming at the mouth and biting her tongue in half.

"Yes," she assured her. "I have a drug that is administered as an intramuscular injection that prevents and treats seizures in patients with toxemia. However, I want to warn you it can make you feel flushed, nauseated and groggy. Also, your vision could be blurred. This doesn't mean anything is wrong; they're just side effects of the medication." She couldn't recall how many times she had given this same speech while working as a labor nurse, but it always helped if the patient was expecting these symptoms.

The fear Annatha was experiencing at the moment was indescribable. Anticipating the labor and delivery of her son in the basement had been scary enough, but this elevated her impending doom to a whole new level. The nurse seemed knowledgeable, but she just didn't feel safe in her hands. She wanted to be taken to a hospital where there were trained doctors and nurses.

"If you really cared about this baby," she argued, "you'd take me to a hospital. I care enough to promise I won't say anything."

"That's not going to happen," Wendy snapped. She got up from the bed and walked over to the stairs. "I have to get my supplies. Lie on your left side until I get back."

Annatha leapt out of bed with surprising agility considering her size. She was unconcerned about exposing herself.

"Take me to a hospital, Wendy!" she cried as she headed towards the stairs, where the nurse was watching her with a stunned expression.

Wendy held up her can of mace and pointed it at the girl, who recoiled when she noticed it. "I suggest you do as I say," she warned. "You're about to have enough pain without pepper spray in your eyes."

Annatha fell to her knees and sobbed for herself and her son. This was turning into the worst nightmare she could have imagined. The book had said her condition required intensive observation and treatment in a hospital by an obstetrical specialist. Women still died of toxemia, and the only thing standing between her and a potentially fatal pregnancy complication was this former labor nurse who planned to treat her in a basement! The thin carpet provided no insulation from the cold floor beneath it and when she slumped backward, crying bitterly, it felt like she was sitting on an icy lake surface against her bare bottom. Between halting sobs, she cursed the day she met the cruel nurse.

Wendy watched for a minute. *What a drama queen*, she scowled. There was no reason for this kind of outburst. She knew what she was doing. Shaking her head, she headed up the stairs to gather her supplies. When the metal door slammed behind her, the girl's wailing disappeared with it. *Thank God for that*, she sighed.

****

Rachel rode the elevator, surrounded by white coated medical students at the University of Washington (UW) Medical Center. Her destination was the sixth floor L&D unit. This was her first time at the hospital located along Montlake Cut, a channel that connected Portage and Union Bays just north of downtown Seattle. For days now she had waited patiently to speak with Wendy Malloy's former unit director. When she phoned a week or so ago, the director was out of town at a conference. The unit secretary she spoke with informed her she would be returning today. This morning she had placed a call before leaving home and secured an appointment. The nursing director had volunteered that some of Wendy's former coworkers were working today also. Rachel waited patiently as the elevator stopped at every floor until it reached the sixth. Each time a few white coats would file out and start chattering the moment they left the elevator. The delays didn't bother her; patience was an acquired skill and she had plenty of practice. Resisting the urge to impulsively stalk the nurse before questioning her former coworkers was just such a lesson in patience. It had been a long week sitting on her hunch about Wendy, but soon she would have a better idea if she needed to pursue it or file it away permanently.

The bulky doors lumbered open at her intended floor. She pushed past some of the students and then through the double door entrance for the L&D unit on her right. She made her way to a woman sitting behind a long counter that appeared to be the reception desk. She smiled pleasantly, presented her badge and informed the unit clerk she had an appointment to see Sara Jordan. She was directed to an office down the hall. A woman with light brown hair, streaked by blonde highlights was sitting behind a desk; her face buried in a file. The door was open so Rachel knocked once and walked in.

"What is it?" she demanded and glanced up with an annoyed expression to confront the intruder.

Rachel held out her badge again and introduced herself. Sara acknowledged she was the unit director and quickly apologized for her manners. She gestured for the agent to have a seat. Before sitting down, Rachel closed the door. She divulged her purpose for being there and the reasons why. A sixteen year old girl was missing after an appointment to see about having an abortion. Wendy Malloy was the last person to speak with her but claimed she had no idea where she was. She wasn't a suspect, she half-lied, but protocol required a background check on her.

"Wait a minute," Sara exclaimed. "Did you say this was a clinic that performs abortions and Wendy works there?"

"Yes," Rachel admitted curiously. "Why?" She reached in her briefcase to take down notes.

"When Wendy worked here," she explained. "She was a staunch pro-lifer. I mean the kind who doesn't believe in abortion under any circumstances."

That's odd, Rachel thought. The nurse had given her the impression she wouldn't have an abortion but never let on she was against it altogether. *Why would she be working at a clinic that performed them? Another inconsistency,* she noted.

"You're certain about this?" she asked.

Sara nodded. "In fact," she elaborated, "she got in several heated debates with some of her coworkers. It got so bad I had to call them all in and tell them to put a stop to it because we were getting complaints from patients."

"Have you spoken with Wendy in the past several months?"

Sara shook her head. "No, Wendy wasn't the stay in touch kind."

"So you don't know she's pregnant," Rachel offered.

This time the director's expression was one of amazement. She stood up and walked around to the front of her desk and leaned against it. Rachel observed her sage colored blouse looked wrinkled, as did the dark brown, knee-length skirt she was wearing. It was definitely an unkempt look, which was surprising, given her position. She appeared to be in her mid-forties and the bulges born of time and having babies were worn unashamedly in the form-fitting clothes.

"You could knock me over with a feather, Agent Gray," she admitted. "Wendy went through a horrible divorce because she had been diagnosed as infertile. The doctors told her the only way she could get pregnant was with IVF."

"What did the divorce have to do with her not having babies?" she asked.

The director's eyes flashed angrily as she explained. "Her dickhead husband, excuse my language, wanted babies so he had an affair and the little home-wrecker ended up pregnant." She made a gesture like she was cutting off something with a pair of scissors. "They should all be castrated, the whole horny lot of 'em."

Rachel was amused at the director's bluntness. She could definitely relate to the feigned castration. It crossed her mind Sara might be a lesbian.

"What is IVF?"

"A test tube baby."

"Ah hah," she remembered. Her sister was infertile and had IVF. In a cruel twist of fate she had ended up with a set of triplets. Her life had never been the same.

"Well," Rachel disclosed, "Wendy did say she had help. She told me they used donor sperm and inseminated her."

Again, Sara seemed surprised. "That's weird, Wendy told me her tubes were blocked and for IUI to work the tubes have to be open."

Another contradiction, she noted. *They sure were piling up.* Next she quizzed the director about the kind of employee Wendy was. The same accolades she had heard in Olympia were repeated. Her fund of knowledge was vast; her clinical skills outstanding but an additional item was revealed. Wendy had a sterling bedside manner.

"Any problems you remember?"

Sara thought for a minute before she replied. "Besides the abortion debates, there was one more thing, but I always wrote it off to the fact she couldn't get pregnant. I would find her rocking babies in the nursery more often than any of the other nurses. When I asked her why the baby wasn't with the mother, she would tell me they asked her to take the infant so they could get some rest."

"Sounds reasonable," Rachel offered.

"It did," Sara admitted, "but only until I received a complaint from one of the patients that her baby was being taken to the nursery more often than she thought was normal." She returned to her desk chair and sat down again before she continued. "I called Wendy into my office and confronted her about it. She started bawling. That's when she told me about the infertility problem and her husband's affair. I think the straw that broke the camel's back was the fact her husband left her for a woman who was pregnant with his child. She just couldn't get past it. Not that I blame her." She repeated the scissors routine.

"Did she stop the behavior?" Rachel asked curiously.

"I guess," Sara ventured, "but shortly after that meeting she gave notice and moved to Olympia. I haven't heard from her since." She regarded the agent for a moment. "You've spoken to her?"

"Yes," Rachel admitted.

"What did you think?"

She hesitated. It wasn't that she didn't trust the director; she admitted she had no contact with Wendy, but this wasn't the time or place to discuss her suspicions.

Sara waved apologetically. "Sorry, Agent Gray," she said. "I guess you can't answer that, but my impression of Wendy was an outstanding person professionally, but a little short on interpersonal skills."

That summed up perfectly what Rachel had gathered thus far. She stood up, thanked the director for her time and supplied her with a business card and the usual "call me if you think of anything else."

"Agent Gray?" the director called after her and Rachel turned around.

"Did you want to speak to any coworkers?" she offered. "They might have some other insights."

She shook her head. "No thanks," she declined. "I think I have everything I need." In fact, she had a good deal of conflicting information that needed to be examined and all the motives commonly seen in women who took other people's babies.

On the ride back down the elevator and long walk to her car in the visitor's parking lot, Rachel's mind was racing. She might be on to something with her hunch about the nurse being involved somehow. First of all, Wendy shouldn't even be pregnant according to the information revealed by Sara. Sure, she could have been lying to save her ass when confronted with the patient complaint, but if she wasn't? Then there was the bitter divorce because she was childless, which could make her desperate for a baby of her own. But why go to work in a clinic that does abortions? It seemed each fact had a codicil. And how did this information factor into Annatha's disappearance?

Next there was Wendy's coworker Traci. She had expressed some concerns about the nurse never allowing anyone to touch her, the refusal to be monitored at a hospital nearby after her fall and risking her baby's wellbeing by driving to Tacoma, and the secretive weekend use of the ultrasound unit. An idea flashed through her mind for the second time in the midst of her analysis. *Was Wendy really pregnant or was she faking it? If she was pretending it would certainly explain Traci's observations. Wait a minute,* she reigned in her exuberance. *Why would she fake a pregnancy?* Then she suddenly remembered. *Annatha's due date was the exact same one as the nurse's. Had she convinced Annatha to give her baby up for adoption and live with her until it was born? She couldn't let her coworkers and doctor know she had persuaded a patient to give a baby to her. That would be unethical and the Washington State laws on adoption might prohibit it. Perhaps her sadness at the prospect of never having her own child had clouded her judgment and caused her to take drastic action,* she reasoned.

When she thought about it some more, Rachel realized an

abortion clinic would be an ideal setting where a patient might be convinced to give her baby up for adoption instead of terminating it, especially if she was conflicted. Annatha was alone, in trouble and hated living at home, anyway. She would have been easy prey for the nurse. A niggling fact she had picked up at the first clinic interview from the receptionist set off an alarm deep in her memory banks. It was an innate talent she had that served her well. Annatha had not made a return appointment, despite going there to have an abortion. Summer claimed the nurse could have done it but Wendy had offered some convoluted excuse why she didn't. *She wouldn't have made another appointment if she knew the girl was coming home with her!* Despite the multiple giant leaps in her logic, Rachel felt there was some validity to them.

She allowed this potpourri of conjecture to sizzle a bit while absently watching a few boats motor down the cut on their way to Lake Union. The sun was down and their running lights drifted through the darkness as if they were floating on air. The brightly lit, serrated downtown skyscrapers and towering Space Needle provided an impressive backdrop to the surreal scene. A gust of cold marine air brushed her hair roughly and Rachel buried her face in her overcoat collar. She longed to feel the warm air blowing from the heater vents in her car and quickened her pace.

Turning the ignition switch to start the engine, she experienced an ominous feeling wash over her as a morbid thought entered her consciousness. If the suppositions she had just formulated were correct, was Annatha giving the baby to Wendy of her own free will? *That's kind of farfetched, Rachel,* she had to admit, *but she couldn't dismiss it out of hand.* If the girl wasn't there voluntarily, it would certainly explain the lack of communication from Annatha, and her disappearance into thin air right after the July appointment with Wendy. This only spawned more questions, though. *How did she manage to coax the girl into going to her house? And where was she keeping a feisty, resourceful sixteen year who would likely escape the first chance she got? Was she restraining her? Drugging her?* She quickly ruled out the last one since Annatha was pregnant. The nurse wouldn't want to have a baby born addicted to drugs.

Rachel realized she needed more than the thin air she was working with to get a search warrant for Wendy's home, but she felt compelled to get a look around despite this limitation. The nurse was on maternity leave so she was probably there all day, which ruled out a clandestine breaking and entering scenario. She decided to visit her at home under the guise of needing to ask more questions, and snoop around as much as she could. Of course, everything was riding on Rachel's suspicion that Wendy wasn't really pregnant. Tomorrow she would go to the obstetrician's clinic in Tacoma that faxed the nurse's maternity leave release form, and confirm if Wendy was pregnant or not. If she was, her hunch would be shot down for good. However, if she wasn't, Rachel would drive to Olympia and have a chat with the good nurse.

It was too late to drive down tonight, and she needed this final piece of information from the Tacoma clinic before confronting the nurse. Besides, she had to get home and cook Mazy some dinner before they went to her school play. However, if she was a betting person, she'd wager everything she owned Wendy wasn't pregnant.

She put her key in the front door deadbolt lock and turned it. *Shut off the music, Rachel,* she ordered. It was time to devote her energies to the precious daughter waiting for her. She stepped inside and called out Mazy's name.

****

Annatha had managed to calm down and was lying quietly on the bed. The nurse had covered it with a protective sheet made of plastic and it felt sticky against her skin. The one exception was her butt cheeks. A flimsy, blue square pad with cotton lining on one side had been placed under her bottom. She was informed it was a "chuck" and would serve to absorb any fluids that leaked out. It had been no small feat to compose herself after the desperate crying jag but she finally decided to surrender her will, trusting a higher power would keep her safe. There was no other choice.

The night stand had been cleared to hold supplies needed at the bedside. A metal pole towered over her with an IV bag hung from a hook at the top of it. The TV tray held a tackle box and some weird looking instruments Annatha had never seen before. In a few short minutes, her basement prison cell had been transformed into a makeshift labor room. She watched while the nurse expertly hooked up the IV tubing by piercing a sharp plastic tip through a rubber nipple at the bottom of the fluid filled bag. Then she took the end of the tubing and placed it on the bed next to her. A syringe was produced from a Rubbermaid tote on the bedside table and used to draw some medicine from a small vial. Next, a tourniquet was tightened around her arm just above the elbow and an orange colored disinfectant painted on her hand.

"I'm going to start an IV now but first I'm going to numb the skin," Wendy instructed. "You'll feel a slight bee sting now."

Annatha winced at the burning sensation in her left hand. Thankfully it was brief. She saw the nurse open a much larger needle that appeared to be encased in a plastic sheath. The needle pierced her skin but she didn't feel anything but pressure. Maybe the nurse knew what she was doing after all.

Dark blood appeared at the open end and Wendy removed the needle from the sheath then quickly attached the IV tubing. She fiddled with a blue plastic device that appeared to control the rate of fluid administration and confirmed the IV was dripping at an acceptable rate into a small chamber at the top of the tubing. Satisfied, she secured the needle and tubing to the girl's wrist with some paper tape.

"There," she announced, "all done."

Wendy checked the volutrol she had attached between the IV bag and main tubing. It held 100cc of fluid at a time, which would allow her to control the rate of pitocin more accurately. The next few minutes were spent mixing the correct concentration of pitocin in the volutrol chamber then adjusting the rate to deliver it safely. It wasn't as accurate as the pumps used in L&D when she worked at UW, but at least it wasn't as random as buccal pit. Some of the older labor nurses had regaled their younger coworkers with stories about the "old days" when they used buccal pit. It was the same drug she was using now but in a tablet form that was placed against the cheek. The absorption was erratic and a much higher dose of pitocin resulted. They complained it was a safe method and the conversion to more exacting, low dose regimens was a lot of fuss over nothing. Wendy had never used it, but if buccal pit was discussed at a conference she attended, the speaker would always say it was being mentioned only to be condemned.

The next problem was preventing a seizure. She had four bags of magnesium sulfate ($MgSO_4$) with twenty grams (20G) in each. The usual loading dose in cases of pre-eclampsia was 4-6G IV (intravenously), followed by 2-3G IV an hour. If too much of the drug was administered, Annatha would stop breathing, so she didn't want to risk giving it that way. The seasoned nurses had told her they used to give 5G of $MgSO_4$ intramuscularly (IM) every four hours as long as the patient had a knee jerk when the reflex was tested, but the loading dose was 10G. It had to be given deep IM in the hip region, which wouldn't be a problem in her petite patient. The one and a half inch needles she had would do just fine. The total grams of $MgSO_4$ meant she had sixteen 5G doses. Subtracting the two for loading, this left her with fourteen; enough for about sixty hours. *That should be plenty*, she decided.

She was gambling the girl's blood pressure wouldn't go too high in labor because she had no anti-hypertensives. A sedative might help, but it wasn't an ideal choice. The $MgSO_4$ prevented seizures, but had no effect on blood pressure. It wouldn't require treatment as long as it stayed below 160/110, but if it crept above this critical mark, Annatha could have a stroke. She drew up the $MgSO_4$ from its bag into two separate syringes.

"This is the medicine for seizure prevention," she warned, "and it's going to hurt a bit. I need you to roll on one side or the other."

Annatha turned away from the nurse and felt strong fingers pressing on her skin. A stabbing pain was quickly followed by a deep burning sensation that hurt like hell. She moaned audibly.

"Sorry," Wendy apologized. "Now roll to the other side."

The same procedure was repeated. Annatha grabbed the plastic sheet in her hand and squeezed tightly. *Jesus Christ, that hurts,* she cursed silently. *Does everything have to be so painful? Stupid question, girl,* she grimaced. Scouting the room after the pain subsided, she searched for Taz's familiar form. He was fast asleep on top of the recliner headrest. *What a traitor.* She considered calling him but decided his presence would be too distracting.

Now that the essential therapeutic regimens were completed, Wendy stood for a moment, wondering why she felt something was missing. It was a few moments before she realized what it was. She wasn't charting anything. During her L&D days there was constant monitoring and recording of the baby's heartbeat, the maternal blood pressure, pulse, intensity and frequency of contractions, medication sheets, and when an epidural had been placed, the mother's oxygen saturation. Before leaving UW, the L&D unit had converted to electronic medical records with bedside computers. Afterwards it seemed like she spent most of her time pecking on a keyboard. Medical liability risk management had driven these changes, but to her way of thinking, it only resulted in less "face" time with the patient. Without these mundane and all-consuming duties under the present conditions, she could spend one hundred percent of her time tending to Annatha and her unborn son.

She decided to check the girl's vital signs, contractions and the baby's heartbeat every fifteen minutes. There was no electronic fetal monitor (EFM) to continuously record this data, but intermittent auscultation wasn't all that bad. It had been the standard of care until EFM came along. In fact, the old "pit" nurses talked about only using their hands and a fetoscope to monitor patients getting pitocin. At least she had a Doppler. Years of training and experience counted more than monitors, anyway, she asserted. She was amply qualified to manage this labor, despite the unexpected complication. The only thing she was worried about was the amount of time pitocin would take to efface (thin out) and dilate the cervix. It wasn't going to be easy. She steeled herself to be objective and diligent, no matter how long it took. Her son's life depended on it.

Annatha was lying on her side, facing the staircase. The light was on so she could see the basement door. It was closed. Even now the nurse wasn't taking any chances. She thought of how many times she had schemed to get it open, but every time the plan had fallen apart with further deliberation. She felt a warm rush and the basement door blurred, then melted into a hazy glow from the stairway light. *It must be the effects of the medication Wendy had warned about,* she realized, and shut her eyes to stave off a wave of nausea that resulted. Thus far she had only felt some mild abdominal cramping from the induction drug. Nothing near the intensity of a labor pain she had read about. She squinted hard to clear her vision and saw Wendy coming down the stairs with a chair she recognized from that first night when they arrived from the clinic. It was from the nurse's kitchen table. She situated it at an angle next to the bed and sat down.

At regular intervals, she would feel Wendy's hand on her tummy, checking for a contraction. It felt like her abdomen was tightening but she couldn't tell for sure. Next her blood pressure was taken and then the Doppler's speaker would broadcast the baby's heartbeat. It sounded strong. Her eyes felt heavy and she fought to keep them open but found herself drifting in and out of consciousness. She felt so groggy and weak, but it wasn't anything like a "high on." It felt awful. She heard the nurse's voice, but it sounded like she was calling to her from down a well.

"Your blood pressure isn't going up," Wendy informed her. She noticed the girl opened her eyes when she spoke.

Annatha tried to focus, with little success. Her mouth was so dry. She tried to moisten her lips with her tongue but it was like licking a rock.

"Can I have some water?" she asked weakly. It was hard to mouth the words with her lips glued together by an unknown sticky substance that had replaced her saliva.

Wendy got up and went to the bathroom. She soaked a washcloth in cold water and wrung it out enough to keep it from dripping all the way back. When she returned, she held it out and told Annatha to put it in her mouth and suck on it. Once it was dry, she would wet it again.

Annatha clenched her teeth on the washcloth and chewed on it gratefully until she had extracted every drop of fluid. She asked Wendy to drench it again and the nurse complied. After a second round of greedily sucking as much water from the rag as she could, her thirst wasn't completely quenched, but it was better. She even felt a little more alert and propped her head up a little.

"I'm going up on the dose of pitocin rather quickly," Wendy cautioned, "so the contractions are going to get stronger. We need to get your cervix dilated some so I can break your water."

"Do you have one of those crochet hooks?" Annatha asked thickly. She thought she remembered something about that in her pregnancy book.

Wendy nodded. "Yes. You've been doing some reading?"

"Where did you get all this stuff?" she ignored the nurse's observation and motioned at the room in general.

"Online at a midwifery website and eBay," she answered. "I got the medications from the clinic."

"Oh," she acknowledged absently, then her eyes squinted. "Why is the room so dark?" The only illumination Annatha could see now was a thin shaft of light escaping beside the almost closed bathroom door.

"Toxemic patients need dim lighting and quiet," Wendy

explained while she situated the blood pressure cuff on the girl's wrist. "What you don't realize is that I've managed many patients with toxemia and even delivered at least ten babies by myself when the doctor didn't make it in time. So don't worry or your blood pressure will go up. I'll tell you if there's anything you need to know. The good Lord will take care of the rest."

After finishing the vital signs, Wendy reached in the tote and pulled out a tongue depressor. She turned so Annatha couldn't see what she was doing then wrapped one end of it in cloth tape to a thickness of about an inch. In case the girl seized she wanted something to shove in her mouth so she wouldn't bite her tongue. It was a bloody mess when that happened. She had seen it before. The thought of having to deal with a grand mal seizure made her stomach knot up, but she had to be prepared.

Annatha was suddenly awakened by a painful cramping in her abdomen and moaned. It was worse than any period she had ever experienced. She realized she was finally having a strong labor contraction. The nurse was watching her reaction over a newspaper she was reading at her bedside chair. *It's that bitch's fault,* she seethed and gritted her teeth harder.

Wendy heard the girl's verbal response to the pain and reached over to palpate the uterus. It was rock hard. *Good,* she thought, *the pitocin is kicking in.* She adjusted the flow valve to increase the rate then applied the Doppler so she could listen to the baby's heart beat after a contraction. It was still strong with a rate of 150 bpm. Next she took another blood pressure reading and frowned when the display read 150/102. It was probably from the pain but she mouthed a quick prayer it would not continue to climb.

"Did you read about the breathing exercises?" she asked. Even though the girl had ignored the question about the pregnancy book before, she decided to press the issue again.

"Yes," Annatha grudgingly admitted. No use being defiant now. She wouldn't tell her about the yoga breathing exercises she had practiced, though.

"Use them your next contraction, and I'll help with the timing if you need me to."

She didn't have to wait long. A few minutes later the pain started again. Now that she was awake she felt the full progression of her contraction. It started in her lower back and radiated around to her lower abdomen. She remembered the book's instructions and began shallow breathing, using the "hee hee hoo" technique each time she exhaled. The crescendo of her voice and the tempo increased in concert as the contraction strengthened then dissipated slowly as it abated.

Wendy watched the girl with reluctant admiration. She had handled that fairly well without the benefit of attending a childbirth class. However, it remained to be seen how well she dealt with the active phase of labor when contractions really got intense.

"You did well," she complimented her. "Next time focus more on the breathing and less on the pain."

Annatha glared at her. "Like that's going to help."

Wendy smiled. "I've taken care of plenty of patients who only used breathing for pain control."

"They had a choice," she shot back. "If I had a choice I'd choose an epidural."

"But you don't," she admonished, "so I suggest you listen to me and focus on your breathing more."

"What the hell do you know?" Annatha cried. "You've never had a baby before."

"Calm down," she said evenly. "Your blood pressure's going to go up. Don't worry, I've got some pain medicine if things get too bad."

"Well, give it to me now," she ordered.

"It's too early," she replied, grabbing the washcloth and disappearing into the bathroom.

Bad, Annatha cursed silently. *How bad does it have to get?* That last one hurt like shit even though she knew she was doing the breathing thing right, and worse still, she wasn't even dilated yet. She had never been one for pain. Her father told her when she was little the screams were so terrifying when she fell off her bike, it sounded like she was dying. She wished silently for skinned, bleeding knees instead of this pain. It couldn't possibly hurt as much. The TV program's image of a baby's head crowning popped into her head and she groaned. *This was going to get much worse.*

Wendy returned with the damp wash cloth and applied it to the girl's forehead. She sat down and resumed reading the newspaper. It kept her from worrying about everything that could go wrong. She continued her vigilance and constant attention to the girl as the hours passed slowly.

Annatha used every ounce of willpower to breathe away the increasingly painful contractions that seemed to be back to back now. She was losing control. At the peak of the contraction, she felt herself collapse mentally and abandoned the breathing with stuttered gasps. The cramping was so intense she wanted to run somewhere and hope everything just stopped. She wished her mother was there to comfort her. It was the first time she remembered thinking that for a very long time, but the urge to hear her mom's soothing voice and touch was overwhelming. *That's not going to happen*, she told herself, she had to get a grip. She could beat this thing. Another contraction started and she felt her resolve melting again like butter on a hot skillet. She was unable to prevent a bloodcurdling scream at the apex of the contraction.

Wendy started when the girl cried out. *The contractions must really be strong now,* she thought and pressed on her abdomen. It felt as hard as the steel basement door that had served so well in keeping the girl captive. She turned down the flow of pitocin and listened to the fetal heart rate (FHR). It was still in the 150s. The blood pressure cuff had been left on the girl's wrist for the past several hours for convenience, and she pressed it for a reading. The display showed 155/108 now, and she felt a twinge of panic. It had to be the pain driving it up. She decided to give Annatha a dose of Nubain. It wasn't going to hurt anything to expose the baby to it this early in labor, but she had to limit the dosage or face a depressed newborn scenario. She had the pediatric Ambu bag, and a bottle of oxygen had been delivered a few days ago, but she didn't want to have to use either one of them. Her baby needed to be born strong and crying from the second he came out. She would only use the narcotic sparingly. The girl would have to suffer through somehow. Retrieving the drug from her tackle box, she drew up a dose and injected it through a port in the IV tubing. In less than a minute, Annatha relaxed for the first time in hours and her eyes closed. Wendy took another blood pressure reading five minutes after the Nubain was administered and she breathed a sigh of relief. It was 140/95 now. It had been the pain and not the toxemia. She uttered a silent prayer of thanks.

Annatha couldn't keep her eyes open. She saw the nurse give her something through the IV and a weird sensation had followed within seconds. Another contraction started and she found it even more difficult to focus now. She felt drugged and her mind was sluggish. She struggled to perform the breathing technique but faltered badly. Even though the pain was still intense, she did feel the medication had taken the edge off a little. *Thank God for that*, she thought as she dozed off.

She found herself sitting on her bed at home in front of a laptop. It wasn't hers; the screen was too big. The LCD displayed a panoramic scene of Wendy's basement. She tried to focus and moved the cursor over the bed. It zoomed in when she clicked on it and suddenly she was watching a close up of herself during a contraction. Her face was contorted and she was trying to get the nurse to lift the covers. When Wendy finally raised them up, a puppy was struggling to get out of her vagina. She began thrashing around and moving up the headboard to dislodge the tiny creature.

"Annatha!"

She opened her eyes when she heard the nurse call her name and realized she had been dreaming. Wendy was holding her legs down firmly. She must have been kicking them for real. *That was weird,* she thought. It was like an out of body experience. She appreciated the pain killer's help with her contractions, but the drug dreams it caused were freakin' bizarre.

"You back to reality now?" Wendy asked. She released her grip and stepped back.

"Yes," she replied, still shaken by the drug induced vision.

She sensed the aroma of coffee and looked up at the nurse. Wendy was staring at her curiously while sipping on a cup. *She must have brewed it down here,* she thought.

"What the heck were you dreaming?" Wendy sat down again.

"Nothing," she lied.

It wasn't that she didn't want to tell the nurse because she was being defiant. All that rage had faded with her first painful contraction. The nurse had displayed an unexpected competence and compassion thus far. She tended to her every need and supplied pain relief that eased her suffering. Sure, she wasn't allowing her to be cared for in a regular hospital, but it was doubtful a labor nurse would have been more attentive. Strangely enough, Annatha viewed Wendy as her lifeline now. Her fate as well as her baby's was in this woman's hands. It wasn't easy to admit this transformation in her perception, but this new reliance had been born of necessity. The onset of her toxemia had produced a reflexive fear that threatened to overwhelm her, but the nurse seemed up to the task despite her initial misgivings. Unlike the long months prior to this moment when she dreaded each time the nurse came to the basement, she felt some measure of comfort at her presence now.

A cold rush shocked her lower body and she glanced down to see the nurse removing the covers.

"I need to check you," Wendy said.

Annatha cooperated and assumed a frog leg position. Once again, the cold, slimy gloved fingers entered her and she tensed up. It felt like the nurse was trying to reach her tonsils. She watched as Wendy grabbed something wrapped in paper about the length of a ruler from the top of the night stand. The nurse didn't remove her gloved hand and with her free one, held the strange object up and opened it with her teeth. It was a yellow plastic device with a small hook at one end. She inserted it alongside her gloved hand and Annatha felt more pressure followed by a warm, liquid sensation bathing her perineum.

"Did I just pee?" she gasped.

"No," Wendy smiled. "I just broke your water. You're two centimeters dilated, seventy-five percent effaced and the baby's head is at a minus one station." (2/75/-1 Vertex)

Annatha was relieved. That would have been a particularly embarrassing labor moment to deal with. Surprisingly, the warm fluid continued running out and soaked her bare butt, along with the pad she was lying on.

Wendy took a small penlight and shined it on the white part of the chuck. It was stained a light green color. Meconium, she frowned. The baby had a bowel movement inside, probably due to the toxemia. She couldn't see any particulate matter and it wasn't deeply stained. As a precaution, she would suction her son's nose and mouth thoroughly before she delivered the chest just to make sure he didn't suck any of the noxious substance into his lungs with those first gasps for air. Although current standards didn't dictate this maneuver anymore if the baby was vigorous, she didn't want to take any chances where her son was concerned.

Annatha felt more alert and the contraction right after her water was broken let her know the heightened awareness was because the Nubain was wearing off. She panted hard and flavored her breathing with several four-letter words. The nurse scowled but didn't comment.

"What time is it?" she asked after a long cleansing breath.

"Two am," Wendy replied absently as she timed the baby's heartbeat.

Eight hours, Annatha calculated. She had been in labor that long? On the one hand it seemed like an eternity of unrelenting pain, but with her brain fading in and out of consciousness she had lost track of time and it was later than she anticipated. Another four hour segment meant another shot of seizure medicine and she saw the nurse was drawing up the dose now. She winced as the deep burning pain exploded in her left butt cheek.

"Jesus," she exclaimed while she rubbed the injection site, "that seems like a barbaric way to treat toxemia in the twenty-first century."

"It's given as an IV infusion in the hospital," Wendy admitted, "but if the dose is too high it can make the patient stop breathing and I don't have a pump to control the rate accurately. This is the safest way for you to get it."

Swell, Annatha grimaced as another contraction started. They were stronger now and she noticed a new part of her body was throbbing almost continuously in her lower back. Forcing herself to assume the knee chest position; she managed to replicate a yoga pose and do the associated breathing with it learned from the TV program. It didn't work as well as she had hoped, so she cursed and turned onto her back again.

"Can I have the washcloth wet again?" she glowered.

Wendy obeyed her request and returned with the soggy rag in hand. She changed the girl's fluid-soaked pad and replaced it with two more dry ones.

Annatha shoved it in her mouth and almost choked when she bit down. The washcloth was so saturated the cold water poured down her throat and she gagged. A contraction started and each time she coughed, the warm amniotic fluid squirted out. *How much more of that crap is in there?* she wondered. The pitocin didn't give her any time to recover now, and the contractions were much stronger. With each one she swore at the nurse through teeth tightly clenched on the damp washcloth. The muffled curses had replaced any attempt to utilize the Lamaze breathing.

"I need a pain shot!" she removed the rag and screamed at the nurse.

"It's too soon," Wendy declined. "You need to buck up."

"You're a fucking bitch!"

She ignored the girl's profanity. It was a common occurrence in laboring patients and she had been cursed at many times. She had often seen a patient turn on their spouse or other family members as if possessed by the devil. It wasn't comical to her like it was to some of the other L&D nurses. She didn't like the disrespect they displayed, no matter how much pain they were in. The girl glared at her menacingly for a few moments, then replaced the rag as another contraction began.

"You'll get another shot when it's time," she announced while she checked the FHR. It was still normal.

During the next few hours, Wendy kept herself busy preparing a vaginal delivery tray in between her labor tasks. She neatly laid the instruments out and when she was finished, covered them with a sterile drape. Everything was ready for the birth. At fifteen minute intervals like clockwork, she checked Annatha and the baby. The girl's blood pressure had been stable through the night, but was starting to climb again; her brow furrowed deeply as the latest display read 152/100. Annatha was wide-eyed and staring at her with pleading eyes. *Maybe she'd give her another dose of Nubain after the next exam.*

Wendy poured herself another cup of coffee. She wasn't sleepy; she was too excited for that, but the warm beverage was soothing in a way. It reminded her of the months she had been on night shift before transferring to days. She glanced at her watch and saw it was almost 6 a.m.; time for another cervical exam and MgSO4 shot.

"Good," Wendy announced with a pleased look on her face, "you're 5/100%/+1 station." She administered another dose of MgSO4.

When Annatha turned back over after receiving the shot, she begged Wendy to give her something for the pain. The labor was progressing well and now that the girl was in the active phase, she should dilate more quickly. It wouldn't hurt to give her one more shot. She drew it up and the girl blinked through moist, grateful eyes as the medication was pushed into the IV line.

If Annatha delivered within four hours, she wouldn't need another dose of MgSO4. It was usually continued for twenty-four hours after delivery; then the risk of seizure fell even if the blood pressure didn't normalize. However, in the girl's case, it wouldn't be continued since she wasn't going to be alive very long after she delivered the baby. First she would make sure her son was healthy and vigorous, then she would turn her attention to ending Annatha's existence on earth.

She shook off the gruesome plan, refocused on the task at hand and went to the bathroom to get a bedpan. When she returned, she instructed the girl she to empty her bladder so it wouldn't get distended and obstruct the baby's descent in her pelvis.

"Fuck off!" she screamed. "I don't need to pee."

Wendy ignored her and insisted, "Please do as I ask."

Annatha glared at the nurse. *Was there no end to this humiliation?* She struggled to lift her butt and felt the cold plastic bedpan sliding under her. When she sat down on it the inside edge cut into her skin and she swore loudly. *How the hell did anyone pee with this contraption digging into their ass?*

Wendy felt sympathy for the first time. In a hospital setting, every patient on MgSO4 had a catheter inserted so the urine output could be measured. She didn't have that luxury here. It was asking a lot, she knew, but the girl had not urinated for twelve hours as far as she could tell. Sometimes it was difficult to know with all the fluid coming out down there. But each time she changed the chucks, she smelled the used ones and had not detected a urine odor. She knew from experience that a distended bladder could delay the second stage of labor, so despite the embarrassment she knew the girl felt, this was necessary.

"I'll get you a fresh washcloth," she announced and disappeared into the bathroom to give Annatha some privacy.

After Wendy was gone, Annatha strained to empty her

bladder but nothing came out. Something was pressing on it and she just couldn't push past it. To make matters worse, she had a contraction and felt so much pressure in her current position she thought she was going to shit the baby out. When it was over, she angrily removed the bedpan and flung it across the room.

Wendy heard the commotion and when she came out, saw the bedpan lying upside down near the stairs. It was obviously empty so she left it.

"If you need to pee, just go in the bed," she offered out of pity. "I'll clean it up."

Annatha was furious. "This whole thing sucks," she cried. "I'm constantly leaking water down there so my bottom is soaked; I'm sweating like a pig and my hair is all matted. Why the hell would anyone do this more than once?"

"You're doing fine," Wendy reassured her. "All of this is normal."

During her attempt to mount a withering response, Annatha was cut short by a painful contraction. She stuffed the rag in her mouth again and screamed against it. When the contraction reached its nadir, she removed the washcloth and glared at the nurse.

"The breathing shit doesn't work," she swore. "Whoever invented that crap obviously never had a baby."

Wendy patiently took a blood pressure reading, since the contraction had subsided. The numbers were going up again, so she decided to give her one more dose of Nubain. She wouldn't tell her it was the last one.

Annatha realized after only two contractions that the last dose of pain medicine, administered only a few minutes ago, wasn't working as well as it had before. She begged Wendy for more but she declined. The nurse explained that the baby was three weeks early and would be more sensitive to narcotics. It might not breathe when it came out. She believed her but didn't know how much longer she could take this. The contractions were one on top of the other and she didn't feel like she was getting enough time between them to recover.

Wendy noticed the same thing and palpated the girl's abdomen to time the contractions. She knew the baby's oxygen reserves were tested each time the uterus squeezed off its blood supply when it contracted. There had to be enough time in between for the placenta to maintain a healthy oxygen level to the baby. She counted one and half minutes from the start of one to the beginning of another. *They're too close*, she calculated and turned down the pitocin.

Annatha drew on every ounce of mental, physical and emotional reserve in her possession. If only she could will her mind to find a safe haven from this torture--but she was exhausted and unable to fight against the pain anymore. It was futile to even pretend the breathing exercises were helpful. She had given up on them a few hours ago. Now she felt like a coastal beach during a hurricane surge, battered in waves with no defense. The only choice the beach had was to wait for the surge to end and assess any damage done. Other than that it was at the mercy of nature's wrath. She was feeling the storm's ruthless fury, and her biggest fear was that it would never end.

Chapter Twenty-Six

Thirty-seven Weeks One Day (37W1D)

Wendy was feeling the strain. Her patient's blood pressure was climbing again and she was too afraid to give her any more narcotics. She knew the girl was frightened and had no skills to deal with the pain, which caused her pressure to rise, but she had no safe alternative other than to get her delivered as soon as possible. Fortunately, Annatha had not complained of a headache thus far. She had never witnessed a patient seize who didn't first report a severe occipital headache. They usually didn't remember that fact, but a witness would divulge the eclamptic patient had grabbed the back of their head just before the seizure started. These were encouraging signs, but there was still the risk of a stroke if her pressure went too high. First she had to coax the girl's body to give up her son, then it wouldn't matter what happened.

She poured another cup of coffee and looked at her watch. It was 7 am. A brain fog was trying to move in and she fought to keep it away. The stress of caring for the girl throughout the night without any rest was beginning to take its toll. Despite the large intake of caffeine, she felt her eyes tearing from lack of sleep, and she was constantly fighting the urge to yawn. When she pulled the graveyard shift, she used cigarette breaks to battle fatigue. A good shot of nicotine seemed to be more effective than a whole pot of coffee. However, she ditched the unhealthy habit a few years ago, so that wasn't an option. She shook her head to clear the cobwebs. It was time for another exam.

Annatha had assumed a knee chest position again and was gently rocking back and forth. She found it helped relieve the incessant throbbing in her lower back, but afforded no respite from the abdominal pain during contractions. At least she didn't feel like shooting herself anymore. However, a new sensation was growing stronger with each contraction, in the form of intense pressure in her rectum. It caused an urge to bear down that was hard to resist. She was afraid of emptying her bowels all over the bed, but that's exactly what it felt like was going to happen if she gave in. Her face was buried in the pillow, so thankfully she wouldn't be able to see if she soiled the bed. She felt the nurse's hand on her back and was able to make out through the muffled effect from the pillow draped over her head that she needed to perform another cervical exam.

"No need to change positions," Wendy said while she inserted her right hand in the glove and applied the lube. "I can check your cervix like this."

The baby's head was low in the pelvis now and Wendy spread her two fingers as far apart as they could stretch but didn't feel any cervix. Annatha was completely dilated now with an exam of C/C/+1 OP. This meant the occipital fontanelle was closest to the rectum or OP (Occiput Posterior), instead of nearer to the bladder or OA (Occiput Anterior). The girl would have a more difficult time pushing him out from this orientation, she realized. If the head didn't rotate during its descent, her son would come out looking directly at the ceiling or as they called it when she worked in L&D, "sunny side up." It made sense the girl had ended up in a knee chest position. The back pain from an OP presentation was sometimes relieved by this maneuver.

"You're completely dilated now, Annatha," she said calmly

and leaned down close enough for her to hear. She felt the girl's hot breath on her face and smelled the unpleasant odor that occurred after hours of mouth breathing. It was something she was accustomed to from L&D experience, so it didn't faze her. When Wendy saw Annatha acknowledge her words by nodding her head against the pillow, she began to explain the process of pushing. The girl was to take a deep cleansing breath when the contraction started, then bear down as hard as she could into her rectum, like she was having a bowel movement, and hold it to a count of ten; take another deep breath and repeat the process. She should get in three pushes with each contraction.

"You are in a good position to push," she continued. "Just remember, it's up to you now to get this baby out. Everything depends on how hard you try. Do a good job and it will all be over soon." Wendy placed the Doppler on the bed so she could monitor the FHR every five minutes now. She had decided not to take the girl's blood pressure anymore, there was nothing she could do anyway.

Annatha focused on the nurse's voice. When a contraction started, Wendy began counting and she followed her instructions. She strained down with all of her might and wondered if her eyes might pop out of her skull. The pressure in her rectum increased when she bore down and it felt like she was trying to expel a watermelon. It was tempting to abandon the pushing and scream at the top of her lungs in despair, but she used the steady cadence of the nurse's voice to keep her from giving in to the urge. When the contraction ended, she collapsed forward, panting from the effort. She felt lightheaded and tried to slow her breathing down.

Her mind wandered to what her son would look like when he finally appeared. From her reading she had learned that most newborn babies had cone heads and their faces were scrunched from travelling through the birth canal, but she knew he would be the most beautiful thing she had ever seen. It occurred to her he would never know the suffering his real mother endured to bring him into this world. She quickly brushed this disturbing thought aside to concentrate on the task at hand. Her son was counting on her to help him in his struggle to be born. She wouldn't let him down.

****

Rachel flipped the visor up when she turned off the interstate at the exit for Tacoma General (TG) Hospital. The dazzling brilliance from the morning sun had revealed its unbridled ecstasy at finally being exposed from behind a gloomy veil vanquished by a crisp northerly breeze that scuttled the thick, gray clouds over the shadowy Cascade mountain range. However, it had forced her to deploy the visor on the drive down from Seattle to keep the glare from blinding her. Now that she was headed west and away from the bright orb that scarcely revealed its celestial radiance during Pacific Northwest winters, it was no longer needed.

She was almost there. It was just after 9 am and she had just hung up the phone after speaking with the receptionist at Tacoma Perinatal Associates, located across the street from TG. It was the clinic Wendy's maternity leave form had supposedly been faxed from. Dr. Elizabeth Wells' signature was on the fax; she was one of the perinatologists who worked there. Rachel had informed the receptionist she was an FBI agent and needed to speak with Dr. Wells regarding an urgent matter. The receptionist relayed that Dr. Wells was due any minute from making rounds, but to call when she got to the parking lot and she would confirm if the doctor had arrived or was still tied up at the hospital.

She had tossed and turned all night. The suspicions provoked by her visit with Sara Jordan yesterday were racing through her mind despite several feeble attempts to shut them down so she could get some sleep. At times during her fitful night, the jumbled facts fell together in a neat package and she felt certain Annatha was at Wendy Malloy's home either by choice or against her will. But when she played devil's advocate with this theory, she could shoot so many holes in it the whole mess fell like a house of cards. The nurse could very well be pregnant and Annatha's visit with her just before disappearing might turn out to be a weird coincidence. However, despite any misgivings she had about her tenuous nocturnal speculations, the need to rule out Wendy's involvement in this case had to be pursued.

Rachel had found it even more difficult to sleep after playing out the scenario of Annatha being held against her will all this time. What a horrible thing to happen if it was true. It also begged the question of how Wendy had succeeded in keeping the girl captive for this long. She almost had to be restrained. Another aspect that occurred to her in the wee hours of the morning was to keep the kidnapping a secret meant Wendy had to deliver the baby at home, not unheard of and she was a former L&D nurse, but poor Annatha would probably be scared to death. If any complications arose, the nurse couldn't risk taking the girl to a hospital for fear of being arrested. However, the most terrifying realization to intrude on her slumber had been that in this scenario Wendy couldn't allow Annatha to live. The nurse was smart enough to know if the girl was freed, she would go straight to the police and report Wendy's crime, and the nurse couldn't allow that to happen. It was a conscious nightmare that had caused Rachel to toss and turn for hours. Her dogged insomnia had required an extra shot in her latte that morning.

Her visit today with Dr. Wells would provide the critical piece of information that either gave her the ammunition needed to tackle the nurse head on or put her suppositions to rest for good. She thought back over the months since taking Annatha's case while she waited impatiently at a traffic light. After Loftin's polygraph and her first interview with Wendy, she had felt the girl was deliberately hiding or had become the victim of foul play. It didn't make sense to her that she would keep the pregnancy and strike out on her own, so the latter fate had haunted her as the most likely one. Weeks of no new leads had stretched on and she had not been able to shake the feeling something had been missed. Succumbing to her obsessive tendencies, she had struck out again and revisited the clinic. There she had taken a closer look at Wendy Malloy, and her investigation into the nurse's past at UW's L&D unit had revealed more contradictions that pointed to Wendy as a person of interest. For the first time in months she had hope that there just might be an explanation for Annatha's disappearance. She knew better than to jump the gun and barge into the nurse's home armed with her suspicions only to witness Wendy lift her shirt and expose a pregnant belly. It was imperative she follow a logical process and let the evidence guide her.

Her destination was nearby so she scanned the numbered addresses as she slowed down. She spotted the clinic building and maneuvered into a parking space. Retrieving her cell phone, she called the clinic number and was informed Dr. Wells was in her office. It was time to settle this thing once in for all, she resolved and strode purposefully towards the front door of the building.

****

Wendy felt like her stomach had as many knots in it as a one hundred year old sequoia. Her worry meter was rising now that the magical two hour mark for Annatha's second stage had come and gone. After two and a half hours of pushing, the baby's head was still at a +2 station; there was marked edema of the scalp, known as caput succedaneum, and the skull was molded as the uterine forces caused it to lengthen in order to squeeze through the girl's birth canal. The swelling made it almost impossible to establish landmarks by finding the saggital suture on the baby's skull to determine the presentation. She feared this degree of molding also indicated the mid portion of the vertex, marked by the location of the baby's ears, was probably at the level of her ischial spines, which served as the reference point for determining station. So more than likely, the true station of her son's head was still at zero.

It wasn't for lack of trying. The girl was giving it everything she had, and her knee chest position was the best one for pushing out an OP baby. Each time Annatha bore down, her perineum bulged and the vagina heaved open slightly; indicators the maternal expulsive efforts were strong and correctly focused. The fact the two hour limit had been broken did not necessarily mean the baby couldn't be born vaginally, but the chances of a normal delivery decreased and the risk of complications increased in her experience. A C/Section was an option under normal circumstances, but these were not normal circumstances. No way would she even consider doing the procedure herself with no effective anesthesia. The girl had to push the baby all the way out or low enough for her to try a vacuum-assisted delivery; however, an attempt with this maneuver now would be futile. The head was too high and OP deliveries required more traction. All she would accomplish would be to pop off the vacuum cup and risk injuring her son's fragile scalp. It might come to this but only if the FHR dropped or as a last resort if the girl was unable to achieve a vaginal birth after four hours of pushing.

She watched Annatha straining down for the third time with this contraction. After it was over, the girl fell forward.

"I can't hold myself in that position anymore," she gasped for air.

"Turn over on your back," Wendy instructed and helped the exhausted girl.

She gave in and decided to take another blood pressure. This time the reading was 160/112. Silently, she prayed the girl had strong blood vessels in her brain that could withstand this amount of pressure without rupturing. She possessed no therapeutic maneuver in her arsenal to lower it and this made her feel helpless. It was time to see what progress could be made with Annatha on her back.

Wendy leaned over and made direct eye contact with the girl. At this distance she could make out her battle scars even in the dim light. Her sclera were bloodshot from the hours of bearing down and the skin on her face was dotted with small petechia, or hemorrhages, for the same reason.

"When you have your next contraction, grab the back of your thighs and pull your legs towards you," Wendy's voice failed to conceal her rising alarm after witnessing this sight. "This will help open your pelvis."

Annatha sensed a change in the nurse's usual reassuring tone. *Was something wrong?* It seemed to her this was taking a lot longer than normal, but she had no point of reference.

"Am I going to be able to push out the baby?" she asked, her voice trembling slightly.

"You have to," Wendy managed to compose herself and tried to placate the girl. "It's your first baby and they always take longer. You can't give up now."

Annatha nodded weakly. She was dripping with sweat and beyond exhaustion. This experience had no equal in her previous existence. Sometime during the relentless efforts to move her baby down the birth canal, an unseen switch had been thrown that disconnected the present reality from her mind. Her body cried out against the onslaught of pain caused by the contractions and intense pressure in her rectum, but her brain ignored the desperate pleas for mercy and forged ahead with its reflexive commands to push. She had discovered untapped strength and willpower unfamiliar to her before today, but it was in danger of evaporating if this ordeal didn't end pretty soon. A cool, wet sensation on her forehead caused her to open her bloodshot eyes. The nurse was placing another rag on her overheated skin.

"You have to keep going," Wendy encouraged her. "Once you get the head rotated it should come down quickly and you can get this over with and get out of here soon. Your son is depending on you; don't let him down."

Another contraction started and just when Annatha thought it couldn't get any worse, it did. In this position, the stabbing pain in her back dug deeper still and she unleashed a shrill "FUUUUUUUUUUUUCCCCCCCCKKKKKKKK!"

"Keep your mouth closed and focus all that energy in your rectum," Wendy said firmly, ignoring the profanity, and began counting to ten. To her relief, the girl gathered herself somehow and complied.

Annatha experienced a curtain fall between the physical agony and her mental determination. She could hear a distant, steady cadence from the nurse's voice and was vaguely aware of her hands pulling both knees back to her stomach, but she transcended to a surreal plane where a primal force wielded its power and provided her with the ability to exercise her maternal duty. It was as if Mother Nature had created a special fantasy land for mothers to enter where She could help them overcome their selfish urges and sacrifice everything so that their baby could have new life.

Reality came rushing back when the contraction stopped, and Annatha grabbed the washcloth and stuffed it in her mouth. She bit down hard to squeeze the water out and eagerly drank it. Despite the nurse's reassurance, she suspected Wendy was patronizing her. It was obvious she was unnerved, and that heightened her own anxiety. She had no idea how long this could go on or what the nurse would do in the end if she couldn't push the baby out. Would she really let them both die here? It seemed unlikely, given her investment over the past months so she could have her own child. A thought suddenly interjected itself that was almost too sinister to consider. *Would the nurse dare to perform a C/Section here?* If she did, there was nothing to keep her from feeling everything, not to mention the fact she likely wouldn't survive. This horrifying realization steeled Annatha's resolve and she pushed harder than ever with the next contraction, praying her baby's head would turn so she could push him out.

Wendy urged her on, but a growing dread was creeping into the basement despite her fervent prayers. Things were looking bleak and she had to come up with a way to deliver this baby without causing harm. Just how she was going to accomplish this wasn't settled yet.

****

Rachel was ushered into Dr. Wells' office by the receptionist, who seemed very curious about the FBI agent's visit. The physician was dictating and waved for her to have a seat. She sat down and waited, but her gut was churning in anticipation. After a few minutes, Dr. Wells hung up the phone and introductions were dispensed. She looked at the agent with a puzzled expression.

"What can I do for you?"

Rachel took a deep breath. She had to convince the doctor to divulge if Wendy Malloy was a patient.

"I'm investigating a missing teenager," she began. "One person of interest is a nurse at a women's clinic in Olympia. To make a long story short, this nurse claims she has a high risk pregnancy and is a patient of yours."

"I'm sorry, Agent …"

"Gray."

"Agent Gray," she smiled. "Unless you have a warrant I can't give out protected health information."

"I'm aware of HIPAA," Rachel replied evenly, "but I think there is a way you can help me without breaking the law."

"I guess you would know about that," Dr. Wells offered.

"Some," Rachel admitted," but I propose to ask you a question I believe does not violate HIPAA regulations."

"Let's hear it," the physician agreed and leaned forward.

"I'm not interested in any health care information or whether this person is a patient of yours," she said earnestly. "I just want to know if she is not a patient here."

Dr. Wells contemplated the question. It didn't seem to her that any privacy laws would be violated by cooperating with the request. The FBI agent was not demanding or pushy about it, either. She decided to help if it meant solving a crime.

"What's her full name?" the physician asked.

"Wendy Malloy."

Dr. Wells shook her head. "I know all of my patients, Agent Gray," she replied firmly, "but I don't recall a patient by that name."

"Could you humor me and check? It's very important."

She nodded and quickly typed the name on her computer keyboard. After hitting "Enter," she waited until the screen changed.

"I don't have anyone with the last name Malloy here." She gazed steadily at the agent.

"I know I'm being picky," Rachel smiled but inside her guts were twisted like a pretzel, "but I just want to be sure. You confirm identification with your patients with a driver's license or such?"

"Without exception," she replied and leaned back. "Does this help?"

"Absolutely," she affirmed and stood up, offering her hand. "Thank you for your cooperation, Dr. Wells, and I'm sorry to rush out, but I have somewhere to go."

They shook and Rachel hurried from the office and pressed the elevator button several times like it would make a difference. *Her suspicions had been confirmed. Wendy wasn't pregnant!* The floor lights above showed the elevator was on the eighth floor and it wasn't moving. She strode quickly towards the exit door and flung it open, flying down four flights of stairs to the lobby. As she crossed the parking lot and approached her car, Rachel warned herself to put the investigative brakes on. All this proved was that Wendy had lied about her doctor. It probably meant she was lying about being pregnant at all, but she had to deal with the evidence no matter how much she wanted to stretch it to confirm her suspicions. Still, she would confront the nurse with this information and see where things led. It gave her an excuse to show up unannounced at her home and at the very least, try snooping around.

Just as she secured her seatbelt, Rachel's cell phone ring tone sounded. She looked at the caller ID and saw it was the Seattle field office number. Oh yeah she recalled, Jim Dalton wanted her to let him know if she was driving to Olympia after her interview with Dr. Wells.

"Yes Jim," she answered.

"Hey," he replied. "I just got a call from a Sara Jordan."

"L&D director at UW?" she was puzzled.

"The same," he admitted. "She wanted you but I told her you were busy."

"Go on."

"She says a former coworker of Wendy Malloy's who wasn't there yesterday found out you were asking questions and claims she knew her pretty well." He paused but she didn't respond. "Anyway, the coworker …"

He stopped and Rachel heard the sound of papers being shuffled. She sighed impatiently.

"I heard that," he chided.

"Good detective work," she shot back.

He ignored her comment. "Betty Lewiston is the name Sara gave me. Anyway, she claims Wendy Malloy had a hysterectomy just before she moved to Olympia."

Rachel gasped. *What the hell? Why didn't anyone else know that?*

"Is she certain?" she demanded.

"Hell, I don't know," he replied, "I didn't interview her, but Sara said Betty Lewiston would know if anybody did."

"I'm on my way to Olympia," she announced as she turned the ignition.

"You want me to get a warrant?"

"No time," she objected and gave him Wendy's home address. "If I strike out we can get it then. If you don't hear from me in an hour, call me. If I don't answer, call the local police and dispatch them to that address."

"Be careful," Jim warned, "and please wait for me.

"Always," she replied and hung up. Next she punched Wendy Malloy's home address into her navigator. The calm, expressionless voice commanded her to turn right out of the parking lot and she dutifully obeyed. The evidence was overwhelming now that she knew the nurse couldn't possibly be pregnant. This meant she had kidnapped Annatha somehow and was keeping her locked up. No other scenario made sense now that she knew the nurse had undergone a hysterectomy. Even though the girl had a troubled home life, Rachel couldn't imagine why she wouldn't have contacted her mother if at all possible. Armed with this knowledge, it fell in her lap to rescue Annatha. Although it was still three weeks or so before Annatha's due date, Rachel felt an urgency to get to Olympia as fast as she could. She didn't want the girl or her family to suffer one moment longer than necessary. Wendy would likely resist any attempt to be questioned or allow Rachel into her home for fear of being discovered. She would need every skill learned over the years to force her way in without a warrant. It was too ominous to consider the baby had already been born, because even though the nurse would be arrested, Annatha would not be alive. Rachel floored the accelerator as she merged onto I5 and into traffic.

****

Wendy shielded her eyes as she emerged from the dark basement and turned towards the kitchen. It felt like she had just stumbled out of a tomb. The morning sun glared through the windows and seemed a thousand times brighter after being in the gloomy basement for so long. Mesmerized by the obtrusive sunlight, she gazed blankly at the countless dust particles dancing about in the sharp, jagged rays that pierced the wood-framed kitchen window and reflected off the stainless steel range. She was refilling the large cup of ice shavings she doled out to Annatha between contractions. It wasn't because she was asked to do so; she needed some time away from the intense drama and growing pessimism downstairs to get her bearings.

In a split second, her mind felt a million miles away. She recalled the story of Abraham and Isaac in the Bible. God had demanded Abraham kill his son to test his faith and love. At the last moment, Isaac had been spared as his father was about to carry out God's command. Was this a test of her faith? Did God want her precious son to enter His kingdom? Her mind was so fogged by the hours of unrelenting emotional stress she found it hard to consider the questions she was asking of herself. After all, she only wanted to do His will. But how could it be His will? She had spared this child of God from certain death, and was she to believe he was to be taken from her now?

Shaking her head in frustration, she opened the freezer door and a blast of cold air escaped. It felt good on her face. She scooped ice shavings into the cup with her bare hand. The wet, frigid sensation against her palm stirred exhausted senses and she quickly finished the task. Setting the cup down, she opened the window over the sink and leaned forward. She drank in the fresh scent of cedar as it wafted across her face, carried by a gentle morning breeze.

Rejuvenated by the stark contrast of nature's brilliant canvas in front of her with the dank, ominous scene downstairs, Wendy experienced an awakening in her soul. She realized all the years of suffering and disappointment were almost at an end. At long last she would have the child she had always dreamed of. Countless fantasies had consumed her the past several months as she imagined what their life would be like. She longed to stroke his soft baby skin and feel his tiny hand squeezing her finger. Her breasts were full and swollen nipples tingled in anticipation of his hungry mouth latching on to feed. The sweet aroma of baby powder and lotion after a bath filled her senses and she blinked away tears of joy. She wiped her eyes on the scrub top she had changed into for the impending delivery and her fanciful daydream was brushed away, too, as the grim reality of a critical situation in her makeshift delivery room returned full force.

The past several months she had devoted every ounce of her being to nurturing and protecting her son, all for this moment. She had spared him from the abortionist's instruments of death and she wasn't about to let him down now. In order to accomplish this she had to adapt a mental and emotional toughness if she hoped to succeed.

During her L&D tour, the obstetrician always made decisions

regarding management. Sure, she had a good idea when a patient needed a C/Section, and this certainly met the criteria. The girl had been pushing for three hours now and the baby's head was still high and so molded she couldn't find any familiar landmarks to judge position. However, it was her sole responsibility to call the trial of labor a failure. In a hospital a routine surgery would be performed and mother and baby would most likely be fine. However, this was not a hospital and executing a major operation with crude anesthesia was going to be the greatest challenge of her life. She had the IV tranquilizer Versed to sedate Annatha and some local anesthesia, but it was a given the girl would not be able to hold still. Even though she had witnessed countless numbers of C/Sections and knew where to make the incisions, the task would still be difficult and almost impossible in a moving patient. The only solution would be to restrain Annatha after sedating her. It seemed cruel after the heroic efforts made by the girl to push her baby out. Maybe she would put the vacuum on and try to pull her son out from below, even though she was sure the attempt would be futile. Wendy reminded herself Annatha was planning to suck her defenseless child out with nothing to numb his pain and this thought emboldened her to press on with her plans. She straightened up and looked at the full cup of ice on the counter. It would likely be the last thing Annatha ever put in her mouth.

****

Annatha gradually slowed her breathing as a contraction subsided. She was too tired to push anymore and simply endured the pain as best she could. Her eyes burned as briny sweat dripped down from her forehead. She squeezed a wet wash cloth over them to irrigate the salty fluid out. Every muscle in her body ached and her vagina had swollen to a grotesque size. Despite the physical suffering she endured it was nothing compared to the fear that threatened to overwhelm her. *Something was wrong. The baby should be out by now.* Wendy kept encouraging her to push but it wasn't doing any good, even though the contractions were relentless and more painful than ever. Long hours of exertion had resulted in a fatigue so overpowering she was drifting in and out of consciousness, but she had enough control of her faculties to understand this couldn't go on forever. She tried not to speculate about what the nurse would do to deliver the baby but she couldn't help but wonder if Wendy was crazy enough to do a C/Section in the basement.

She turned her head and through half open eyes saw the nurse's chair was empty. *Where had she gone?* Another contraction started and despite the intensity she dealt with it by closing her eyes to shut out the pain. She found herself thinking about the past months and how much she missed her mom. The timeless hours of reflection in the basement had made her realize the really important things in life. She had an unfinished life and looked forward to continuing it with an entirely new point of view. Her son was to be taken from her, but she would always remember him and the time they spent together during the pregnancy. By loving her unborn son unconditionally, she had thrown away her immature selfishness and learned what it was like to place another person above everything else. It was a rebirth of sorts for her, a gift she would forever cherish.

Annatha was jolted from her self-induced trance by the most painful contraction she had experienced yet. She shut her eyes tightly but was unable to escape the horrifying pain that wracked her body. Breathing rapidly, she became frightened when it failed to lessen as usual. Instead, it continued building fiercely and surged past her breaking point with a vengeance. She struggled to get on top of it but lost total control, and from deep inside her soul an agonal scream erupted and filled the empty basement. Her surroundings began to fade and she experienced an overwhelming sense of doom. *Was this what it felt like to die?* She felt her numb lips mouth the word "Mommy" and everything went black. She was a little girl again running to her father's open arms …

****

Wendy was at the top of the stairs securing the steel basement door when she heard a primal scream. She knew immediately something was very wrong and flew down the steps, terrified by the bloodcurdling sound. When she arrived at the bedside Annatha was lying motionless and all the color had drained from her face. She activated the blood pressure cuff but decided not to wait for the reading and pressed two fingers against Annatha's neck to find her carotid pulse. It was present but very thready. The cuff beeped and she glanced down at the display; it read 100/60. Even though it was normal for most patients, the girl had been hypertensive so this confirmed, along with the weak carotid pulse, that she was going into shock. She grabbed Annatha by the shoulders and shook her several times while calling her name loudly, but her body just flopped limply like a rag doll.

Wendy felt panicked. What was going on? She grabbed the Doppler and smeared gel over the girl's abdomen. The baby's heart rate sounded fine but a thought crossed her mind that it might be Annatha's pulse she was picking up. If she was in shock her heart rate would be as rapid as the baby's. She felt for the girl's carotid again and to her horror it matched the Doppler's rate beat for beat. Moving the device around she searched frantically for the FHR. Finally, a much slower pulsating sound was discovered and when Wendy timed it on her watch, the rate was down to 60 bpm. *Oh my God,* she realized, her son was in distress.

Wendy stepped back and surveyed the scene in front of her. Annatha was unresponsive and in shock, most likely due to internal bleeding which meant the baby was not getting enough oxygen. Something catastrophic had just occurred to cause this. Wracking her brain, she could only think of two situations that would create this clinical picture: the placenta had separated due to her high blood pressure, or the uterus had ruptured from long hours of pitocin and pushing. It didn't much matter which one it was, her son was in mortal danger and if she didn't get him out quickly he would suffer brain damage or die.

Wendy moved rapidly. She switched the bedside lamp on, grabbed the #10 scalpel, some scissors and tissue forceps from the tote. Standing over Annatha, who was now trapped in the clutches of death's unforgiving grasp, her hands were shaking uncontrollably but she knew if she didn't get to her son in time her dream would be over. She pressed the scalpel against the girl's abdomen just above her pubic bone and pressed down firmly. The skin split beneath the sharp blade like an orange rind and she carried the incision along the linea nigra that ran down the midline of her abdomen all the way to her belly button. The fatty tissue oozed fluid that had accumulated from the girl's toxemia; Wendy noticed it was a pale yellow and didn't bleed as expected, probably due to hypotension. She continued dividing the muscle layers, searching for the thin band of connective tissue that held the rectus muscles together. It was difficult to identify and because time was critical, she abandoned the effort and began slicing through the thick muscle. Fortunately, it didn't bleed much either. Once through this layer, she encountered a large, over-distended bladder and before she could stop it, the scalpel pierced the bladder wall and urine gushed out. Shaken briefly by the inadvertent injury, she told herself it didn't matter anyway and resumed the incision above this point where the peritoneum, a thin sack that lined the abdominal cavity, was ballooned out and appeared bruised. She stabbed the scalpel into the reddish purple bulge and opened the abdominal cavity. Immediately after the entry was made, dark red blood mixed with amniotic fluid gushed out of the wound, along with clots the size of baseballs. Wendy gasped. Annatha's uterus had ruptured.

****

Rachel knocked for the third time on Wendy Malloy's front door; still no answer. She knew the nurse was home because her car was parked in the driveway. Jim Dalton had specifically asked her to wait for him, but she couldn't justify delaying this any longer. After months of investigation she had finally located Annatha and felt certain the girl was being held against her will. This was no time to wait for the cavalry since she couldn't be sure something untoward had already occurred. She mentally prepared a list of evidence that gave her probable cause to enter the house without a search warrant. Satisfied she was legally protected, Rachel turned the knob and opened the door. She entered the front room and shouted "hello" several times. No one answered so she quickly walked down a hallway and scouted each room. She noticed the nurse had decorated and furnished a nursery in one of them and glanced in the crib to make sure it was empty. Returning to the hallway, she noticed a steel door that was closed and walked over to study it. It appeared to have two deadbolts securing it. There were two key holes and one had a key in it. The other lock seemed to be a special deadbolt latch plate of the type that had a key pad on the other side. *This amount of security was designed to keep someone in,* she surmised.

She turned the knob and pushed but the sturdy metal door didn't budge. The keyed deadbolt wasn't locked, but she realized the plated one must be opened from the other side by a key pad. Pounding on the steel door with her fist, she identified herself as an FBI agent and demanded Wendy let her in. After repeating her command a few more times Rachel stepped back and assessed the situation. If she continued now, it wasn't an open door she was walking through. She had to have a really good cause to disable the deadbolt and violate Wendy's right to a reasonable search and seizure. *Come on, Gray, there's plenty of cause here,* she decided. She had to get that door open, but how? Discharging a bullet into a metal door would be a bad idea. No telling what kind of ricochet she would get. Then she remembered there was a drill in her trunk. She had used it before to disable locks.

Striding rapidly out of the house, she opened her trunk and rifled through a box of tools until she found the drill, with a bit already in it of the size she would need. She tightened the grips snugly around the bit and shut the trunk. It was time to bust this crazy nurse and return Annatha to her family. She hurried back into the house.

****

Wendy didn't have time to put gloves on before she made her incision. Sterile technique was far down her list of concerns. A ruptured uterus meant the baby was floating free somewhere in the sea of blood pouring out. She reached inside and felt the warm liquid up to her elbows as her fingers searched frantically. It was only a few moments before she located her son's torso and walked her hands down his body until she felt his feet. She pulled with both hands but they slipped off due to the oily blood that bathed his skin. Crying out in desperation, she grabbed the washcloth from the girl's forehead and plunged it into the bloody mess and used it for traction to deliver her son's body feet first. Using the rag, she cleaned the blood from his face but his tiny head was limp and rolled back and forth as she wiped.

Wendy screamed "NO!" as she scooped up his lifeless body and placed him in the makeshift warmer she had prepared. She squeezed the base of his umbilical cord between her thumb and forefinger but could not feel a pulse. If he had lost a lot of blood from the ruptured uterus, she had no way of resuscitating him with fluids. In order for him to have any chance of surviving, she would need to initiate CPR. She grabbed the Ambu bag and plugged in the oxygen tank tubing, turning the valve on full flow. *Concentrate, Wendy*, she braced herself. Everything she'd worked for the past several months would be gone if she couldn't bring her lifeless son back.

She placed two thumbs over the baby's lower sternum and pressed three times, then used the Ambu bag to force a breath into his tiny lungs. Suddenly, she was distracted by someone banging on the basement door. There was a muffled voice in between the pounding but she couldn't make out what it was saying. This was most unexpected. *Who on God's earth could it be?* Wendy shook her head and resumed CPR on her son. She couldn't stop now; everything rested on the next few minutes. Her son's life depended on the skills she had honed as an L&D nurse. She had witnessed severely depressed babies before who didn't seem to stand a chance, but using these same techniques minus an intravenous line, they had been brought back to life with no residual neurologic injury.

After what seemed like an eternity, she heard a muffled cry beneath the Ambu bag mouthpiece. Again, she felt for the base of his umbilical cord and this time she could feel a faint pulsation. She timed the beats and gasped when the count totaled ninety-two. There was hope, she rejoiced silently, and stopped the precordial compressions. She popped the tubing off the Ambu bag and held it over her son's face, bathing him in oxygen-rich air. His fingers were moving now and he was breathing on his own. The blue color of his skin had turned a healthier pink shade. She rubbed the bottoms of his feet to stimulate him and weak cries became stronger as the irritating maneuver awakened his life force. He pulled his feet away and began kicking his legs. Wendy felt the tears streaming down her face and the struggling infant's figure blurred. She donned a stethoscope and listened to his chest, since she couldn't see well. A strong heartbeat was easily heard but his lungs sounded a little gunky. She found the bulb syringe and began sucking out his nose and mouth, which made him even madder, and he cried out in protest. Wendy heaved a long sigh and relaxed for the first time since the ordeal had begun. It was even more satisfying than she had ever dreamt to watch her son as he blinked curiously at his new home while protesting her efforts to clear the mucus from his mouth. His close brush with death had been terrifying but she managed the crisis expertly and rescued him. She resisted the urge to pick him up and hug him tightly. He had just gone through a pretty severe trauma and needed to breathe in pure oxygen for awhile longer.

Her joy was cut short by the sound of something grinding against metal, and she recognized the high-pitched whine of a drill. The shrill noise reverberated in the closed room and she held her hands over her ears. She suddenly realized someone was trying to get into the basement. It had to be the same person who was banging on the door while she was performing CPR. Whoever it was had no business there. A horrifying thought crossed her mind that a burglar might be trying to break in. She eased over to the bed and found the bloody scalpel lying in a pool of blood next to the girl's lifeless body. Picking it up, she moved in front of where her son was lying just as the drilling stopped and the basement door swung open. An unwelcome silhouette appeared at the top of the stairs and she heard a woman's voice shout "FBI!" in a firm voice.

Rachel bent down to look into the dimly lit basement. The only thing she could see from her vantage point was a bed. The lamp on a night stand next to it provided enough illumination and she could make out a frail figure lying motionless in the bed. A chocolate-syrup colored stain covered the sheets and spilled out onto the floor. She knew from experience blood assumed a dark brown color in the dark. There was so much it looked like someone had been slaughtering cattle. Her heart fell as she realized it was Annatha and from all appearances, she was dead. *What the hell had happened here?* The horrifying sight of her lifeless missing girl drenched in blood took the wind out of her sails for a moment. *Keep sharp,* she reminded herself and struggled to control her emotions. She inhaled a deep breath to regain her composure and took another step down just as the sound of a baby crying echoed in the room.

Rachel almost vaulted down the remaining stairs and turned to survey the room. She spotted the nurse, who seemed to be guarding something, and decided it was probably the baby. It was hard to tell with just the two lights on, but her right hand was clutching something that appeared shiny and the left was hidden from view. What was she holding?

"Wendy Malloy, this is Agent Rachel Gray of the FBI," she announced loudly and flipped open her badge.

Wendy took four long strides towards the intruder who had just identified herself as the pesky FBI agent she was interviewed by at the clinic. Her eyes were wild with rage as she prepared to defend her baby and her home. She swung her left hand around from behind her and emptied the mace can from a distance of several feet, catching the agent completely by surprise.

Rachel felt her face explode in pain and realized immediately she had been maced. She groped for her 9mm service revolver and simultaneously slid backwards up the stairway while the sharp edges of the hard, wooden steps dug into her back. A hazy figure loomed over her and she pushed frantically as hard as she could but not before something sharp bored into her upper thigh. She cried out in pain and kicked wildly with both feet until she felt one contact an arm. A clattering noise alerted her that the weapon she had been stabbed with was probably knocked loose for the moment. She took the opportunity to escape her assailant, quickly turning around and crawling on all fours as fast as she was able with her limited vision. When she reached the top, Rachel grabbed the side of the steel door, slammed it shut and propped her legs against it. Her revolver was still in its holster so she took it out and released the safety just in case she was unable to secure the door. It was difficult to focus with her burning eyes filled with tears. She felt like she was trying to see through a pouring rain. Suddenly, she felt tremendous pressure against her feet. The nurse was still after her, trying to open the door.

Wendy pounded and shoved against the steel door. She grunted and fumed against it in vain. It wouldn't budge.

"You can't have my baby!" she cried out in desperation.

"Drop your weapon, Wendy," Rachel ordered, "it's over." She felt a warm liquid on her thigh and wished she could see how much the stab wound was bleeding. Instead, she pressed her hand firmly on top of it and winced at the pain elicited by her maneuver.

"You will not take my baby!" Wendy shrieked. "His mother was going to kill him and God commanded me to save him."

Rachel knew she was dealing with a crazed psychopath, which explained the powerful thrusts she felt against her legs. Insanity seemed to provide superhuman strength to its victims as a way of making up for their mental anguish. Her thigh was throbbing and she knew it wouldn't be long before the nurse overpowered her efforts to keep the door closed. For the first time, she wished Jim Dalton was around.

The nurse's last effort almost succeeded and Rachel made a split-second decision to remove her legs and wager the nurse would crash through the doorway out of control and injure herself. It worked, but not as well as she had hoped.

Wendy pushed mightily against the door and felt no resistance. Her momentum carried her forward with no time to retreat and she slammed into the wall across the hallway. The blow almost caused her to lose her balance but she deftly resisted falling and righted herself. Fortunately, the scalpel had not been dislodged by the sudden jolt and she turned to face her enemy. This time she would find the agent's neck and inflict a mortal wound.

"Drop your weapon or I'll shoot," Rachel warned. She couldn't make out the nurse's position clearly enough to fire at her shoulder and disable her. It didn't matter anyway, as she was fighting for her life. Unless her attacker surrendered in the next few seconds she would have no choice but to defend herself with deadly force.

Wendy raised the scalpel and zeroed in on the agent's neck where the carotid artery was located. She lunged but never heard the shot that pierced her throat underneath the chin and ravaged her brain matter.

Rachel felt the nurse's flaccid body as it came crashing down on top of her. The smell of gunpowder was thick in the air and she lay back gasping for breath underneath the dead weight that pinned her against the hardwood floor. She groped blindly for the nurse's head and when she moved her hand down to find a pulse she felt the sticky, warm blood oozing from the entry wound in her neck. Ignoring the sick feeling in the pit of her stomach, she confirmed there was no hint of a beating vessel against her index and middle fingers. Wendy Malloy was dead. She shuddered and wiped the bloody hand on her pants.

This was the first time she had killed anyone in the line of duty and Rachel knew she would probably experience some remorse down the road, but after witnessing the sight of Annatha's lifeless body in the basement, she only felt satisfaction this evil woman was gone. Rachel suddenly remembered through the roar of adrenaline that coursed through her body that she had a crime scene downstairs as well as a newborn baby, but first she needed to be able to see. She shoved with all her might and the nurse's body flopped against the floor with a loud thud. Once free of her attacker, she replaced the revolver in its holster. Climbing slowly to her feet with the injured leg protesting all the way, she limped into the kitchen and turned on the faucet. She cupped her hands and splashed water in her eyes until the unbearable stinging ceased and groped for a dish towel to dry them.

"Hello?" Jim Dalton's baritone voice shouted from the open front door.

"Come in, Jim," Rachel blinked her eyes rapidly and was grateful she could see fairly well now.

The stocky ex-Marine entered the house and spied his fellow agent standing in the kitchen. Her eyes were bloodshot and she was bleeding from her right thigh.

"What the hell happened to you?" he asked, dumbfounded.

"Call 911," she ordered without responding to his question. "There's a newborn infant in the basement that's probably less than an hour old."

Dalton didn't hesitate. He could tell by her voice she wasn't in the mood to go into any details right now. Flipping up his cell phone he dialed 911 and described the situation to the dispatcher while he walked to the basement door behind Rachel. He checked the nurse's pulse to see if they needed more than one ambulance but there was none.

"She's as dead as Judas Iscariot," he stated flatly then looked up at Rachel. "Want me to take a look at that?" he motioned at her wound.

Rachel didn't acknowledge his flip remark or the offer for first aid. She was anxious to survey the bloodbath downstairs and tend to the baby until the EMT's got there. The bleeding from her leg had slowed but she groaned when she stepped over Wendy's body as the injured muscles protested the effort. She took each step one at a time and winced with every inch of progress. It seemed an eternity ago she was scrambling up them in fear for her life. Nothing this intense had ever happened to her before and she felt a mixture of fear and relief all at the same time. *That was a very close call.* At the bottom of the stairs, she stopped to catch her breath.

"You okay?" Jim asked.

"Yes Jim," she said crossly. It wasn't his fault her leg hurt, but his attention was annoying. He needed something to do. "Call the Thurston County CSI team. They'll need to work this scene."

As she walked across the basement floor, Annatha's body lay like a ghoulish shrine to the ultimate sacrifice a mother could make for her child. She knew it was inevitable that the girl would have to be examined, but for now she turned her attention to the baby, who was whimpering all alone in his makeshift crib. His entire body was covered with dried blood from his dead mother. Rachel picked him up and took him into the bathroom. She ran the water until it was tepid and used a wet hand towel to wipe off the blood. This made him start crying again and he released a stream of urine that almost caught her in the face. Never having raised a son herself, she didn't anticipate this and quickly aimed the flow away from her. Next she dried him off with a clean bath towel and wrapped him tightly in it to keep him from getting cold. She knew babies also lost heat from their scalp too so she took a wash cloth and fashioned a small cap. Her heart was heavy as she carried him out of the bathroom. He would never know the suffering his mother went through to have him. Even though she knew Wendy would have loved him in her own crazy way, it wasn't right what the nurse did. Sure, Annatha was going to have an abortion but that was no reason to kidnap her, hold her in this basement for months and kill her with secrecy. Even though the investigation into Annatha's death had yet to begin, Rachel sensed something went very wrong during the birth process and the lack of a safe hospital environment had been a fatal omission. Reluctantly, she knew it was time to turn her attention to the grisly murder scene.

"Here Jim," she handed the infant to the startled agent. "You're a dad, act like one." Rachel sneered but didn't let the agent see her. He acted like she was handing him a ticking bomb.

She spotted a box of exam gloves next to the bed, plucked two out and slipped them on. This was perhaps the most difficult case from an emotional standpoint that she had ever dealt with, and standing over the dead girl's body she experienced a sudden rush of grief and anger. Annatha's eyes were closed and her facial expression was peaceful, in contrast with the macabre picture displayed by the rest of her body. Her skin was sallow from being drained of its life-giving blood that was spilled out around her. Rachel studied the crude incision on her abdomen. Apparently this was how the nurse delivered the baby, she deduced. Wendy must have been desperate to attempt major surgery in this setting. She mentally recoiled at how horrible it must have been for Annatha to be cut open without adequate anesthesia. It wasn't clear at the moment whether the girl bled to death from the operation itself, or if something hemorrhaged from the pregnancy. She didn't know enough about the medical aspects of childbirth complications so she elected not to explore the wound. That would be left to the coroner. She knew despite her best efforts to prevent it, the grisly scene was now burned into her memory and would haunt her for some time to come.

Rachel shed the gloves and glanced over at Dalton. He was still holding the baby like a priceless Ming dynasty vase and she couldn't help but smile. She walked over, relieved the agent of his burden and cradled the infant in her arms.

"Isn't he beautiful," she cooed and poked his soft cheek.

Jim shrugged. "I guess," he agreed. "Did you see the cat?"

Rachel shook her head. "Where?"

"Over by that recliner," he pointed.

Walking over, Rachel spotted the cat crouching underneath the chair. He was trembling so she tried to soothe him as best she could while clutching the newborn tightly in her arms. It seemed likely the nurse had provided Annatha with her favorite animal to appease her over the long months. Unless she did something, he would be taken by animal control and possibly euthanized. She couldn't let that happen.

One of the EMTs emerged at the top of the stairs. "You guys the ones who called?"

"Yes," Rachel replied and flashed her badge. "We're FBI and I have the newborn down here."

Now both of them appeared and made their way down the steps. When they reached the bottom, they both gaped in horror at the gruesome sight on the bed.

"What the hell happened here?" one of them managed after a few moments.

Rachel informed them the baby had been born within the hour and his mother was obviously dead from blood loss.

"Who shot the broad at the top of the stairs?"

"I did," Rachel shook her head at the calloused remark. "It's a long story. Why don't you people do your job and get this baby to a hospital?"

"Yes ma'am," the taller of the two replied.

They asked Rachel to place the baby in the crib Wendy used and began assessing his status. She watched for a minute then went upstairs to wait for the CSI team. Eventually, she would have to give Meredith the sad news but she wanted to do it in person. Maybe she would take Annatha's cat.

Epilogue

Rachel stood silently beside Meredith as they both gazed at Annatha's infant son in his nursery crib. She had driven straight from Wendy Malloy's house to Meredith's residence on Mercer Island to deliver the tragic news personally, and offered to drive the grief-stricken mother to the hospital in Olympia where her grandson was being treated. Meredith begged Rachel to inform Dee about her stepsister's death and have her meet them there. When offered the cat found in the basement where her daughter died, Meredith didn't hesitate and gratefully accepted him.

The baby was sleeping, and Meredith placed her hand over his bare chest. His skin felt toasty against her bare palm under the crib warmer. She didn't think she had any more tears but her eyes blurred anyway. It was almost too much to bear to think of her precious daughter held captive all alone in a basement for months. How frightened she must have been. The guilt she felt for not calling the FBI sooner threatened to overwhelm her. Fearing Brandon's reaction and going along with his rationalization Annatha had just run away; pouring booze and pills down night after night angry with her daughter for not contacting her; all of these excuses and pathetic reactions resurrected themselves and broadsided her full force with self recrimination. She knew this was only the beginning of a never ending process that would shower her mercilessly with doubts and guilt for the rest of her life. Her only comfort was that the blossoming spirituality, born while she was in treatment, provided her with the tools to face this tragedy sober as well as the fervent hope Annatha was somehow reunited with Bill. Still, it was almost too much to bear.

"I know you feel responsible," Rachel offered sympathetically as if reading her mind, "but hindsight is always twenty-twenty."

"Thank you," she smiled weakly.

Rachel put her arm around the grieving mother and squeezed. Actually, that was good advice for her to follow. She alone had to deal with the regret of not seeing through Wendy Malloy sooner. Many hours of self reflection and what-if's lay ahead for her; it was her nature and she couldn't change it.

"Meredith?" Dee's voice called behind them.

They both turned and Meredith gathered her stepdaughter in her arms and they both hugged each other tightly. Dee began to sob and Meredith joined her. Rachel swallowed hard as she fought her own tears. After a few minutes they released their grip and Dee looked down at the sleeping baby.

"He's so little," she choked back sobs.

"I'm going to name him Anthony William," Meredith announced as she dabbed her swollen eyes with a tissue that was already soaked.

"Hi Anthony," Dee cooed and placed a finger in his tiny open palm. He reflexively closed his hand around the finger and she smiled through mournful tears.

"He's all I have left of my girl," Meredith's voice broke and Dee squeezed her hand.

"Agent Ward," Dee turned and faced the agent. "I don't know how to thank you enough for not giving up."

Rachel felt her heart melt. "I'm so sorry I didn't find her in time."

Meredith took the agent's hands in hers and gazed directly into her eyes. "You listen to me," she said firmly. "If it weren't for you we would never have known what happened to Annatha or about this precious child. That horrible nurse would have gotten away with this. We owe you a lot, Agent Ward, and we won't forget what you did for us."

The agent nodded humbly and Meredith released her grip. She turned her attention to the baby again. Dee put her arm around her and they both gazed at Annatha's son with wonder and sorrow.

As Rachel silently watched them, thoughts that nagged her during the drive to pick up Meredith surfaced again. A conscious decision to have secrets had destroyed more than one life here. Annatha had secretly gone to the clinic to terminate her unwanted pregnancy, a pregnancy caused by a lying philanderer who cheated on his wife. Wendy Malloy had furtively imprisoned her and schemed to keep the baby herself. In the end, Anthony was the one pure being who survived the horrific ordeal. Cruel twists of fate had thwarted each one of their choices designed to resist the inexorable current of life's flow that ultimately swept them away, leaving Anthony alone in a basket on the shores of his own River Nile.